'All the songs about he
thunder claps had sunl
of it. Now all the crowd
with crazy eyes and she had to escape . . . she pushed the
table back and ran to the door.

Railway stations. This is where the dramas are carried
out. Not in drawing-rooms or even bedrooms, but on
draughty stations with the five forty-five coming in and
people milling around with suitcases and bags.

She couldn't stand the crowds. She went to the ticket
office, handed in her ticket. Stefan had to search for his
warrant, so he was held up. She walked outside to the
piece of waste ground which led to a bombed area,
where grass and ragged robin already covered the
rubble. Here she stood, drawing great, shuddering
breaths. Here it was quiet.'

Joyce Bell was born in Nuneaton, Warwickshire and as a child, she had two ambitions: to travel and to be a writer. At the end of the war she married a Polish airman and they went to live in Argentina for several years. On their return to England, and after winning an award in a Festival of Arts competition, Joyce began to write seriously. She has now published over 200 short stories and serials, and eight novels. She has three children and one grandchild.

By the same author

The Calder Boats

THE GIRL
FROM THE
BACK STREETS

Joyce Bell

ORION

For Michael, Julie and Tony

An Orion paperback
First published in Great Britain by Orion in 1994
This paperback edition published in 1994 by Orion Books Ltd,
Orion House, 5 Upper St Martin's Lane, London WC2H 9EA

Copyright © 1994 by Joyce Bell

A CIP catalogue record for this book is available
from the British Library.

ISBN: 1 85797 418 2

Printed in England by Clays Ltd, St Ives plc

BIBLIOGRAPHY

The books and diaries I consulted are too numerous to be listed in the bibliography below, but especially helpful was *Courier from Warsaw* by JAN NOWAK and *Dark Side of the Moon* compiled by ZOË ZAJDLEROWA, for its records of life in the Siberian prison camps.

ACHERSON, N. *The Struggle for Poland*, Michael Joseph
CALDER, A. *The People's War*, Jonathan Cape
CIPKOWSKI, P. *Revolution in Eastern Europe*,
    John Wiley & Sons
CRAWSHAW, S. *Goodbye to the USSR*, Bloomsbury
GARTON-ASH, T. *The Polish Revolution: Solidarity*,
    Jonathan Cape
LAYBOURN, K. *Britain on the Breadline*, Sutton
NOWAK, J. *Courier from Warsaw*, HarperCollins
ZAJDLEROWA, Z. *Dark Side of the Moon*,
    Faber/Harvester Wheatsheaf

ACKNOWLEDGEMENTS

I would like to thank the following people for their help: Boleslaw and Maria Krzesinski, for telling me of their experiences in a Siberian prison camp; Michael Burdett (formerly Barewski), who escaped through Rumania to England in 1939; J. Bingel and his Polish family; M. Karpinski, Chairman of the Polish Air Force Association (Leicester branch); Iris Yorke, and the many other friends and relatives who related their memories of life in and around Coventry during the war years.

PROLOGUE

1989

The house stands on top of a hill and looks over four counties, five if you count the West Midlands. But although so near to Coventry and its small neighbour, Chilverton, the view is purely pastoral, the green heart of England. Marged opened the door to breathe the sun-washed air of the June morning, and idly watched the young man walking up the lane towards her. Then, as he drew nearer, she stood still, rigid with shock. He walked on ... and on ...

And all the clocks ran backwards.

Now he was in the doorway, tall, fair, grey-eyed. 'I'm David Forrest,' he said. 'Your grandson.'

She let out a sigh which could have been relief that he was not a phantom from the past, but a living, breathing human being. He went on: 'I don't think we've ever met.'

'No.' The world was swinging back into focus. 'I would have come to the funeral but I was abroad – I didn't know there'd been an accident. I only heard yesterday – from friends.'

He shrugged. 'It doesn't matter. I know you and Mother didn't get on. She wouldn't ever let me see you—'

'It wasn't my doing.'

'She did have a reason. You wouldn't tell her who her father was.'

The net curtains swayed in the breeze. Funny how she'd

always stuck to net curtains, even when they went out of fashion. Funny how the cravings of childhood never left you: if you lacked cream buns then you spent the rest of your life eating cream buns – and they never satisfied you. It was too late.

'Come inside,' and she led the way to the room she liked best, the one with the wide picture windows and the panoramic views. She had been listening to the news on the radio and she stood now, one hand on the switch. 'The results of Poland's first free elections to be held under Communist rule have now been declared. Solidarity is victorious with 260 out of 261 seats. Now the weather ...' and she turned it off. 'Sit down—' She pointed to the chintz-covered chairs. 'Is that why you've come – to find out about her father?'

'My grandfather.' She liked his direct gaze. 'Why didn't you ever tell her?'

'Oh, I don't know.' She did, of course. She'd made a promise. And besides, she hadn't wanted to talk about that shimmering dream of love, and certainly not to Marie. Maybe I was wrong, she thought now, we always did get off on the wrong foot, Marie and me. I suppose I disliked her for being unlike *him*. So unlike that she'd almost come to wonder if she could possibly have made a mistake ... Now he was here, reborn in Marie's son. It could have been him but for his clothes. She'd never seen *him* out of uniform ...

'Would you like a cup of tea?' she asked, to gain time, and when the boy nodded she went into the kitchen with its modern units and windows overlooking the woods. She walked twice round the large room, unseeing. Was it possible that life, after snatching so much from her like a spiteful child, was now handing something back?

When she returned with the delicate china cups, the toast and sandwiches, she had regained a measure of calm. 'Quite the lady's tea, you note,' she said in her usual sardonic manner. 'Even though it's breakfast. I expect you just have coffee in mugs.' David looked faintly puzzled ... *he had that look too* ... so she added: 'Take no notice of me. I never did learn to say one thing and mean another.'

But he wouldn't be deflected. 'I didn't come just to find out your secrets, Gran.' The word came easily, naturally. 'I've only just found your address. And I would like to get to know you. I've got no one else now. My father's dead, I was an only child, don't seem to have any cousins.'

'Not on your mother's side, certainly. I never met your father.' She poured out the tea.

'You see,' he said, 'I don't know if I'm funny or something, but I always feel different, somehow.'

'Different? In what way?'

'I don't feel I belong – anywhere. Sometimes I don't even feel English—' her head jerked up '—then I think it must be my age, you know—' He smiled for the first time and she caught her breath. 'Age is always to blame for everything, isn't it? When you're young, when you're middle-aged, when you're old ...'

She was no longer listening. He'd called her Gran. She felt an inordinate sense of happiness that he had come. She had never admitted, even to herself, how much Marie's rejection had hurt. How much she'd hidden under that sardonic exterior. Clowns weren't the only ones to mask their sorrows. No doubt most people did. No doubt most people were quite different from how they appeared ... But for him to come today – it was extraordinary.

David said, 'I wonder if you'd feel like telling me?' and she blinked, restored to the present.

'It's a long story,' she hedged.

'I suppose it is.'

'What do you know about me?'

'Very little. Mother wouldn't tell me anything. Not even where you were born.'

She grinned maliciously, her momentary vulnerability

forgotten. 'No, she wouldn't, not Marie. Wouldn't tell you I wasn't born in a nice house like this one. That I came from the back streets of Chilverton.'

'Did you?' He was leaning forward now, interested. 'And you had this dream of making money, getting on in the world—'

'Oh no,' she contradicted. 'That's fiction, it wasn't like that before the war. We never dreamed we would move out of our place in life. All we could put our energy to was to survive.' *It took the winds of war to blow us around, and when the dust settled we were in quite different places – even different countries.* She was silent, remembering how many things she had seen and heard; she'd been a part of history.

David went on: 'Your name's Marged, isn't it? Is that Welsh? But you're not—?'

Now she smiled. 'No, I'm not Welsh. I was once called Marged, and it stuck. My name is Marguerite.'

'That's nice,' he nodded, and she remembered the other man who'd said those same words. So long ago. 'I was named after the flowers in the garden,' she went on. 'Marguerites are big daisies. You don't see many of them today. The kids used to call me Margie, and my brothers Margerine.'

'I'd love to hear about your childhood,' David said. 'Was it grim?'

'Not at first. We had fun. And there was my dancing.'

'You were a dancer?'

She laughed. 'Ballroom. The culture of the back streets. We had a high standard. I wanted to make a career of it. Of course, dancing *was* dancing then, very professional. And very sexy, not that we ever used that word but we knew what it meant. Then you kids think you've invented it.' Her eyes twinkled. 'I could tell you things that would make your hair curl.'

He was silent and she said softly, 'I used to think I was searching for the rainbow.'

4

'And did you find it?'

Now it was her turn not to answer. She looked through the window into the blue distance as though she were thinking. When she turned she changed the subject. 'You must be eighteen now. What do you plan to do? Go to university?'

'I hope to, in September.'

'I wondered – if you'd like to stay with me for a while, then we could get to know each other.'

'And you'll tell me about my grandfather?'

'I'll tell you the whole tangled story. Though I'm not sure if you'll thank me for the telling. You may think I've thrown away your inheritance.'

'Tell me anyway.'

'Tomorrow,' she said, 'I'll show you the street where I was born.'

Chapter 1

Victoria Street was the children's world. They played there, went to school round the corner, ran along the canal bank, or in the back field where the horses grazed and at night galloped under the moon.

The street was vivid and lively, with its two lines of terraced houses marching down to the canal, straggling over the bridge to end in the squat little building that was Grant's Clothing Factory. There were corner shops, windows filled with fat glass jars of multi-coloured sweets, the ceilings inside festooned with bunches of kettles, saucepans and balls of string. You could ask for anything in the corner shop and not be disappointed, from teapots to paraffin, children's clothes to jugs (all sizes).

The street was full of characters: the Italian ice-cream man who trudged along with his gaily-coloured wheelbarrow, the little window-cleaner with ladder and bucket, the occasional knife-grinder, and the gipsies with paper flowers who pulled pieces of privet from your front hedge and sold them – paper flowers attached – to you at the back.

Cars were seldom seen, the midwife travelled by bicycle and, it was rumoured, carried babies in the black bag strapped to the back. Milk was brought round in churns and poured into jugs; horses still pulled the dustcart and the baker's van. Funerals were the grandest spectacle of all, the shiny coaches drawn by jet-black horses with tossing manes, black-plumed, while all the people stood still and men removed their hats. Comedy and tragedy, all life was in Victoria Street.

They were in the street when Margie first met Roberta. It was June 6 1930, eight months after the New York crash started the world Depression, the same day Margie's dad had his accident. And she was nine years old.

School was over for the day, the girls were playing hopscotch, Margie, Amy Barton and Vera West, who always had several younger members of the family in tow, two of them sat now in the gutter watching Martin and John bent double, rolling marbles. 'You're out,' Amy said to Vera.

'She's not,' Margie defended. Vera was a quiet girl, pretty but looking undernourished, without the energy to protest.

'She put her foot on the line.' Amy tossed her fair hair, her thin, peaky face pouting.

'She did not.' The girls stood deadlocked, so that when a voice said: 'Excuse me, where am I?' they all jumped.

They turned from the hopscotch squares. A girl stood behind them, possibly of their own age, but obviously not of their world. Her long plaited hair shone with constant washing, her skin was as clear as porcelain. She wore, not the flowered cotton frocks of Victoria Street, but a plain blue dress with spotless white collar, neat white socks and black shoes. She made Margie feel grubby. The girls all stared, but the stranger seemed quite self-possessed. 'Perhaps you could tell me where I am,' she said.

Martin gave a hoot of laughter and Amy mimicked: 'Perhaps yoooo cad tell me—'

'Shut up,' Margie ordered. And to the girl: 'Where do you want to go?'

'Park Manor.'

'Well, you've taken the wrong turning. Park Manor Road is down at the end, opposite the factory.'

'Thank you.' But the girl didn't go, she stood there watching as Amy and Vera turned back to their hopscotch and the boys rolled their marbles.

It was hot for June; the horses swished their tails and the ice-cream man trundled his cart, wearing the same shabby overcoat and battered trilby he had on whatever the weather. Margie said, 'Let's play battledore and shuttle-cock.'

'No, mine's in home,' Amy pouted, and Margie, huffed, turned to the stranger. 'Do you want me to show you where to go?' she offered.

'Let her find her own road,' Martin put in. 'We don't want Park Manor kids here.'

'Tek no notice of him,' Margie said loftily. 'He's always the same. Come on, what's-your-name.'

It hadn't been a question, but the girl took it literally. 'Roberta,' she whispered as they fell into step. 'What's yours?'

'Marguerite. They call me Margie. I don't know how you came to mek this mistake,' and she looked round, puzzled.

Victoria Street was surrounded by small branching roads, all terraced. Park Manor Road was very different. Its houses were mostly detached, mock-Tudor or mock-Elizabethan, with little turrets and gables and latticed windows, and big gardens at the rear.

'I was curious.' Roberta had halted. 'Who are the boys?'

'They're my brothers. John's a bit older than me, and Martin's the same age.'

'You're twins, then?'

'Well, really we're cousins, but Martin's mam died, so my mam brings him up with us.'

'He's handsome.'

'Who, Martin? Don't tell him that, he'll get too big for his boots.'

'And the girls?'

'Amy's the fair one. She lives at number eighteen, two doors away from me.'

9

'She's spiteful.'

'Ye-es.' Margie wasn't sure if she wanted this self-possessed newcomer to talk about her friends, even if what she said was true. 'Vera's the other one,' she hurried on. 'She lives in the council houses opposite.' *And her mam has nine kids and her dad knocks 'em all about when he drinks. Where he gets his money from to drink nobody can understand.*

'So they're council houses?' Roberta looked a little supercilious. 'Aren't they for slum-clearance people?'

'Some of 'em.' And people like the Wests were the lowest grade in Victoria Street; the children were ragged and humiliated by having to apply for free boots from a charity in the town. Vera carried the shame of this on her face. Respectable children wore shoes, not pumps, not even boots, but shoes. Margie pitied Vera and the rest of the West children who could be seen daily running off to school in grubby, holey jerseys, either too big or too small, usually carrying a piece of bread in one hand and, if girls, holding up their knickers in the other. Margie's mam didn't like her to go in the Wests' house. 'You never know what you might pick up,' she'd say mysteriously.

But this Victoria Street lore was not for outsiders so, as Margie stood, lips pressed together, Roberta said, 'Well, thank you for showing me. Goodbye.' She hesitated. 'Perhaps I'll see you again.'

'Maybe.' Margie retraced her steps, stopping to watch a narrow boat being pulled along the canal, its horse with nose-bag shuffling in front, its little cabin spotless and shining, a woman in a dirty overall at the tiller. Margie waved then went on, wondering if her mam would give her a ha'penny for ice-cream. They all had their Saturday pennies, except for Brenda who was at work, but Mam often gave extra to spend at the corner shop's wonderland of chocolate drops, everlasting sticks and the like. But it was the carnival on Saturday, they'd need some money then. They'd go down into the town proper, over the canal bridge, into the High Street.

Chilverton was a small town. Its hand-loom silk-weaving, spread from its large neighbour, Coventry, had long since gone. Now it had one silk-weaving factory, several small engineering factories, also spread from Coventry, and one larger one, Mordant's, where her dad worked. You could see the lights of the factories at night, and hear the whirring of the machines as you walked past, the constant throb of industry that ruled their lives. Outside the town were a few coal mines, with the pit banks often smouldering with little fires, smelling of sulphur.

The High Street contained a Woolworths (nothing over sixpence), a Marks and Spencer (nothing over five shillings), one or two fine old buildings, and a large Co-operative store where Mam obtained her groceries for the 'divi' it paid. But on Saturday all the town would be decorated with flags and bunting, and they'd roast an ox in the market-place. Margie sang as she walked, one foot on the pavement, one on the road, full of the joy of life, of carnivals and Saturday pennies and ice-creams. *Blow away the morning dew, how sweet the winds do blow*, sang Margie.

She was back in her own end now, and she looked up from the pavement. The children were no longer playing, they were gathered in a crowd around one of the houses ... was it a wedding that she'd not heard of? No, it was *their* house! A few women had joined them; a bicycle stood by the railings around the tiny front garden. A policeman was just entering the front door and policemen, to Victoria Street, meant only one thing – trouble.

Margie forgot the heat and ran. The front door was closed now, so round the entry to the back-kitchen, into the kitchen where the policeman stood and John and Martin, white and worried, were staring up at Mam, who was just putting on her hat. Margie was filled with terror. The police put people into prison, and that was the worst thing that could happen to anybody. Was he taking Mam?

'Mam,' she cried, anguished. 'Don't let him take you.'

Her mother looked down and her eyes seemed somehow funny, as if she couldn't see properly. 'It's all right, Margie,' she said. 'I'm just going to the hospital. Your dad's had a bit of an accident. You be a good girl and stop with Martin.'

She skewered a hat-pin into her hat, turned and stumbled. The policeman put out his hand. 'Steady now, missus,' he said. 'Come on, I'll take you to the bus.'

'Oh, I can walk,' Mam said. 'I always do.'

'You'll be better on the bus. Quicker, too.' He waited, and Mam gave in.

'Yes.' She drew a breath. 'John, run and tell Grandma. Oh, and Aunt Mary.'

They left by the back way, and Mrs Harvey next door was out in the shared yard, wondering what had happened. 'Shall I see to the children, Mrs Fennel?' she asked.

'No, they'll be all right, thank you,' replied Mam, and Mrs Harvey turned away, disappointed. Trouble with neighbours, Mam always said, they wanted to know all your business, and she liked to keep herself to herself.

John ran out too, and Martin and Margie sat in the kitchen. It was a pleasant room with its horsehair sofa, its dresser displaying the big blue vase, its scrubbed table, covered now with a chenille cloth. The singing kettle on the hob of the black grate, the patterned lace from the market screening the sash window, the rag rugs and coconut matting over the red tiled floor, were all signs of a happy, well run home.

This is where they sat in the evenings, reading the *Happy Mag.*, with its cheery stories and *Just William* series. They hadn't a wireless yet, but they did have an old gramophone and several records, *Wedding of the Painted Doll* and *Yes, We Have No Bananas*. Then Dad would come in from the garden or allotment and sit in his armchair, the wooden one with the high back. No one sat in this chair but Dad, and there was a lot of laughter and fun.

Now Margie stared at Martin, still afraid. She said, trying not to let her voice quaver: 'I wonder what it is, they don't have accidents at Mordant's. The men at the pit have accidents, but not in a factory.'

'You can at Mordant's,' Martin replied. 'Our dad says Mordant is an old slave-driver, he's horrible. He says—' Then, seeing she was on the verge of tears, he stepped towards her. 'Look, a blood ally,' and he held out his hand, showing his most treasured marble. She smiled waveringly, and he began to walk round the room, whistling tunelessly, until Margie, edgy, said, 'Shut up!'

'Shut up yourself, Margerine.'

Margie and Martin might well have been twins. Born in the same week, both had the same dark hair and eyes, the same oval face. But their smiles were different. Margie had an urchin look with a gamin grin. Martin seldom smiled and when he did, the corners of his mouth turned down and not up. Both had hot tempers and they fought with each other more than with John or Brenda, who were quiet, even placid. Their relationship could be described as love-hate; they fought, but there was always a feeling of closeness, the closeness that came from sharing the same pram, if not the same womb, though at first Margie had believed they were twins, that the nurse had brought them together in her little black bag, and she couldn't understand why. 'Did you order two?' she'd asked Mam, but Mam only laughed and said sometimes you got more than you bargained for. Then Dad laughed as well as if it were some secret joke.

Margie liked her dad. Pleasant and smiling, he took the children with him to the allotment at weekends, and they helped bring the vegetables home for their Sunday dinner. Tasty carrots, which she liked to eat raw, peas and beans in season, lovely fresh celery, gooseberries and raspberries for Mam's pies. Last week, he'd dug up the first of the early potatoes and wheeled them home with Margie sitting triumphantly on top of the wheelbarrow, Dad pretending to tip her off, making her laugh. Dad made Mam laugh too. She would say, 'Oh go on, you silly thing,' and, 'Mind out of my way, I've got the washing up to do.' But she didn't mind, really, Margie knew; one of life's great mysteries was that grown-ups seldom meant what they said.

The door opened and John came in. 'Grandma's not in, so I left a message with next door,' he said.

Margie opened the cupboard by the fireplace where they kept their toys, and took out a book. But she couldn't concentrate, not even on *Black Beauty*; she was thinking of her dad at the hospital. She'd never known anyone in her family go to hospital before, hospitals, like doctors, cost money, and were to be avoided. John had a bad cough every winter, but Mam didn't take him to the doctor. She rubbed his chest with Vick and bought a bottle of 'cough-stuff' from the chemist.

'Why did Dad have to go to hospital?' she asked.

''Cos he hurt his leg,' John answered. 'The policeman told Mam.'

'Well, I hurt my leg last week but I didn't go to hospital.'

'P'raps he had to have stitches,' John told her. 'They'll stitch it up, then he'll come home. Don't suppose he'll be long,' he added kindly. John was always kind.

Martin, pretending nonchalance, walked outside into the yard. He banged the tin bath hanging on the wall, dabbled in the wooden tub which Mam rolled inside every Monday to do the washing, and passed the coalhouse and the lavatory to wander aimlessly into the garden, where the mock-orange-blossom tree with its waxy-white flowers stood.

At a quarter to six Brenda came in. Fourteen years old, her intelligent face was pleasant rather than pretty, and would have been unremarkable but for her beautiful grey eyes, which didn't seem to belong with the somewhat sturdy figure and sensible air. She was apprenticed to the tailoring at Grant's, and took charge now in the capable way of the eldest of the family.

'You should've got your tea,' she scolded Margie, once they broke the news that Dad had had a little accident but would soon be home. 'Get the bread out now while I light the fire for cooking, Dad'll want his dinner when he comes home,' for he took sandwiches for his midday meal, as there was no canteen. Brenda put a match to the sticks while Margie laid the table with the starched white cloth. But no one ate. And as the hours passed even Brenda began to look uncertain.

'Run and see if they're coming,' she ordered Margie. 'Don't go away, mind.'

Margie ran to the bottom of the entry. The sun was a great red ball hanging low in the sky like a big lantern, and as she watched, it sank out of sight behind the council houses. The street scene had changed with the onset of evening, the children had gone, courting couples walked past, off for a stroll or to go to the pictures, a few men sauntered down to the club or pub. Margie's dad never went out on his own, never left Mam with the children, as so many did.

The lamplighter rode up on his bicycle, stopped to light the lamp with his pole, then the bus trundled up, a red double-decker with open top. It stopped, and Mam got out alone. She walked with the same lost air she'd had before she went, as though she didn't know where she was going; indeed, she almost passed the entry till Margie ran to her and guided her in home, watched by Mrs Harvey through the net curtains.

Eva sat down. The heat outside had lessened, but now the fire kept the kitchen warm. 'Dad?' asked Brenda.

'He's got to stop in hospital,' Mam said.

The children stared. Eva's face was white, her lips were trembling and they stood by, alarmed. Women in Victoria Street weren't given to crying, except at funerals; they bore their lot in stoic silence. So the children didn't know what to say or do. Brenda put her arm round her mother, John stood on a chair and lit the gas.

Then Grandma came in like a breath of fresh air. Grandma, who had had six children and twelve grandchildren, who was used to adversity and death and illness. She sat down on the horsehair sofa – no one sat in Dad's chair – and took off her hat. Margie noticed her mother's, left on the dresser instead of being put away. Mam set great store by her hats, they all joked about it. 'A new one every year,' laughed Dad, and it was true. They all sat upstairs in the bedroom clothes closet, blues and greens and browns. Only one remained unchanged, her black funeral hat.

Grandma took charge. 'Have you got some tea made, Brenda? That's right. Here, Eva, drink this. Pity we've not got anythin' stronger. Now—' as Mam's colour returned. 'How is he?'

'Bad.' Mam turned to her, mouthing the words as she did when she didn't want the children to hear. Brenda and John, who had learned to lip-read, could understand, but Margie was unable to follow. 'His leg is crushed. They thought at first he'd lose it ... he'll be in bed for weeks ... weeks,' she ended aloud.

Even the shocked children knew what this meant. No work, no pay. Grandma said, 'So how did it happen?'

'Well, he tried to tell me, best as he could. His machine's at the end, and they all have belts and pulleys going to a shaft along the roof. Frank said he knew the – the piece at the top was loose. He'd told the foreman more than once. Nobody did anything. So today it broke and—' She returned to the mouthing. 'It fell on him, all of it.'

There was a stunned silence. Margie looked round at the grown-ups, bewildered. Grandma said, 'But he'll be all right?'

'I think so – in time.'

Grandma leaned back, one work-worn hand smoothing her black skirt in a habitual rhythmic movement as though trying to smooth away the cares of her family once and for all. Then she asked bluntly: 'So how will you manage for money?'

Eva hesitated. 'I don't know. I – I've hardly got anything saved now. Frank had weeks of short-time in winter, he always does ... we were banking on the summer's work to put us right again.' She shook her head from side to side, dazedly. 'I don't know what I'm going to do,' she whispered, and Margie was alarmed to see her mother, who knew everything, did not now know what to do.

Grandma said. 'You ought to get compensation.'

'Yes, but you know Mordant's—'

'Old skinflint Dad calls him,' Margie put in.

'There'll be a bit of benefit,' Eva said doubtfully.

'A bit, yes!' snorted Grandma. 'And you'll have to wait for that. No, you ought to get compensation,' she repeated forcefully. 'Go and see Mr Mordant.'

Eva looked dubious; she was the quiet sort, like John. But then Aunt Mary called round and seconded it, so it was decided. Aunt Mary was the eldest of the family, second in command to Grandma. 'Bit too much in command if you ask me,' one of the uncles was heard to mutter at a family gathering.

The clock struck nine, and Grandma said, 'These children should be in bed long since. Come on, Margie,' and she took her into the back-kitchen, gave her a quick wash, then up to the room she shared with Brenda. 'Say your prayers,' she ordered as she put the lighted candle by the bed, and as Margie knelt and went through a long litany of God Bless, mentioning by name all her relations, ending with: 'Please send Dad home soon,' Grandma patted her head. 'Don't you fret,' she said, and left.

The candle flickered, making shadows march across the ceiling. Dad said they'd put in the electric one of these days when he had a good week. Margie didn't know how much a good week would be, her parents never talked about money problems before the children, but she knew his wages were higher than those of the men in the pits, so she always had a nice new frock for the church sermons in summer, and there was always food on the table and coal for the fire.

She could hear a mutter of voices downstairs, heard Martin come to bed, then John. Grandma and Aunt Mary went home, and Brenda came in. 'Aren't you asleep yet?' she asked, as she slipped into bed beside her.

'Will Dad be home soon?' Margie asked.

'Soon, yes.'

'Will he be back in time for us to go to the seaside?' They didn't go for a week's holiday in August, but there were day trips, when they walked down to the station to catch the early-morning train, to spend a lovely day at Blackpool or Skegness or Yarmouth. Living in the middle of the country they had a long way to go to the coast, either way, east or west.

'I don't know,' Brenda said dismissively, and Margie knew she wouldn't say any more. Not Brenda, her grown-up sister. 'Go to sleep now,' she told her, and blew out the candle. Margie was left in the deep blackness and the sighing shadows from the orange-blossom tree. And she knew, with a child's intuitive studying of the grown-ups, that something terrible had happened, and that it would change all their lives.

Frank Fennel had been heard to say that Margie resembled her mother, but that Eva didn't have her daughter's cheeky look, and it was true that Eva was quiet and shy. This was due in part to a somewhat domineering mother and elder sister, and in part to the fact that she went into service at the age of eleven, and you don't answer the master back if you want to keep your job. But being quiet did not mean she could not think, or have any opinions: she had been a supporter of the suffragette movement in her twenties, and now all women had been given the vote, she was delighted. A quite beautiful girl in her youth she had, as soon as possible, left service to work in the silk-weaving factory, and had several boyfriends before she met Frank Fennel in 1911.

Frank had had an unhappy childhood, his mother dying when he was a baby, his father remarrying a woman who, with sons of her own, did not want stepchildren. Frank also left school at eleven and his father sent him to Mordant's, not to serve an apprenticeship, but to become a semi-skilled worker. He met Eva, knew this was the girl for him, and they married in 1912.

Brenda was born in 1916, and John in 1919 when Frank came back from the Army and put his gratuity as deposit on the terraced house in Victoria Street. All the houses on the right side were privately owned; it was easy to buy a small house in the twenties once you had the deposit. It was there Margie was born, and where Frank agreed to take the baby Martin, even though it meant another mouth to feed. Frank worked hard, gave most of his pay to Eva, seldom drank, smoked Woodbines, and was determined to make a better home than the one he'd left. He never spoke of his unhappy childhood, even to Eva, of the parents who fought, the stepmother who never gave him enough to eat, but the memory was there, helping him keep his own temper in check, to do all he could for the family he loved. His wages were good enough when he was in work. Eva managed well and saved for the weeks on short-time, bridging carefully the gap between adequate living and poverty. So even with the short-time they managed, provided he was not ill, and he hadn't been ill – until now.

Now there was this accident and Eva was worried sick, for the doctor hadn't been optimistic. She was nervous as she walked to Mordant's early on Saturday morning, through the market in the centre, on to the far outskirts of the town. She had never talked to a manager before. At the weaving factory she had dealt with the overlooker, and he was one of them, rough and ready, outspoken, harsh if necessary, but you knew where you were with him. You never saw the manager. And Mr Mordant was reputed to be a holy terror. She remembered Frank telling her how he'd inherited the business from his father and uncle, and the first thing he did when the father died was get rid of the uncle who'd started it!

She arrived at the long grey buildings that were Mordant's, and halted at the gates, peering inside at the trucks, components, all the paraphernalia of an engineering works, all grey in the bright sunshine. The gatekeeper came out of his office and Eva said bravely that she wanted to see Mr Mordant.

The gatekeeper clucked his sympathy when she told him who she was, and muttered it was a bad business. He telephoned through and said, 'You'll have to wait, Mrs Fennel. He'll see you later if he's got time. You can wait in the yard, if you like.'

So Eva stood inside the gate and waited for three hours, staring at the greyness. Eva hated factories; she hated working in them, felt it was like being in prison, shut away from the sunlight. She would have liked to work in a flower shop, or draping silks and satins over models, arranging the colours. Eva never told anyone of these pipe-dreams. What was the point? There were no flower shops or models in Chilverton anyway, and now all her energy went into working for her family, doing the heavy housework, dollying and mangling the clothes, scrubbing floors, none of which she was strong enough to do, and which left her weary, thinking sometimes of her father who'd died of the consumption, wondering if that's why John was so quiet – would he go the same way?

Occasionally, if she had a shilling or two to spare, she'd take the children on the train to Birmingham to the Art Gallery where she'd stand in wonder before the pictures, still saying nothing. But now she had the vote and she knew what she wanted – a better world for her children. She'd sent Brenda to Grant's because it was the best she could afford with three younger ones, and the tailoring was a good trade. She hoped the younger ones would do better, perhaps even enter the scholarship for the grammar school – that would be a step up indeed for Victoria Street.

The doors were opening, men were rushing out to the bicycle sheds, then streaming through the gates as if they couldn't get away quickly enough. As the last ones filtered through, the gatekeeper said to Eva: 'Mr Mordant will see you now. Come with me.'

He led her into an office, a small room with table and chairs, and left her. Mr Mordant came in.

And Eva quailed. This was no overlooker but a man who, though no older than herself, was immaculately groomed. His thinning hair was slicked back from his forehead, his white shirt was spotless, his suit uncreased. She had worked for such as he when in service. Not a member of the nobility, who treated their servants well, but one of that vast class of people who were not so much deliberately cruel as indifferent. Frank Fennel to Mr Mordant was a number, no more. He walked round the table and turned to face her. 'Well?' he snapped.

Eva swallowed nervously. 'I've come about my husband's accident, Frank Fennel.'

'Well, he's going on all right, isn't he?' Mr Mordant sat down but he didn't ask her to sit, and this put her at a disadvantage immediately, kept her in her place.

'It's a question of money,' she stammered, hating to talk of *poverty*. 'He's going to be off work for weeks.'

'He'll get benefit.'

'Yes, but we have to pay the hospital.'

'Then you'll have to apply for public assistance,' he said carelessly.

Eva cringed at the thought, and said, bravely, 'But he was hurt at the factory.'

'It was his own fault entirely, Mrs Fennel.'

Eva hesitated. You didn't argue with bosses nor masters. But she was a mother hen defending her family, and she strove to attack this fox who would tear them to pieces. 'F-Frank is a good worker,' she said. 'The – things fell on him.'

'But he'd tightened the belt, you see,' explained Mr Mordant, as if to a backward child. 'I've looked into it all. Then the belt pulled it down.'

Eva hesitated again, out of her depth but knowing that Frank had said it was in no way his fault, rather that of the unsafe practices in the factory. She wished someone was with her, someone who would know what to do or say. This man's superior attitude diminished her. 'We wondered about compensation,' she faltered.

Mr Mordant had been watching her. He seemed to ponder. 'Well, I tell you what I'll do,' he said. 'I'll give you something to tide you over. I don't have to, you know. There's no liability.'

'Oh,' said Eva, who didn't know.

Mr Mordant opened a drawer and took out a typed sheet and several five-pound notes. Eva didn't stop to wonder when this had been prepared. She was trembling now, thinking she had misjudged him. He was going to help, after all.

He handed the white notes to her. 'There you are,' he said. 'Twenty-five pounds.'

Twenty-five pounds! She had never seen so much money in her life, and was overcome with gratitude. 'Oh thank you, Mr Mordant,' she gasped.

'Just sign this receipt, will you?'

Eva signed the typed sheet and left the office. She was still trembling, but this time with relief. Now she could pay the mortgage and feed her family; she wouldn't have to apply for that ultimate of shame and humiliation, public assistance. She walked back to the market and bought some tomatoes for tea. At home she told the waiting children: 'He's not so bad after all, he gave me some money, and it'll be a godsend till your dad can get back to work. I'll put it in the Post Office, draw some out every week.'

★

Summers were golden, with long sunny days, picnics with sandwiches and bottles of cold tea. The canal lay heavy and still in the heat, and the children would take off their shoes and paddle. Everyone was happy in summer. There was more work; less coal was needed, for Mam had a gas-ring to boil the kettle, and doing the weekly wash was easier. There were Sunday-school 'treats', with processions and tea before going to the field with its brass band ...

Margie thought this summer would be the same once her dad came home, even though he had to stay in bed for a time. The front downstairs room had been prepared for him, for they had no indoor lavatory or bathroom, so Mam would have to carry all the water from the back-kitchen. They borrowed a commode from Grandma, Aunt Mary lent them a single bed, which they placed near the wall over the thin carpet – Mam's pride and joy – and the sideboard was pushed back. Mam put her blue vase on the sideboard and filled it with orange-blossom. Mam loved flowers.

Margie was at school when he came home, and she ran straight to the front room, eager and happy. 'Dad!' she shouted, then stopped, dismayed.

For the pleasant smiling Dad had gone. She hardly recognised the man lying in the bed; his face was so thin and grey, his hair had been cut short and a thick plaster covered his forehead. The part of one arm she could see was black with bruises, while his legs lay inert under the bedclothes. She repeated, 'Dad,' uncertainly. He muttered, 'Hallo,' and that was all.

Eva came in. 'Don't bother your dad,' she admonished. 'He's in pain.'

'I want to get up,' Frank grumbled. 'People die in bed.'

'You know the doctor said you'd got to stop—'

'What does he know, old fool?' Frank shouted.

Margie stood, undecided, the scent of the orange-blossom was heavy in the still air. She was hurt; she had always been Dad's favourite. He noticed her woebegone face and said, more gently, 'Come on, little wench, come and sit by me.'

Yet he had changed, and as the days passed his anger was always near the surface while Eva nursed and tried to soothe him. The children had less time to play as they were given more jobs to do. Margie helped her mother in the house, the boys worked on the allotment, Uncle Harry helping to plant the potatoes and celery. They needed the food now more than ever.

Life had taken on a new dimension, but the children adjusted, they had to. Their home life was changed, Mam began to look worried as she drew out more and more of the money in the Post Office, there was no talk of seaside trips this year or even new clothes. Margie, as yet, wasn't too unhappy. Like most children she had the sense of wonder to come. Of walking towards the rainbow and one day being able to clasp it in her arms when she'd understand the meaning of the universe.

In the street games varied, not from any fixed date of the calendar but from a spontaneous moving of the blood of the children. Battledore and shuttlecock had long since gone, as had whips and tops, but skipping stayed with them all the time. So did Roberta.

She turned up again one warm day in July. Dressed now in a pretty plaid frock, she stood watching the girls play higher and higher, but when Margie took pity on her and asked her to join in, Amy snapped: 'We're going in the back field.'

'And we go through our gardens, so you can't come,' said Martin, lounging by the fence.

Roberta turned away but Margie shouted, 'Why are you all so rotten to her? Come on, Roberta, I'll take you round the road.'

Yet she understood Amy's hostility. Roberta wasn't one of the gang, consisting as it did of Amy, Vera, Margie herself, and a few more girls who lived nearby, Edna Farmer

24

and Rosie Brown. She was an outsider, even more so than the alien kids from York Street School, or the High School, those snobby girls who would never deign to mix with Victoria Street and were not allowed to play netball or hockey matches with them. Chilverton in the thirties consisted of myriads of small groups never mixing. Margie, not an introspective child, wasn't sure why she allowed Roberta to play with them; she supposed she felt sorry for her, looking so forlorn and alone. In Victoria Street you were never alone. Or perhaps it enhanced her own superiority as leader of the gang. Perhaps because she didn't like Amy.

But she took her round the road, and they wandered through the fields, picking stray buttercups; on towards the pond where the boys caught tadpoles and brought them home in jam jars. Roberta, always pernickety, wanted to know who the fields belonged to. Margie had no idea. No one ever stopped them, she explained kindly.

Eventually the girls and boys separated, the boys to climb trees which Margie enjoyed but Amy did not. She suggested they play 'I wrote a letter to my love', and they sat round in a ring, a little uncomfortably because the whole of the back field consisted of ridges and furrows, and Roberta said she didn't know how to play.

Amy tossed her shoulder-length ringlets. 'Don't you know anything?' she asked sharply, so Roberta glanced at her wristwatch and said, 'Look at the time, I'll have to go.'

'Show off,' muttered Amy. 'Just to let us know she's got a watch. I'm going to have one at Christmas.' But Margie knew she wasn't showing off; the watch was just a normal part of her life. And she kept coming, in spite of Amy's dislike.

One thing puzzled Margie about Roberta. She wore the same plaid dress every time she came. And this wouldn't have mattered, but it was never washed. The children all played in old clothes, but even Vera's went into the weekly wash. No one asked Roberta about this, not even Amy;

however badly a child might be dressed it wasn't done to mention it in Victoria Street. Who knew what the reason might be? A drunken father, abject poverty. Margie was puzzled how this would apply to a girl from Park Manor Road, but she shrugged it off. You never knew. And the plaid dress grew dirtier and dirtier.

Roberta never said anything about her home, yet she seemed avid for news of Victoria Street. She listened as the girls sat in the back field, gossiping about Mrs Trigger who had a fancy man. 'He's the father of her two kids,' said Amy, and Roberta frowned and asked, 'How is that?'

The girls, who didn't know, who were just repeating their mothers' talk, nodded sagely and said that's how it was, and Rosie Brown put in: 'Her husband doesn't mind. He'd never satisfy her, our Jess said.'

Roberta pursed her lips. 'I don't know what you mean, and I don't think you do, either,' and now Amy's long hostility came to the surface.

'What's it to you?' she asked hotly. 'Who are you, anyway? What do you come here for?'

There was a sudden silence, but Roberta did not flinch. 'I like coming here,' she said.

'I asked you who you were,' Amy persisted. 'You live in Park Manor Road, right? Where do you go to school?'

'Miss Shipton's,' replied Roberta, then added, 'It's a private school.'

Was she showing off now, or being apologetic? Margie wasn't sure, but Amy, thinking the former, became more inflamed.

'I bet that's a potty little school. I bet it's no good. So why don't you play with the kids from there, then?'

'Mummy won't let me,' said Roberta.

This flummoxed Amy for a moment, and Rosie Brown asked: 'You mean she won't let you play with *anybody*?' Visions of Roberta being shut away in some house, neglected, flashed through Margie's mind, and never quite left her.

She asked, 'What about your dad? What does he say?'

'I don't see much of him. He's always working.' The girls nodded: this they understood. 'I'm very fond of my father,' Roberta ended.

'But you don't like your mother.' It was a statement.

'No.' Pause. 'She goes out a lot.' Margie shot a glance at Amy. Amy's mother went out a lot. She worked in a pub in the town and it was rumoured that she seldom came straight home. Amy's dad, unlike Mr Trigger, was always rowing with her about it.

'So who looks after you?' asked Rosie.

'We have a housekeeper,' said Roberta.

The girls blinked. They had never heard of anyone – outside books – having a housekeeper. 'What's she like?' asked Edna.

'Oh!' and now Roberta's voice held passion. 'She's a perfectly dreadful woman, dressed in black, absolutely terrifying,' and the girls sucked in their breaths in enjoyable horror.

'So your family don't know you come here, then?' asked Margie.

'Oh no, I slip out. I came first because I was curious. Now – I like being here. I like being able to run about and get dirty—'

Now the subject of dirt was out in the open, Amy stared at the plaid dress, so grubby now it smelt. 'We're not dirty,' she said, affronted. 'It's you who's dirty.'

Roberta looked down at her frock. 'I put this on so no one will notice,' she explained. 'Then I hide it.'

'You could wash it sometimes,' Margie told her gently.

'I wouldn't know how.'

Margie tutted in exasperation at this helpless female. 'How old are you?' she asked.

'Nine.'

'So am I. Well, you ought to know how to wash a frock, a great girl like you.' Margie was quoting her own mother,

27

enjoying feeling superior. Not that she could have done a week's wash, not that Mam would have let her, but she knew enough about it to know that you could wash anything with soap. 'Don't you watch your Mam?' she asked.

'Mummy doesn't do the washing. She sends it out.'

Margie could understand that too. Mrs Bradley at the corner shop sent her washing to Vera's mother and paid her five shillings a week.

But what a funny way to live. Yet she had to admire Roberta for slipping out from what seemed like a prison. 'If you're not supposed to go out, what do you do?' she asked.

'Oh, just stay in the garden or the nurs— my room,' Roberta answered.

'And you en't got no brothers nor sisters?'

'I have one brother. He's away at school.'

'And en't there no kids to play with in Park Manor Road?'

'Well, we don't play in the street.'

'Why not?'

'Mummy would say it was common.'

'Would she? Why?'

'I don't know,' said Roberta.

Well, parents had their funny ways. Distinction of class was strong in the thirties, but such things have to be learned and the girls were only nine. By the very fact of her living in a close community, Margie knew little of any other. She knew there were people higher up – the doctor was one of them – and such people were high up because they knew everything. But Roberta didn't know *anything*, she couldn't play any of their games, didn't even know how to wash her frock. Margie was puzzled.

But Amy had returned to the attack. 'Common?' she cried. 'Don't you call me common, you stuck-up little cat. You're stupid, that's what you are. And I don't believe a word of what you've told us, so there. *My* dad's an engine driver, that's a good job, and we go away to the seaside for a week every year. And I always wear clean frocks, not like yours. So clear off, go on. We don't want you here. You're a ligger.'

Roberta rose to her feet and, watched by the others, walked away, over the ridges and furrows, through the boys playing rounders, past two yapping dogs . . .

Margie said, after a pause, 'I don't see why she can't play with us. She must have a terrible life, she's like an orphan.'

'I read a story about an orphan, she hadn't got no home,' put in Rosie.

'Well, no use having a home if you can't *do* anything,' countered Margie. 'I bet they shut her up in a room.'

They were silent, thinking it over. Margie pressed her advantage. 'I think we should let her come,' she ended. 'What about you?'

The girls looked at each other. 'I don't mind,' said Edna. 'Nor me,' added Vera, who enjoyed seeing someone in a worse plight than she. Rosie nodded.

'So it's only you, Amy,' said Margie.

Amy tossed her ringlets. 'Oh please yourselves,' she pouted. 'But I still don't like her, and I think she tells lies. And Martin don't like her, either. He thinks she's awful.'

'It's nothing to do with Martin,' said Margie. 'I'll go and talk to her, see what she says.'

She caught up with Roberta as she was leaving the field, and the two fell into step together. 'Was it true, all you told us?' she asked.

'Yes – except I have a nanny who looks after me.'

Margie stopped, thunderstruck. 'A *nanny*? You have a nanny, a great girl like you?'

'She takes me to school,' Roberta said apologetically.

'Can't you go by yourself?' Margie knew nothing of the world where nannies took the place of mothers.

'Well, you see—' Roberta didn't know enough of Margie's world to explain. 'When we come back I find a way to avoid her. I have tea and then I go to my room – or say I do   and she doesn't check. As long as I'm back at seven to get ready for bed ... I didn't tell the others that.'

'You did right.' Margie could imagine Amy's mockery, and as for Martin, he'd laugh his head off. 'I'd keep quiet about a nanny if I were you. Well—' offhandedly. 'We were talking about letting you come again.'

For a moment the two girls faced each other, as if sizing the other one up, trying to fathom what lay beneath the surface. They stared. Margie held the power and Roberta knew it. For a moment the friendship hung in the balance, the friendship that would, had they been able to see into the future, change both their lives, even become a matter of life and death.

Roberta said, 'What did Amy mean when she called me a ligger? Is that a swear-word?'

'No, it just means fibber. She thought you weren't telling the truth.'

'Oh.' Roberta paused, then, 'I'd like to learn some swear-words.'

It was the first hint of devilment she'd shown, and Margie grinned. The scales banged down on the side of friendship.

'You can come again,' said Margie, and walked away.

Roberta walked back to Park Manor Road, determined to return to Victoria Street. A lonely child, the finding children of her own age who participated in splendid games with no one around to say, 'Don't do this, Miss Roberta. Little ladies don't run and jump,' was like entering a land of glorious freedom. The corner shops, the coal wagons, the ice-cream man were all part of this wonderful world, and she loved it.

At home it was always, 'Don't bother me, Miss Roberta. Run away and play.' It was the story of her life. On the infrequent occasions when she saw Mummy it was, 'Run along now, dear. Where is Nanny?' Mrs Stanway the housekeeper

30

did frighten her, Cook didn't welcome her in the kitchen, and the maids were always busy – at least when she approached – she often heard them giggling in corners when Mrs Stanway wasn't around, and this simply added to her loneliness.

There was no question of bringing her schoolfriends home. Mummy wouldn't allow it. Adela Mordant was the daughter of a small squire, but the granddaughter of an earl, and to her way of thinking none of the little girls at Miss Shipton's was good enough to mix with a member of the landed gentry, not daughters of doctors and teachers and even – oh horror – tradespeople. Roberta never quite realised this. She thought, from Mummy's constant belittling of her, that it was she who was not good enough for them. As for the common children who played in the street, they existed in Mummy's eyes solely to grow up and become maids to serve Mummy.

Roberta was afraid the servants might know what she was doing, so she crept behind the curtains to listen to their conversation while they cleaned the downstairs rooms, and learned a lot about her family from them.

'Meks you wonder why she married him. She don't mix wi' anybody. An' her family don't want to see her now—'

'Reckon they were glad to get her settled with somebody, flighty piece that she is. Reckon they thought she was expectin', and palmed her off on him.'

'It's the child I feel sorry for. Stuck with that old soak of a nanny. Not much of a life for a kid.'

'Where does she go when she's out?' Roberta jumped.

'Who, Lady Anne? Fancy men, I expect.'

These conversations were very puzzling. Who was Lady Anne? What were fancy men? But at least they told Roberta the servants didn't know about her escapades.

But she had to be careful. There had been that dangerous occurrence when she said 'ain't' before Nanny, then had to make the excuse that she'd heard it from one of the maids.

Nanny said Mummy would be most annoyed if she picked up the local accent and Roberta, who had been trying to modify her tones because the Victoria Street children made fun of her, was forced to become bi-lingual – as well as deceitful.

She had been born with a passionate, loving nature, but the search for love led to deceit, the passion was forced underground. But, like a banked-down fire, tiny gleams would shoot up from time to time and, given the right spark, promised to burn strongly.

Roberta returned to Victoria Street the very next day, and gradually Amy accepted her. Now only Martin was hostile.

But Margie had her way, and the friendship went on. They never suggested visiting each other's homes: obviously Roberta, not being allowed to do anything normal children did, couldn't ask her there, while Margie's home, which up to three months ago had always been a merry place, full of children and clatter, was changed now. Dad was up, but still miserable; he couldn't walk properly yet, and he sat for much of the time, brooding. Margie brought him books from the library, for they all liked reading, but now he never touched them. He couldn't work in the garden, so Mam looked worried and home wasn't such a pleasant place.

Yet Roberta's having such an odd lifestyle brought her closer to being one of them. They all had something to be a little ashamed of: Amy's mother at the pub with her men friends, Vera's big family and awful dad, Margie with her own dad's problems, and now not working, for being off sick was almost as bad as being on the dole – you dropped in the Victoria Street social scale, from a respectable worker's family to people to be pitied, and the ones who'd looked up to you before were the first to look down on you now.

It was in September, just after the holidays had ended, when Margie came home from school alone. John and

Martin had gone to the allotment. She walked in the back-kitchen, and both the doors were open. She stopped. Dad was in the kitchen, standing by the table, trying to propel himself along without his stick. His face was white with pain, he was gasping for breath as he forced himself along. His pain was almost a tangible thing; it seemed to reach out and touch her as she stood, alarmed. It both awed and terrified her to see her dad, the strong and powerful, reduced to this pitiful wreck. She didn't want to pity her dad, she wanted to admire him. And at that moment, something of her childhood left her for ever. She put away childish things and became, as so many did in Victoria Street, old before her time. Outwardly she appeared the same, inwardly she was *old*, older than her parents who, she saw now, were not infallible beings, but small cogs in a giant wheel that could crush them as easily as anyone else. And she knew in that instant, that in future she'd always have to rely on herself.

Margie never let her dad know she'd seen him that day, and slowly his leg improved. He was desperate to go back to work, for the Post Office money had dwindled. Brenda's wage, as an apprentice, was six shillings and to help out, John had started collecting manure from the streets, left by generous horses, and, after taking what they wanted for the allotment, he sold it to other gardeners for a few coppers. Martin would never join him, however, though he'd help on the allotment, and they grew all they could to help their finances. But not only were there no day trips to the seaside this year, there was not even an outing to Coventry or Birmingham. Roberta had gone to France for a month.

Margie decided to help her dad. Again she went to the library and this time tried a bolder plan. She came home with a large heavy volume and set it on the table near to Dad. 'Look what I've got,' she said.

'What?' asked Frank, without interest.

'It's a children's 'cyclopedia. Look—' She turned the pages. 'Lots of pictures. And,' she ended cunningly, 'maps. Remember how you used to say you'd like to travel?'

'Fat chance of travel now,' Frank said.

'But I'll take you when I'm grown up and go to work. I shall have pots of money. Now, where shall we go?' These were the let's pretend games they used to play, but now he was silent. 'France?' Margie asked, and waited for an answer.

'No, I had enough of France in the war. All that mud—'

'Germany then,' she interrupted. 'No, you wouldn't want to go to Germany, would you?' Anti-German feeling was still strong in the thirties – so many had lost loved ones in the war. 'Well, where else is there?' She pored over the book. 'Russia?'

'I think it's a bit cold in Russia.' Frank was beginning to thaw; he moved his chair nearer so that he could see the book. 'And they had that revolution, I don't think they have much food there now, either.'

She returned to the map. 'What else then? Poland—' doubtfully, for she had never heard of Poland. 'Do you know anything about that?'

'I remember a few years back they got free – 1920, I think it was.'

'What do you mean, got free?'

'Well, they'd been occupied by Germany and Russia for a long time, hundred years or more. After the war they got their country back, threw the Russians out. I remember reading about it in the paper.'

At last he was interested. 'Shall we go there then, Dad?' When I'm—' she sought in her mind for a great age.

'Eighteen?' he asked.

'Yes. When will I be eighteen, Dad?'

'In 1939.' Frank was smiling now, and she was happy. They both knew it was make-believe: people in Victoria Street didn't go abroad. But he was *interested*.

'We'll go then, Dad. In 1939. When I'm grown up.'

'All right.' Frank gave in. 'We'll go to Poland. But I don't know what it's like there . . .'

Chapter 2

The Kowalskis' house was larger than its neighbours, so that a visitor might wonder what its original purpose had been. Not grand enough to be a palace of the old Polish nobility, nor yet a merchant's dwelling – or it would have belonged in a wealthy trading centre such as Plock instead of out in the country – its façade came to an abrupt end as though part of it had been destroyed. The porch which had once been in the middle was now at the end, and the overhanging shingled roof was somehow lopsided. Fat cattle grazed in the meadows that led down to the river flowing towards the Russian border; the stables were old, but the barns were new. So, if in the past it had once been a manor house, now it was just a working farm. From the kitchen came the smell of fresh baked bread, the sound of a woman's voice lifted in song. The children sat together, looking lazily at the hay drying in the fields.

'Let's go down to the river,' suggested Stefan who, although not the eldest, was obviously the leader. He moved forward, full of restless energy, but Stanislaw, thin, bespectacled, a book in his hand, was reluctant. 'Come on, Professor,' called Stefan, so Stanislaw stood up.

Tadeusz, at seven the baby of the family, with a round open face and an eager-to-please air, scrambled to his feet. 'I'm coming too,' he called.

'I'm going to catch fish,' said Stefan. 'Last time, you fell in the river.'

'Don't tease him.' Janina was protective. 'Come on, Tad.'

They all loved the river, loved to dabble in the clear water running over the pebbles in summer, to skate on the ice in winter. As they reached it Stefan mused, 'Wonder why Mama sent us to the village? Old Pietr always takes the horses to be shod.'

Not that they minded taking the horse to the smithy; in fact they enjoyed watching the fiery furnace, the huge bellows, hearing the clang-clang of the hammer on metal, the sparks flying. Josef the blacksmith was a giant, easily the biggest man in the village, and they stared in awe at his rippling muscles, his bare chest. And when he'd finished the shoeing Tadeusz said: 'Let me ride,' so Josef gave his big rumbling laugh and lifted both him and Janina on to the horse's great back.

They set off, Stefan holding the bridle, Stanislaw walking at the side, reading. 'I saw Pietr by the stables as we came out,' Stefan remarked. 'He isn't ill or anything.'

'Mm?' Stanislaw didn't look up. 'I didn't see him.'

Stefan gave a little snort. Stanislaw wouldn't see him. He lived in a world of his own, so that Mama sometimes lost patience and said: 'Do you walk around with your eyes shut?' And Father, peace-making, would say it was because he was so clever.

As the horse slowly meandered along the country road, the fields around them shimmering in a heat haze, Stefan would have liked to jump over the ditch at the side of the road, simply for the sheer joy of living, and he knew that even if he released the bridle, and if Stanislaw kept his eyes shut the whole time, the horse would still find his way home. But he didn't jump. Stefan felt responsible for the children.

He took his responsibilities seriously. After all, Father

worked all the time with Pan Lenski and Pietr. Stefan knew they couldn't afford more help, yet *he* didn't want to work on the farm when he grew up, and this troubled him sometimes, for Stanislaw was already earmarked to be the professor Stefan laughingly called him. With his brains, his poor health, his dreaminess, Stanislaw would make no sort of farmer.

But Stefan himself had musical talent, his music teacher had already told Mama he needed better teaching, and frowned at the tinny old piano which was all they had. Stefan frowned at it too when Mama wasn't looking. It was permanently out of tune because the wood inside was rotting away and the flat notes jarred on him every time he played.

But whatever they did in the future would depend on Mama. Father was quiet, firm if necessary, but they all knew that Mama was the dominant partner. And Mama – Stefan's face creased in a puzzled, amused frown – Mama in no way walked around with her eyes shut, yet she did sometimes have grand, even wild schemes, which made living with her such fun. Stefan loved his mother dearly. He would have done anything in the world for her.

As they reached the house, Mama was still singing. Father said she'd been singing ever since they regained their freedom, all of ten years ago. And it was true, Barbara Kowalska was happy these days. Born under Russian occupation, their home taken from them, they had been forced to live in a tiny cottage where Barbara scrubbed floors and consoled her mother after her father was killed for participating in one of the many uprisings. Jan Kowalski, whom Barbara married in 1913, took part in the final miraculous battle after the Great War and the Russian Revolution, when the Bolsheviks invaded on their way to conquer Germany and the world. The Poles had stopped them and regained their country.

The Kowalskis had been able to get Barbara's old home back and, while the country began its mammoth task of uniting its three divided sections, they worked and struggled in a penniless society, with high inflation and shortages of food, to make the farm prosperous, and to give their children a good start. Barbara felt the world was before them, so she sang . . .

Father met them at the door. He lifted the two youngest down from the horse, but instead of letting them go indoors he said: 'Run out and play for a little while. We'll call you when tea's ready,' and he led the horse away.

'Can't I come with you?' asked Tadeusz, for he loved helping on the farm, but Father said no, so, a little disgruntled they went down to the meadow.

'Why can't we go in?' Stefan wondered, throwing himself down on the grass.

'Mama wants us out of the way,' said Stanislaw, sagely.

'It's your birthday, Stefan,' piped Tadeusz.

'I know it's my birthday, silly. Oh, you mean she's planning a surprise? I'm too old for birthday parties, I'm twelve.'

'Wait and see,' Stanislaw told him. 'And you, Tadeusz, say no more,' and he opened his book again.

The sun was hot. Tadeusz rolled on his back. 'I'm hungry,' he complained.

'You always are,' said Stefan, unfeeling. 'No wonder you're fat.'

'I'm not!'

Janina wanted to protest but she was a little in awe of Stefan, the lordly one, so she said nothing.

'I love holidays,' said Tadeusz.

'I do too,' agreed Janina.

'I love the summer holiday, it goes on for ever and ever.'

'I wish it did,' said Janina wistfully, and she lay back too. If only life could always be like this, playing in the fields in summer, no school ever . . .

'I like Christmas,' said Stefan.

'Oh *yes*,' breathed Janina. 'Oh *yes*.' The celebrations on

39

Christmas Eve when they waited for the first star to appear in the sky, then went into supper, with the extra plate always laid for an absent friend or for any stranger who might come. The Christmas tree with its angel on the top ... 'The presents the angels bring,' she said. 'And going to Midnight Mass in the snow '

'And making snowmen and skating,' added Stefan, smiling tolerantly at the little girl. He jumped up, went to the river and lay on the bank, cupping his hands in the water where the fish were running. 'You two stay there,' he ordered Tadeusz and Janina. 'Don't go into the water.'

But Tadeusz was restless too, so he stood up and walked carefully to the river's edge, followed by Janina, his shadow. 'Can you bounce stones?' he asked, and skimmed one over the water.

Janina picked up a small stone. It fell with a plop.

'No, like this,' Tadeusz said, demonstrating. 'Put your hand under like this, see, turn a bit, then throw.'

Janina tried, she turned her body, swung too hard, lost her balance and fell into the water.

In seconds Stefan had raced back and hauled her out. 'I told you to keep away,' he said crossly.

'I'm all wet,' wailed Janina. 'Mama will be angry.'

'Take your clothes off. They'll dry in the sun,' ordered Stefan and, as she hung her head, said, 'Well, go over there behind that tree trunk if you don't want us to see you.' Janina trailed away, and when Tadeusz made to follow Stefan held him back. 'Let her go,' he said.

Behind the tree Janina divested herself of her frock and knickers and spread them on the grass to dry.

She sat for what seemed a long time; she couldn't see the others, she might have been alone. It was very quiet, she could hear nothing but the sounds of the country, the cheep of the waterbird, the buzzing of bees in the clover, and she was suddenly filled with panic. Maybe they'd all gone and left her, and she dared not peep round the trunk, not without her clothes. A feeling of dread came over her at being left alone, the same feeling she got at the little village school when Pan Nowak the headmaster came into the classroom to give one of his tests, and he would ask the children questions at random. Janina would sit quivering, eyes tightly closed, praying that he wouldn't ask her, because she might not know the answer.

Then the sickening dread when he called her name, the relief if she knew what to say, the shame if she did not, while around her, the other children sat complacently. Tadeusz, who didn't care very much whether he knew the answers or not, sympathised, but could not help.

So Janina sat now, wondering if she had been deserted, knowing she could find her own way home, she, a big girl of nine, but afraid of being unwanted.

Then she heard Stanislaw say quite clearly, 'Mama is calling,' and Stefan shouted: 'Come on, Janina!' and hastily pulling on her clothes, she ran to join the boys.

'Are you dry?' Stefan asked and she nodded, her anxiety forgotten. Of course they would not leave her; they never had. So happily they wended their way back to the farmhouse.

'Wonder if we shall have a history lesson today?' Stefan said, and the boys grinned. When their mother was a girl, Polish was a forbidden language, and no Polish history could be taught at the Russian-dominated schools. Now they had their own schools again but Barbara, to make absolutely sure, still taught her children at home, as she had been taught. She would sit them down in the evenings and begin the lessons they all knew by heart.

'When did the kingdom of Poland begin – Stefan?'

'King Mieszko I was baptised in the year 963, thus making Poland the bulwark of Latin Christendom. The kingdom grew and prospered, uniting with the Duchy of Lithuania to become a commonwealth.'

'Good.' And so they would go on, through all the kings,

the battles with the Turks, even touching on the ancient Persian trade routes through Lwow to the important markets at Cracow.

And at some point Tadeusz who, even though he was lazy and uninterested in academic work, knew all the answers, to tease Mama, would pretend he did not. So, when she asked him to tell her about the Golden Age in the sixteenth century, he would say 'Um' and 'Er' until Stanislaw, who wanted to get back to his own books, intercepted with 'I'll tell him.' Then Tadeusz would regret his action, knowing that Stanislaw, if unchecked, would recite pages of history, just go on and on and end up coughing, for Stanislaw was asthmatic.

So he would gabble hastily: 'The Golden Age was when Polish armies occupied Moscow and it was a haven of religious tolerance. The monarch was elected by the nobility and the power of kings limited by charters, and great matters decided by votes. Only Britain had an equal system of early democracy.'

'Good,' said Mama. 'But that was the end of Poland's glory. Her greedy neighbours, Russia, Prussia and Austria, split the country in three, and for over a hundred years Poland disappeared from the map of Europe.' And then Mama would talk about the many uprisings, and the children listened in silence, for they all loved to hear of their turbulent, romantic history.

'Tell us about Great-grandfather, in Siberia,' Stefan would interrupt at this point, and Mama smiled.

'Your great-grandfather was a de Reszke,' she said. 'A member of the gentry—'

'Minor gentry,' murmured Stanislaw, but Mama ignored him.

'In the 1863 uprising, which was very serious and very bitter, he was captured, and sent to Siberia by the Czar's men, and his house – this house – was confiscated and partly burned down. In the wretched Siberian prison – for

42

under the Czar Siberia was just the same as now – he somehow managed to escape.'

'Into the snow,' prompted Stefan, who was never really sure whether this part was true, but loved to hear it nevertheless.

'Into the snow,' replied Mama equably. 'He lived with the peasants, he worked his way back till, after two years he reached St Petersburg. There—' she paused, dramatically, 'he met a group of revolutionaries, or at least people who wanted a revolution, because the Czar was a tyrant, who owned everything and everybody—'

'So he urged them on,' intervened Stefan. 'He encouraged them to rebel, he helped cause the revolution.'

'And now we have our home again,' said Mama. 'Not as it was formerly, alas, with little of the original furniture left, just the old clock, the Louis Quinze chairs, the chest. But ours once more,' and she'd wipe a tear from her eye which they all knew were tears of happiness. They loved the story, it made their home doubly precious.

But today there was to be no history lesson. As they approached the house they saw that their neighbours, the Lenskis, were also standing in the doorway with Mama, and Stefan wondered again if it was going to be some sort of party. They were very friendly with the Lenskis, whose farmhouse, though much smaller than their own and with a thatched roof, was so close, their lands running alongside.

The children reached the porch and went inside, through to the large parlour with its open fireplace and wide windows, double-glazed in winter to keep out the bitter winds that swept from Siberia. The old clock ticked away, the chairs and chest stood along one wall, but the rest of the furniture was modern and cheaper, and did not fill the room, there were large gaps in the corners.

Until today. Mama said, 'Stefan,' and he looked across to where she pointed.

There in one corner was a grand piano.

They were all standing round now, looking at him. The boys, Janina, Pani Lenska with her dumpy little body and round face, her husband not much taller, Stefan's own father, an older version of Tadeusz. Stefan cried, incredulously: 'This is for me?'

'For you.' Stefan was the one who resembled his mother in looks. He had her fair hair, her grey eyes, her easy charm. And he was the closest to her heart. 'I have spoken to your music teacher,' she said. 'And I have talked with the masters at your school. They all think you have a good chance of getting a place in the School of Music in Warsaw as soon as one becomes available. But you must practise and practise ...'

'Oh, Mama!' A place in Warsaw ... she had arranged this. 'How can I ever thank you?' he asked.

'Well, just for now, why not show us what the new piano sounds like?' she asked, smiling.

And Stefan went reverently to the piano and began to play.

Chapter 3

It was a grand day towards the end of September when Dad started back to work. He was up bright and early, and though he still limped badly, he had persuaded the doctor that he'd be fine; his job was standing, not walking. There was a bus running to Mordant's for the workpeople, so he took his bag of sandwiches and said, 'So long,' trying to hide his limp. Eva said, 'So long, Frank,' but she still looked worried. Margie felt happy. Things would be back to normal now.

The children came home for dinner as always. They sat round the table. Mam was putting out the potatoes and new fresh carrots, her back to the window, while they watched their plates eagerly, knowing there was blackberry pudding with custard to follow. None saw the shadow come across the yard, but they heard the back door burst open, then the kitchen door, and they turned, startled.

It was Frank. His face was grey and twisted. He looked for one of the chairs by the dresser, but Martin was sitting on it at the table. 'Get up, Mart,' said Eva and Martin, frightened, stood up. Eva asked, 'What is it, Frank?'

He looked round, fiercely. 'I've got the sack,' he said. 'And it's all your fault.'

'Frank!' cried Eva, shocked.

He sat on the chair, his hands twitching, and began to

speak so forcefully that they could all see just what had happened. The gateman stopping him, Frank asking why. 'You're finished,' said the gateman. 'Sorry, mate, that's my orders.'

Frank had stood amazed, alarmed. 'Finished? Why?' Though he knew there didn't have to be a reason. If you were sacked, you were sacked. Little red spots danced before his eyes. 'I want to see Mordant,' he said. 'And I'm not going till I do.'

'Wait a minute.' The gateman disappeared and soon the foreman came out. 'What's all this?' he blustered.

'I don't want to see you. I want Mordant. You're the bugger who should have reported that machinery but lied about it—'

Frank raged on, refusing to go till he'd seen Mordant. The gateman had to open the big gates for the delivery lorry; men were staring. In the end Mordant came.

'There's no point your waiting there, my good man,' he said. 'You couldn't do your job any longer with your leg, and anyway, I set another man on. We couldn't wait for ever.'

'So can I have another job?' asked Frank.

'I've got nothing else.'

'Then I should have compensation. That machinery wasn't safe.'

Now Frank paused and looked at his frightened family. 'He told me that he'd given me compensation. And that you – Eva – signed a paper to say that you wouldn't ask for any more. You see what you've done.'

'Oh, Frank,' whispered Eva.

'Did you sign that?'

'He said it was a receipt.'

'Didn't you read it?'

'No. I was upset, Frank, I didn't think—'

'You should think when you deal with a man named Mordant. That twisting lying sod!' Dad was shouting now.

'Twenty-five pounds. Twenty-five bloody pounds to last me a lifetime.' He stood up, face twitching, picked up Eva's blue vase from the dresser and smashed it on the floor. Then he fell down.

Margie heard someone screaming and knew it was herself. Martin put an arm around her. She was terrified. Dad was twitching and jerking; his face was purple. His breathing was stertorous, little bubbles of froth came from his mouth; his hands were clenched. Mrs Harvey heard the commotion and knocked at the door. 'Is there anything I can do, Mrs Fennel?' she asked. And Eva, as terrified as the children, called her in. Mrs Harvey was good with illness.

'It's a fit,' said Mrs Harvey. 'Loosen his collar, he'll be all right when he comes round. There,' as the convulsions subsided. 'He's coming to now. Come on, let's get him on the sofa. Fetch a drink of water, you kids.'

The doctor was sent for and he agreed it sounded like a fit. Perhaps Mr Fennel had hurt his head in the accident, he suggested. And would there be others, they asked anxiously? He shrugged: who could tell? He handed over a prescription for tablets and left.

And Frank and Eva faced each other, stark fear in each pair of eyes. Fits were something you kept quiet about, together with insanity in the family, prison sentences, workhouses and public assistance. If you didn't, you'd never get a job. And when you had a bad leg as well, you were as good as dead. You'd never work again.

Home now became a miserable, even a frightening place. Frank was angry all the time: he raged and even swore in front of the family as he'd never done before. Eva cried, Grandma came and tried to smooth him down.

'It's no good you going on at our Eva,' she said. 'If she hadn't got that twenty-five pounds you'd still have had the sack and you wouldn't have got nothing.'

'I ought to've had more,' Frank said sullenly.

'We know that, but how would you get it? Pay a lawyer,

when you haven't got a penny to bless yourself with?' But Frank wouldn't be soothed.

He had another fit and Eva, terrified, dared to send for the doctor again. Dr Healey hadn't much time for his panel patients – workers whose fees were paid through this comparatively new-fangled insurance scheme instead of cash like his private patients – and he drove up to the house on his morning rounds.

'Take the tablets,' he ordered. 'There's no need to send for me again. There's nothing I can do.'

'Then there should be,' Frank shouted. 'Call yourself a bloody doctor?'

'If you don't watch your language I'll cross you off my panel,' Dr Healey said curtly.

'He didn't mean it, Doctor. He's not himself,' Eva put in, hastily, placatingly, for everybody knew that once you were crossed off, no other doctor would take you on. 'He's worried about not being able to work—'

The doctor snorted and left. Martin asked: 'Why is everybody so nasty to you when you're poor?'

No one answered. Perhaps there wasn't an answer. And Martin walked into the garden, pondering. He had pondered a lot since the day he overheard Mam talking about his parentage. Brought up to think Frank and Eva were his real parents, he hadn't taken much notice the day Mam told him that his real mother – her sister Grace – was dead, that's why he lived with them. He hadn't wondered about his father till the day he was sitting on the stairs, and Aunt Mary and Mam were discussing his latest prank – scrumping apples, being caught by an irate farmer and towed home by one ear, to be suitably admonished by Dad then sent to his bedroom.

Aunt Mary had sniffed: 'Trouble with children like that, you never know what bad blood's in 'em.'

'Oh come on, Mary, you don't know there's any bad blood at all.'

'No, she wouldn't tell who the father was, would she, our Grace? But you know and I know, Eva, that she was going out with some posh chap. Remember the time he brought her home in a cab? Then when she was expecting he didn't want to know.'

'We reckon he was married,' Eva murmured.

'Well, he would say that, wouldn't he? He must've thought she wasn't good enough.'

'We don't know—'

'You know as well as I do, that a posh chap wouldn't marry a girl from Victoria Street.'

Their voices were lowered, and when he could hear again they had changed the subject. And Martin went up to his bedroom, where he was supposed to stay for a punishment. Why wouldn't this man marry his mother 'cos he had money? What difference would that make? The only photograph he'd seen of Grace had been taken as a child, and showed a pretty fair girl, with a sweet trusting expression. He could never think of this child as his mother, not this little girl. Eva was his mother.

But it seemed there was something wrong about not having money, something to be ashamed of. He hated that man who'd been so unkind to pretty little Grace, and it was then his hatred of authority was born. It didn't apply to his school, for he knew the teachers tried to help. Why, only yesterday Miss Baines had said, 'You're a clever boy, Martin. You'll be one of the half-dozen children picked to enter for the scholarship to the grammar school.'

Now he walked upstairs and spread an old newspaper over the bed he shared with John. There were pictures in it of Amy Johnson, whose flight to Australia in May had created such a sensation. He cut the picture out and pinned it on the wall, next to that of Colonel Lindbergh, who'd flown the Atlantic in 1927. He'd like to fly an aeroplane, he'd like that more than anything. He'd be famous then and nobody would refuse to marry him because he was poor.

49

But he said nothing about these dreams except to Margie, his confidante.

Frank signed on at the Labour Exchange and drew dole of thirty-two shillings a week. Eva tried to get work, without success. The Post Office money was gone now and things grew tight. Christmas approached, and there was little hope of presents, though Margie made paper chains for decorations, and Eva bought a little Christmas tree from the market.

And then, as a cold wind blew from the north and the skies were full of snow, two of Dad's workmates came to see him, Bill Jackson and Fred Moreton. They sat on the horsehair sofa and Mam made them a cup of tea as they talked about the accident.

'We knew that machinery was loose,' Fred said.

'And we had a word with the foreman after,' put in Bill. 'He said he'd told Mordant, but he wouldn't have it done. You know Mordant, allus penny-pinching.'

'So there was nothing we could do,' added Bill.

'*You* could have gone to see Mordant,' muttered Martin from his seat on a stool by the fire.

The men looked down at him and laughed. 'Hark to the young 'un,' said Bill. 'You know what 'ud have happened if we had – *we'd* have been out. And wouldn't have got another job, neither.'

'Not if you're branded as a trouble-maker,' agreed Fred.

'But what we've done,' Bill went on. 'We had a collection round the blokes—' and he put a canvas bag on the table. 'Now,' he cautioned Frank. 'This en't charity. Call it a leaving present, if you like, somethin' for Christmas, for the kids, like.'

They stood up to go. The bag lay on the table, bulging with coins, sixpences, shillings, even half-crowns. Margie watched her dad anxiously but Frank said, standing, 'Thank you, chaps. Thank you all ...'

'Ah well,' Fred said, at the door. 'We know you had a

rotten deal, Frank. Maybe he'll get his come-uppance one day, Mordant. Maybe this young lad here will give it to him,' he nodded at Martin and they all laughed.

All except Martin. 'Maybe I will,' he muttered.

Another bright spot was going to Grandma's party. They walked along the road and from every house came the sound of singing – the Salvation Army band was playing carols on the corner. At Grandma's all the family were there, aunts, uncles, cousins, and they all gathered round Uncle Harry's piano and sang. Grandma gave the grown-ups home-made wine and mince pies, and when they walked home it was snowing. A real Christmas.

The New Year brought more snow and ice, and though it was fun to make snowmen and slides, at home hardship returned. The allotment vegetables were finished except for potatoes, stored under the bed, and bottled fruit in the pantry. Mam no longer bought best butter, creamy and yellow, tasting of clover meadows, nor good cuts of meat, but cheap pieces containing little nourishment. They paid visits to the market at half-past eight on Saturday evening, just before it closed, when the stallholders had to get rid of the perishable goods, the banana woman practically giving them away.

As the winter wore on Margie had another worry. Her shoes were getting too small, but she dared not ask for a new pair. Mam had bought John and Martin new ones and said with a weary sigh, 'They'll have to last, I can't buy any more.' Margie was terrified the teacher would give her a ticket for free boots – the ultimate shame. So she walked on through the winter in her tight shoes, thinking that if they lasted till spring she'd be all right, she could wear her sandals then. Sandals were acceptable.

She worried about her mother, who was getting a beaten air, like Vera West's mother. You had to fight when you were poor, she realised, like Grandma did. Grandma, who had nursed three children with diphtheria and two with scarlet fever all at the same time, and only one died. Grandma, who had lost one son in the Great War and a daughter – Grace – in childbirth but who, at sixty-four, was bloody but unbowed. Widowed, she lived with her youngest son Harry, and Margie visited her often, gaining sustenance from her bold attitude to life, listening to her words of wisdom. 'It won't always get dark at six,' said Grandma.

Grandma was full of such sayings. 'Catchpenny,' she'd snort at the door to the salesman offering cheap goods, and more mysteriously, 'Wheels within wheels.' Grandma thought the whole world was in league against her and she fought them gloriously, single-handed. Grandma didn't believe in turning the other cheek. Hit them before they hit you, was her motto, though she didn't put it quite like that. 'Don't let them do you down,' she'd cry. Margie began to model herself on Grandma and grew more impatient with her own mother.

It wasn't Grandma, however, but Frank who resolved the problem of the shoes. He watched her as she walked home from school, one rainy day in February. She hobbled across the yard, entered the kitchen and took off her coat – one which had been Brenda's, and was really too big, but it kept the rain out – and Frank asked abruptly: 'Have you hurt your foot?'

'No,' Margie said, taken offguard and surprised that her dad had noticed.

'Take your shoes off,' he said, and to Eva: 'This child's being crippled. She must have some new shoes.'

'I can't, Frank, not yet. Unless I get a check from the Co-op, pay so much a week. And I know you don't like the never-never.'

Frank walked to the window, the rain pelted down in an icy stream. 'Two shillings I'm allowed for each child,' he said. 'And a pair of good shoes costs ten. Cheaper ones don't last five minutes.'

'But she grows out of them,' said Eva.

Margie walked up to the fire. It was cold outside and the cheap coal Mam bought now didn't give off much heat. 'I expect it's my chilblains makes me limp a bit,' she said.

Frank made a strange sound that was something between a sigh and a groan. Then he said: 'Get some shoes. We'll have to take lodgers.'

Lots of people took lodgers in Victoria Street. The lodgers had the front room up and down but the Fennels were handicapped by having their bedrooms full. So Brenda went to live at Grandma's, their parents moved in the back room with Margie, and the Evans came. And in the short time they were with them, they changed Margie's name and changed their lives.

Mr Evans was a Welshman who came to the Midlands to find work in the pits, his wife a small dark woman with curly hair. Usually, the lodgers were kept separate. They had to use the same back-kitchen with its sink – they cooked on their own open fire – but they were not allowed to walk through the living-kitchen – they had to go round the entry in all weathers.

But Eva wouldn't have that, not with snow and ice on the ground. Eva quite liked having lodgers. It removed the immediate money worries, though the long-term one remained: what would they do when Frank's benefit ran out and they had to apply for public assistance? But she let the Evanses use her oven and come through the kitchen, and in return Mr Evans gave her some of his allowance coal (strictly forbidden). And sometimes they'd sit and talk.

Frank began to come out of his silent misery when he talked to Mr Evans. He understood, he'd been out of work for a long time. 'You should have a union,' he advised. 'They'd have seen you got compensation. Seen the machinery was safe in the first place.'

'Mordant won't allow 'em,' said Frank.

'We have the same trouble in Wales,' Mr Evans nodded. 'Treat you like dirt, they do.'

Mr Evans was an intelligent man. He and Frank would discuss the events of the day, world affairs. 'It's this Depression,' Mr Evans said. 'Same all over the world, they say. Bad in Germany, cos they have to pay back such a lot after the war.'

Frank sniffed. 'Well, they shouldn't start wars, then. We didn't want it. I was there in the trenches.'

'No, but it's when people are so poor that trouble starts. That's what caused the revolution in Russia.'

'You don't think Germany is likely to turn communist?' asked Frank.

'Depends on who they get for a leader,' answered Mr Evans. 'A man named Hitler is promising all the people work, but Hindenburg's against him, so he doesn't seem to get anywhere. But I reckon something's got to change, else there'll be trouble,' and Margie, in later years, thought how odd it was that an ordinary man like Mr Evans sensed what the men in power didn't, that the world was ready to blow up.

'Same as here,' the Welshman was going on. 'All these hunger marches, I went on one last year.'

'The government says they're communist-led,' said Frank.

'Well, they would say that, wouldn't they?' asked Mr Evans. 'I went, and there was a contingent of women as well.'

Eva looked up. 'I wanted a vote,' she said, 'and now I've got it and what good's it done me? If there's another march I think I'll join.'

There was a silence. Frank looked at Mr Evans. 'See what kind of a family I've got?' he said. 'Communists all, all in the pay of Moscow.' But he was smiling, and there was laughter, and it was like the old days, when they *laughed*.

But Eva was thoughtful, and the following week she joined the Co-operative Women's Guild, because they

54

fought for women's rights – votes for women, money for women. They alone of the banks and societies paid the dividend to the woman only, and many a working-class wife was thankful her husband couldn't get his hands on it.

As spring approached, Mr Evans persuaded Frank to start going out. Like so many miners, he had a gentleness within his strength, loving the country and wildlife.

'Come on, man, there's nothing to be ashamed of in having a gammy leg,' he said. 'Many a miner walks on crutches and is proud of it – it's a badge of honour. And pleased to be alive he is, to be walking on God's good earth.'

So they walked together when Mr Evans finished his shift, and some of the pain was lifted from Frank.

And it was Mr Evans who changed Margie's name.

It was a cold evening, too cold to be out, and Martin, frustrated, had been particularly devilish. He pulled Margie's hair, he called her Margerine. Mr Evans said, 'It's a nice name you have. I had a sister named Marged, a Welsh name,' and after that he always called her Marged. She liked it, and gradually the name stuck.

Nineteen thirty-one was the scholarship year. It was also the year of the Means Test. Martin and Marged were among the few children chosen to enter for the exam, and sat the written test in a local hall. The results came in a buff envelope.

Frank opened it. 'You've both passed,' he told them.

Now started days of discussion. Eva said, sadly, 'We couldn't afford it. Not now your benefit's running out, Frank.'

'I'll still get something,' Frank replied. 'From the—' he couldn't bring himself to say the dreaded words *Public Relief*.

'You don't know,' Eva said, whose sleepless nights of worry left her white and tired. She thought of Mrs Brown up the road who also had money worries; in the end she tried to kill herself and they took her off to the asylum.

'I want to go,' Martin said.

'There's still the interview. That's where you're all weeded out,' said Frank. 'And they won't take you, not with me out of work. They want children who'll stop on and go to college. I'd have to sign a paper saying you wouldn't leave before you were sixteen, and we couldn't afford that.'

Afford, afford. Did their lives have to be run by the word afford, thought Martin, resentfully. 'I want to go,' he repeated.

'It's a great thing, education,' agreed Mr Evans. 'It shouldn't be just for those who have money.'

John said nothing. Neither did Brenda.

Marged did not mind too much about the scholarship, but her dad took her into the garden, saying he wanted to look at the flowers. It had rained in the night, and little droplets sparkled on every leaf. Frank bent awkwardly to pick one of the roses and, with his head turned away said, 'I wanted the best for you, Marguerite,' and she trembled at the pain in his voice, yet she knew she had always been his favourite. He endorsed this now. 'You are the baby, see. The others are good, but . . .'

'Bren and John couldn't go, Dad. They passed.'

'No, we couldn't manage it then, not with you younger ones to keep. But you were the baby . . . Oh, the dreams I had.' She stood silent. She had never heard her dad talk like this. 'I thought, later, we'd get a better house, a nice little semi like those in Marbourne Road. We could have too, if I'd been able to keep on at work, and saved . . . we could have sold this one—' his voice broke. 'Now, to be like this . . . not even a man, your mother having to put up with lodgers in her home . . .'

'Dad, no, Mam doesn't mind.' Yet she understood his loss of dignity, that he should be almost deformed, he who had been so proud of what he had done for them. Tears suddenly blinded her eyes, and now it was she who turned away.

But it was Martin who was hit the hardest. He repeated: 'I want to go.'

'We can't, Martin,' Eva said. 'It would mean both of you going. It's impossible.'

'I needn't go,' said Marged.

'One's not going without the other,' Frank stated, and Marged knew he meant that if his own child couldn't go, then Martin shouldn't, either. And she was sorry, as Martin walked away into the front room to talk with Mr Evans, watched uneasily by Eva.

That night Martin went up to bed early, refusing to speak to anyone. Eva made him a cup of Oxo and sent Marged up with it. She opened the door. Martin was sitting morosely on the bed. 'What's the matter, Mart?' she asked.

He shrugged, and she went to look at his pictures of planes which now covered one wall. His chief interest at the moment lay in war planes, the history of the Royal Flying Corps, the beginning of the RAF, the Bristol Fighter, and the new Hawker Hind.

Not knowing what to say, she moved to the window. In the back field, boys were playing cricket with an old bat, using shabby coats for wickets. Their cries echoed in the summer air. She said, 'It'll be better later, Mart,' knowing it wouldn't. His one chance – like hers – had come and gone. There'd be no other.

'It won't,' he contradicted. 'It'll be worse.'

'Why? What do you mean?'

'It's something called the Means Test.'

'What's that?'

'When you've been on the dole they stop your money, then a man comes round to see if you've got any other funds coming in, like lodgers or anybody working. If you have, they cut your pay. The Evanses'll have to go.'

'How do you know?'

'Mr Evans told me.'

She was silent, shocked, knowing how much her mother depended on the few shillings their lodgers paid. *Means Test*. The words filled her with dread, all the more so because she didn't understand their meaning, only that they were going to do terrible things to their home-life.

Martin said, 'We'll be poorer than ever. And it's all Mordant's fault.' He stood up, came to her. 'Swear that you'll get your revenge on Mordant,' he hissed, pushing his face close to hers.

She stared at him, wide-eyed, half-afraid of his intensity. 'What can I do?' she whispered.

'Swear,' he insisted. And she said softly, 'I swear.' Then she remembered her father's pain and repeated, strongly now: 'I swear that someday I will be revenged on Mordant.' Martin clasped her hand and they stood together, a bond forged.

And now she didn't see so much of Amy and Vera, much less Roberta, it was Martin who became her friend, and Martin's friends. She followed them over the fields, with them she climbed trees, was dared to do reckless things. Her mother protested at her torn frocks, her dad was angry, but she kept on, hitting out at life which dealt such blows, in the only way she knew. For it was all true: the Means Test came into being, the Evanses had gone.

There were many outcries and protests all over the country, more marches were held, two men were put in prison. But to no avail. The Means Test was here, and Frank was interviewed. He was asked about all his assets, how many were working, what they earned, what money he had in the bank ('that's a laugh,' snorted Frank). An officious little man inspected their home to see if anything could be sold. 'Take our beds, we'll sleep on the floor,' grumbled Frank. But Mam had packed her treasured tea-set – a wedding present from the family – the wall clock, a couple of favourite ornaments and her best white tablecloths, to be hidden at

Grandma's or the Means Test man would order them to be sold.

Brenda stayed with Grandma, or her earnings would have been subtracted from Frank's relief, but it was not the same, being forced to go, and Marged, in the bedroom on her own, missed Brenda, turned out of her home, and her unhappiness turned to wildness.

The climax came when she was over in Farley's meadow where the boys were bathing in the canal without their clothes. Marged didn't take off her clothes. She sat at the side, watching.

And someone told her mother.

That night, when Frank was in the shed and the boys were going out, Eva said to her daughter, as she was about to follow: 'Just a minute, I want a word with you.'

'What?' She stood sullenly by the door. She didn't say much to Mam these days.

'What's this about you being by the canal with all the lads and them with no clothes on?' And as she didn't answer, 'You should be ashamed of yourself. What do you think people will say?'

'Who cares?' began Marged.

'Don't take that attitude with me, milady. You should care. Running about with no clothes on!'

'I didn't take mine off.'

'You should have come home.'

'But Mam, the lads always go swimming like that.'

'The lads, yes. Then leave 'em alone. It's time you did, anyway. You're getting too big to play with lads now.'

'We don't do nothing,' Marged said sulkily.

'I should hope not. Anyway, be told. I don't want to tell your dad. You know how he'll create.'

But she did tell Grandma. Grandma often came down since the Evanses had left. It was Grandma who advised Dad to start repairing cycles in the shed, although it was strictly against the rules and the Means Test officials always asked the neighbours if a man was earning a shilling or two extra. But no one shopped Frank, and it was rumoured that they were afraid of Grandma. Grandma prided herself on being respectable but she would swear black was white if it meant outwitting 'Them'. 'They're all hand in glove,' she'd cry, 'They' being the vast army of employers, petty officials and doctors who had dealings with Victoria Street. But she was respectable even so, and she turned sternly to her erring granddaughter.

'Well, miss, what's all this about your going with lads with no clothes on?'

'Oh, for goodness sake, Grandma, it was—'

'You're nothing but a great Tom-lad these days. You should be ashamed of yourself. Why, when I was your age I was at work, your mother as well.'

'I wish I was at work.'

'You will be soon enough. And you'll be working for the rest of your life, remember that.'

'I wish you wouldn't keep on at me.'

'Your mother only wants the best for you. Don't want you to make a mess of your life,' – which last left Marged mystified, as she confided to Brenda in the silence of their candle-lit bedroom. For though officially Brenda still lived with Grandma, she came home at weekends, giving up all her earnings to be divided between Mam and Grandma.

'Well, it's your own fault.' Brenda was unsympathetic. 'What do you want, to be talked about like Film-Struck?'

'Film-Struck' was the nickname of a half-witted girl who wandered the fields and lanes. Named after Film-Struck Fanny, a character in a comic, she was an unpleasant girl, with a deep interest in sex, and the boys took advantage of this, taking her over the fields at every opportunity.

'Why should I be like Film-Struck?' Marged asked.

Brenda drew a breath. 'Because of what she does with the lads.'

The candle flickered, the chest of drawers threw strange

shapes on the wall. Marged whispered, 'What does she do, Bren?' knowing she was penetrating one of life's mysteries.

'You shouldn't ever touch the lads when you see 'em naked,' Brenda said repressively.

'I don't.' Marged was surprised.

'Or let them touch you – down there.'

Marged burst out laughing. 'You mean touch their things? Oh Bren, as if I would.'

'But Marged, that's how you have babies. That's what Film-Struck does.'

'What, just touching their things?'

'It's when they put theirs to yours,' said Brenda.

'Oh.' Marged nodded, having no idea what she meant. And for a long time she thought that to touch a boy *there* meant she would have a baby. And she knew that was wrong if you weren't married, her mother said so. Some girls did have babies before marriage, and there was a lot of talk, then somehow the baby was fitted in the family with the others and gradually people forgot.

As winter wore on it became too cold to run wild with the boys. But she walked down to school with them, rather than with Amy and Vera, and was always ready these days to quarrel. The boys and girls were separated in the play-ground but in the street she'd pick a quarrel, even fight. Her schoolteacher, Miss Anson, asked her why she was suddenly being so naughty. Marged said nothing.

How could she explain the miserable life where not only every penny counted, but every farthing? Where Dad had to stop repairing bicycles, as it was too dangerous having people call at the house where everyone could see; where the Means Test men, like the secret police, watched your every move; where even if the local councils – who ran the Public Assistance – wanted to raise their payments, the government stopped them. Benefits were cut, teachers' pay was cut, pay of the armed forces was cut and led to a mutiny in the Royal Navy at Invergordon. Life was dreary when you didn't dare buy anything for fear of Them, when Brenda now handed over all her wages as Grandma and Uncle Harry gave her food while she stayed there, and Eva grew more and more tight-lipped.

The months slid by. There were still protests all over the country, and a national hunger march was planned for October 1932. It was to be the largest, best-organised march to date. On a chilly day in September, when the leaves were turning brown, and Eva had to light a fire – she had been cooking on the gas-ring through the summer – the family were sitting in the kitchen when she returned from her Co-op Women's Guild meeting.

'This march they're planning for next month,' she said baldly, hardly stopping to take off her last year's hat. 'There's a women's contingent, and I'm going.'

There was dead silence in the kitchen. Marged stared, literally open-mouthed at her usually quiet mother, then turned to Frank, waiting for his explosion.

Frank blinked. Eva took off her coat unconcernedly, and Marged knew – they all knew – that she would go whether her husband approved or not. Frank said, 'I wish I could come with you.'

Marged jumped to her feet. 'Let me come too,' she begged.

Eva hesitated. Frank said, 'You can't walk all the way to London. It's a hundred miles.'

'I can if Mam can. I'm strong. Oh, please let me go.' Please let me *do* something . . .

'But you'll wear your shoes out.' Even in protests you had to think about money.

'They repair them on the way,' Eva said. 'They did it at Leicester on the last march. There's always people to help.' She turned to her daughter. 'How about if you come part of the way?' she asked. 'Say to Stratford-on-Avon? Then you can come home.'

'How would she get home?' Frank asked, practically.

'They collect money. Lots of people sympathise, even if the government doesn't,' said Eva.

'They don't know nothing about us in London,' Frank said. 'Don't know we exist.'

'So she can come back on the train,' Eva went on, and Marged knew she had won.

Two more local women were marching. Both from the Guild, neither on Means Test. Mrs Jenkins was the secretary of the Guild and Mrs Cooper, a former suffragette, was an ardent supporter of the women's movements. They called at the house.

'We shall join up with the women south of Birmingham,' said Mrs Jenkins. 'There's been a bit of trouble on the way. The women were told at Burton-on-Trent they'd have to give their names at the workhouse, and they refused to be treated like tramps. We have to sleep in the workhouses, you see, if the reception committees can't provide anything else. They call them institutions now.' She smiled.

'Has there been any more trouble?' Frank asked.

'Well, the Lancashire contingent met violence at Warrington, though when they got to Birmingham workhouse, sorry, institution, the chairman of the Public Assistance Committee gave them ham for supper – his gift. How about that? Anyway, are you ready?'

'I think so.' Grandma, who would have loved to join them but was prevented by her 'rheumatics', borrowed mackintoshes for both of them, and filled haversacks with sandwiches.

They set off, walking two abreast, Marged with her mother. Behind them a woman pushed a pram containing blankets. At the front two others carried a huge banner, reading: 'Women's Contingent marching to London against the Means Test.' Most of the women were dressed as she was, in coats or raincoats, with berets on their heads.

People stared as they walked, some cheered them, others turned their noses up, but the women marched on.

63

Sometimes they sang: *These things shall be* and *Jerusalem* and Marged felt uplifted, proud to be part of the marching women.

Sometimes they rested, and Marged was glad. Her legs ached, and she realised that the soles of her shoes were thin. They halted outside a village, near a stream, and several of the women took off their shoes and dabbled their feet in the water, Marged among them, and it was relief indeed.

Two workmen walked by, and stopped. 'Hey, missus, this ain't the seaside,' called one.

'We thought it was. Thought the tide was out,' riposted the women.

The men stepped closer and saw the banner. 'Marching to London?' asked one. 'You'll never do it.'

'Oh yes, we will!' cried one of the paddling women. 'I'm from Burnley and I've worn out two pairs of clogs so far. I've got sore feet and blisters, but I'm going to get to London if it's on my hands and knees.' And the women cheered.

'Want a drink of tea?' asked the man. 'I'll send my missus,' and sure enough, down came village women with jugs of tea and plates of bread and jam.

But at their next halt, the leader came to talk to them. 'There might be trouble ahead,' she warned. 'The police have had instructions from the Home Office. Last year Coventry put the marchers in a school and paid for the food supplied by the Co-op; now they've had a telegram from the Ministry saying the Council will be surcharged if it repeats this action. And the Chief Constable of Warwickshire has sent a strong body of police to Stratford, and that's our next stop.'

'We carry on,' said the women, for Stratford was where they were to stay the night. 'Are you all right?' Eva asked Marged, and the woman with the pram of blankets said: 'Put her on here. Give her a ride.' So, amid laughter, Marged was hoisted on to the pram.

The Lancashire contingent was already in Stratford when

64

they arrived, and there was no reception committee. The women marched to the workhouse, only to find eighty-seven police billeted there, and outside, the Police Superintendent and the Public Assistance Officer of Warwickshire facing a group of the Lancashire men.

'We want a hot supper,' one man said.

There was a consultation before the PA Officer agreed, and the Superintendent told the crowds: 'You can have a hotpot for supper and bully beef for breakfast.'

'Can we have tea with our supper?' a woman asked. 'We're dying of thirst.'

Another consultation. The Superintendent said they could have tea, but not the meat for breakfast. Marged was so hungry she could have eaten a horse. She followed the crowd into the long room with tables, thankfully ate the small plate of hotpot, drank the tea, and helped clear the tables away so they could sleep on the floor. Now she saw the reason for the blankets.

She awoke, cramped and aching. The women were already astir; they followed the others into the yard where the men were assembled around tables and benches. There was bread, margarine and buckets of tea, but no meat.

'There's bound to be trouble,' the leader told the master and the Superintendent. 'These marchers are weak and under-nourished as it is. They need meat to sustain them. How can they march forty miles on bread and marge?'

He was right, the men were angry, were shouting for food. Someone broke a table, then a bench, and the police turned up. A fierce battle broke out, but the men's walking sticks were no defence against truncheons. 'On your way,' the police yelled and the marchers were herded out of the workhouse, out of the town, limping and bleeding.

As they left, Marged felt a blow on her head from a truncheon. She screamed, and her mother shouted: 'Look what you've done, you great bully! She's only a child.'

'Are you hurt, lovey?' one of the women asked, and Marged shook her head.

'She'll have to go back,' Eva said. 'Can we pay her train fare?'

''Course we can. Come on, we'll take you to the station, then join up with the others.'

'Will you be all right, Mam?' Marged asked anxiously and Eva said, 'Don't you worry about me. You look after yourself.'

They saw her on the platform, where the train was coming in. She climbed aboard, waved, and sank down on the seat, her feet and legs aching, her head paining from the blow. But when she arrived in Chilverton, Martin was waiting on the platform.

'How did you know when I was coming?' she asked. 'We couldn't tell you.'

'I met every train.' He noted her limping. 'Are you all right?'

'I'm fine.' And she staggered home.

Frank met her at the door. The neighbours came in. Brenda was home in the dinner-hour and it was she who brought a bowl of hot water, who peeled off Marged's stockings and shoes, and then it was the loveliest thing in the world to soak her aching feet while Brenda brought cups of tea, and Dad said, 'You did well.'

'Did I?' Marged's eyes shone.

'Yes. I read somewhere how it is better to light a candle than lie cursing the darkness. Sometimes you have to protest – but there's a right way.' And she knew he was referring to her running wild over the fields with the boys, that he understood her motives even more than she did herself.

Eva carried on to London, and now workhouse masters were instructed that walking sticks should be taken from the marchers because reports said the Yorkshiremen had strong sticks, the Scots had cudgels, the Tynesiders broomsticks, while the woman pushing the pram holding the blankets was an object of suspicion. 'Think I've got a bomb?' she asked the police who stopped her. The

66

Metropolitan Police banned the carrying of sticks, so the men hid theirs inside their trousers; the women could not, so their sticks – used to help them walk – were confiscated. The men from South Wales, who Eva thought the thinnest and weakest of all the marchers, were described as those to be watched, professional agitators, dangerous men. Detectives and informers swarmed all over the haunts of the Communist Party in London. 'We'll all be on the files now,' laughed Mrs Jenkins to Eva.

Eva missed the assembly in Oxford Circus, and was glad she had when she heard that mounted police had attacked the marchers, who fought back with bricks and stones. Forty were arrested. Onlookers were hurt. Some people in the neighbourhood opened their homes to shelter the marchers, and pelted the police when they banged on their doors. There was a debate in the House of Commons.

But Eva was with the columns of marchers on Thursday 27 October as they rounded Marble Arch and entered Hyde Park, and she saw masses of people, a crowd of a hundred thousand gathered, and two thousand police, including mounted police and special constables. And she saw it was the specials who first struck out with their batons, then mounted police charged into the crowds. The marchers fought back, tearing up railings to defend themselves. Many were hurt. Eva was amazed. She had thought it would all be orderly, that they'd be allowed to meet and take their petition to the House of Commons.

And thousands did march to the House of Commons to present the petition, but the police confiscated it. *Hunger marchers backed by red gold*, thundered the *Sunday Despatch*. *Five thousand pounds of hard cash smuggled from Moscow to Britain*.

The House of Commons refused to see the petition. There was nothing to do but go home. Eva came back tired, hungry, aching from head to toe – and angry. Frank said simply: 'I'm proud of you.'

She was angry because she thought it had all been for nothing. But it had not. The marches had aroused middle-class and influential supporters, well-known writers Storm Jameson and Vera Brittain wrote: *Can it be that the government is so anxious to silence them because it would rather not hear too much about what it feels like to try to feed a child on two shillings a week?* Other well-known writers joined in, H.G. Wells, A.P. Herbert, and politicians Clement Attlee and Edith Summerskill. Together they started the Council for Civil Liberties, protesting at police intimidation of hunger marchers.

Frank said to Marged, 'When you're an old woman, you'll be able to tell your grandchildren that you helped to make history.'

Marged went back to school, and her schoolmates eyed her with awe. 'Tell us about it,' they begged. 'Were you hurt?'

But the glow of heroism soon wore off as more down-to-earth matters reasserted themselves. Her shoes were letting in water badly, for no one had repaired them in Stratford-on-Avon. She said nothing to her mother but several days later as she was leaving the classroom Miss Anson stopped her. 'Just a minute, Marguerite.'

She waited till the class had emptied then pointed to a white ticket on her desk. 'Would you be interested?' she asked. *Free boots.*

Marged drew back as if stung. 'No, miss.'

'No, Miss Anson,' corrected the teacher, a grey-haired spinster of some fifty years. 'It isn't really charity,' she said.

'I don't want to wear boots,' Marged said.

Miss Anson pondered. She knew and respected the feelings of her poorer children, knew that if you lost your pride you lost everything. You had nothing else. You felt worthless. 'I was thinking,' she began. 'You were top of the class last year, and you had a prize.'

'Yes, Miss Anson. A book.' *You bought it.*

'It was small, I thought, for a year's work. Supposing we got you another prize, say a pair of shoes. Quite plain. Lace-ups,' Miss Anson hastened to add lest Marged plump for ankle-straps, a great favourite with the girls this year.

Marged blinked, but try as she would she could see nothing wrong with this novel suggestion. 'Well, yes, thank you,' she said.

'Now.' Miss Anson knew there was no point in asking the girl to walk home with her, as the others would want to know why.

'How about if I get one or two pairs, then you can call at my home and try them on.'

So it was agreed, and honour was satisfied. Even Frank could not argue with a prize.

Miss Anson lodged in a semi-detached house in a pleasant avenue not far from school. Marged knocked at the door and was ushered into the front room. And stood still.

She thought it was beautiful. There were fine net curtains at the windows, not cheap lace like her mother had, and more surprising, all the room *matched*. Pale green paper on the walls, a green carpet, and though the settee and arm-chairs were covered with chintz, they had a green motif, too. Marged had never seen a room that matched. Her own home furniture was bought for cheapness, from sales; even the wallpaper was any colour that was going. This was a palace.

She tried on the shoes and thanked Miss Anson with a fervour that surprised that lady, who didn't realise that Marged had found her dream home.

Marged did not return to running wild with the boys. She was changing, the world was opening up. And something more important happened at the same time. She went to the church fête and watched couples dancing in the little hall. The music was like that which came over the neighbour's wireless, smooth and graceful, with piano, sax and drums.

Marged was fascinated by the rhythm and movement. She caught a fleeting glimpse of the rainbow. Here was another world she hadn't known existed, a grown-up world of long dresses and high-heeled shoes. She felt she had been stumbling around for so long like a blind person, not knowing where she was going or why, the only reality being the poverty and harshness of the world. Now she found a respite in the beat-beat of the music, solace for the grim reality of life in the back streets. 'I want to dance like that,' she murmured.

Gradually her interests changed. She began to watch Brenda as she prepared for Saturday evenings at the dance – her one outing – noting how carefully she made up her face, how she hitched up her dress so it wouldn't show below her coat, making Dad ask where she was going. And when Brenda had gone she experimented with Pond's face powder (used by Society ladies), the Tangee lipstick (new, natural). The adventures with the boys began to seem childish, immature; she drifted back to the girls, and though they'd still join in the odd game of hide and seek in the winter, they preferred to stand talking by the front gate, looking forward to the next year or so when they would be grown-up, would have periods like the older girls in the top class, would be women. On Sunday afternoons they joined the promenade round the Park, and Amy began to make eyes at John.

Marged had seen little of Roberta over the past year or so. When she was running with the lads she ignored her, knowing Martin wouldn't want her with them. Sometimes she'd have a word with her when Roberta stood on the corner, making no apology for her neglect. After all, she wasn't one of the gang. And now with the spring, as Marged entered her thirteenth year the old childish games disappeared for good. The patterns were changing. Boys were not just other kids who wore trousers, but an opposite sex whom you started to notice because they had handsome faces, and Marged began to fall in love. She fell in love regularly two or three times a week. She pinned pictures of film stars on her bedroom wall – Tyrone Power, Gary Cooper. The world was changing completely, and she wasn't sure that Roberta was changing with it.

She was hovering around on the Saturday morning Marged had to go to the Co-op in the town for Mam. 'Bring the bacon, cheese and lard,' instructed Eva. 'The rest is to be delivered.'

'I have something to tell you,' Roberta said, catching up with her, and Marged replied, 'Come on then, I'll walk along with you.'

She didn't have to go via Park Manor Road to get to the town, but Roberta was saying, 'I'm going to boarding school.'

Marged knew all about boarding schools; they featured heavily in the girls' weeklies that she read. 'I shall soon be going to work,' she countered, not to be outdone.

'Will you? Where?'

'Brenda will get me in at Grant's.'

'Will you like that?'

Marged shrugged. It wasn't a question of liking, it was what you had to do.

'Will you write to me?' asked Roberta. They were walking along Park Manor Road with its detached houses with their little turrets. Halfway along, she stopped. 'I live here,' she said.

Marged looked round: there was nothing but one huge house, the biggest in the road. '*Here?*' she asked. 'In this mansion?'

'This is Park Manor. The road was named after it.'

Marged stared thunderstruck at the building. Set well back from the road, it was so huge that she could not imagine anyone actually living in it. It was as big as a prison or the workhouse. Where would you put the front room or the kitchen in a place like this? She repeated, 'It's a mansion.'

Roberta shrugged. 'I don't want to go to boarding school.'

'Don't you? I'd like to.' Midnight feasts in the dorm, jolly japes. Marged thought it sounded fun.

'Brian's at school. That's my brother, and he doesn't like it,' Roberta said. 'But you will write to me, won't you?'

'If you like. But I don't know your name.'

'Don't you? I thought you did. I know your name. It's Marguerite Fennel, and your brother's name is Martin.'

'He's my cousin.'

'Oh yes. Well, my name's Mordant.'

Mordant.

Marged stood transfixed. Around her she could hear birds twittering in the many trees. Mordant. Not ... *him.* She asked, carefully, 'Where does your father work?'

'He owns his own firm, engineering. I expect you've heard of him.'

Oh yes, I've heard of him. We've all heard of him. He's the man we hate above anyone ...

Without a word Marged turned on her heel and ran. Along Park Manor Road into the High Street and the Co-op. Once she halted and looked back. Roberta was standing there, a silent, lonely figure. Marged was outraged. To think she'd befriended this girl, and all the time she was the daughter of *that man.* So Roberta was going to boarding school! And if it hadn't been for her father, Marged might now be at the High School, going out into the world, preparing to be somebody important. Now, thanks to him, she'd have to stay in Victoria Street all her life, work at Grant's, marry and live up the road like Brenda ...

But in Germany, the man named Hitler was working his way doggedly towards the position that would empower him to reshuffle Europe, and move millions of people around on a vast human chessboard.

The rippling notes of Chopin filled the parlour of the

Polish farmhouse, the candelabra on the piano the only light in the room, making the corners shadowy in the twilight. Stefan swung into a waltz, thinking as he played of the crinolined ladies who'd flirted behind their fans ... here? When this parlour was a drawing-room? The shadows held their secrets.

Now, dreamily, to a nocturne. Had perhaps Countess Marie Waleska called here on her way to meet Napoleon, whose mistress she was for many years? When the Polish legionnaires marched under the French tricolour?

Abruptly he switched to Chopin's *Revolutionary Étude*, written for the 1831 uprising against the Czar, in bitterness and anger. His mother looked up with a start at the sudden change, but Tadeusz came to the piano and began to sing. He had a sweet treble voice, and when he stopped, Mama said: 'Why did you play that now, Stefan?'

'I don't know, Mama. Just a—' He broke off. A what? Premonition? 'Just remembering the gallant battles,' he ended.

'Would you fight the Russians and the Prussians?' asked Tadeusz beside him.

'Of course I would. I'd be in all those battles. I'd be there—' Stefan rose to his feet, posing, a stick held like a sword.

'My dear boy,' said his mother, 'you have just heard that you are going to Warsaw to study music. That will be your life from now on.' She put her hands on his shoulders and kissed him on both cheeks.

'Like Paderewski,' said Tadeusz, who had a gift for putting his foot in things, for Paderewski was also a politician.

'They've made a song about Paderewski in London,' Stanislaw intervened hastily.

'I'd like to see London,' said Stefan. 'What sort of country is England, Professor?'

'Very rich,' replied Stanislaw. 'With a mighty empire.

All the people must be rich there too,' and he looked a little ruefully at his shabby suit. Some sacrifices had to be made.

'I'd like to go there someday,' repeated Stefan, still standing. Maybe he would, too. When he was a famous pianist, maybe he would travel to London and Paris.

Mama switched on the light, and the shadows of the past vanished. 'It's nearly time to eat,' she said, and disappeared into the kitchen with its blue Delft tiles and large stove which heated the radiators. But Stefan walked outside and stood watching the sun sink in the west, the sky suffused with red and orange.

Behind him Stanislaw said, 'You're in a funny mood, Stefan. What is it? Don't you want to leave the old home?'

Stefan shrugged. 'I'll be back. You as well, Stan. You've got what you wanted too, a place in the University of Cracow.'

'Yes.' Stanislaw began to cough.

'Just watch that asthma of yours, you know,' Stefan said, concerned.

'I will.'

Stanislaw moved back into the house, but Stefan still stood, watching the storks fly overhead, the storks that came in with the spring and nested on the barn roofs. He could hear the mutter of his parents' voices in the kitchen, through the open window.

'It will be all right,' Mama said more loudly.

'If the Kilinskis wait for payment until the Slowackis pay us—' said his father.

'It will be all right.' Mama was very strong-willed, and when she'd made up her mind that something had to be done, then done it was. But she knew how Father loved the farm, and her voice softened as she added: 'We've done very well, Jan. *You've* done very well.'

'We need more land,' his father said. 'We need to expand to make it really pay.'

'But we can't. There's the river and the road round two sides, and the Lenskis on the other—'

74

'Yes, the Lenskis ... I did wonder—' He broke off.

'Wonder what? Not to buy out the Lenskis? Why, Jan, it is their home, and I don't want to take anyone's home, even if we could afford it. I know what it is like to lose a home.'

'No, no, I didn't mean that at all. All I meant was, well, the Lenskis have only one daughter. We have three sons.'

'Well?' There was a clatter of dishes as Mama put something on the table and waited.

'What better way to join the two farms?' asked Father. 'Anyway, it did belong to you once, to the de Reszke estate, did it not?'

'Yes, I suppose so.'

'I'd like to get it back – for you, Barbara. Your old inheritance. You've worked so hard, all these years ... it would be for you ...'

'Why, Jan ...'

Stefan moved away. Soon he would be in Warsaw. He knew his parents were sacrificing a lot for his career. He hoped he'd soon be successful and able to repay them.

'Come, boys,' Mama called. 'Supper is ready.'

Stefan turned and Tadeusz, who had also moved outside, followed more slowly. He wasn't musical and he wasn't clever and he didn't want to be. He just wanted to work on the farm with his father, milking the fat cows, turning the good earth to make it produce wheat for bread, oats and barley for fodder, watching the constant cycle of the seasons, being a countryman. A satisfying life.

The autumn sun glinted on the stork's nest on the barn, the river rippled in the dying afternoon, but the boys were careless of the beauty; they knew it would always be theirs. However far they travelled, they would always come back. This was home.

Chapter 4

Dusk was falling on Victoria Street. Lights glimmered in the little houses, and children ran home from school to where a bright fire would be burning, the curtains drawn against the chill afternoon.

The machines whirred in the little factory; a few girls were singing. On the sleeve table, Marged put her foot on the pedal and guided the sleeve carefully through the machine. She liked the factory when each little lamp shone over the machine, leaving pools of shadow. It was somehow cosy. 'Roll on six o'clock,' said Mrs Grey, who sat opposite.

'Roll on eight, I'm going dancing,' said Marged.

'You and your dancing.' Mrs Grey pulled out a sleeve, snipped off the ends of cotton and placed it on the pile at her side. 'How often do you go?'

'As often as I can without me dad moaning,' said Marged.

'That's right, enjoy yourself while you can,' called Mrs Pearson, a fat, overblown woman at the end of the table.

'I used to go dancing. Now we're saving up to get married,' said twenty-year-old Doris. 'My chap says there might be a war.' It was March 1939.

'There won't be no war,' Mrs Grey contradicted. 'Hitler's got Czechoslovakia, says he don't want any more.'

'Yes, but if he invades Poland—'

'We'll tell him not to, so Doris can save and get married,' shouted Mrs Pearson.

'I'd like to get married,' put in Mary Dane, who was only fifteen, just starting on sleeves after a year in the brushing room. 'Don't you want to, Marged?'

'Not me,' Marged answered, 'I want to have a good time.'

'Wait till you fall in love,' said Doris sentimentally.

'Pooh, love,' scoffed Marged. 'There ain't no such thing.' Though she supposed she would get married some day – what else was there to do, after all? You could stop at home then if you wanted, and she let her mind wander to Miss Anson's semi, the matching room, the chintz-covered chairs ... Pipe-dream, that. Most of the couples she knew started off in two rooms, then the woman kept on working till they could put a deposit on a house of their own. That's if you were allowed to work; some factories wouldn't employ married women.

'Your John's courting, en't he?' asked Doris.

'Yes. Amy Barton. She's been runnin' after him since he left school.'

'He's got a good job, en't he, in an office?'

'Yes. The headmaster got it for him.' Not that a clerk's pay was much, but it was a secure job and you got paid for holidays and illness. The Fennels' lot had improved now they were all working. Eva had gone back to the silk factory; she left home at seven in the morning and returned at seven at night. Now they were better off they had a new long tin bath and a wireless, and they had electricity installed in place of gaslight and candles.

Frank resumed his bicycle repairing in the shed, earning a few shillings, helping him to forget that his wife and children were entirely supporting him, for once John started working the Public Assistance was stopped, so Brenda came home. The Means Test was still in operation, and men still marched, but they had more support now from the middle

77

classes and people who were worried about the rise of the right wing in Germany.

Frank did a certain amount of housework. He cleaned the black grate with Zebo polish, but he would not cook, so Eva and the girls peeled potatoes before they left in the morning, to be ready for the evening. Marged and Bren did the bedrooms and scrubbed the floors at the weekend.

Brenda was courting too. Jack Morris, who worked at a Coventry factory, one of a thousand similar factory employees in the district. Tall, thin, intelligent, good workers. His parents were known to the Fennels. They'd been at school together, and Eva went through all their details: his mother had been one of the Talbot Street Greenwoods, his father one of the Morrises – you remember, Frank? – they were a big family, all boys, all good at football.

'Mam goes through their pedigree as if we were aristocrats,' laughed Marged, but she knew it was always done. There were good families and bad families even in Victoria Street, and the Fennels were all relieved that the stigma of Public Assistance had been lifted from them, though they were still pretty hard up. But Jack Morris would make a good husband, giving his wife plenty of housekeeping money – when he had it – helping his widowed mother, having for himself one night out with the lads and the football match on Saturday. That's if they ever got married; they seemed no nearer now than when they met.

Yet Bren had been lucky with her job. When she'd started at Grant's it was as an apprentice, with proper indentures, the lot, and she had learned every aspect of the trade: sleeves, linings, coats, she was a fully trained tailoress. Now things had changed. There weren't the orders for made-to-measure suits these days. It was all mass production, and though Grant's did some of these orders it wasn't the same, and more than one woman in the factory wondered where it would all end. The dole queue? True, the girls did learn most things even so. Marged had been on linings, though not yet on coats; now she was back on sleeves to finish this order, and sleeves was perhaps the easiest of all jobs, except little ones like button-holing, given either to kids or, in one case, a handicapped girl. But she could earn up to two pounds a week on piece-work.

The women sat around long tables, facing one another, so they were able to talk as they worked. Mr Levy the manager, Sammy to the irreverent work-girls, walked up and down, holding pieces of coat or sleeve in his hand, but he was all right really. He'd go up in the air if you made a mistake but he soon simmered down. There were worse places than Grant's. Far worse.

'If you girls get married,' said Mrs Pearson, looking round the table, 'mek sure you get hold of a good bloke. Not like the one I picked.' She roared with laughter.

'How can we tell, Pearie?' asked Mary Dane.

'Well, don't pick a handsome 'un. He'll be conceited. Don't have one who drinks, or you'll never have any money.'

'What's your old man like?' asked Doris.

'My old man – him,' snorted Mrs Pearson. 'If I had my time over again I'd marry a foreigner.'

The girls shrieked. 'Why?' asked Mary Dane.

'Because they know how to love.'

'Ooh!' they shrieked again. 'How do you know, Pearie?'

'I went out with an Italian once. He thrilled me.' Her great laugh boomed out.

'Where did you meet an Italian?' asked Sue.

'In Coventry. He'd come to work in a hotel.'

'So what happened?' asked Sue.

'I can't tell you any more. Mek you dissatisfied.'

'If I got married again it'ud be for money,' said Mrs Grey. 'Marry first time for love, second for money.'

'Ah, when you've got more sense.'

'I was reading today in a magazine how to keep your man happy,' said Sue.

'Only one way to mek a man happy,' pronounced Pearie.

'What way's that?' asked Mary Dane, who was naïve.

'Bolster his ego,' said Mrs Grey.

'Rub his chest with camphorated oil,' said Pearie, and the girls shrieked again.

Then they all began singing:

I wish I had someone to love me, someone to call me his own.
Someone to lie in bed with me, for I'm tired of sleeping alone.
I don't want an old man of sixty, nor yet a young boy of
  sixteen
But a nice handsome lad about twenty, who knows how to use
  his machine.

Marged joined in with the rest, smiling to herself. If you didn't know the facts of life when you started at fourteen, you soon learned them from the married women; they talked about men the whole time. She wondered what the husbands would say if they knew how the women talked. Life wasn't like the pictures, that was for sure, nor the books when they talked about love. She liked the pictures, especially the Rogers-Astaire ones. They could dance, those two, and the songs were grand, *Night And Day, Smoke Gets In Your Eyes, Lovely To Look At.* She thought sometimes she danced to the best songs ever written. She was lucky.

Bren used to go dancing, then when she started courting she stopped. Jack didn't like it. Girls would say this sort of thing with pride. 'My Jim (or Bob or Bill) won't let me do this or that ...' Marged didn't intend to stop, not for any man. She still searched for the rainbow, and the nearest she came to finding it was in her dancing. But Marged admired her sister. At twenty-three Brenda was capable, intelligent and good-looking, too. Not exactly pretty, but she had those wonderful eyes that looked like the sea on a stormy day, Marged thought poetically. And she never moaned about the years she'd had to hand over all her money, before

Mam got her job. Yes, things were easier now, but they'd never forget the bad years, none of them.

The women were singing again, a modern popular song. *South of the Border* ... they'd be playing this at the dance tonight ... Martin went dancing too, and all the girls fell for him with his dark good looks and his angry eyes. Martin *was* angry, though perhaps only she knew why ... Martin, her twin. Before he left school the headmaster told him he'd obtained a technical apprenticeship for him at Mordant's. 'I tried Rolls Royce and Morris in Coventry,' he'd told him, 'but all their places are filled. But, as you know, a technical apprenticeship is better than a craft apprenticeship. You'll have to go to technical college once a week, where you'll learn draughtsmanship and so on ...'

Frank hadn't wanted him to go to Mordant's, but Eva had been all for it. 'Once he's served his apprenticeship he can move,' she said. 'And the drawing office will be better than the machine shop, which is all he'll get from the other.'

Martin said nothing. He went to Mordant's, came home and said sullenly, 'I'm not a technical apprentice, I'm craft. They said I didn't have the qualifications.'

Frank was indignant. 'You should tell Mr Cook,' he said.

'What's the use?' Martin asked. 'Headmasters don't understand what things are like in these places.' He laughed scornfully. 'They teach us about honour and to do the right thing ... Do they really think people in the world know anything about honour?'

'Not at Mordant's,' Frank agreed.

Martin stayed. A job was a job in 1935. But when Marged sympathised with him one night he said, 'I wanted to go to Mordant's. I'm going to get my own back on them. I told you.'

'How?' she asked sceptically.

'I don't know yet. But I will.'

The women had stopped singing. 'Six o'clock,' announced

Pearie. 'I'm off. Get my old man's tea. He won't like it, allus grumbling, damn his eyes.'

Slowly the machines ground to a halt. Marged finished her seam, placed it on the pile, ran a comb through her hair and stood up. She made her way to Brenda at the other end of the room. 'Coming?' she asked.

'Not for a minute. I want to finish this side. Sammy needs them tomorrow, rush order.'

'M'm.' Marged envied Brenda, good enough to work on special orders, then she buttoned her coat and walked to the door.

The women filed out, chattering. Marged joined a group and began to walk along the road. It was a dull day, yet lighter outside than in the factory. As she reached the end, where Park Manor joined the road, she stopped. Standing on the corner was a tall girl in expensive clothes, beige wollen calf-length dress under a short coat, smart brown hat. Roberta.

'Don't go,' Roberta said. 'I had to see you.'

Marged paused. She'd never answered the letters Roberta wrote from boarding school, had spoken to her only once since the time she'd learned her name. She'd often hung around Victoria Street but Marged had ignored her, had passed her by until one day Roberta had stopped her. 'Tell me what's wrong,' she'd said.

'All right.' Marged had stopped, too. 'I'll tell you what's wrong. Your father, that's what's wrong.'

'My *father*?' Roberta was mystified.

'Don't you know how people hate him?'

Roberta's face showed hurt. 'He is a most respected man in the town. A member of the Round Table, Rotary—'

Marged gave a scornful laugh. 'Maybe with those sort of men. Maybe they're all the same.' *All hand in glove*, Grandma would say. 'But not the people who work for him. Like my dad, who had an accident and hasn't worked since.'

82

'But that's not my father's fault!'

'Yes, it was. The machinery was faulty and he wouldn't repair it.'

'I'm sure you're mistaken,' Roberta said. 'My father would always see things were all right.'

'Oh no, he wouldn't!' Marged shouted. And then, as she saw people staring, 'Oh, you don't know nothing. Nothing. And you don't care.'

She walked away, for she saw that in any argument Roberta would always side with *Them*, the ones she belonged with, and would never see the other point of view.

Roberta had never come again. Not until today.

Now Marged hesitated, and Roberta said, 'I'm sorry about your father's accident. But there's no reason why *we* shouldn't be friends.'

'What do you want to be friends for? You don't belong round here,' Marged answered sullenly.

'I used to like hearing about the neighbours. Does Mrs Trigger still have her fancy man?'

So she remembered all that. 'She has that one or another. But I don't have much time to talk now. I go to work.' And if it wasn't for your father I wouldn't be working here.

'What do you do on Saturday afternoons?'

'I go to the pictures sometimes.'

'My mother wouldn't let me go to the cinema.'

'No, I don't suppose she would.' Marged stiffened at the correction. *Cinema*, indeed. Yet she knew a sense of power that Mordant's daughter should be here as a supplicant. She felt immeasurably older than Roberta now, a schoolkid at eighteen, for heaven's sake. The women from the factory had all gone now, Brenda would be coming out in a minute. She turned to go, but Roberta said: 'My father says there's going to be a war.'

'Oh, he knows, does he?'

'I should be glad if there was a war, I could leave school then.'

83

'Well, you'll leave anyway, won't you? You aren't going to school for ever.'

'Yes, but I can get a job instead of going to finishing school.'

'You can get a job anytime.'

'Oh no, Mummy wouldn't let me.'

Marged sighed. 'Your mother won't let you do anything. Why don't you leave home? And what do you want to go to work for?'

'I'd love to.'

'You don't know what you're talking about.' Marged paused. Roberta wouldn't work in some little factory, slogging away from eight till six. She'd get some fancy job somewhere.

'Well, you see, there's nothing to do at home. Mummy's always out or away.'

'Have you still got the nanny?' Marged asked maliciously.

'No, she's long gone,' Roberta answered seriously. 'So you see I get pretty bored. I thought that once I was home I could have parties and so on, and Daddy wouldn't mind, but Mummy says no.'

Marged stiffened at the mention of Daddy; she thought Roberta might have shown enough sensitivity not to bring him into the conversation. Aloud she said: 'Mummy sounds a bit of a martinet.'

'Between you and me I don't think she likes the idea of a grown-up daughter. What do you do in the evenings?'

'Go dancing.'

'Oh, where?'

'At the Co-op Hall. I suppose your mother would say that was common.'

'I'm afraid she would.' Roberta smiled. 'But she wouldn't know, would she, if I came with you, and I'd like to. I've made an arrangement with Brian, my brother. He tells Mummy he escorts me when I go out, and in return I don't tell Mummy how much he drinks.'

84

Marged stared at this new Roberta. There was something different about her and she wasn't sure she liked it. She herself had another friend now, Corrie Thompson, who, she guessed, wouldn't take to this young lady with her la-di-da ways, and her more pronounced southern accent. Why did she want to come with them anyway? She asked, 'Can't you go to dances with your friends? Or your brother?'

'I have been to the Majestic.' That was a large hotel near Coventry.

'What's it like there? I might try it sometime,' Marged said.

'We-ell, it's a little exclusive.'

Marged was furious. Did Roberta say these things deliberately? Or, what was worse, did she say them unconsciously, not even realising people had feelings? She said, annoyed, 'I have another friend now and she might not want you with us. I'll have to let you know.'

Suddenly Roberta tensed. Marged turned her head and saw, in the half-light of evening, Martin walking towards them, pushing his bike. He had seen them and halted, while Roberta grew more tense.

'Bike broke down?' Marged asked unsympathetically.

'Yes, puncture.' He looked at Roberta, and the air was charged, electric. 'Hallo,' he said.

'Hallo.' Roberta sounded breathless.

Marged opened her mouth to tell Martin that Roberta was Mordant's daughter, then closed it again, wanting to see what was happening. 'You remember Roberta?' she asked.

'Of course.' Martin was looking into her eyes.

'Martin,' said Marged, 'is a one for the girls. Don't let him fool you.' And to Martin: 'Come on, I'm off. I'm cold and I want my tea.'

He glanced at Roberta again, shrugged in a comical way, grinned and followed Marged. Roberta walked on to the tree-lined Park Manor Road.

*

When she was sent to Melbourne Boarding School for Girls, Roberta was with what Mummy called girls of her own sort. She liked Melbourne, it was better than home, but there were still holidays. One girl asked her to her own home for a week, and she enjoyed this – little Pamela had a nice Mummy and Daddy – but Mummy couldn't be bothered to ask her back, so the invitation wasn't repeated. Roberta never asked herself why her mother didn't want to bother with her; this rejection simply added to her lack of self-esteem.

But Melbourne changed her. She no longer envied Marged, no longer regarded her as an equal and this showed in her remarks about the Majestic. She didn't come to see Marged, but Martin.

When had she fallen in love with Martin? Do children fall in love? Sometimes she felt she'd been in love with him since the day they met. Certainly, as Melbourne moulded her into the model of a young lady, her interest in Victoria Street would have waned had it not been for him. After Marged's defection she still hung around the street, but it was to see Martin, not Marged. And when he turned into a handsome youth, with dark upper lip and a look in his eye that she'd never seen before, she was lost. It was the look he gave to all the girls, but Roberta wasn't to know that. She only knew that he made her feel like a woman, and she liked the feeling. She wanted him.

Roberta knew nothing about sex. The girls whispered at school, but they knew no more than she. Nor did the boarders from the nearest boys' private school, who once a year were herded into the hall and held the girls amateurishly in a dance. What happened in the bedroom was never touched upon in the films she saw surreptitiously. The hero might clasp the heroine in his arms and plant a chaste kiss on her lips, but that was all.

Yet it was enough. Roberta dreamed of being held in Martin's arms while he kissed her feverishly and the thoughts gave her a strange feeling in the lower part of her body, a throbbing, yearning for something she knew not what, but she would hold her pillow and press herself into it, then, half-ashamed, pull away, only to start dreaming again.

Her thoughts did not go past the wanting of him, unlike most girls whose dreams were always of marriage, as in all films and novels of the time. Roberta knew that some day she would get married – it seemed the only way to escape from home – and that Martin would never be approved of as a suitable husband. Not by Mummy. Nor was Roberta sure she wanted it herself. As a child she had loved Victoria Street but now, instructed in the ways of the world, she did not want to live there in a terraced house with neighbours like the Wests.

So she shelved the future and thought only of the present. And the present meant making up to Marged to try to get her to take her along to the dance. Roberta knew that Martin went dancing, just as she knew where he worked. Her walks around the town had in reality been to follow him. She wished sometimes she had someone to confide in, but the one girl who might have understood – Marged – was barred.

She was jealous of Marged. Marged lived in the same house as Martin, shared his thoughts. They lived as brother and sister. Indeed, Marged said the reason they were so close was because they were twins. The family regarded them as twins. But they were not brother and sister. They were cousins. And cousins could, and did, marry. Sometimes she hated Marged for her very closeness to him, and for this reason she would never tell her of her feelings lest she put ideas into Marged's own head about her attractive cousin.

But she wanted Martin, and she was determined to go to the dance somehow if that was the only way to get him.

★

Weekends were always pleasant. The factories finished at one o'clock on Saturday, then Marged and Brenda walked into the town to do the weekly shopping. Round the market with the multi-coloured fruit stalls, the bargains in 'seconds' from the Leicestershire hosiery factories, the crockery stalls ... They halted before a mound of bananas. A woman stood at the top of the yellow pyramid shouting: 'How much for these, then? Penny each? Two a penny? You can have the whole bunch for thrippence.'

'What a mouth she's got,' chuckled Marged, and laughed louder as a man climbed up beside her and began to ram bananas down her throat.

As they walked Brenda said quietly: 'We're thinking of getting married.'

Marged stopped laughing. 'When?'

'Soon. Jack's work's been good lately. He thinks there's going to be a war, says the parts they're making are for planes, not cars. Anyway, we've waited long enough.'

'Does Mam know?'

'Not yet. I'll tell her tomorrow. So don't say anything now.'

'She was just thinking of giving up her job.'

'I know.' Brenda stopped to look at a woman selling bunches of daffodils. 'But there's always something. When our John got a job he couldn't pay much because he has to have good clothes in his office. Then you and Martin, well, I doubt if Mam sees a penny from Martin.'

'He is an apprentice, Bren.'

'Yes, and he'd be the same if he earned twenty pounds a week. He's a selfish little so and so.'

'I give Mam a pound, and I keep myself in clothes and spending money out of the rest.'

'I know, Marged. But we're all working now. Even Dad earns a bit with his repair jobs. Anyway, I shall keep on working, so I'll help if I can.'

They reached a cheap-jack stall where the man was

shouting: 'Do I want five shillings for this tea-service? Do I want two shillings and sixpence? No, I'm giving it away. One and elevenpence for this beautiful set of cups and saucers—' and they had to push their way through the crowds round him, enjoying the patter as much as wanting to buy.

'Where are you going to live?' asked Marged, once they were free.

'You know Mrs Timkins at number forty, died a couple of weeks ago? Her house is up for sale. Two hundred and fifty pounds they're asking. Well, as I said, Jack's work's been good lately. He's been doing overtime, so he's saved a bit – enough for the deposit and p'raps a bit of furniture.'

'Oh Bren, that'll be great, having a house. Can I come and help you get settled in?'

''Course you can. Come on now, or we won't be home till tea-time,' and they pushed on through the crowds.

Dinner was a makeshift affair on Saturdays, usually fried eggs and tomatoes or even fish and chips, and everyone was talking and laughing. In the afternoon, Marged went to the pictures with her new friend Corrie Thompson to see Fred Astaire and Ginger Rogers in *The Gay Divorcée*, where she sat entranced.

The Thompsons had recently come to live in the street. Mam didn't altogether approve of Corrie, and perhaps she did use a bit too much make-up, while her clothes were often too tight on her curvy figure. She had a mop of curly flame hair the colour of Frank's chrysanthemums. But she was an excellent dancer. Marged had met her at the Co-op Hall, asked if she were on her own, and then they had walked home together.

'Who are these Thompsons?' Mam asked, frowning. 'I don't know them. What do they do?'

Mr Thompson used to work on a fair, but Marged didn't tell her mother that. Anyway, Corrie said he *owned* the fair. They sold up and settled in Victoria Street. Mr Thompson was a large fat man with a florid face and red nose. 'He's got a shop,' Marged told her. 'Furniture.'

'What, that second-hand place in the High Street?' Her mother sniffed. 'Lot of junk, if you ask me. And those other Thompson girls, they look flighty to me, Corrie an' all.'

'She's all right,' Marged defended her friend. And indeed, Corrie was good fun. They laughed together at the swains who begged for their favours. There was Funny Fred and South American Joe and Bashful Bill ... oh, and Corset Cuthbert.

'Well, just you be in at half-past ten, not a minute later.'

'Oh Mam—'

'Never mind "Oh Mam". Half-past ten or you know your dad'll create.'

She never was back by half-past ten, of course. Not when the dance didn't end till twelve. But Frank was usually in bed, and Martin, who could stay out as long as he liked, lied unblushingly and swore Marged was in when he arrived.

'It's not fair. Martin can stop out late,' Marged complained, and Eva said succinctly: 'Girls bring their trouble home, boys don't.'

Marged had learned dancing at the local church halls, then she graduated to the Co-op Hall, where the standard was high. Dancing was the culture of the back streets, taken seriously by the working classes of the thirties; all the artistic longings, the love of beauty, the flair for colour that was crushed by dull factory work was put into the dance. Every slow step was a masterpiece of precision, every twirl a *pas-de-deux* of delicate movement, perfected by hours of patient practice.

Her first efforts had been humiliating. Either no one asked her to dance, or she had the attentions of a slow stumbling boy who was a learner like herself. She couldn't afford to pay for lessons at first, for at fourteen she had given her mother all her wages, receiving one shilling back for pocket-money. This had gradually increased over the years until now, aged nearly eighteen, she paid her board.

At the Co-op Hall, as a newcomer she stood at the back, for there was a protocol in dance halls, and only the best of the males dare approach the females who stood in the centre. But patience and persistence, practising with girl friends, plus a natural talent, moved her slowly to better and better partners till now she was one of the top dancers. She spent all her money on dresses and make-up, and had a regular partner, Ken Phillips, a miner's son from one of the villages.

She and Corrie walked to the hall to the strains of *Music, Maestro Please* from Jeff Marsden and his Band, a five-piece local outfit. Into the cloakroom to be immediately enveloped in the atmosphere, scent from face powder and perfume, and girls' chat before the mirrors, of who took them home last night and what sort of time they had. Marged left her coat with the little woman behind the counter, smoothed her hair, added a touch of Evening in Paris, then into the hall, its floor newly polished, its row of red plush tip-up seats round the edges waiting for the girls and boys to arrive.

There were only a few here yet, and Ken was not one of them, so Marged and Corrie, disdaining the young hopefuls – after one quick glance to see what type of dancers were there – took the floor together, as much to show how good they were – beginners keep away – as to the actual dance. Then they stood in the centre.

Ken arrived. He claimed Marged and together they went into a tango. She liked the tango, liked the slow dragging of the feet just a fraction behind the beat, liked the sensuous rhythm. Few attempted such a difficult dance, so she and Ken had the floor to themselves. She said, 'I saw Ginger Rogers and Fred Astaire this afternoon.'

'I saw it in the week.' The tango finished and they stood

while the onlookers clapped. 'Listen, kid, you know we were talking about entering a competition? Well, there's one at Birmingham in a few months' time.'

'Shall we enter? Are we good enough?'

'If we practise. We'd have to come every night. But the winners go on to the semis, then the finals in London.'

Marged stared thoughtfully at Ken. Tall, good-looking, he was a perfect partner, but she wondered what her dad would say. She had said little to her family about her dreams, and never took Ken home to meet them – that was reserved for when you were 'courting serious' – as they were dancing partners, no more. But it would mean being out late on more nights, and Dad wouldn't like that. Well, she shrugged, he'd just have to lump it. She was grown-up now, nearly eighteen. She'd been working for almost four years. Her life was her own affair.

'I'd love it,' she said.

'If we were successful for a few years' amateur, then we could turn professional, exhibition dancing,' Ken went on.

A glittering world opened before her, crowds, success, travelling . . . 'Oh yes,' she breathed.

'I don't see what can stop us,' said Ken, as he swung her into a waltz.

Sunday was the best day of all. No need for anyone to get up early, no mad rush to get to work. Just a slow waking, the thinking over the night before, the movement downstairs, the leisurely breakfast. Then the starting on the Sunday cooking, the fire to be made up to heat the oven, the joint to roast, Bren seeing to the vegetables while Marged and Eva made the pies with the last of the bottled plums. One pie for Sunday, two for other days, stored in the cool pantry. Then cakes and jam tarts and Martin coming in to pinch one and Bren slapping his hand. Marged put the tarts into big tins, wondering how on earth she'd manage to buy a posh dress suitable for dancing competitions.

Afternoons were lazy too, when the washing-up was done and they sat in the front room, even managing a fire when it was cold. Eva went to bed, while Frank settled for a snooze in the comfortable chair, part of a three-piece suite bought second-hand a year ago. Brenda was sewing, so Marged went up to their bedroom and studied her reflection. Chaps found her attractive, she knew, but she could find no trace of beauty. The urchin look of childhood had never quite disappeared, though her dark hair was longer now, permed into waves. Perhaps it was the eyes men found appealing, what in the twenties were called bedroom eyes, or the mouth that was at once demure and – to quote her mother – cheeky. Or maybe the ready wit. She smoothed her hair, and decided to try to improve her appearance with a home-made face pack – oats, egg-white and lemon – which looked revolting but seemed to whiten the skin. She opened the door to see Martin on the landing. 'I want you,' he told her in a stage whisper.

'All right. What?'

He followed her into the room and closed the door. 'That girl yesterday. Who is she?'

She hesitated before answering. Then, 'Roberta. You remember, she used to come and play with us. You hated the sight of her.'

'I thought it was. Well, who is she? What does she want?'

'She came to see me, to be friends again.' Who was she? Marged hesitated. If she told Martin, how would he take it, when he hated Mordant's so much? Better he remained in ignorance. So she said casually, 'You know as much as me. Anyway, what's it to you?'

He shrugged. 'Just wondered.'

She was a little alarmed. 'Do you fancy her? If so, lay off. She's from Park Manor – Road.'

'So? That might be fun.'

'Don't you have enough girls?'

'I never have enough.'

Marged paused. She knew that to most men – and certainly to Martin – the more a girl was forbidden the more they'd want her. She said, feigning indifference, 'I don't know anything about her. Now go away, I'm going to the back-kitchen,' and she walked downstairs.

As she mixed the face pack she was thoughtful. If Dad ever found out who Roberta was there'd be one almighty row, and she couldn't risk that, not just when she was needing his approval for more nights out dancing. They'd have to do something to get rid of her, she and Corrie, so she'd never come again. Corrie would think of something.

John brought Amy back for tea and they sat in the kitchen while Brenda and Marged cut bread and butter and opened a tin of pineapple in the back-kitchen. 'She might offer to help,' Brenda grumbled. 'Every Sunday for tea and never a hand.'

'Our John's miles too good for her,' Marged said gloomily.

Amy at eighteen was little changed from the child who'd played in the street. Her hair was still fair, hanging now in a pageboy bob, her pretty face was spoilt by the petulant mouth. She had long slender fingers and showed these off to the best advantage now she wore an engagement ring, touching her hair, her blue rayon dress, her necklace.

'Are you going to tell them your wedding plans while Amy's here?' Marged had asked Brenda, and she replied, 'Yes, I promised Jack.'

It was as they were finishing the sponge sandwich that Brenda broke the news. 'We're thinking of getting married,' she began. 'There's a house up for sale—'

Marged looked anxiously at her dad. She knew he wouldn't like her telling them while Amy was here, showing up his helplessness, his dependence on Brenda. He would never reveal his feelings any more than she herself would;

he'd cover up with anger. Sure enough, he said grumpily: 'That's right. Just when we're getting on better, now you leave home.'

'Well, they can't wait for ever,' Eva said peaceably.

'We've been courting six years,' cried Brenda. 'What do you want me to do? Wait till we have to get married, like so many do?'

'Just as your mother was thinking of giving up her job —'

'We'll manage all right,' John said. 'I'm still here.'

Amy pouted, and Frank noticed. 'You'll be the next to go, I don't doubt. And we'll be left struggling again, thanks to Mordant.'

'Oh Dad, don't start all that again.'

'The twins are here,' John went on. 'Martin should be earning more when he's finished his apprenticeship.'

'If I know Mordant's I'll be out when I'm finished,' Martin put in.

'That's enough from all of you,' said Eva firmly, glancing towards Amy. And Frank said, 'I won't say another word.'

He turned from the table, went to his chair and sat silent. Marged sighed. Dad was going into one of his depressions. Sometimes they lasted a few hours, sometimes days, and during this time he wouldn't speak to anyone. She was the only one who could talk him out of it, and she went to him now.

'Come on, Dad,' she said, as Amy and John went into the front room. 'You know you don't mind, really.' Yet she understood her dad's attitude even as she tried to talk him out of it. Once you've known poverty, you're terrified of it coming back. And, she reflected ruefully, if Brenda and John both went – for once married, John would no doubt live at Amy's as she was an only child – and if Mam stopped working, with Martin still an apprentice, then she, Marged would be the chief breadwinner. Yet she persisted. Brenda had done her bit.

'But this isn't the best time to get married and buy a house,' Frank said. 'Suppose there's a war? Jack'll be the first to go. He's in the Territorials, en't he?' Jack had joined the 'Terriers' several years ago during a spell of unemployment, for this meant not only pay but a week's camp in the summer.

Brenda had been clearing the table. Now she stopped, dishes in hand. 'I know, we have talked about it,' she said. 'But we still want to go ahead.'

'And be left with a mortgage to pay on a soldier's money?' asked Frank.

'I shall work.'

'And if you have a baby?'

'I shan't.'

'Oh, got it all planned, have you?'

Marged patted her dad's hand. 'Maybe there won't be a war. Dad – do you remember when I was little, and we were talking about going on a holiday?' Why had this stuck in her memory? 'We said we'd go to Poland, remember? I said I'd never heard of it. Well, I've heard of it now.'

'Yes.' But Dad gave a faint smile. 'As I remember, you were going to take me.'

'Well, I can take you somewhere, if not Poland.' She drew a breath. 'I want to enter a dancing competition in Birmingham. Why don't you come and watch me?' She waited for the wrath to fall, but at least she'd turned it away from Brenda.

But surprisingly he wasn't too upset. 'I can't go to Birmingham,' he protested.

'Yes, you can. You can get a bus to the station. Will you come, Dad?' Though God knows how I'm going to pay for my dress now, she thought.

'I might.' The family gave a concerted sigh of relief, and Frank switched on the wireless.

The little church in the Polish village was full. Janina and

96

Tadeusz knelt together near the back. They were thinking, they were all thinking, of the German tanks now rolling into Czechoslovakia, so near to them. 'Dear Lord,' intoned the priest. 'Let us pray for peace.'

Janina clasped her hands together. What was happening to the world? She prayed earnestly, her lips moving slightly, yet when she stood up she did not, for once, feel comforted.

They sang the last hymn. Behind Janina, Pan Nowak the village schoolmaster sang loudly, his voice trembling slightly on the high notes. The children used to laugh at him – though not to his face – and call him the Martinet as he walked along with his military bearing, his bristly moustache. Janina remembered how scared she used to be of him in school, yet he was a nice man really, an old man now, long since retired, living alone.

As they left the church the priest was standing in the porch. 'Janina, Tadeusz,' he greeted them. 'Pani Kowalska not here tonight?'

'No,' Tadeusz answered him. 'Father isn't well, so Mother decided to stay with him.'

'Oh dear, nothing serious, I trust?'

'We think he's just tired.'

Outside, the March breeze blew the women's clothes, tried to take the hats from their heads. Janina and Tadeusz walked along the road where a little snow lingered, nodding to Pani Berman, the Jewish lady who had come from the west side to stay with her brother, to escape the Germans – if they came.

'They won't invade us, will they, Tadeusz?' Janina asked.

'No, of course not. Hitler promised ...'

'You'd have to go, Tadeusz.'

'Well, I'll have to do my military service anyway.' Tadeusz was philosophical. 'Like Stefan now in the Air Force.'

'Everyone's going away,' mourned Janina.

'It was always agreed that Stefan and Stanislaw would leave,' Tadeusz said. 'And Stanislaw's doing well at university. Failed his medical, poor old Stan. Me, I'm just a farmer.'

Janina said nothing. She liked farming too; the warmth of the barn when she milked the cows, helping Tadeusz with the calving, seeing the calf slip into the straw, then nuzzle up to his mother. She and Tad took the milking in turns, which meant they didn't usually go to evening service together, not that Tad went very often anyway.

The schoolmaster passed them, marching briskly along, nodding his good evening. They watched him silently. In the sky clouds gathered in the west, blotting out the spring sun. A low rumble of thunder was heard in the distance.

'You know he volunteered for the Army again?' said Tadeusz.

'I know, and he must be seventy.'

'He's not well really, though he pretends to be.'

They walked along in silence; a few birds twittered from the trees. Then Janina said abruptly, 'Do you remember Christmas?'

'Christmas? Yes, of course.'

'We had supper, and we put out an extra plate as we always do for those not with us—'

'For Stefan, who couldn't get leave,' Tadeusz replied sombrely.

'Tadeusz, I saw Stefan sitting there in the empty place.'

He turned to look at her, concerned. 'Janina – you imagined it.'

'Yes, I suppose so. But it worries me. I feel something bad is going to happen.'

'You should get out more,' he told her. 'You don't go anywhere except to church. Why don't you try the dances in the villages?'

'You know I don't like dancing,' and indeed, Janina was content to stay on the farm. Her life revolved around home.

'Anyway, you don't go out either, not since you've had your radio.' Janina had been surprised at Tadeusz's new hobby; radio didn't seem to fit in with farming, somehow. But he said he'd learned all about it at technical school – Tadeusz hadn't passed for higher education at the *liceum* any more than Janina herself. 'All you seem to do is get old ones, dismantle them and put them together again,' she ended.

He grinned. 'To learn all I can,' he said, and then, more seriously: 'I wonder, when I'm in the Army, if I could be a radio operator. After all, I'm nearly seventeen.'

'But you won't have to go till you're twenty-one,' she said, alarmed again.

'Just thinking,' he answered hastily. 'Anyway, this new radio I've got is great. Do you know I can get London?'

'And what do they say?'

'They are shocked at what Hitler's done. Outraged. After his promises to Chamberlain.'

'Tadeusz.'

'Yes?'

'Is it true that Hitler is demanding Danzig? Our free city?'

Tadeusz paused. 'There is a rumour,' he began delicately. 'I've heard nothing definite.'

A flock of birds wheeled overhead as they reached the farmhouse gate. 'Spring,' Janina said dreamily. 'I always love the spring.' She drew a breath, thinking of new growing things, baby lambs, yellow ducklings on the pond. It was easy to forget distant wars if you thought of pleasant things.

Tadeusz's voice interrupted her reverie. 'What's that at the door? It's the doctor's car. Father must be worse. Come!' and he began to run, Janina panting behind.

The doctor came to the door as they reached it, climbed in his car and drove away. They burst inside where Pani Kowalska was wringing her hands and crying. Tadeusz stood, shocked. His mother never cried, never grew hysterical. Pani Lenska was fussing round her like a little hen, trying to soothe her, saying, 'Calm down. It will be all right.'

'Tadeusz,' Barbara cried. 'Your father – he's been taken ill, his heart . . . it's serious, Tadeusz.'

'Shall I go up to see him?'

His mother seemed not to hear. 'It's all my fault,' she said.

Tadeusz turned on his way to the door. 'How can it be your fault?'

'He worked too hard. All the time he worked too hard. And it was I who arranged for Stefan to go to the School of Music in Warsaw when he should have been here, helping. Stanislaw couldn't, but Stefan is strong . . . it's all my fault.'

'Come now.' Pani Lenska put her arm round the weeping woman. 'You did your best for all of them.'

'But it has killed my poor Jan—'

'*Matka.*' Tadeusz's voice was calm and strong, so that Janina, shaken herself, was impressed. 'Please, no more. It is not your fault that Father is ill. Now, may we go up to see him?'

Barbara nodded. 'Yes, but I must make it up to him.'

Inside the bedroom Tadeusz seemed less sure of himself. 'Father,' he said uncertainly. 'How are you?'

The man in the bed gave a faint smile, 'You'll have to do all the work now, Tadeusz. You and Pan Lenski.'

'Of course I will, Father, until you're better.'

'I shan't be better in this world, my son. There now,' to his wife, 'don't cry. We've had a good life.'

She moved to the bed. 'Tell me, Jan. Is there anything you want? Tell me, and I'll get it for you.'

He smiled, tried to speak, but his voice was faint, and she had to bend her head to hear him. Tadeusz and Janina stood in the background.

When they went downstairs Barbara seemed to have a grip on herself. 'Tadeusz,' she said. 'Go to the Post Office and send a telegram. Get Stefan home.'

Tadeusz and Janina stepped outside just as Pan Lenski came running from next door. 'The news on the radio,' he gasped. 'Hitler is demanding the Polish corridor – our only outlet to the sea.'

Tadeusz stopped. His mother looked from one to the other. 'Wait!' she cried. 'Wait. I must speak to Stefan myself. I'll go and telephone.'

'We'll come with you—' Tadeusz began, but his mother brushed past him.

'No. You wait here. Both of you. I'll see you when I come back.'

A big black crow flew overhead and Janina watched it fearfully. Another bad omen. She felt hardly able to grasp the things that were happening; her life seemed to be being taken out of her control, and she gave a sob of fear. 'Tadeusz,' she said. 'I'm afraid.'

He put an arm around her shoulders. 'Don't be afraid Janina,' he said. 'I'll always take care of you.'

The aerodrome was situated to the west of Warsaw, and Pilot Officer Stefan Kowalski was in the mess with some of his friends. Now in his early twenties, he had a finely carved face with high cheekbones, a firm mouth and clear grey eyes.

'There might not be war,' said Antoni Dabski, his wireless operator.

Stefan twirled a glass of vodka and said ruefully, 'These are the last months of my national service. I'm due for demob in September.'

'You'll be lucky. They're recalling men now,' said Jan Puchowski caustically. 'But even if that mad Hitler does invade, Britain and France have guaranteed our frontiers now.'

'Yes.' And this news, coming on the last day of March, two days ago, had cheered them immensely, cheered all Poland. In Warsaw, English visitors were fussed over;

people in the street shook their hands, they were given favoured treatment by droshky drivers and waiters – drinks were free.

Learning English became fashionable and Stefan, who already spoke the language, was in great demand. Noël Coward came to visit and was warmly welcomed. There was no fear. The whole country was stimulated.

'After all,' said Antoni, 'if it did happen, our army could hold up the first Nazi onslaught until Britain and France had gained time to attack.' They had great faith in French infantry and the British Navy. With such friends their cause could never be lost.

'We're on night manoeuvres tonight,' Jan said, and Stefan nodded. They sat, waiting.

Stefan had enjoyed his years in Warsaw, studying music. He liked its gaiety, the elegant cavalry officers in their military cloaks, the men in fur hats, the women in Paris fashions, the nightlife with gipsy music.

Above all, music. He had visited Chopin's birthplace, just a few miles away. Then there was the Lazienki Park, with its beautiful Palace on the Water, summer residence of Poland's last king, and the Chopin monument where there was always an open-air piano recital by eminent pianists.

Stefan sighed. He was ready to fight for his country, if necessary, but part of him was sad to lose the enjoyments of youth, the long summer evenings when he'd sat in Lazienki, beneath statues of classical and contemporary dramatists, watching plays being performed on a tiny islet on the lake, where an open-air amphitheatre had been built by the same king within sight of his summer palace.

But it was only April. Six months to go before his demob, and it might still be all right. He was wondering about his mother's last letter. She'd sounded worried, yet didn't say what was wrong. Was it Stanislaw, now at Cracow University, one of its youngest members of staff, but still suffering from asthma. Was he ill?

The next morning brought another letter. *My dear Stefan, I have been trying to telephone you for days and cannot get through. What is happening, Stefan? I am sorry to have to tell you that your father is seriously ill, and has only a few weeks to live. You must come home, Stefan. We want to see you urgently. We have a great favour to ask of you. You always say how much you want to repay us. My dear son, I have never wanted repayment, yet now there is something you can do for your father. It means a lot to him. And to me ... Please, Stefan. Love, Matka.*

The next day Stefan went home on compassionate leave.

Chapter 5

Marged, dressed in her pale blue coat, walked in the Park with Corrie. It was the recognised rendezvous for young people: girls walked two by two, boys in twos and threes; they eyed each other, sometimes they 'got off' and went home together. Many couples started courting this way, and were married. As they walked, Marged explained about Roberta.

'You don't want her around,' stated Corrie.

'Well, it was all right when we were kids. Now, I don't know. It's never been the same since I heard who she was. I mean, we can't forget what happened; every single day when we look at Dad—' She broke off, and they circled the Park, with its borders of wallflowers and multi-coloured tulips.

'He must have hurt his head,' she went on, remembering that Corrie hadn't been there at the time. 'He had several fits at first. Now he's changed. He gets depressed, or bad-tempered. Sometimes he's all right, just like he used to be, then—' She shrugged. 'If it had been an ordinary accident, he'd have come to terms with it. We all would. But the machinery was faulty and Mordant wouldn't have it repaired.'

'Does Roberta know?'

'Oh yes, but she doesn't seem to think her dear daddy

could do anything wrong. She's changed. More snobby. She says she goes to the Majestic, but it's rather exclusive. No, I reckon it's Martin she's after now.'

'Then let him deal with her.'

'But she comes to me. And if me dad finds out who she is, then bang'll go my plans for the competition. Just as I'm getting him in a better mood about Brenda and everything . . .'

The sun shone fitfully. Spring had been late this year, but the Park was a pleasant place even so. In the bandstand in the centre, Chilverton Silver Prize Band played marching songs with gusto. A few hardy souls were sitting on the benches, but most people were walking.

Corrie said, 'I know how to frighten that Roberta off.'

'How?'

'Well, she wants to see life in the back streets, don't she? As a change from the Majestic. Slumming, ain't she? Let's take her to the Red Cow. They have dances there.'

Marged was aghast. 'My dad would never let me go there.'

'He won't know, will he?'

'Oh . . . I'm not sure. Eh, I'd love to see it, though.' Marged's eyes sparkled.

'It'll be fun. When will you see her?'

'Dunno. She'll be round soon, I expect. I wish she wouldn't. She stands outside the factory and all the women want to know who she is. If they find out, if Brenda finds out—'

'We'll stop her,' said Corrie confidently.

Roberta was outside the factory the next evening, and the women in their shabby working clothes stared. Marged went to her and said offhandedly: 'You can come dancing with us Wednesday. Wait at the end of the road. Eight o'clock. Wear a short frock.'

Roberta was waiting, wearing a green dress with a bolero lined with green and white check. Marged and Corrie both wore flowered dresses. The three eyed each other then Marged said, 'We're going to the Red Cow.'

'Where's that?'

'It's a pub just outside the town. They have dances. It's great there but it's a bit rough.'

'What do you mean, rough?' asked Roberta.

Corrie was giggling. 'There's a rough crowd gets there. The men are like those in a George Raft film,' improvised Marged.

'George Raft's a good dancer,' supplied Corrie.

'And some of the women are pros.'

'Pros?' asked Roberta.

'Prostitutes. The lowest sort. Common.'

'Do you go there often?' asked Roberta hesitantly.

'Often,' lied Corrie. 'It's great. Don't you want to come?'

'Ye-es. But I thought you were going to the Co-op Hall.' Roberta wanted to ask where Martin went, but didn't dare.

'Not tonight,' Marged was saying. 'Come on, got to get the bus.'

The pub stood on the outskirts of a mining village, and looked quite ordinary, but for the sound of music coming from inside. Roberta stared at the name. 'Black Bull?' she asked. 'But you said—'

'That's its real name,' Marged explained. 'They call it the Red Cow, you know, like they call the Black Swan the Dirty Duck.' Roberta blinked. 'Come on,' Marged ended. *Before I lose my nerve.*

They entered. There was a bar at one end of the long room, and little tables and chairs around the walls, while in the centre couples were dancing. The air was heavy with cigarette smoke; the smell of beer was strong. Men weaved through the tables, carrying brimming pint glasses. 'Where are the prostitutes?' asked Roberta.

There were several girls standing at the bar. They all had peroxided hair, with split ends and dark partings. They wore low-cut dresses, skin-tight, and their faces were caked with make-up. Somehow they didn't look over-clean, not dirty exactly, but as if they never did much in the way of washing. Crikey, thought Marged. My mam 'ud go mad if she knew I was here.

Roberta was blinking. Corrie said, 'Shall we have a drink?'

'We're not old enough,' protested Roberta.

''Course we are. Anyway, nobody asks questions here. What are you having, Marged?'

She wasn't sure. Port and lemon was a popular drink for women. 'Gin?' queried Corrie, and she hesitated. Gin was common, though suitable perhaps for the Red Cow. It was what the pros were drinking. Gin, mother's ruin ... 'Gin and lime,' she amended.

Corrie went to the bar and came back with three drinks. Marged sipped hers and thought it was horrible.

Then one of the men asked her to dance.

He was a little fellow, dapper with smooth black hair, not unlike George Raft, probably worked at the pit, Marged thought. He wore an ill-fitting blue suit, and she would have refused but Roberta was staring open-mouthed, so she went with bravado.

And surprisingly, he was a good dancer. Nor did he say anything out of place. Marged relaxed. Just went to show that the rumours about the Red Cow were false. Though those women up at the bar didn't look false. She returned to the girls.

'How did you get on?' asked Corrie.

'All right,' Marged said. 'He was quite a gentleman. We shan't be shoved off to a white slave place at this rate,' and she slid a glance at Roberta, but she was quite unmoved.

'It's when they take you home that the trouble starts,' Corrie said darkly.

Then George Raft asked Roberta to dance, and now it was Marged's turn to stand open-mouthed. For Roberta danced quite well. Marged watched George Raft's reaction when he talked to her. He seemed almost respectful, and she knew a sudden sense of annoyance and was surprised at herself. It seemed her feelings about Roberta were more complex than she realised.

And as she pondered, the trouble started – and started with Roberta. Several youths carrying glasses filled with beer were crossing the floor, threading through the dancers, and they appeared half-drunk. None of this would have been allowed at the Co-op Hall, Marged reflected. An MC stood in the middle of the floor, and was big and burly. Nor was there a bar at the Co-op. One of the youths bumped into Roberta, who turned and said in her clear carrying voice: 'Oh, *do* be careful.' This set the youths off in a cacophony of sound. 'Eow, dew be careful,' and the first one emptied the beer over Roberta's dress. She stood, horrified, and her partner stepped towards the youth, telling him in no uncertain terms to clear off. The youth promptly punched him on the jaw.

George Raft, though small and thin, was a miner, used to hacking coal all day long. His arms were solid muscle. He hit back and the youth slumped to the floor, and now a free-for-all began.

Marged stared, appalled, saw one of the barmen come to try to restore order, but it was hopeless. Someone had blown a whistle and, by the speed at which they approached, the two policemen could not have been far away. And at the same moment as they ran in the door, Marged saw Martin entering. 'Oh hell,' she groaned.

'Let's get out of here,' said Corrie feverishly.

They had little choice. People were pushing now towards the door and the two girls were swept along with them. Marged was just in time to see Roberta being grasped by one policeman, while the other grabbed the youths. They were pulled out of the door towards a waiting van and Marged, horrified, gasped: 'We can't let them take her!'

'Don't be soft. What can we do?' asked Corrie.

And then Martin was before them, saying in an awful voice, 'What are you doing here?'

Marged ran. A bus was just pulling up. She clambered aboard, Corrie behind her. They rode back to the town in silence, and Marged ran in home and went straight to bed, where she lay appalled, thankful that Brenda was not back yet. What an awful thing to happen, dragged off to the police station ... Roberta ... They'd let her go, surely? Marged was uncertain about police procedure. They wouldn't put her in prison, would they? What would her 'mummy' say? What would her own mother say, come to that, if she ever found out? Why had she let Corrie talk her into going there ... She'd known it wasn't respectable – but she'd never go again, that was for sure. Shivering, Marged closed her eyes as Brenda came in, and pretended to sleep.

She saw Martin in the morning at breakfast, but knew he wouldn't say anything before the family. She worked through the day automatically, oblivious to the talk around her, to Mrs Pearson asking her if she were in love. And when she came out of the factory, Martin was waiting for her. He must have pedalled like mad to get there first.

The Fennels couldn't afford the local evening paper as well as a daily, but Mart had a copy in his pocket. 'Come on,' he said grimly, and they walked on together, past a group of girls playing skipping, past the boys with their marbles, on to the road which led to the back field. Martin steered her towards the opening.

March had gone out with the proverbial lion, and even now, in early April, a strong wind made the budding branches creak and groan, blew Marged's hair into her eyes as Martin put down his bike and handed her the newspaper

There were several paragraphs on the front page about the disturbance at the Black Bull. She skimmed through the names and addresses of the youths, who were each given a heavy fine with the alternative of prison, till she reached what she sought. *The girl, Roberta Mordant, was fined ten pounds and released, the magistrates saying they were surprised that a young lady of good family should be in such a place. Asked if she had anything to say in her defence, the girl said, 'I was deceived.'*

'So,' Martin's voice was savage. 'Who deceived her?'

'It was just a joke,' Marged said feebly.

'Roberta Mordant,' he stated. 'How long have you known?'

'Oh, a long time.'

'Why didn't you tell me?'

Marged brushed the hair out of her eyes. 'At first I didn't think ... I was just shocked,' she replied honestly. 'I just wanted to forget it – and her. Anyway, you always detested her.'

He ignored this. 'And now?' he asked.

'Well, she came back, as I told you. But I didn't want me dad to find out. You know how he'd make a fuss. That's why I thought better say nothing, just get rid of her.'

'So,' he accused, 'what was the idea of taking her there? You know the sort of place it is. Got a bad name and everybody who goes there gets a bad name.'

'You seem to know all about it.' Marged was sulky.

''Course I do. But I don't particularly want to hear my sister's name mentioned at the Red Cow.'

'Oh, who cares!'

'Those girls at the bar would go with anybody for a shilling.'

'I thought they charged half a crown.' She tried to be flippant.

'Do you know what me dad would say if he knew you went there?'

A group of boys playing rounders in the field knocked the ball towards them. Martin threw it back and Marged said, 'All right, it's a rough place, I know. But we thought it would be fun—'

'Who's we?'

'I don't see that it's your business, but Corrie and me—'

'Corrie Thompson. She's a bit of a gay girl herself.'

'No, she's not.' Marged defended her friend.

'I know chaps who've been with her.'

'Is that all you talk about, who you've been with?' Marged asked angrily, and for a moment Martin grinned.

'Most of the time,' he admitted. His face went serious. 'And what was the idea of taking Roberta?'

'Oh, it's Roberta now, is it? Why shouldn't we take her? She's always pestering us to take her somewhere, so now she's been. She likes slumming.'

'You little devil.'

'Fancied her, did you? Well, now you know who she is. Got off with a fine, paid for by her daddy, Mr Mordant. Your boss, the man you hate, remember?'

The boys were shouting; the ball rolled towards them again, and again Martin threw it back. 'She can't help her old man,' he muttered as he threw, and the words were caught and blown away by the wind. But Marged grasped his meaning.

'You do fancy her, don't you?' She laughed. 'Fat chance you've got with her!'

'Oh, shut up. Go on home.'

'You should have gone and rescued her,' jeered Marged. 'Like they do in the pictures.' Then she ran.

But she was angry. With Martin for being so sympathetic towards Roberta, with Roberta for causing trouble between them, and with herself for agreeing to go to the Red Cow in the first place. She should have known better – though she'd never admit that to Martin.

Anyway, it was over now. Roberta wouldn't come again, and Martin wouldn't want her now he knew. It was all over.

Marged settled down to serious practice for the competition

dance which was to be held on 10 September. With Ken, she travelled to Birmingham to see two famous exhibition dancers, and she studied the female dancer's dress as she was swept round in a tango. Black, low-cut with shoulder straps, it fitted her body closely, to swirl round her feet in flounces, Spanish-style. And that night she pondered aloud to Brenda the problems of buying such a fabulous dress. 'There'll be the bridesmaid's one too,' she added mournfully.

'You could combine the two,' Brenda said thoughtfully. 'A pastel shade for the bridesmaid's dress, then have it dyed.'

'Yes. Backless, with a little bolero for the wedding. Boleros are all the rage. Goody-goody. How's the house coming on?'

The house had been bought with a deposit and a mortgage. Just a little farther up the road from their home, on a bend, it was similar in type, except that it had a private yard. The entry went between the two houses instead of four as in Marged's home. An old lady, Mrs Travers, lived in the next house, and Virginia creeper covered the back walls.

'It's lovely,' enthused Marged. 'You won't have any nosy neighbours. How about furniture?'

They were able to afford a table and chairs for the kitchen, a sideboard (second-hand) and two beds, double and single. 'I want to get a wardrobe as soon as I can,' Brenda said, and Marged sighed at this luxury. 'I shall come and stay with you,' she said.

The wedding took place at the end of July because Jack had to spend his August holidays with the Territorials. Yet Victoria Street didn't really think there'd be a war, even though Hitler kept making speeches, and now he had his eye definitely on Poland. The weather was glorious, and everyone who could went for a holiday. They sat on the sands, children making sandcastles, dads with handkerchiefs over their bald heads.

The wedding breakfast was to be held at the Fennels'. Eva had bought a large piece of ham which was boiled in the copper, and, with Marged and Brenda, spent the whole of the Friday evening making cakes and tarts. Mrs Sheldon up the road made the wedding cake. She used to work in a baker's; now she made cakes at a reasonable price for neighbours.

The ceremony went off without a hitch. Brenda and Jack left to spend a weekend in Blackpool. The relatives of the two families crowded into Eva's front room, so many they had to borrow chairs and glasses. They ate in the kitchen, then sang the night away, getting more than a little merry.

The weather continued fine. Brenda returned to her new home, and Marged sang as she helped her mother in the house.

And on 28 August Roberta came back.

She always seemed to turn up at important times in the world's history, Marged mused. She was waiting outside the factory and Marged remembered the date – it was just when Hitler began making trouble on the Polish border.

It had been hot in the little factory; all the windows were open but no breeze came in from the huddle of surrounding streets. Working with heavy cloth, trying to keep sweating hands from marking the linings was a strain. The women were more than usually pleased when six o'clock came.

And outside they all stared at the elegant girl waiting across the road, a picture of coolness in her pale lemon dress – 'That's not from Marks and Spencers nor the market,' muttered one girl – her large brimmed hat, her white strapped sandals. 'Crikey,' another voice said audibly. 'Has she come for a job?' and there was laughter.

Marged, flushing, walked over to her and halted, unsure. Then, 'Hallo,' she said.

'Hallo.' Roberta seemed as cool as ever.

'Look – I'm sorry about that business at the Red Cow.'

'Don't worry about it.'

'Did – did you get in any trouble at home?'

'My mother was livid. I've been sent away.'

'Away?'

'To a finishing school.'

And this brought a quick question from Marged, fascinated as always by the other's lifestyle. 'What did you do there?'

'Oh, cookery, dressmaking—'

Marged gurgled, remembering the plaid dress episode. 'So your mother paid money to servants to do your cooking and sewing while you did nothing and now you have to pay to learn all about it. Wouldn't it save money if you learned at home as I do?'

Roberta didn't smile. 'We are taught to set a table—'

'My mam learned that in service—' Marged couldn't resist a little gentle mockery.

'How to receive people and so on. But I'm home for the holidays now,' Roberta changed the subject, 'and for good if I can manage it.'

Marged wanted to go. She was tired and hungry and, after a long day in the factory, felt grubby beside the immaculate Roberta. But she had to settle the affair of the police court. 'Did your mother ask how you'd got to the Red Cow?'

'Of course. And I told her I'd become acquainted with some common girls from Victoria Street.' Marged looked to see if she were joking, but Roberta seemed perfectly serious, so she laughed uneasily. 'Why I've come,' Roberta was continuing, 'is to invite you to a party I'm giving. It's next Saturday, the second of September.'

'A party, where?'

'At my house. You and Martin.'

Marged brushed back her hair from her eyes. A passing cyclist whistled at the girls. 'I don't know,' she said. 'Have you asked Martin?'

'I don't see him. I thought you could do that.' *You owe me*. The words hung in the air, unspoken.

Marged deliberated. It was so unexpected. Entree to the Mordants' house, as an equal. She eyed Roberta curiously, unable to penetrate that calm exterior, the bland expression. Was that what her finishing school had taught her, to be poker-faced? Marged felt a spurt of irritation. What was the point of all this? Their worlds were too different now, had always been different. So why? Did she fancy Martin, was that it? If so it would be the biggest waste of time ever thought of.

'I'll see,' she hedged.

'Let me know,' Roberta told her. 'Give me a ring – oh, you wouldn't be on the phone, would you? You'll have to drop me a line. Goodbye now,' and she left the heat of the little factory street for the cool shade of Park Manor Road.

Marged turned towards her own home, entered it to find both Frank and John sitting before the wireless, listening intently to the news. 'Where's Mart?' she asked.

'Upstairs, getting ready to go out,' Eva replied. No one else took any notice; they were still, tense, as the news droned on.

'Germany today closed the frontiers with Poland ... cordoned off the free city of Danzig – now under German armed guard. Nazi authorities have cut off Poland's outlet to the sea ... All major roads are blocked and guarded by German troops ... Polish goods trains seized by Germans ... vital railway line to Gdynia, Poland's only port, is also cut ...'

Marged moved to the stairs, the announcer's voice following her. 'The Cabinet met today and are warning Germany to stop this aggression or Britain will go to war. Our Ambassador has flown to Germany ... with a message. "Britain will stand by Poland whatever the consequences."'

Since their quarrel about Roberta, Martin had said no more

on the subject. What he thought, Marged had no idea – one never did with Mart. She went to his door. 'Mart,' she whispered.

'What?'

'I've got something to tell you, a message.'

He opened the door, and she took in the sameness of the room, the pictures of aircraft on the walls, the pile of books on the chest of drawers. Martin looked smart, as he always did, wearing a white shirt and blue tie. He went to the mirror and began rubbing Brylcreem into his hair, trying in vain to smooth back the black waves. Martin never had his hair cut short, so it was always falling over his forehead, when he'd push it away with one hand. 'Roberta's asked us to a party at her house,' Marged said.

He put down the Brylcreem jar and walked to the window, staring out at the back field. She went on: 'I didn't tell her how you felt about Mordant's.'

'Good of you.' He was sarcastic.

'Well, it's up to you to tell her yourself. I didn't say whether you'd go or not.'

He turned back, said slowly: 'Perhaps I will.'

'You *will*?' And then, 'Don't make any trouble, Mart.'

'I'm not intending to. Why should I?'

'Because I know you. You're not going out of love for Roberta.'

He gave a snort that could have meant anything, and Marged was baffled. But she wrote to Roberta, saying they'd be there.

In the next few days Britain prepared for war, while still hoping for peace. All road signs were removed; everyone was issued with a gas mask. The Territorials were called up, and Brenda looked worried. The Germans stepped up their movements. In Warsaw there were bombs on railway lines; by Wednesday, Danzig was under German control. Hitler received Chamberlain's document but took little heed. He built up his troops along the Polish border. And on Friday, 1 September, he invaded Poland.

On Saturday Frank and John were again sitting before the wireless. Amy, who had been waiting for John, came up to see what he was doing. Eva was fitting the blackout curtains, yards and yards of material she'd bought from the market, so Marged and Martin's going out together caused little comment. Marged wondered what her dad would say if he knew where they were heading, but Frank had other things on his mind now. John, was call-up age, he'd be the first to go if there was war. Perhaps there wouldn't be. Chamberlain seemed to be hesitating. He sent another note to Hitler, an ultimatum ... Pull out of Poland or Britain would declare war.

It had been another hot day, though there seemed something almost menacing in the oppressive heat. Marged did not wear a coat, and they walked along the road, curbs newly painted white for if and when the blackout was begun. She said, as they turned into Park Manor Road, 'If this was a film we'd buy out Mordant's and get our revenge,' and Martin answered, 'I'll get my revenge one day, don't you worry.'

She stopped walking. 'Mart, what are you planning? You can't marry her and you wouldn't get her in trouble, would you?'

He laughed shortly. 'Not got much of an opinion of me, have you?'

'I go around with girls, remember? They say you're the hottest thing in town.'

'Yes, well, so long as they don't say it about you.'

They had arrived. The drive which circled Park Manor was filled with cars. Marged began to sing a song softly about the Vanderbilts asking us to tea ...

Martin said, 'Don't worry, Mordant's only one man if he's got six shirts on,' and she giggled nervously.

They entered a hall and immediately a man approached

them. 'Your card, sir?' he asked.

'Card?'

'Invitation card, sir.'

But then Roberta was there. 'It's all right, Jennings, they're with me.' And to Marged, 'Wraps in the cloakroom there. I'll be waiting.'

Marged was ushered into a room with washbasins and mirrors as grand as the Co-op Hall, if not so big. She touched up her hair and went out again, just in time to see Martin and Roberta disappearing through a doorway. 'Thanks very much for waiting,' she muttered, following.

Now they were in a long room, filled with young people, and she saw to her dismay that all the girls wore evening dresses and the men dinner jackets – all that is except Martin in his best blue suit and herself in a short frock. Roberta might have told me, she thought, then shrugged philosophically. She didn't have a long one anyway, except for her bridesmaid's dress, now in the process of being dyed. Martin and Roberta went on the floor, dancing to the slow foxtrot played by the three-piece outfit at one end of the hall. Marged watched as he pressed his cheek to hers, held her close. 'All over her,' she muttered, and looked for somewhere to sit.

Along one side were sofas, and she thankfully sank on to one. It *was* interesting to see Roberta's home even if she did have the wrong frock on. She looked round, wondering where Roberta's mother was, picturing some stiff elderly woman dressed in black. But who was that? An older woman with one of the young men who quite clearly called her Mrs Mordant. Marged gaped. Fortyish, with black waved hair, wearing a long red dress, skin-tight, completely backless and almost frontless, her mouth a red wound in her white face, weaving in and out of the dancers, a glass in her right hand ... this was Mummy? Marged tried to guess her background, and failed.

Adela Mordant was born in 1898, daughter of a baronet who owned a hall and acres of land in Cumberland. Her mother, a Catholic, sent her to a convent school until she was eighteen. She left her cloistered life to enter a world of Army officers who, in 1916, were billeted at a nearby convalescent centre. A pretty girl, she was soon the centre of attention. She danced with Freddie and Bunny and Johnny, and received proposals of marriage at the rate of three a week. The war ended, the officers dispersed, but Adela, introduced to champagne and flirtations, went to stay with a friend in London seeking more Freddies and Bunnies as the feverish gaiety of the twenties rushed in. No one knew for certain whether she was really pregnant in 1920; she thought she was, and to her dismay, Freddie and Bunny melted away like snow in summer. Her mother, alarmed, pushed her into the arms of Maurice Mordant, visiting on a business conference and he, flattered, asked her to marry him.

It was the one error of judgment he had ever made in his life. Adela soon made it clear that she had no intention of settling down. She craved excitement still, she was – and would be for the rest of her life – seeking Freddie and Bunny and Johnny who had thought her so attractive. She was furious when she became pregnant again with Roberta, and never forgave the girl for being born at all. She left her family for long periods, visiting friends in London, becoming one of the Bright Young Things, dancing the Charleston, the Black Bottom, drinking cocktails at night-clubs, the Top Hat in Soho, the Silver Slipper in Regent Street.

Maurice considered divorce, but Adela's Catholic connection forbade this, and he hesitated to upset her family even though they never deigned to meet him. There might be money to come, he thought, and Maurice Mordant's god was money. So they led an almost separate existence, she agreeing to accompany him on business dinners, he – as he crudely put it – keeping her. He found solace in other affairs, had little time to spare for his children – he despised

Brian though he quite liked Roberta – and left Adela to her own devices.

She was now that pathetic figure, an older woman trying to appear young, still seeking Freddie and Bunny in every man she met. Marged saw nothing of the pathos, just an over-made-up woman who'd obviously been drinking. She was appalled.

A voice said, 'Shall we dance?' and she turned to see a tall fellow, handsome but with a weak chin and foolish smile. He was swaying a little, and she hesitated, but he pulled her to him.

'You're a good dancer,' he said, and tried to hold her closer. She pulled back to get away from his drink-sodden breath. He laughed a little too loudly. 'Whassa matter, sweetheart?' he slurred.

Marged said nothing.

'I say, who are you?' he asked.

'I'm Marguerite Fennel. Who are you?'

'Brian Mordant. And where do you come from?'

'Victoria Street.'

'I thought you had a funny accent,' he said. 'Like the blokes in the factory.'

She drew a breath. 'You've been drinking,' she accused and as he stumbled, 'Shall we sit down?'

They sat on one of the sofas and she glanced round. How could she get away from this oaf? If she left him no doubt he'd follow her. She looked for Roberta, but there was no sign of her, nor of Martin. Brian put his hand on her knee and she pushed it away angrily.

'Don't be like that, li'l girl,' he said thickly.

Another fellow, seeing her predicament, joined them. 'Hallo, Jeremy old friend,' said Brian.

'You're drunk,' remarked Jeremy, sitting beside him.

Brian laughed. 'I only came for the beer.'

'You mean the old man's best whisky. And who's the girlfriend? Introduce me, do.'

'This is Marg – Margreet Fennel. From Victoria Street.'

'Hallo, I'm Jeremy Spencer.' The young man shook her hand. 'Can I get you a drink?' And as she hesitated, 'Champagne?'

'Yes, please.'

He went to the buffet and Brian put his arm around her. Again she tried to pull away, and to remove his hand from her knee. Jeremy returned with the champagne and sat down. 'Hear you're helping the war effort, Brian.' He tried to take his friend's attention away from Marged.

'Yes, the old man dragged me into the firm. 'Course, it was intended all along: Brian Mordant, son of the big man. I loathe the place.'

'Can't you do something else?'

'How can I when I've no money?' The band was playing a waltz and Brian's arms crept round Marged's waist again, one hand dropped to her knee. Jeremy said, 'Shall we dance, Marguerite?'

'Oh no, she's staying with me.' Brian's arms held her tighter. She had to lean back to save the champagne from spilling, and Brian leaned over her. He whispered in her ear, a few words so obscene that she jerked back, amazed. Then – Crack! As the music ended her hand struck his cheek with the sound of a whiplash. It cut through the talk and everyone turned. 'You drunken fool,' Marged cried, pushing him off. She stood up, threw the champagne into his face, and he slid to the floor.

Out in the garden, Roberta and Martin were in each other's arms. She pressed close to him, and his leg pushed between hers, forcing them apart. One hand held her, the other clasped her breast, inside her dress, the nipple between his fingers. He kissed her, and she put her arms round his neck, holding him tight. 'You love me,' she breathed. 'I knew you did.'

'Where can we go?' he muttered.

'Go?' She was bewildered. 'There's nowhere ... is there?'

A couple came through the open french windows, laughing. 'What happened?' someone was asking.

'Some little girl slapped Brian Mordant's face. Don't know who she is, never seen her before. Wearing a short dress. Mamma Mordant is bearing down on them like an avenging angel – just as she was trying to seduce young Crabshaw ...'

Martin pushed Roberta away and ran back to the room, taking in the scene. Adela Mordant was helping her son to his feet. 'What's going on?' she asked. And as he was incapable of answering she turned to Marged. 'Who are you?'

'Marguerite Fennel.'

'I don't know any Fennels. Where are you from?'

Marged saw Roberta standing in the doorway. 'Victoria Street.'

'And how did you get here? I didn't invite you.'

Marged looked at Roberta, who was silent. 'Roberta asked me.'

'I don't believe you. I expect my poor daughter picked up some undesirable people at that dreadful public house known as the Red Cow. And now you are trying to cash in. Go away, we don't want your sort here.'

Marged's lips pressed together in a thin white line of anger. The crowd stood, watching. And still Roberta was silent. It was Martin who came forward, took his sister's arm and said loudly, 'As you are so bad-mannered we'd rather not stay,' and he marched her to the door.

Outside, Marged stood still. 'Nobody talks to me like that,' she said.

'All right, calm down. She's just ignorant.'

'And Roberta stood there and said nothing.'

'Maybe she was scared.'

'Oh no, Roberta isn't scared. She did it deliberately.'

'Well, she's a Mordant, isn't she?'

'But you were with her?'

He shrugged. 'That doesn't mean I trust her.'

'No, you were right at the start, wanting to get your own back. Well, I'm with you now.'

'Come on, don't let it worry you.'

'You don't care, do you?'

'What that lot think? Not on your life. Come on, are you going home?'

'Yes, of course.'

They walked to the end of Park Manor Road, and there didn't seem to be many people about. The sun had gone now, the sky was dark. From the distance came a rumble of thunder. Martin said, 'It's early yet. If we both go in together, Mam'll wonder why. How about coming to the Co-op Hall with me? Have a dance.'

She shook her head. 'No, I don't feel like dancing. I'll go home.'

He held her arm, repeated, 'Don't let it upset you, they're not worth it,' and he strolled away, whistling.

Alone, Marged walked towards their house. The sky was black now, the thunder louder. Had Roberta been trying to get her own back for the Red Cow business? She realised that their friendliness was really the fascination of enmity between her and Roberta. It didn't affect Martin; it could not happen between a man and a woman because of the sex thing, but between two girls there was no barrier to the fight. And it was a fight. 'I hate her,' she muttered. 'I really hate her.' Martin was right, she was a Mordant.

Frank and Eva took no notice of her coming in, for they were still listening to the wireless. *Mr Arthur Greenwood asked in the House of Commons how long were we prepared to vacillate at a time when Britain and all Britain stands for are in peril?*

The Cabinet rebelled and told Chamberlain war must be declared.

The next morning, Britain was at war.

Chapter 6

Stefan Kowalski could still see the rubble of Warsaw, feel the shuddering impact of the huge bombs that had wiped out their aerodrome, together with bridges, trains and civilians. How many days had they been travelling on this track through burning villages and crowds of refugees, one day ... six days ... ten? He rested his smoke-blackened head on the strut behind him and tried to think clearly. On 1 September, Poland took on single-handedly the might of the German Army and Air Force, trying to hold out until the Allies came to her aid. She clung on against all odds, but no help came. There had been days of heroic fighting while the Germans surrounded them on three fronts, Czechoslovakia, Prussia and the Reich itself. Days of hell.

But the Polish soldiers were dogged and enduring, their self-reliance was extraordinary, able to reorganise into ever smaller units and go on fighting. The Germans were disconcerted by their capacity to carry on, in spite of their hopeless inferiority in weapons. Part of the Polish Navy had escaped and reached British and French ports, whilst all the aircraft remaining – about a hundred – flew to Rumania.

Stefan's own aircraft was lost, and when the aerodrome was gone the order came to move eastwards: 'Destroy everything that could be of use to the enemy.' And here they were, hoping to make a stand ...

They had heard there were attempts to organise some resistance on the line of the River Bug, the last natural obstacle before the frontier between Poland and Russia. On both sides of the river lay nests of camouflaged machine guns and the houses were manned by numbers of soldiers, but they wouldn't be able to resist long for they lacked both guns and equipment.

The truck was ordered to stop for the night. 'Why here?' wondered Antoni.

'We're sheltered,' replied Jan. Even so they could hear firing. The Germans weren't far away.

They tried to sleep. Stefan wondered how his family were, his father, dead now, Tadeusz, too young for call-up, working the farm, Stanislaw, rejected because of his weak chest. His mother ... Janina ... He fell into an uncomfortable doze, but wakened to hear shouts and cries. 'What is it?' he asked. 'What's happening?'

The squadron leader entered. 'Russia has invaded us in the east,' he said.

'To help us fight the Germans?' asked someone.

'That's what we thought at first. But communiqués issued in Berlin and Moscow say that the Red Army's come in by agreement with Hitler. It's going to occupy the eastern part.'

'Hell. My home's there.' Stefan was aghast. 'Can I go to them?'

'No. We have our orders. We're heading for the Rumanian border. It's the only way.' He turned at the entrance. 'No use your going home,' he added to Stefan. 'The Soviets are deporting Polish forces to Russia.'

Nightmare now, through rain and sleet and mud ... What could he do ...? What of his family ...?

Stefan and his group escaped the Russo-German pincer and arrived in Rumania, only to be immediately interned. Rumania was a poor country, they could see, but they were not treated badly, the food was adequate. At night they slept in tents, and Stefan lay awake, thinking.

'I can't stay here for the duration. I want to get to England, to fight ... for my home ... how is my mother ...?'

He tossed and turned, hearing the shunting of goods wagons somewhere nearby. Hour after hour it went on ... trundle, trundle, clang!

The next morning he whispered to Jan: 'Did you hear the shunting last night?'

'Yes. Kept me awake.'

'Wagons mean railway lines. Railway lines mean trains. We've got to get out, Jan.'

They thought, they discussed, they walked to the fence. 'It wouldn't be too difficult to get over, and the Rumanians are sympathetic to us. Once over the fence, we could go down to the railway—'

'And get on a train somehow.'

They bided their time, Jan, Antoni and Stefan. They hoarded their food, waited.

Their chance came on the night of a terrific thunderstorm. The noise was so bad no one could hear as they slipped out, climbed the fence, and made off towards the sound of the trains.

The rain poured down, but they didn't mind. They were free! Free to carry on the fight ...

They walked along the track, not knowing where it would lead. 'I think that's the station ahead,' said Jan.

'And I hear a train.'

A whistle, a steady chug-chugging, the train slowed down as it neared the station. The three jumped aboard.

To be confronted by the guard.

Stefan had prepared for this. He held out his gold watch. 'Take it,' he said. 'Get us to Bucharest. Bucharest. Please ...'

The guard eyed the wet, bedraggled figures before him. Then he took the watch.

He led them into the guard's van, pointed to a large

crate. Opened it. It was empty. And they crammed inside, with their hoarded sandwiches between them; soaking wet, but free.

They travelled for six hours before the train slowed down on the outskirts of a big city. Bucharest.

They jumped off, mingled with the crowds. A taxi stood outside the station. 'Polish Embassy,' Stefan ordered, and they were driven off without question. The Embassy staff paid the taxi and led them inside to a bath, dry clothes, and a hearty meal.

Over the meal they learned that there was a good network set up for escaping Poles, and within a week they had joined a group which was transported to a villa on the Black Sea port of Tulcia and told to wait for a British ship.

Now they could breathe again. Now they were on their way. The ship took them to Malta, and another wait. Then the SS *Franconia*, with a two-destroyer escort, landed them at Marseilles, more trains to Lyon and Cherbourg and they finally faced the English Channel.

I'd like to go to England some day. Stefan thought of his childhood dream and chuckled ironically. The ferry ploughed through a grey and stormy sea to Plymouth.

They had arrived to join the Polish Air Force in Britain.

Victoria Street was dark. The blackout was in full swing, and even in daytime there was a difference. The cars which had been increasing in number were fewer, and people carried gas masks, though not in the original cardboard containers. Smart imitation leather ones were on sale.

The Fennels' life had changed immeasurably. None of them would forget the day when Frank walked in and beamed: 'I've got a job. Old crock like me.'

They crowded round, laughing. 'Where, Dad? Where?'

'At Billings', in Coventry. I'm in the stores, so I can sit down. With all the young lads being called up, they need us old 'uns.' His voice was tinged with sadness, for John was one of the young men. And he was planning to marry before he left. Brenda's Jack had already gone, and they were all sorry for Brenda, who had had only one month of marriage. She said little. Brenda did not wear her heart on her sleeve, unlike Amy, who was already in tears at the thought of being left alone.

Frank did not say to Brenda, 'I told you how it would be.' He took her aside one afternoon and murmured, 'If you need any help you know where to come,' and slipped her a pound note from his new wage packet. And Brenda, understanding how he enjoyed being able to give, thanked him and tried to smile.

Martin said nothing either, but one day he called Marged into his room. 'Don't tell Mam and Dad,' he began. 'I volunteered for the RAF as a pilot.'

'Oh Mart, you'd love that!'

'They turned me down.'

'Why?'

'Because I didn't have a grammar-school education.'

'Oh, Mart.' She felt his disappointment. 'Seems a silly way to run a war, not taking chaps who want to go,' she said hotly. 'I bet you could fly a plane from all the studying you've done,' and she turned to the wall pictures, brought up to date now with the latest in war planes, then the books on the chest of drawers. Martin was plane mad.

'Well, I shan't volunteer again,' he said.

She walked to the window where the back field was dull and grey, tinged here and there with frost. They said it was going to be a bad winter, the old folks who read the signs. 'You'll have to go if you're called up,' she returned.

'Want to bet? Anyway, I shall be reserved.'

She turned, stared. 'How do you know?'

'Because Mordant's are keeping everybody they can. All the good workers, and I'm one. That's why they won't pay me off when my apprenticeship is finished.'

'You mean they fiddle it?'

'Naturally, knowing Mordant's.'

'Well.' She tried to smile. 'You'll be able to take over the firm.'

'Yes, won't I?' And I know just how I'm going to do it, he thought savagely.

Marged understood Martin's disappointment, but she had her own setback. The dance halls and cinemas had closed on the outbreak of war, but the Co-op Hall reopened, and when she went as usual, Ken was waiting for her. 'I reckon this'll put paid to our competitions,' he told her.

'Have they stopped them?'

'Seem to think we're going to be bombed. The September one was cancelled, so with some halls closing I can't see them going on. Not to mention the chaps being called up.'

He looked down at her wryly. She hadn't grasped yet just what being at war meant.

She said pettishly, 'Why does stupid Hitler want to invade everywhere? Where's he going next, Russia?'

'Russia's signed a pact with Hitler, remember?' asked Ken, and she knew a moment's disquiet that she couldn't understand, a fear of wild winds unleashed in space, quaking earths squashing little people into dust.

'Why?' she asked. 'Why?'

They learned why when they heard that the Russians had invaded Poland from the east on 17 September, and Chilverton, who had hardly heard of Poland before the war, now wondered uneasily how the people were faring there.

The Kowalskis' farm was quiet when the Soviet tanks rolled in, and when they first saw the invaders approaching, Tadeusz wondered if the Soviets were going to help them drive out the Germans, to make Poland free again. He walked outside. The soldiers looked tired and dirty, and as they halted, children from the village ran out to see these strange people, and the soldiers talked to them, asking where they could buy watches. Tadeusz returned home, where his mother stood by the window, Janina by her side.

'It's the same as before,' Barbara Kowalska said. 'Poland split between Russia and Germany.'

It was obvious that the Soviets had come to stay. The family locked the door and waited. Until a Soviet officer strode up the path, knocked on the door, entered without waiting to be asked. He looked round the big kitchen, walked into the parlour, then to the window where he could see the chickens clucking in the yard. 'A big house,' he commented. 'You are nobility?'

'No,' said Barbara quickly. 'We are peasants. Like you. Farmers. We work hard.'

He looked at her suspiciously, opened the drawers in the bureau and began to rifle through the papers. They watched, fearfully. 'You'll have to go,' he ordered. 'We need this house for our headquarters.'

'Go? Go where?' asked Tadeusz.

The officer shrugged. 'Where is the master of the house?' and Tadeusz answered, trying to make his voice firm and deep, 'I am.'

The officer snorted. 'A boy. Come on, get moving—'

'But we must pack our things—'

'Hurry.'

'But what about the animals? The cows will soon need milking, taking to the barns—'

'We'll see to them,' and he waited as they grabbed a few clothes in a bag, but when Barbara tried to take some of her papers from the bureau he stopped her. 'Go,' he commanded, and they were hustled out of the gate. They stood, bewildered, then began to walk forlornly down the road, past the tanks and the vigilant soldiers. The Lenskis were at their door, and Pani Lenska called, 'Come in. Come and stay with us.'

They stepped inside the little house, Barbara, Tadeusz and Janina, and watched as the soldiers looted their home, took their beloved possessions; the old clock that had survived the Czar's men, the antiques, the radio that was

Tadeusz's pride and joy. The cows lowed in agony, for they needed milking, but next day they were slaughtered for food. Tadeusz observed it all, dry-eyed. He knew every cow by name.

And then the rumours started. Warsaw had capitulated and a German-Soviet treaty was concluded, dividing Polish territories between the two aggressors. The division of the spoils was arranged by a German-Soviet convention signed on 28 September. Now millions of Poles were under the rule of the Soviets who were already deporting people to Siberia, to labour camps and jails. And though this stab in the back made Polish resistance hopeless, it was continued in many places, above all in Warsaw. The Kowalskis waited.

But some days later, other men came into the village, men from the NKVD*, the secret police, and they also began knocking on people's doors in the night, making arrests. Pani Kowalska said, 'We must go to Warsaw, to my sister.'

'But *Matka*, Warsaw is surrounded, they say. The Germans—'

'Tadeusz, you are only sixteen. I am nearly fifty. I was born under Russian occupation. I hate the Germans, but I fear the Russians more. We must go – while we can.'

'And leave our home?'

'Our home is already gone.'

They had not unpacked their bags; they stood them near the door. They huddled round the table as night fell, they and the Lenskis. It was getting cold; the storks had gone from the roofs, a few flakes of snow were falling. And at midnight came the knocking they dreaded, that they'd waited for yet hoped would not come.

Tadeusz was nearest the door. He opened it and the whole family crowded behind him, as if they would find safety in numbers. A man in the uniform of the NKVD stood there.

* NKVD – predecessor of the KGB.

131

'Janina Kowalska?' he asked.

'Yes, that is me.' Janina, now a pretty girl of eighteen, came to the door, her eyes dilated with fear.

'I have a letter for you from Stefan Kowalski in England.'

'From Stefan? Then he is safe?' And now they all stepped forward, hope and joy on each face, Kowalskis and Lenskis alike.

'Come out here,' called the officer. 'Come and fetch it.'

'But why—?'

In reply the officer dragged her outside, Tadeusz, his mother and the Lenskis following, trying to hold her, being stopped by soldiers with bayonets.

'Where is the letter?' asked Barbara.

'Oh, I must have lost it.' The officer was laughing. 'Now,' he stopped suddenly, still holding Janina, and the smile left his face, to be replaced by a cruel sneer. 'You should not communicate with the likes of Stefan Kowalski. He is with the reactionary forces in the West.'

'You mean Britain?' Tadeusz cried. 'They are all fighting the Germans, as you are.' Then he remembered the treaty.

'Come.' The officer pulled Janina out to the road, where they could see a truck waiting with people standing inside, including the priest, the schoolmaster. It was all happening so rapidly, they were bewildered. Barbara Kowalska shouted, 'But Stefan is my—' and Tadeusz put a hand over her mouth. Janina was pushed into the truck, and Tadeusz slipped beneath the soldier's rifle and ran to her. 'Let her go! Where are you taking her?'

He grabbed her arm, and the soldier brought the rifle down on his head. Tadeusz rolled in the road. Pani Lenska rushed to the truck with the bag, pushed it into Janina's hands, then fell back as it lurched forward. It drove away, towards Russia.

Tadeusz got to his feet dazedly. 'We mustn't stay here,' his mother said, 'or they'll take us all. We must go to Warsaw.'

'But Janina—'

'There's nothing we can do. I've seen it all before.'

They huddled together in the little house, shocked, fearful. And when all the secret police had gone, Tadeusz and his mother slipped out – the Lenskis refused to leave – and walked to the station where they asked about a train to Warsaw. But most of the railway lines had been destroyed, bridges blown up, so they would have to get there by a roundabout route. They travelled for hours, and at length found a train that would take them nearly to Warsaw.

The train was crowded; they had to stand. Tadeusz glanced at his mother in the dim blue light. How must she be feeling, to regain her home only to lose it again? After all her work ... He was glad his father was no longer alive. Barbara's face was impassive. It was a strong face; she would bear this as she'd borne so many troubles. He leaned towards her and touched her hand and she looked at him and smiled faintly.

And what of Janina? Was she even now being taken to some Siberian labour camp? He'd heard of the labour camps, the inmates, who, if they survived, suffered from frostbite, starvation and exhaustion, working in 65°C of frost, wrapped in rags. He knew about the Purges. And if Stalin could do this to his own people, what horrors were in store for foreigners?

But Janina ... why her? He liked Janina, she'd always been kind to him when his brothers teased him. She was a simple girl, fond of farming as he was ... *Don't think of the farm. Don't think of Janina. Not now ... Concentrate on survival.*

The train stopped some miles outside Warsaw, and the passengers were ordered out; they could not go any farther. There was a curfew, so they would have to wait till morning. Tadeusz and Barbara spent the rest of the night with a crowd of refugees who filled the small waiting room, most without money or food. Many were elderly, but there were also young babies. And in the morning mother and son set out to walk to Warsaw. It was cold, a little snow was falling. 'Courage, *Matka*,' said Tadeusz. 'We won't be long now.' But he wondered what they would find when they reached his aunt's apartment.

They walked all the way, there were no buses, only crowds of refugees. The streets were filled with abandoned guns and huge barricades. Fires were still raging, whole streets were reduced to rubble where the Germans had bombed with their powerful Luftwaffe. The last Polish troops had been taken prisoner.

Tadeusz's heart sank as they picked their way along. He had visited his aunt several times; the last occasion had been when he went to see Stefan, and together they sat in Lazienki Park by the Palace on the Water. Maria Bilska was the widow of a lawyer, she had been quite comfortably off.

They turned into the small road where she lived, stepping carefully through the rubble, tired, dirty, dishevelled. Then: 'Look!' he cried. 'Aunt's apartment. It's still standing.'

For the first time since the Russians had come in, something like a sob caught at Barbara's throat. 'Maria, my sister,' she murmured. 'Will she be there?'

They stood on the corner surveying the devastation, and a truck carrying prisoners rolled by, men standing crammed together inside. Barbara took one look and cried: 'Stanislaw was in that truck! My son ... but he's not a soldier, he's a professor, a sick man ...'

Janina had been pushed into the truck with such force that she almost fell. A man helped her stand upright and she saw it was Pan Nowak, the schoolmaster. Beside him stood the priest, blood flowing from a cut on his head; next to him the Bermans, the Jewish merchant and his sister who had come east to escape the Germans. In a corner an old woman nodded over her rosary.

Some of her terror left Janina at the sight of these familiar faces. Pan Nowak, who used to frighten her at school, now seemed like an old friend. 'Where are they taking us?' she asked.

'I don't know, child. I can't think that I've done any harm to anyone. I'm not even rich.'

It was bitterly cold, and the truck jolted into Pinsk station where they were herded out, heavily guarded, Janina clinging to Pan Nowak as to a lifeline. There was a train waiting, long and dark green, and crowds of people were being pushed along in a confused, shouting mass.

Janina was appalled; never in her life had she seen anything like this. They were being propelled on to the train by the soldiers, families forced apart, screaming children driven to one end, their frantic mothers to another. Still Janina clung to Pan Nowak, as around her people were crying and groaning. One old lady fell and was lost to view. Relatives crowded the barriers, holding out food and bags, but were forced back by the guards with bayonets. The guards seemed indifferent to the suffering, as if they were used to such work.

Inside, the doors came together in the middle of the carriage, and the outer doors clanged shut. The train began to move. It was still dark, but as Janina's eyes grew accustomed to the gloom she could distinguish the shapes around her, about fifty herded together so close they had to stand. She could see no sign of the priest or the Bermans, nor of anyone else she knew, apart from Pan Nowak. The air was close and foul, for all it was so cold outside. Children screamed and wept, especially those who had lost their mothers.

'Why are they taking the children, Pan Nowak?' Janina asked, and he replied, 'They seem to be taking whole families.'

'Where are we going?'

He paused. 'I don't know.'

'We're going to Siberia,' cried a woman. 'You know what Siberia is, prisons.'

Janina shuddered, but her sense of disbelief continued. This couldn't be happening to her – why should it? You didn't go to prison unless you had done something wrong, and what had she done? What had Pan Nowak done, or the priest, or these children and old people? She began to shiver.

Pan Nowak sensed her distress, and tried to comfort her. For himself he wasn't too upset. He was an old man and if they wanted to kill him, so be it. But these young ones . . .

'Look,' he said, pointing upwards. A little light was seeping in from high up in the roof. 'It must be morning. We'll feel better if we can see.'

But they still couldn't really see; there were no windows. 'I'm hungry,' one child cried. 'Mama, I'm hungry.'

They were all hungry, and worse, Janina's body had another need and she didn't know how to ask the way to the lavatory, or how she'd get there through this crush. A child solved the problem as he asked his mother. His mother didn't know. 'We'll have to wait till the guard comes in,' she said.

They waited for two hours, when a guard entered with a dirty basket containing small pieces of dry bread. 'Where is the lavatory?' asked the child's mother.

The guard laughed and pointed to the floor. In the middle was a small round hole.

Janina's eyes dilated, and there were loud cries of protest, and questions about where they were going and why. The guard answered nothing, merely laughing and leaving them. Their cries turned to anger, but they were helpless, small pieces of human cargo being taken out of their own country. 'So this is what it means to be invaded,' said the mother of the child.

The bread was divided among them, not satisfying their hunger in any way, and their attention turned back to the hole in the floor. The children used it unselfconsciously, but the adults refused – at first. Then they realised there was no alternative. Pan Nowak and another man tried to rig up a makeshift curtain using their coats, and one by one the people entered the still public space.

Janina was one of the last, and she was filled with shame. She knew she was painfully shy, and sometimes wished she was not, but now she wondered why such things should happen to such as she, who asked for nothing but a quiet life. When she staggered back to the side, the foul air and the stench hit her nostrils so that she wanted to vomit; she was dizzy and felt herself falling. Pan Nowak caught her and managed to prop her up. 'All right, Janina,' he said. 'Don't think about it. Think about nice things, your home, your mother, the farm, Tadeusz . . .'

'Yes,' she gasped.

'Look,' he said thankfully. 'We're stopping.'

The train pulled up, the doors were opened. They could see the platform, but were not allowed to get out; instead, more people were pushed in. As before, women tried to bring food, but were roughly thrust away.

Now it was just a nightmare of shouts and cries and sobs and smells. Janina wanted to sit down, but she could not or she would have been trampled. An old lady in the corner who steadfastly refused to eat or to use the hole, was moaning. Now night merged into day, with stops and starts and an occasional meal consisting of buckets of nauseous soup with fish heads and bones in it.

They crossed the Russian border, and when they stopped now, the Russian people did not come to help or even stare; they just passed by. 'I expect they're used to it,' said Pan Nowak.

They reached Kharkov and were told they had to change trains. Thankfully they stepped on to the platform, breathing in the cold, freezing air with gratitude. More and more people were hustled on to the platform, and the guards were pushing people here and there. 'Over here,' they cried, and Janina found herself knocked away from her friends. 'Pan Nowak,' she screamed, feeling she could bear these outrages more easily if she could stay with people she knew. But the guard pushed her on with his bayonet. 'All of you into the cells,' he rapped out.

The cells were dark and cold, but there were so many people they warmed each other. A little light crept in through a tiny grating at the top of one wall. Janina felt abandoned, lost.

Then one of the women started to sing one of the old Polish songs, and it was taken up throughout the prison. The guards yelled at them to shut up, but no one did. 'Let them shoot us,' cried one man. And they began to scratch their names on the prison walls, and those of their native towns, so that in time the cell would be covered with names – Crakow, Katowice, Tarnopol, Wilno, Lwow, Lida, Lomza ...

In the morning they were pulled out again, herded on to another train, and now there was no sign of her friends from the village. Janina never heard of them again.

The second train was the same as the first, unlit, unventilated, with a hole in the floor. They were given a little drinking water; never enough, so if rain or snow fell, as it did with increasing rapidity, a hole was carefully made in the roof and a piece of rag stuffed into it and sucked for its moisture. But they had to be careful; if the guards saw them they would be shot.

On and on, sometimes stopping, night and day merging into one. And people began to die. First the old and the sick, then the children. The rest were reduced to animals, squatting over the hole in the floor, or, when in open country, forced to get out and crouch in rows while the soldiers stood on the steps and shouted orders and jeers. The bodies of the dead were left at the side of the track.

The journey went on for weeks, but Janina had lost all

sense of time. She could no longer think clearly, though she tried to remember her home and the village with its little white-painted houses and the flowers in the gardens, the scent of woodsmoke. Tadeusz, who had said, 'I'll take care of you.' She brightened at the memory.

Sometimes she felt so cold she could hardly breathe, and she thought it must be Christmas. They'd soon be celebrating; they'd go to Midnight Mass and the church would have the little crib, surrounded by candles. Other times the foul air was so thick she thought it must be summer and they'd be making hay with Tadeusz laughing down at her from the wagon, the huge horses lumbering past.

The train arrived at Vladivostok and they were told to get out. This was the end of the line. Janina had never heard of Vladivostok, but it seemed to be a port for she could see the sea, and someone said it was in the Far East, near to Japan.

It was cold; a bitter wind blew from the water. 'Wait there,' called the guard. 'Wait for transport.'

Huddled together, cold, hungry, dirty, they waited.

Chapter 7

In England, nothing was happening. British planes were dropping leaflets over Germany, not bombs. The phony war. In October there were appeals for war-workers, and this was discussed at Grant's.

'Maybe women will be called up,' said Mrs Pearson. 'They can take me to the forces any time they like, put me with the soldiers.' Her great laugh boomed out.

'Lots of girls are joining up,' Doris put in.

'To get the men,' snorted Mrs Grey. 'That's all they take women for, to keep the men happy.'

'You should go in munitions in Coventry,' Mrs Pearson advised Marged. 'You'd get good money.'

Marged pondered the conflicting opinions. 'I remember the last war,' said her mother. 'I worked in munitions, on inspection. They brought girls down from the Highlands of Scotland to work on the top floor, putting gunpowder into shells. When there was an air raid they locked them in. Said they'd go up anyway if they were hit.'

'Why don't you try for an office?' suggested John. 'You get better conditions, war or no war. Though not more money.'

There seemed few prospects at Grant's. Work would be falling off as the war went on, since men wouldn't want suits. They'd all be wearing khaki, and Grant's had no

Army orders. 'We might close down,' opined Mrs Grey lugubriously.

Now advice came thick and fast. 'Don't go too far away,' Marged's mother pleaded. 'There's a lot to do at home, and now Brenda's gone ...' Still the housework and shopping to do, and shopping would be getting more difficult. Marged studied her mother, thought how tired Eva looked. She had at last given up her job, but the years of scrimping and saving had taken their toll. Just over fifty, she looked sixty.

'Try for the office,' John repeated. 'It's a chance for you.' And Marged saw that the war was, in fact, bringing unheard-of opportunities. She no longer had to stay in her station in life; she had missed out on education, now was her chance to catch up. She enrolled at Mrs Dailey's secretarial school for shorthand, typing and book-keeping, three hours a week, Monday evening and Saturday afternoons, at one shilling and sixpence an hour. It meant sacrificing her lovely Saturday afternoons with Brenda, but she worked hard, practising her shorthand whenever she had a minute to spare.

John was married at Christmas. Amy wore white and Marged was her bridesmaid, wearing the same dress she'd worn for Bren's wedding, though Amy pulled a face at that. The reception was held at the Co-op Hall, and all the family were there, Grandma enjoying herself hugely. The couple went back to live at Amy's.

But early in the New Year John left for the Army, as a private in the Royal Warwicks. He came to see the family before he left, Amy clinging to his arm, crying.

John kissed his mother. 'It won't be for long,' he said.

Eva clung to him for a long moment, and Frank shook his hand. He went to the door with Amy, the front door, used only on special occasions, through the tiny garden to the gate, where he turned, the wintry sun gleaming on his fair hair. 'See you soon,' he called.

The family watched him all down the street. Eva

murmured, 'I wish he hadn't said that. My brother said it in 1915 and we never saw him again.' And she stood there even when he'd disappeared from view, and a cloud covered the sun.

'Come in, Mam,' called Marged. 'It's going to snow.'

It was the coldest January for fifty years. In Chilverton there were 25° of frost, and snow stacked up by the roadside. Only skeleton bus services could run, and whole villages were cut off. Main-line trains ran a day late, causing shortages in the shops, rationing had begun. But there were still no air raids. Cinemas reopened, even on Sundays, for the benefit of the forces now coming to the area. An army camp was constructed in the grounds of a stately home, and a new aerodrome had been built two miles away. The blackout was lightened by the snow, though Frank had difficulty getting home from Coventry. 'You'll be stupid if you try this,' Frank told Marged.

She went to the local Labour Exchange to ask about jobs.

'There's a vacancy at Mordant's for a clerk-typist,' she was told.

She hesitated. She didn't want to go to Mordant's. But it would be a start. She could move if she didn't like it.

She walked to Mordant's, and as she reached the factory she stared at the place that had ruined her father's life – and Martin's. The locked gates, the notice saying you could be searched ... like a prison, she thought. But she went through the small open gate to the gatekeeper's office. 'I've come to apply for the job as clerk-typist,' she announced.

The gateman picked up the phone. 'Mr Walters? I have a girl here ...'

She was taken along the yard, past the grey buildings where grey lorries stood waiting beside piles of grey metal. Through a door into a long room pretty much the same as the one she'd worked in at Grant's, but these workers had typewriters, not sewing machines, and she was led through them to a small office at the side. A grey-haired woman whom Marged thought looked about ninety, came forward.

'Miss Sansome,' said the gatekeeper. 'This is the girl applying for the job.'

'Thank you. I'm Mr Walters' secretary. If you'll wait here, he'll be with you in a minute.' And she gave a frosty smile.

Marged waited, and Miss Sansome began to type at a speed that left her gasping. She had done three letters before Mr Walters opened the door and ushered Marged inside. His office was small and dark, lined with brown cupboards and cabinets, with one small window at the far end. He sat at his desk in the middle of the room, pointed her to be seated opposite, and said, 'Right, Miss – er. You want a job. Qualifications?'

Marged studied him as she told how she was learning shorthand and typing. A portly man around fifty, his face at first glance appeared pleasant and smiling, but his eyes never quite met hers; and looking at him in profile she found a foxy look that she did not like. Marged sometimes felt that her lack of education had sharpened her perceptions, and she sensed that this was not a man to be trusted.

He asked where she worked now, and what she earned. Two pounds a week? 'I'll offer you two pounds five,' he barked. 'Right.' He picked up the phone. 'Get me Mr White. Cliff? I have a typist here. Yes. Get rid of her.' He turned to Marged. 'Start a week on Monday,' he said.

Marged went home uneasily. She had learned in the first hour that all her dad's warnings were true. This wasn't a good place to work at – they sacked someone just to take you on. And they'd get rid of you just as easily, no doubt. Still, did it matter? She could learn her job at Mordant's, use them as they'd used her dad. Her lips tightened. If she didn't take the job someone else would. It was a cut-throat world she lived in. Nevertheless, she didn't tell her dad that piece of the story; he wouldn't like that at all. Had his principles, her dad. Look where they got him.

Martin said, 'You're going to *Mordant's*?'

'Oh come on, Mart, you know it's the only big place round here. I shan't stop if I don't like it.'

'You won't like it,' he said.

'We can't get away from Mordant's, can we?' she asked. 'It's like some evil power holding us.'

'You'd be better in the forces,' Frank muttered. 'Even the Army treat you better than them.'

Poland was divided into three. The east was occupied by the Soviets. The western sections had been incorporated into the German Reich, and were to be completely denuded of Poles and resettled by Germans. First there would be mass expulsions, followed by systematic extermination.

But the centre of Poland, a triangle around Warsaw, Cracow and Lwow was, oddly, given a French name by the Germans – *Gouvernement Général*. This was a vast cage, governed by the Reich, where the Poles had no rights whatsoever, but where life was not quite so harsh, for the job of Poles here was to produce food for the Germans, so they were not shot if caught on a train, nor executed if apprehended without a pass in the streets; they were allowed to ride to and from work. But they had to step in the gutter when a German approached.

Tadeusz Kowalski owed his life to his youth. He and his mother had been welcomed by Maria Bilska, and shared her apartment. And one night, they were awakened by a hammering on the door. Two Gestapo men stood outside. They pushed their way in and demanded to see all identity cards, then they searched the house, carefully noted Tadeusz's date of birth, and left. The next day, they heard that all men between the ages of nineteen and fifty were taken away. No one knew where or why. They simply disappeared.

The first priority for Tadeusz was to find work, and his aunt sent him to a man she called Jacek, who not only found him a job, but a German work permit, without which he was liable to be deported to forced labour in Germany. Back in his aunt's flat, Tadeusz listened to the radio; everyone in Warsaw listened to London and Paris services, so they all knew that the new Commander-in-Chief and President of Poland was General Sikorski, that he'd formed a government in exile in Paris, and that a Polish army was being raised abroad.

'I want to do something,' Tadeusz said.

'Do you?' asked his aunt. 'Then you shall.'

He wasn't aware at first that his aunt was in the new underground movement that was springing up. Only when he realised that she used her flat as a listening centre for London radio did he suspect the truth. It was dangerous even to listen to the radio in Warsaw; the Germans confiscated all receivers and announced the death penalty for their possession – and for listening. But the people were desperate for news, so every evening little crowds would slip like shadows into various apartments – of which Maria's was one – and huddle in back rooms waiting for the broadcasts. And when in October the first underground paper *Poland Alive* began to circulate, Tadeusz was one of its distributors. Reading it, he learned that hundreds of smugglers were crossing the frontier daily; they ran through the woods when the German patrols changed, evading raids, hiding, waiting ... He said to his aunt: 'I want to do more than this.'

She sent him to see Jacek again – this was not his real name, they never knew each other's names, and the man was expecting him.

'What can you do?' asked Jacek.

'I worked on the farm all my life, but I know a lot about radio. It was my hobby.'

'Can you use a transmitter?'

'I can.'

'Would you be willing to send messages? You know that if you are caught you'll be shot.'

'I'm willing.'

And, as was to happen in England, people stopped being afraid when faced with death and danger. And as in England, pre-war political antagonisms were suspended. All worked together.

Tadeusz fitted up a transmitter in his aunt's apartment and tapped out messages to London, eagerly, hopefully.

London was their lifeline. They clung to it as drowning men to a straw. London – their hope, their only hope.

Mordant's general office was a dismal room with no windows, and it was cold. Nor did it ever seem to get warm. Dozens of men and women sat round tables pretty much the same as at Grant's. Marged was shown to a place with a typewriter, two girls at her side, three men opposite, and was given some cards to type. It was a simple job presenting no problems. She wasn't very fast and the cold numbed her fingers. But no one seemed to be hurrying.

'Office is over-staffed,' said Mr Blake, the little man opposite. 'You won't have much to do. It's the war, you see. Government pays. Never used to be like this, used to be a real slave-driving place. But everybody's coming in now for one reason or another. That bloke over there is a retired colonel, come back to do his bit. Lives in a hotel and has a week off every month. Says he has malaria, but he really goes on a drinking binge. Some of 'em have come to escape the call-up, women as well as men. And some of 'em have never worked before in their lives. Like her—' He nodded over his shoulder. 'At the back, see, that's the boss's daughter,' and Marged looked up to see Roberta.

'Perhaps she wanted to work,' she defended.

'And the band played believe it if you like,' snorted Mr Blake. 'Anyway, watch what you say. She'll report it all back.'

'She wouldn't . . . would she?'

'Very likely that's why she's here. It's all tittle-tattle. You can't trust anybody.'

'I'm Miss Fennel now,' Marged told Corrie that evening. 'Never been Miss Fennel before in my life. Five days' work plus Saturday or Sunday and I'll be paid overtime for that. It's money for jam.'

'I thought about joining up,' said Corrie. 'All those officers —' Her eyes grew dark with longing.

'I've had to change my secretarial classes,' Marged went on. 'I've cut out one hour, but I do more book-keeping—'

'Seems silly to me,' said Corrie. 'I think I'll go in the factory.'

'We've got a canteen. You should see it. Well, two canteens really, one for the workers, that'll be you, Corrie, self-service and bare tables, and another for the staff, table-cloths and waitresses. Then the senior staff have a separate table with a coffee percolator. Do you know what a coffee percolator is?'

'Who's the senior staff?' asked Corrie, interested in spite of herself.

'Mostly women, secretaries of the managers. You should see them, all old maids, all miserable. But they are power-ful,' Marged ended thoughtfully. 'They act for their bosses, so they are over us. Mr Mordant's secretary isn't an old maid, though. She's young and beautiful.'

'Boss's choice, I suppose,' Corrie yawned. 'Come on, let's go to the dance.'

Marged had thought that with the onset of war, all the fellows would be gone. Ken, her old dancing partner, had been one of the first to be called up. But as the weeks passed the Hall filled with soldiers from the Army camp, and RAF men from the aerodrome. All were other ranks, of course, officers and men were not allowed to mix off-duty.

But many of them were excellent dancers from northern and Scottish regiments, who took their dancing seriously. Marged and Corrie were in great demand. Some of the fellows came just for the dance, requiring a good partner.

But most wanted to take the girls home as well, with a goodnight kiss and 'trying it on', as the girls put it. Marged laughed and left them. 'It's here today and gone tomorrow with you chaps,' she told them.

As a bitter cold Christmas led to a snowy, icy January, the first trickle of Poles came to the Hall, and the girls, who had never seen any foreigners before in their lives, went down like ninepins before their old-fashioned courtesy, their gallantry, and habit of kissing the hands. They were rumoured to be good lovers.

But Marged kept aloof from this foreign charm. 'They're not very good dancers,' she said dismissively to Corrie. 'And they don't speak English very well.'

She danced every night, whatever the weather, snow, ice or slush, fitting in her housework and secretarial lessons on top. She was overworked but didn't know it; she did her best in the office and hoped for promotion. She made friends with several of the girls, but not with Roberta. The events of the party still rankled. And when they passed on the first day, Roberta nodded slightly as if she were the merest acquaintance. Be like that then, thought Marged, and made no further effort to be friends.

Roberta had been sadly disappointed with work. When she said she wanted a job, she had no idea she would be sitting in a dark crowded office, where to copy numbers from a card to a long sheet seemed at best trivial, at worst childish. Mr Walters had worriedly asked Mr Mordant what he was supposed to do with Roberta. Her father replied: 'Just find her something. Her mother wants her out of harm's way.' He did not exactly say to evade the call-up, but that was what was meant, and Mr Walters knew it. Nor was it true to say that Adela wanted it. Adela was planning to join what Winston Churchill scathingly called 'the stampede from Britain'. She was waiting for a passage on a ship to America. What happened to her daughter she neither knew nor cared.

'I'm sorry I can't offer you anything better,' Mr Walters apologised to Roberta. 'But you're not trained, you see.'

Roberta realised this lack, and that it was impossible to get a career without it. She had not passed matric. It hadn't been considered necessary. Melbourne girls did not *work*, they were groomed to become the wives and mothers of important men, able to talk on topics of the day, but not to *work*. Now she felt her position keenly that she, well-educated and the boss's daughter to boot, should be in a lesser position than Marged, and it was this as much as anything that made her snub her.

The other reason was Martin. He was behind her decision to work at Mordant's. Though, once there, she realised that she was never going to see him. The factory worked different hours from staff, had different canteens, even different lavatories. But Roberta was determined. It was easy to slip out from her home and wait for him by the gates at seven o'clock when the day shift finished. She dressed in the pale green suit she wore for the office, but added a pretty blouse. Her dark hair was newly waved.

He came out, pushing his bike. 'Hallo,' she said.

He stopped, 'Hello.'

There was a pause, and she felt her heart racing. He was so handsome. Even in his denim overalls and a smudge of grease on his cheek, his hair all tousled, he was handsome. 'I wondered,' she began. 'I mean, we had some unfinished business at the party, didn't we?'

Still he didn't speak, and she went on: 'I must apologise for my mother's behaviour.'

'And for your own,' he said. 'Why didn't you tell her you'd invited Marged and me?'

She flushed. 'I – oh, Martin, I was scared. You don't know my mother.'

He didn't know whether to believe her or not: he couldn't make her out. In some ways so naïve, in others so determined – like waiting for him here. He said, 'Well, I didn't take kindly to being turned out, I can tell you. Nor did Marged. I suppose you forgot to mention to your mother that you'd asked us?'

She hung her head. 'I wanted you to come so much,' she whispered. 'I didn't think she'd turn you out.' Was there a slight emphasis on the you?

'Well, and what do you want now?' She was trembling, and he noticed. 'To see me again?'

'Yes.'

His eyes were calculating as he looked at her. 'All right. Where?'

'I have a car.'

His eyebrows shot up. 'And petrol, I suppose.'

'Of course. My father—'

'You needn't spell it out. Anyway, I can't drive.'

'But I can. I'll teach you.'

'And . . .' he looked round. The snow had gone, but it was still cold. 'Where are you planning we go?'

'My father owns a cottage in Borley village. It's empty.'

The cottage was not only empty, but cold. There was wood, however, so he lit a fire, while she stood watching. He kissed her, and she was as eager as he. 'Well,' he said. 'You're a hot little number and no mistake.'

'I love you, Martin.'

'Do you?' He put her on the floor, he lifted her skirt, let his hands fumble underneath, then slowly he was stroking her, and he heard her catch her breath. Then she sat up. 'Martin – wait.' He stopped. 'I don't want to have a baby,' she said.

He was fully roused now. 'For God's sake – I'll be careful.'

'Martin, can't you buy something? I heard the girls talking—'

'All right, I'll get some. But not now ... just relax ... haven't you ever done this before?'

'Of course not.'

He pressed her close again and she said, 'Oh Martin, I do want you.' Now she was pulling him to her, kissing him, pushing her body to his ... and then passion gripped them both and they clung together on the damp floor, lost to the world.

Martin was at the age when he would have taken out any pretty girl, hopefully for what he could get. He wasn't often successful, girls were too worried about having babies and being left, but there had been a few hurried fumbling affairs before he met Mrs Wilton.

Mrs Wilton was a prostitute and she lived at number thirty-two. Everyone knew what she was, including her husband, who said publicly he didn't mind as long as he had her too. She was plump, golden-haired, pretty and clean. Her clients usually came from the best end of the town and could be seen slipping in and out of the lady's front door by anyone who cared to watch. The women neighbours were tolerant unless their husbands decided to spend a few hours with her, when all hell broke loose, with rows that were heard all down the street. But they did not object to their sons visiting her. Better than having some young girl turn up on the doorstep with a baby, they said darkly.

She was in the front garden one day when Martin was passing, and she greeted him. 'Hallo.'

'Hallo,' said Martin warily.

'Going to the pub?'

'No, the dance.'

'Why don't you come in and see me one evening?'

Martin stared. He was seventeen at the time. 'We-ell,' he began, wondering how much she charged.

'Just for a chat,' she said easily, so he followed her inside. He'd often wondered what her house would be like, but it was just a normal front room, and the bedroom, though full of frilly covers and coloured cushions, was nothing out of the ordinary either. And although the chat turned into several visits, for which she asked for 'something for the kiddies', she did seem to enjoy teaching him the rudiments of love play and sexual games he'd never thought of, all of which stood him in good stead when he tried to seduce the local maidens. He didn't see Mrs Wilton these days. No doubt she was fully occupied with the Army and Air Force, he thought sardonically. But now he had Roberta, and he was puzzled.

Girls weren't usually so blatant, not nice girls, and everyone wanted to be thought a nice girl and not 'get a bad name', with all the mothers talking about them and watching what they did and warning their sons away. So most girls were wary. They might give in at the end, but they were always scared of having a baby. Roberta just gave in. Yet she hadn't been with anyone before, that he knew. And she said she loved him. He whistled to himself as he walked home. She loved him.

He thought of his childhood fear that no one would want to marry him if he hadn't any money. Of his desire to be revenged on Mordant. And here was the daughter falling into his lap like a ripe plum. What did you do with the boss's daughter when you had sworn revenge? You took her out. You made her fall for you. And then ...

He knew as well as Roberta that her parents would never agree to her marrying a factory worker. There might be a war on and the world was going mad, but it didn't make any difference to people like the Mordants. Still, there was always the time-honoured way. Make her pregnant, force the issue ...

So she wanted to be careful. He could wait for his chance. She was, like the song said, very easy to love. Oh yes, he could wait all right. And enjoy the waiting.

Roberta was obsessed with Martin. She had lacked love in her childhood, in her whole life, but now she had someone to love, her whole being was concentrated on him and him alone. She must possess him wholly. She could not bear him even to talk about his family, especially Marged. When one night he mentioned that she was a good dancer, Roberta was wild with jealousy. The fires that had been damped down for so long now burst into flame, and were consuming her.

She hadn't realised that sex could be so enjoyable, and she spent her days dreaming of the night to come. She even began to wonder about the future. *Could* they get married? Not if her mother had anything to do with it, but Adela, who hadn't been able to get a passage to America, was now in a safe haven in Scotland. What of her father? Would he consent? Then what? Even in her passion Roberta knew she would not want to live in Victoria Street, not now. So why couldn't Martin live and work with them? He was bright, though shop-floor workers were never moved to management; it seemed the thought had never occurred to anyone. Yet surely her father could find him something...? In the meantime they had this delicious love-making ... the rest could wait.

Marged bought a fashionable white riding mac to walk to work, and thick pullovers for the cold office. Her department was called Efficiency, probably for want of a better word, she thought, as they seemed to do all the odds and ends left over from other sections. Next to them was the Estimating Department, and several times she was asked to type estimates when the girls were very busy. Her typing had improved immeasurably, even with cold fingers, so she was able to do justice to the long schedules which stated every part of an aircraft component, together with each price. So, when she heard that one of the married girls in Estimating was leaving to have a baby she asked Mr Blake if he thought she might apply.

'Don't see why not,' he answered laconically. 'You can

ask. Might get more money.' So she approached Mr Walters, through Miss Sansome, and put in an application.

Contrary to general belief, Roberta did not go home and tell tales from the office. Nevertheless, it was difficult not to talk sometimes about her place of work. She did not see much of her father, but he was usually in for dinner.

So when her father said, 'Seems we have a bright little worker in your department,' she pricked up her ears.

'Who?' she asked.

'Name of Fennel. She's asked for promotion, apparently, and I'm told she's good.'

And Roberta was suddenly angry. That the little girl from Victoria Street should be promoted while she, the boss's daughter, did a kid's job ... *Marged*. All her jealousy flamed as she burst out: 'I wouldn't have thought you'd have bothered with a girl whose father hates you so much.'

'What?'

Half-ashamed of her outburst, Roberta tried to draw back, but it was too late. 'It's nothing,' she mumbled. 'Just that he was injured at work, but it was a long time ago.'

Her father said no more, but he was thoughtful. He remembered the case, and that the machinery had been faulty. He didn't want a bright young Fennel perhaps re-opening the matter. True, no one could do anything now, it was too late, but with government contracts being fought for with firms in other areas, it didn't do to have any scandal. Governments didn't like that, especially men like Bevan, who was all for the workers. Marged's promotion was blocked.

'It's not fair,' she said hotly to Mr Blake.

'No,' he agreed. 'But that's Mordant's.'

'I'm going to ask Mr Walters why.'

'He won't tell you, nor will the old witch. But she's off this week, so now's your chance.'

'Are you talking about Miss Sansome? She's never absent.'

'Perhaps the Jerries have taken her,' said Mr Blake hopefully. 'Go and have a word with her deputy, Mrs Scott. She's all right.'

Mrs Scott was indeed quite willing to discuss her boss's failings with others. She was indignant at the way he treated the workers, both factory and staff. He was always too quick to say, 'Get rid of that man,' even in wartime. So when Marged asked why she had been dropped, Mrs Scott said simply: 'Mr Mordant intervened.'

'Mr Mordant? But why?'

'Seems he was looking into the past.' She leaned forward at Marged's look of mystification. 'Your father had an accident here, didn't he?'

'Yes, he did,' she said. 'But what's it to do with me?'

'Mordant probably prefers it kept quiet. Thinks you might make trouble.'

'He's put the idea into my head,' said Marged, bitterly. 'But – do you mean to tell me Mr Mordant remembers all that?'

'No, he didn't remember 'cos he came looking for the file. Someone must have jogged his memory.'

'But who would do such a thing?'

Mrs Scott shrugged. 'Do you have an enemy? One who knows Mordant?'

'You don't mean Roberta?'

'I don't know, Marged, honestly. It could have been anybody.'

'It could have, but it wasn't. Who else knows?' Marged flung herself out of the office, and walked up to Roberta. 'You mean bitch,' she hissed. 'Telling tales to Daddy. I'll get you for this.' And Roberta flushed and hung her head, guiltily.

Furiously, Marged poured out the whole story to Martin that evening when Frank was in the shed and Eva upstairs.

'Are you sure?' he asked incredulously.

'Who else could it have been?'

He patted her shoulder. 'Never mind, kid, your turn'll come.'

She snorted. 'I wish a bomb 'ud drop on old Mordant, that's all.'

Eva came in, and Martin walked up to his bedroom. Alone, he brooded. He hadn't told Marged that he was seeing Roberta, and wasn't sure why. He thought of the girl who threw herself into his arms night after night, who vowed she loved him ... what sort of love was that? He knew, guiltily, that his own motives were not exactly pure, yet – he wasn't harming anyone else, was he? His mixed feelings only fuelled his anger, never far from the surface. And when he saw Roberta he let her drive the car a little way out of town then said sharply: 'Stop! Don't go any farther.'

'Why? There's nothing here.'

'I want a word with you. What's all this about your telling your dad about Marged being who she is, stopping her promotion?'

She turned, shocked and surprised that he knew. 'I—' she began. 'I couldn't help it.'

'Course you could help it, and it was a rotten thing to do. We don't tell tales round here. Do you know what you've done? Done her out of a good job, that's what.'

'I – didn't think.'

'Your sort wouldn't. You just don't know, do you? How she's been working night after night, studying. She didn't want to work at Mordant's, but she had no choice. We don't have choices, not like you. Now you – the boss's spoilt little daughter – had to step in and ruin her chances. And for what? Just out of spite.'

Roberta mumbled. 'I'm sorry.'

'Sorry? You think you can put everything right by saying sorry? Like your dad messed up our lives, I'm sure he'd say he's sorry. Except he wouldn't mean it, and neither do you.'

'You think more of Marged than me,' said Roberta, sulkily.

'And why not? She's worth ten of you.'

'She's only your – *sister*.' She said the word deliberately.

'Yes. And a good kid.' He jumped out of the car.

'Aren't you going to see me again?'

'No, I'm bloody not.'

'There's no need to swear.'

'Why not? Hurts your delicate little ears, does it? Doesn't matter what harm you do to someone as long as you talk nice. Oh, sod off, leave me alone.' And, shoulders hunched, he turned abruptly and walked away.

Marged turned to Corrie. 'Come on,' she said. 'Let's have some fun.'

'What, no homework tonight?' asked Corrie. 'You're always late on Mondays.'

'No fear, I'm sick of working. It gets you nowhere. Not at Mordant's. Only way to get on there is to tell tales, crawl around the boss. Well, that's not my way, so they can go to hell. Come on.'

They went to the dance, and however cold it remained outside, in the hall it was warm with so many bodies crushing around. The atmosphere was feverish; everyone was out to have a good time. There were thick blackouts over the windows, the air was heavy with cigarette smoke. Girls wore short dresses and, as stockings became scarce, painted their legs brown, with a black seam down the middle. Married women were there, husbands in the forces; they took their wedding rings off their fingers, and soldiers home to their beds. The band was good, the singer a half-caste boy from Cardiff.

Marged was still in love with dancing and life grew hectic, as she was caught up in the restless frenzy of war. She made dates, sometimes arranging to meet one or two lads on the same night, letting one or both down as her fancy chose. She promised to write to a hundred soldiers and never did, though the postman brought scrawls of undying love which petered out in a week. They laughed; they braved the blackout and didn't care, they sang in the streets: *Bless 'em all, The Washing on the Siegfried Line* and *Roll out the barrel*. Marged hadn't had such a good time in her life.

Her mother began to grumble. 'Late again. You're getting to be a regular gadabout.'

'Gadabout,' scoffed Marged. 'Just 'cos I enjoy myself.'

'Mrs Harvey said she saw you with a fellow last night—'

'Mrs Harvey?'

'Said it was a different one to the one the night before.'

'Oh, so she watched through her lace curtains, did she? In the blackout? Old gossip.'

'Why don't you find a nice chap and settle down?'

'Like who? All the chaps are going in the forces.'

'You don't work at your homework as much as you used to.'

'I used to, you're right. And where did it get me? Doing rotten jobs, that's where. You know what I have to do now? Take on any job where a girl's away, Sales, Buying, Estimating ... but I don't get any more money, oh no. Work? I've had it with work.'

'You're a big worry to me,' said her mother.

'I want to see *Gone With The Wind* when it comes to Chilverton,' Marged told Corrie. 'I read the book and I like Scarlett O'Hara. She's not one of these goody-goody heroines that are in all the other books, she's different.'

'Well, you're not a goody-goody.'

'I know,' gloomily. 'That's what worries me.'

'Oh come on,' laughed Corrie. 'There's a war on. Might all be dead next week. I'm going out with a Pole tonight,' for as spring approached, more Polish airmen arrived at the aerodrome.

Marged sniffed. 'I don't like foreigners. And those Poles

aren't very good dancers.' She paused. 'Is it true what they say about their love-making?'

'Hey, how do I know? I've not got that far.'

'But they kiss your hands and all that. Somebody told me a tale about one girl who went with one of them— no, I won't tell you, it's rude. Anyway, our chaps laugh about them.'

''Cos they're jealous – they're losing all their girls. But they always end up by saying that the Polish officers mix with their men and ours don't. They envy them that.'

By the end of February, a thaw had set in. The roads were clear, and it became warmer for several days. Marged was with Corrie, walking through the town, when they were hailed by two soldiers from the camp in the Hall grounds. Their jeep stopped and two forage-capped heads poked out. 'Come with us to our dance, at the camp in the Hall,' said one.

'Dance? You must think we've come off the Christmas tree,' scoffed Marged. 'You want the Red Cow, straight on for a mile.'

'No, honest, we're on the level. We've got this dance going and we're short of girls, so we're having to look for some.'

'A likely story,' said Marged.

'It's true. Honest. In the grounds of the camp.'

'I reckon it's true,' said Corrie. 'Let's go.'

'My mother 'ud kill me,' Marged muttered. 'She warned me about chaps like you.'

But they went.

And it was as the soldiers had promised, all above board, with an officer to keep order. They danced in the little hall, they had partners galore. There were sandwiches and cakes and lemonade; it was as harmless as a vicarage tea party. A bit of fun for boys departing towards a possible death. Going with songs to the battle.

The girls were enjoying themselves too much to notice

the time, and when the dance finally ended Marged was horrified to see it was one o'clock. They were driven back, past the guard on the gates who oddly insisted on seeing their identity cards, oddly, because he hadn't inspected them when they came in! Corrie couldn't find hers. 'Think we're spies?' asked Marged.

'We should have hid under the seats,' put in Corrie.

'Well, you can't keep us here unless you make us prisoners of war,' laughed Marged.

The guard let them through, but they were late, very late, and Frank was waiting up. His temper had improved since he'd found a job, and the fits had disappeared, but it still didn't do to upset him. 'What time do you call this?' he roared.

'Sorry,' Marged muttered.

'So where have you been? The Co-op ends at twelve.'

'We went to a dance in the camp in the Hall grounds. We didn't know it was going on so late—'

'And how do I know that's true?' asked Frank.

'Because I say so,' flashed Marged.

'Just because that good-for-nothing Corrie Thompson can stop out all hours, that's no reason why you should—'

'We don't want you to get into trouble,' put in Eva anxiously.

'I can take care of myself—'

'Oh yes? With a lot of chaps you'll never see again? Anyway, I'm not having you coming in at this time.'

'All right, I'll leave home. I'll go and live with Brenda.'

'You'll do no such thing.'

'You can't stop me. I'm over eighteen, I can leave home.'

They stood, deadlocked. Eva, always the peacemaker between her hot-tempered husband and rebellious daughter, said: 'Maybe it would be a good thing. I don't like to think of Brenda on her own.'

'But when Brenda's on nights, Marged would be on her own.'

'Martin could go down then.'

'And who's going to help with the housework?'

'I don't need help now. I don't go to work myself. I'll manage,' said Eva.

So Marged packed her bags and went to live with Brenda, where her sister wasn't exactly welcoming.

'You'll have to behave yourself here,' she said sternly.

'Behave myself? As if I didn't. *You* used to go dancing.'

'Yes, I know. But the war's doing funny things to women. Some of 'em at least. Why don't you find a nice—'

'Chap and settle down,' finished Marged. 'Why does everybody want me to get married?'

'Keep you out of trouble,' said Brenda.

'Oh yes? Like the women you were just talking about? Do you know that Amy goes dancing now? And John in the Army. Well, I don't want to get married.'

'I don't know what's the matter with you,' said Brenda.

'That makes two of us,' muttered Marged, turning away. How could she explain that the rainbow she had been seeking seemed forever out of reach? Just as she thought she caught a glimpse of it, a dark cloud rolled up and it was hidden from view. She couldn't explain, even to herself, that she expected more than her life could offer, so she faced the world with defiant eyes, hitting out at Them before they got her down, as long ago Grandma had taught her. She half-expected Grandma to come and give her a lecture, but she couldn't get around so much these days. She was over seventy, and had arthritis.

Brenda said, relenting, 'We'll be able to go shopping on Saturdays sometimes.'

'When you're not working and I'm not working and I'm not going to my classes,' said Marged sardonically.

The weather was still chilly for spring, and now the main argument in the press seemed to be about unmarried wives – a name the respectable objected to – and the great problem of officers and other ranks being together in the same public house. Or rather, not being together, for other ranks were asked to leave when an officer had his drink.

Marged walked down Victoria Street on her way to work, passing her old home without a glance. Once she saw her mother in the front room but she did not stop. Inwardly, she longed to be friends again, and had Eva called out, she would have gone to speak to her. But no one asked her to come back, not even Martin, who seemed to think it was a great joke. So Marged stayed away, pride refusing to let her make the first move.

But as a chilly March slid into an equally chilly April, things suddenly began to happen. Hitler swept through Denmark and Norway, the King of the Belgians capitulated, and the Germans marched through France. The British Army was cut off along the French coast, up to Dunkirk, where all the little boats fetched the soldiers away ... or most of them.

Appalled, Marged sank her pride and went to see her parents. And it was good to enter the warm kitchen again, to look hesitantly at the family grouped around the fire, to wait for their welcome.

'Well, look who's here,' said Martin.

'Took you long enough to come,' said Frank in his gruff manner and Marged smiled. This, translated, meant he was glad to see her again.

She went over to her mother, who looked up, white-faced, wan. 'Hallo, Marged,' she said, and Marged sat down on the sofa.

'Where's John?' fretted Eva. 'We haven't heard from him.'

'We shall,' soothed Marged. 'It's early days yet.' She wanted to ask if she could come back home, but feared a rebuff.

'Would you like a cup of tea?' asked her mother, and Marged said, 'I'll do it,' and went to the back-kitchen. She was accepted again. You only offered tea to those who were accepted. She'd wait a little while before asking anything more.

Now the Germans faced them across the Channel. The people felt the men in power were dithering. In the House of Commons Leo Avery said: 'We must get men of fighting spirit in our government.' He looked at Chamberlain and quoted the words of Oliver Cromwell: '"Depart, I say and let us have done with you. In the name of God, go."' The Labour Party refused to serve under Chamberlain and Churchill became Prime Minister.

Britain stood alone. Invasion was expected. And for a moment, Victoria Street teetered on the edge of panic. Old race memories asserted themselves – fears of Boney, beacons lit on hills to warn of invaders. And over all, lay the sheer excitement of fear. What were they going to do?

Churchill told them in a voice that boomed out, echoing through Time itself. *We shall defend our island home ... if necessary alone ... we shall fight on the beaches, we shall fight in the fields and in the streets, we shall never surrender.*

The country braced itself, the panic subsided. The moment when the war could have been lost was gone for ever. The King wrote: 'Personally, I feel happier now that we have no allies to be polite to.'

'Bloody foreigners,' said Victoria Street more robustly. 'They won't come here. Bloody cheek.'

The phony war was over, the real war began.

Chapter 8

It was weeks before they heard from John, and then Amy brought a telegram. *The War Office regrets . . . Lance-Corporal John Fennel, reported missing, believed killed . . .*

Amy was crying, loud childish sobs, and Eva put her arm around the girl. Marged, who called in every day now when she came home from work, heard the news with horror. He couldn't be dead, not her brother. And she thought, in passing, how little she knew about John. Funny, they lived in the same small house, mostly in the same room, yet how much did they know of each other's innermost feelings? Martin she knew, but John? He'd always been there, the big brother, always reliable, never a hothead like Martin, coughing in the winter but working regularly. She had wondered what John had seen in Amy, yet if he loved her . . .

When Amy had gone Eva sat in the kitchen, tearless, white-faced. The sun poured through the window; the weather was relenting at last, birds sang. Martin said, 'It doesn't mean anything, Mother, he could be a prisoner, or hiding in France somewhere.'

And oddly, it was to Martin Eva turned, rather than to the girls. 'You're the only son I have now,' she said, and Marged noted that she seemed sure that John was dead. How did she know? Did mothers always know? Marged was aware that she had never been her mother's favourite. Eva put the boys first, especially John, and then Brenda, the oldest, the one who helped the most. And when Brenda heard that Jack was a prisoner, she and her mother were drawn even closer.

Eva said to Martin: 'Don't *you* go, Martin. Don't join up, I don't want to lose you, too.' And he put his arm around her shoulders and whispered, 'I won't, Mother. I won't ever leave you.'

Marged said awkwardly to her mother, 'Do you want me to come back, to help you?'

Eva shook her head. 'No, stop with Brenda. She needs someone now.'

Marged sympathised with her sister, but Brenda did not confide her feelings – she never had. She came home one day and said she was going to Passmore's in Coventry, working a capstan lathe, making parts for aeroplanes. The hours were long, twelve-hour shifts, but she would earn up to ten pounds a week.

They still went to the market, when possible, for Marged worked every other Saturday, but it was very different from pre-war days. It no longer stayed open till nine in the evenings, naphtha flares blazing, not in the blackout. The few stalls that did come were forced to pack up before it grew dark; indeed, never again was the market to stay later than four.

The Fennels were not short of food, for all of them except Eva ate dinner in the canteens forced upon firms now, but there were no longer cakes made with real eggs and butter. Eva spent a lot of time queueing, for although some shops were good at putting out their quotas of food and cigarettes when they came in, others hid them immediately under the counter, to save for special customers. Frank managed to grow vegetables in the allotment. Amy's father worked long hours and came home weary from driving a train in the blackout.

Marged was still unhappy at work; she was in the Estimating office again for a week. 'Doing work I should have been doing permanently,' she said bitterly. 'Last week Sales, next week something else. Talk about the war effort!'

'Yes, but look at the experience you're gaining,' Brenda comforted.

'I suppose so. And my shorthand's good now. But I don't feel I'm doing much ... honestly, Bren, the way this place is run! I wonder if I should try for something at Coventry.'

'I should wait a bit longer, see what turns up.'

What turned up was another move, another temporary job. 'You're to take over as Mr Brian's secretary,' said Miss Sansome.

'Brian Mordant?' Marged asked, surprised.

'His secretary's ill. Her husband was drowned – Navy.'

'Oh, poor girl. But why me?'

'You're the only available spare,' said Miss Sansome acidly, and Marged grinned to herself. She wondered if Mr Mordant knew she was to type for his son, though from all accounts Brian hadn't the brains to do much. 'It'll be God help us when he takes over,' said Mr Blake piously.

Brian's office was at the rear of the main block, and as Marged entered on the Monday morning he looked up lazily. He had a comfortable swivel chair, the secretary's typewriter was new and modern, unlike those in the general office, and there was a small electric fire in one corner. 'I say, don't I know you?' asked Brian.

'Yes,' Marged replied sharply. 'Your sister asked me to a party at your home. You were drunk, you were rude, and your mother turned me out when I slapped your face.'

'God, was that you? I was blind drunk and I never remember afterwards what I've done. Why did you slap my face?'

'Because you said something horrible to me.'

'Did I? What?'

'I wouldn't repeat it,' Marged said hotly. 'I might add that I haven't had a sheltered upbringing like your sister. I can talk rough with the best of them, and I've heard some dirty talk. But the men I know always know when to stop, and they'd never say anything like you did.'

'I say, I'm sorry.'

'I should think so. There is a limit, you know. Joking's one thing, but nasty talk's another.'

'Well, don't take any notice of Ma, she's a bad-tempered old so and so. Anyway, sit down,' and she sat in a comfortable swivel chair.

He came to stand beside her, let his hand touch her hair. 'You're a pretty girl,' he said.

'All right, watch it, or I'll slap your face again.' *You could talk to the boss like this in these days when jobs were plentiful, and she didn't care now whether she stayed or went.* 'Is there no typing to be done?'

'I shouldn't think so.' He went back to his own chair, and Marged tidied the papers in her drawer, tried the new typewriter, then waited, bewildered.

'I say, what do you do in the evenings?' Brian asked. 'I've got a car if you want to go for a spin.'

'No thanks,' Marged returned shortly.

The door opened and a girl entered with a folder which she put on his desk. He opened it, sighed, then put it down, unread. When he left the office Marged peeked at the file. 'For the attention of Mr Brian Mordant,' she read. 'Please read and comment.'

'Shouldn't you read this?' she asked when he returned.

'Can't be bothered,' he answered, and the file was left until the next day when it was collected, still unread.

This became the pattern of the days. Files would be sent in for Brian to read; he ignored them, and they were returned. He sat, doing nothing except pestering Marged from time to time. Bored, she began to read the files herself.

They were from Mr Mordant, and it dawned on Marged

that what his father was trying to do was teach Brian the business. If he read all the reports, he would at least grasp what was going on. But he never did. Marged grew exasperated, and in the second week she taxed him with it.

'Why don't you read the reports?' she asked.

'Can't be bothered,' he repeated laconically.

'But what will you do when you take over? You won't know anything.'

He shrugged. 'The old man's good for a few more years yet. Anyway, I don't want the business.'

Marged lost her temper. 'Do you realise that there are still people out there who are unemployed?' she asked. 'Do you realise that other men are fighting for such as you? If you don't want to do anything here, why not join up?'

He had the grace to look a little ashamed. 'What's that file about then?' he asked. 'If it upsets you so much?'

'It's from the Wages Department. And I've been trying to figure out just how and why wage rises are given. There seems no rhyme nor reason to them. They're not given for length of time served – this girl here has only just started. And they're not given for merit – Miss Jones is a good worker, yet she's had nothing.'

She held the file out to Brian, but he didn't take it. 'Read it to me,' he commanded.

So she read out the list of wage rises and at the end, as he didn't speak, she said: 'It's all wrong, there's no system. I mean, why has Mr Barlow been given another rise?'

Brian shrugged. 'I suppose it's a matter of luck.'

'Oh come on, Mr Brian, luck shouldn't enter into it. This is the sort of thing you should comment on. Why—' Marged warmed to her task, for she hated to see a job not done properly. 'When you take over you could put all these things to rights, don't you see?'

Brian initialled the file, but still made no comment. And the next day, when the reports came in he passed them to Marged. 'All right, read them to me,' he said.

And this became the pattern, till Marged began to wonder whether Brian could actually read. She dismissed the idea as fanciful. Hadn't he been to some posh school? He could write, couldn't he?

She began to watch him covertly, and saw that, when he did read a paper, it was slowly, blinking, as though he couldn't concentrate, or couldn't take it in. He'd pore over it like a backward child. Yet when someone came in the office he'd hurriedly pass the paper on, not wanting anyone to see how slow he was. *So he realised.* And he didn't mind her knowing; she was just a temporary help, a little girl from the back streets, a nobody. And, she thought with a grin, when his father finds out I'm here I'll be sent packing. I have to be kept down below.

Mr Mordant did know she was there; he knew everything that went on. He also noticed that his son, at a managers' meeting, made, for the first time in his life, some comments on the files he read, asking about wages. He had begun to despair of his son ever being capable of running the firm, but now he saw there was hope. Was Brian coming to his senses, or was that girl somehow jollying him along? Well, at least she wasn't making trouble. And she was only temporary, a stopgap as they had no one else.

He decided to leave her there, an extra week or two wouldn't hurt. He kept the most confidential files away from Brian while she was with him, and decided that if she put one foot wrong she'd be out, war or no war.

When Brian came back from the managers' meeting he said triumphantly to Marged. 'I asked about those wage rises, and they said it was left to each head of department.'

'So,' Marged answered, 'he can just hand out a rise if he likes the colour of someone's hair. Or if he or she spies for him. It's not right, Brian. There should be some method.'

But she was surprised he'd mentioned it at the meeting. That showed he could remember things, if they were read out to him. Very odd. But it wasn't her business. And he was a bit of a nuisance with his wandering hands that always managed to touch her as he walked past, and his repeated offers to take her out 'for a spin'. 'And I'd be spinning home – on my feet,' she replied shortly, and was glad when his secretary came back and she could return to her own department.

In July tea and cooking fats were rationed to two ounces a week. Marged always took her meat ration to her mother, for although Martin and Frank ate in the canteen, she still had the working-class idea that men required more food, and she didn't want Eva to sacrifice her own rations. Whenever she dropped in on her way to the dance, for she'd started the dances again in June, her parents would be sitting close to the wireless, listening to the news. As if, Marged thought, they'd hear something special, something that would bring John back. Today they hardly turned as she entered, and there was an extra item about the Germans in Paris.

The news ended and Eva sighed. 'All those people who've been invaded – makes you wonder how they're living.'

'Ah, they don't tell you that, do they?' Frank asked. He thought for a moment. 'Don't suppose they know,' he ended.

Stanislaw Kowalski had been lecturing at the prestigious University of Cracow when the Germans took him. He had asked why – or tried to – and in reply received a bang on the head from a gun.

'You know why,' said the little man next to him. 'The Germans plan to eliminate all Polish intellectuals. They say ten thousand have already been sent to Dachau. They mean to wipe us and our culture out of existence – but for the moment we are to work for the Germans.'

Stanislaw's glasses were broken so, as they drove through Warsaw he did not see his mother. At the nearest station they were herded on to cattle trucks by armed German soldiers. Only a tiny ray of light filtered through the dark brown truck. He was jammed into a corner next to the little man, who said his name was Tomasz; he too was a teacher. Men of all ages were there, women and children. 'And these are to work for the Germans?' asked Stanislaw.

The train chugged away. They was no food, just a bucket of water which was soon passed round and emptied. No toilet, either, merely another old bucket in a corner. Stanislaw, a fastidious man, was horrified, but forced to use it. Day passed into night; they only knew because the slits of light disappeared, and now a bitter wind blew through. A baby cried in a long pitiful wail, an old man was moaning. When morning came the guards filled the bucket of water, but brought no food. No one could sit down. They slept, if they slept at all, on their feet. The baby still cried.

The train started again, then stopped and stood waiting for hours, so no one knew how long the journey actually was. Stanislaw was hungry, they all were. On the second day the baby died. The crying stopped abruptly; the mother gave a shriek and carried on screaming while the old man still moaned.

The train stopped. They were forced out, and marched to the camp to the strains of the camp orchestra, through the iron gateway with its slogan *Arbeit Macht Frei* (Work Makes You Free), along the double line of electrified wire-fencing, past the concealed machine-gun nests. Inside, their forearms were tattooed with a camp number, their clothes were taken away and they were given a striped prison uniform. Finally they were marched to the rows of grim prefabricated huts.

They slept on planks. For breakfast they were given a mug of brown liquid that could have been anything, and a small slice of black bread. The same in the evening.

Stanislaw was handed a pick and shovel and spent twelve hours digging foundations for another building. He had never worked like this before; his arms ached, his chest burned, and he was so hungry he wanted to die of it. Little Tomasz, who was a perky, chirpy fellow, tried to cheer him up. 'At least we're alive,' he said.

Day followed day. Stanislaw was perpetually hungry, perpetually tired, coming back at nights in a state of near collapse. On the third night he had a bad asthma attack. Tomasz leaned over to him. 'Do you take anything for that?' he asked, concerned.

'I did. I have nothing here. Do you think I should ask for treatment?'

'No, no, don't do that.' Tomasz didn't like to tell this quiet man that the Euthanasia Campaign was already 'eliminating' all cripples and imbeciles from the country's hospitals. But he tried to warn him. 'Don't let them hear you wheezing,' he said. 'Or ...'

Stanislaw understood. He was to work till he dropped; after that there would be others to take his place. The buildings had been planned to hold fifty thousand prisoners year after year as long as any Poles survived. The present life expectancy was three months.

Stanislaw was a deeply religious man and he prayed for his family and his country. He tried to pray for the Germans, but found this very difficult.

In August 1940 the first bombs came to the Midlands. The sirens wailed. Brenda was at home, so sleepily they put on their coats, walked to the shelter in the garden. They heard a crump in the distance, then all was silent. This became a regular occurrence: the bombers came over, tried for Coventry or Birmingham but were prevented to some extent by ack-ack guns and barrage balloons, so the disgruntled Jerries turned, dropping their bombs casually on the way back. Several people were killed in this haphazard manner.

The shelter, sunk in the ground, was cold and damp even in summer, and in the end they rebelled. 'I'm staying in bed,' said Marged. 'Might as well die comfortable in bed as of pneumonia in a shelter. Anyway, if a bomb's got your name on it—'

Everyone firmly believed this. They had watched as families were bombed out twice, even three times, as if the bomb was following them around. They heard of someone living way out of the cities hit by one of the casual bombs, while others, crowded in homes and shelters, were untouched. It didn't make sense. Nothing made sense any more, so what the hell? They stayed in bed, merely getting up when the raids grew too fierce and going to see if the old lady next door, Mrs Travers, was all right. Martin was out with the ARP most nights anyway.

Life grew more hectic. Marged carried on dancing. Soldiers took her home as before and tried it on. Some would plead and some would argue. Marged said as always, 'No, sorry. It's here today and gone tomorrow with you,' and left them, laughing about them the next day with Corrie.

'Young chap took me home last night,' she confided. 'Only eighteen. He said, "Will you ... you know." Said he'd never done it before, but as all his mates were talking about it he wanted to try.'

'So?' asked Corrie.

'So I said no. Didn't want him practising on me.'

But she was more restless than ever. Her work didn't satisfy her, and her regular nights of pleasure coupled with broken sleep when air raids were on, left her exhausted. The continued presence of boys hot for love-making could hardly fail to arouse her, and she wondered if that was what she really wanted. Did other girls ... they all denied it, of course, even girls who had been courting for years and had to get married in the end, swore it had only happened once.

We were all living on a knife-edge and hardly knew it. The raids kept on and we knew we might die. Oddly, it made us all the more alive. Everything stood out more clearly, like leafless trees in winter against the snow. We demanded more. We took more interest in the Arts, and the government sent us entertainment in our canteens, not all light comedy either. We were, for the first time in our lives, important . . .

The Battle of Britain had begun over the south-east of London. Raids continued in the Midlands, nothing too big as yet, just enough to disturb people's rest at nights. But as the weeks went on, it became obvious that this war was not to be fought on some faraway battlefield, but here at home, with the civilians as targets. The big cities endured raids – even Chilverton had a number of casualties.

But the dances continued as always; if the sirens went, few left the hall. And it was one moonlit night in October, that Marged heard the news that shocked her.

Corrie had called for her, and as Marged took her coat from its peg she eyed her friend critically, noting the tight skirt, the red 'see-through' blouse. These chiffon blouses were usually worn over a fitted petticoat, but Corrie had no petticoat, simply a bra, and that too, looked tight. Marged was thankful for the blackout that her mother couldn't see Corrie, thankful for once that she wasn't living at home.

Once outside, Corrie pulled her coat around her as Marged said casually, 'You must be eating too much of your sugar ration. You're putting on weight.'

And Corrie didn't answer with a joke as she usually did. She said sombrely: 'I've got to get married.'

Marged stopped, amazed, and a woman walking behind cannoned into her. 'Sorry,' Marged said, then to Corrie: 'You're – *what*?'

'Come on, you're blocking the pavement. Well, you might as well know.'

'But who is it?'

'Ron. That bloody soldier I've been going out with.'

'But—' Marged started to say that Corrie hadn't been out with him many times, but bit the words back. 'What's he say?' she asked.

Corrie hesitated. 'Says he won't.'

'Won't marry you?'

'I told him I'd take him to Court. He said—' She gulped. 'Said he'd bring all his friends to swear they'd been with me as well.'

'Oh Corrie – he wouldn't!'

'Says he will. Some chaps do. Anything to get out of paying.'

'But Corrie, what will you do? Have you told your mother?'

'Yes. She says I've got to get married. To somebody.'

They reached the Hall. The band was playing *In the Mood*. Halfway through the dance the sirens sounded, and Marged saw no more of Corrie. She supposed she'd gone with Ron.

She walked home alone, to the drone of planes overhead. And in Victoria Street she heard the sound of shouting coming from one of the houses. Before the war it had been common to hear shouting, from the Wests' in particular, but now, with the blackout, people seemed to be quieter. Funny that. Just as the kids couldn't play in the street after dark as they used to; couldn't hang round the brightly lit corner shop playing guessing games. Marged thought of her own childhood, out in all weathers – hadn't she ever felt cold? Making slides on the pavement, building snowmen . . .

The shouting continued and it seemed to be coming from the Barton's. Marged halted. Mr Barton was such a quiet man, not given to shouting or rowing. But she could hear the words clearly now.

'It's not right, your husband just reported missing and you out with another chap. I've a good mind to give you a good hiding!' – and then came the sound of crying. Amy!

Marged went home.

She did not go to the dance again for several nights, for her mother called in at Brenda's the next day, to say that Aunt Ann had tuberculosis and was in a sanatorium. Visiting days were Tuesdays and Sundays, and Marged promised to accompany her mother.

They went the next Sunday, on Marged's day off. The sanatorium was miles out of Chilverton, in the country, but a special bus ran as so many people in the area had TB. It was a dreary October afternoon when they set out and the bus was icy cold. 'We need fur coats here,' muttered Marged. 'Hope Aunt Ann isn't too bad.'

'She was never very strong,' Eva replied. 'That's why she never had any children.'

Marged would have liked to ask her mother what she did to prevent them so successfully, when Corrie's fellow had failed, but thought Eva would only ask just why she wanted that particular information. Anyway, there were only French letters, and she knew about them. Corrie's Ron couldn't have been using his Army ration. Marged peered through the window at the dull landscape, the bare trees, and wondered what was happening to Corrie. She hadn't seen her friend since her announcement, She hadn't been at the dance, and Marged didn't really want to go to the Thompsons', she didn't like them. Mrs Thompson was 'mouthy' – she talked too much and too loudly. She also wore make-up and high heels as Corrie's sisters did. Marged couldn't imagine her own mother in high-heeled shoes. They weren't for mothers, somehow.

The bus drew up at the sanatorium and they went inside. Long corridors smelling of disinfectant, nurses in starched uniforms, wards full of people coughing their lives away. They were told Aunt Ann was on one of the balconies and they found her in a row of beds, outside.

'Crikey,' gasped Marged. 'You don't sleep out here, do you? It's freezing.'

'Yes, we do,' said Aunt Ann. 'They say fresh air's the only cure.'

They chatted for a while, then left to catch the icy bus. The fog had thickened now, so the driver leaned over the wheel peering into the gloom. 'The nurse told me your aunt isn't too bad,' Eva said, relieved. 'Maybe she'll be home soon.' And Marged knew her mother had worried about John 'going consumptive' and wondered which was better, to be killed quickly in battle or to die a lingering death in a freezing sanatorium. She thought of Amy, and hoped her mother wouldn't find out about her goings-on. Though no doubt some friendly neighbour would tell her . . .

The next evening Corrie came round.

'On your own? Good,' she said, and sat by the fire, which Marged poked to stir it into action. 'This is poor coal,' she muttered. 'Come on, Corrie, tell me what happened.'

'I'm going to get married,' Corrie said.

'Oh good. So he's come round?'

'I'm going to marry Bill Foster.'

Marged stood, thunderstruck. 'Who's Bill Foster?'

'You know. That young soldier I've been going out with.'

'But you said it was Ron—'

'I know what I said,' cried Corrie savagely. 'I wanted to marry Ron. I *like* him.'

'And don't you like – the other?'

'Oh, what's it matter?'

'Does he think the baby is his? Does he know?'

'What does it matter?'

'Oh, but, Corrie—'

Corrie sat up angrily. 'What do you mean, but? It's us against them, isn't it? Every time it's us against them. They beg us, don't they, they go down on their knees. We'll get married, they say. Then they don't want to know.' She sniffed. 'I've got to get married, Marged. My *mother* don't want to know. She won't have me at home. Anyway,' she ended more quietly, 'will you be a witness at the registry office? It's in two weeks' time.'

''Course I will,' said Marged, and wondered what to tell her mother.

'Then I shall go to live with Bill's mother,' Corrie went on. 'She's lives in Grange-over-Sands. I'd never heard of the place.'

So Corrie married Bill Foster the first week in November, with only Marged and a friend of Bill's at the ceremony. Then she left for Grange-over-Sands, promising to write.

Marged told her mother about the wedding, omitting to say there was a baby on the way. Eva sniffed. 'Bit quick, wasn't it?' But these things did happen in wartime – hasty weddings, because fellows were going overseas and you didn't have time to wait. They might never come back.

Marged missed her friend. Corrie had been good fun. And she was shocked by what had happened. So they'd been right all along, her mother and Martin . . . and she hadn't guessed.

But now she was alone and restless, wondering what she did want. She was nineteen . . . what now? More nights of pleasure at the dance? There were other girls to be friendly with, though in wartime you never kept a friend for long, either they went to work on shifts, or started courting like Rose Brown, who'd taken up with a soldier. She went out with him for three weeks till he was posted, and now she was waiting, perhaps for years . . . was that what she wanted?

She knew what she didn't want – the sort of hasty love-making the fellows tried hard to persuade her to accept. Not from any strong moral conviction, but partly in fear of the consequences and partly because anything more than kissing a stranger did not appeal to her. So what did she want? To fall in love? Deeply and seriously? And who with? One of the chaps who came and went in a matter of weeks?

She went upstairs to the room she shared with Brenda. The front bedroom, with its double bed, its chest of drawers, the mirror on the wall. She did not draw the blackout curtains but went to look through the window at the dark houses opposite. At home she'd looked over the back field, but that was ploughed up now, helping the dig for victory campaign, gone for ever, she supposed.

A new moon shone fitfully, the sirens had sounded, and as the bombers droned overhead she wondered if that was what she wanted, to really fall in love? What was love? Was there such a thing? Look at Amy and John ... But Amy had always been shallow. And Marged knew that if she fell in love it would be deeply ... seriously. So where was he, this lover to come?

'I'm getting soppy in my old age,' she told herself, and drew the blackout.

November the fourteenth was a bright moonlit night and the sirens went early. As Marged walked home from work she could hear planes coming over in a continuous wave, and crashings in the distance. Martin came up. 'It's going to be bad,' he said. 'They're over Coventry. Are you coming to Mother's?'

'No, I'll be all right. I'll wait for Bren. I wondered if they'd send them home early.'

'Well, get in the shelter. Go on now, Marged.'

'OK. OK. I'll just fetch Mrs Travers.'

She went next door and brought the old lady and her little dog to the shelter in the garden. 'Might as well settle down for the night,' she told her. 'I've got a flask of tea and some blankets, so sit down, make yourself comfortable.'

Mrs Travers smiled shakily, and Marged pulled the thick oak board Frank had given her over the entrance. She wished Brenda would come, but her sister would know where they were. The little dog whimpered at the noise and Mrs Travers held him on her lap. And they sat through a night of hell.

It was an hour before Marged looked out, and over Coventry the sky was alight. Searchlights criss-crossed with demented rays, and her nostrils stung with the peculiar bombing smell of burning, smoke and dust. She pulled the board back and they sat on through an inferno of noise, noise that deafened, pounded and reverberated, it was like being in the front line without a gun.

It's strange listening to an air raid from an Anderson shelter because you hear everything that goes on. You hear the planes come over, you hear them go back. You hear theirs and you hear ours. You hear the bombs dropping, six in a row, and you begin to count; one two three four five and oh hell, that was near and you wait. Then it comes, the whistling and the whishing, louder and louder until . . . crash . . . and the sound of bricks falling . . .

And the night wore on and they listened; it was a concentrated attack such as they'd never known before, such as no one had known before, ever. The noise was horrific and the smell suffocating. Marged and Mrs Travers huddled together; she put her arm around the old lady, a poor old woman in the front line of the war. The little dog was shivering and whining, but Marged was quiet. It seemed to be almost natural to be sitting in an air-raid shelter in the garden listening to that monstrous din.

Mrs Travers spoke at last. 'Hark,' she said. 'This is the fourth bomb, and the plane's coming our way.'

They listened. *OOoooon-crump.* The fifth bomb dropped with a thud that shook the shelter. They waited for the last bomb. *Ps . . . OOOoooooooon . . .* how slow it was. Eternity in a falling bomb.

'This is us,' said Mrs Travers.

The whine grew louder and they waited numbly to be blown to hell. The crash shook the earth's foundations and the oak board in front of the shelter split in two. Marged's ears cracked and her mouth choked with dust. There was a long tearing sound of falling masonry which seemed to go on and on and on. Mrs Travers said: 'That's our house gone.'

Marged poked her head out of the shelter. Bren's house – her dear house – gaped minus its roof, the windows were shattered. Then she looked over the gardens, and she felt that the world was out of focus. The orderly row of houses had gone, there were strange shapes and holes, and she was afraid, afraid of the mad shapes, the world out of focus. And she ran to the entry, down to the street . . .

Already men were there, and Martin, and where their house had been was a pile of rubble. Already there was a special policeman standing, and he held her and said, 'No, you can't go round.' And she said, 'It's my home, my parents . . .'

'All right, all right, they're doing all they can. Why don't you go and wait—?'

She pulled away. 'No, my brother's there . . .' and she could see him, digging . . .

The planes were still coming over . . . how many bricks were on top of Mam and Dad? 'They were in the shelter,' she said. 'Where's the shelter?'

'Yes, love, I know. They're working on that.'

'It's buried, isn't it? Buried under all that?' And she heard someone say, 'They wouldn't have a chance.'

She waited. She saw them bring a body from the wreckage. It was Amy, bright, pert little Amy . . . then Mr Barton was lifted out, his leg in pieces, and his wife, her face torn and bleeding, her clothes blown off, naked until they covered her . . .

OOoooon-crump . . . 'Go back, Marged,' shouted Martin, and she picked her way to the shelter and Mrs Travers. *OOoooon-crump*. She looked up. Sheet after sheet of red tore the sky like an angry aurora, but the dawn was not yet. It wasn't the dawn, it was Coventry burning.

Mrs Travers was holding her in her arms and pouring tea into a mug, and she drank it. The little dog whined, and Marged shivered as though with an ague.

The All Clear went, and Martin came to the shelter . . . dirty, clothes torn, hands bleeding. 'Marg,' he said. 'Marg . . .'

He didn't have to say any more. She stared at him, but

she didn't cry. They went back into Bren's house, with the roof and ceilings on the floor, covered in soot from the chimney. She said, 'I shouldn't have left home. I should have stopped with them.'

Martin answered reasonably: 'Then you'd have been killed, too,' and she gaped at this ... was it possible? Her own intransigence had saved her life ... *if a bomb has your name on it* ...

Mrs Travers made more tea, they drank it, and she left them to see to her own house. Martin said, 'Listen, Marged, what about Bren?'

Bren! 'Do you think she's all right?'

'God knows. They say it's hell in Coventry, the whole city smashed. We can't let her come home – not knowing ...'

'What can we do?'

'Go to meet her.'

Marged stared. Was it possible? But anything was possible when you lived in a world out of focus. 'How?' she asked. 'By train?'

'Don't know if there are any trains running, somebody said there are bombs on the line. We'll go by car.'

'Car?' Why was her head so fuzzy?

'I can get one.'

Bomb-shocked, she followed him. They walked to the end of the road. Grant's factory had had a direct hit. She stopped. 'Poor old Grant's,' she said.

They moved on into Park Manor Road. There was a fire at one end, firemen working, but no one stopped them. They walked to Park Manor itself, round the drive where a car was parked, keys in the ignition. And when he opened the door and got in, it was all part of the night's dream-like quality that she was getting in, too. She didn't even wonder how Martin knew how to drive, or that there was a car here. She did say, 'Can you drive?' and he said, 'Yes.'

'Bren goes on the bus,' he said. 'And they go the country road.'

They set off. Coventry was still burning, the sky was alight; it was like a picture of hell and they were driving towards it. They could smell the sulphur, and their mouths filled with dust as they turned from the country to a main road.

And now they saw people walking towards them, moving slowly like pictures of a retreating army. Some walked together, in twos and threes, some struggled alone. One woman carried a baby, while an older woman pushed a pram full of clothes. Another woman was holding her head and it was bleeding.

Martin stopped the car. 'Where are you going?' he asked.

'Out,' said a woman dully. 'Just out.'

'Do you know if Passmore's has been hit?'

'Everything's been hit. The whole city's in ruins. My home's gone.'

'Are the buses running?'

A man gave Martin an incredulous look. 'You kidding? There's no buses, no bus station, no nothing.'

'You never saw the like,' another woman said. 'Women's heads blown off, rolling in the gutter. I saw a dog with a baby's arm in its mouth ...'

'I saw a toddler, crying. All his family had been killed ...'

'What you going for?' asked another.

'My sister hasn't been home. We're looking for her. We can give you a lift when we come back. Where are you heading for?'

'Nowhere,' said the woman. 'I'm going to sleep under the first hedge I come to ...'

They drove on towards the sulphur and the smoke, until the road was no more, there was just ruin ... ruin everywhere ... Marged got out of the car. 'Oh my God,' she said. 'All these houses ...' and she thought of all those brave sturdy homes that men had built brick by brick, and all the people like Bren, who saved their pennies to buy one of them, the little gardens bright with flowers and vegetables ... the pity of it, and the waste.

'We can't get any farther,' Martin said. 'It seems there

are no more roads ... no nothing ... not even water – the mains are all burst ... I wonder if I should go and help?'

'We've got to find Bren,' said Marged, thinking of the shelter back home, the dead bodies ... how many dead bodies were in Coventry this night ...? She looked at her watch. It was nine o'clock.

People were walking from the devastated city. Some lived outside and had no transport, some had no homes, some were injured. Martin packed the car with three of the worst cases, then they waited ...

Marged thought, How shall we know? In all this carnage, how shall we know? Will anyone ever know who's alive or dead? Or missing, like John ...? More people came walking through ...

More crowds ...

Bren.

She came to them as if she were sleep-walking, clothes torn, face bleeding. 'Get in,' said Martin, tersely, and she sat in the front seat on Marged's lap, while two women and a man, Bren's friends who had been bombed out, somehow squeezed in the back, lifting the injured three on to their knees. Marged put her arms round Brenda and held her as if she'd never let her go.

'Mam's house was bombed,' she told her. 'They're dead.' And then, loaded, they crawled home.

They dropped off the wounded passengers at Chilverton hospital, then went on to Victoria Street.

'Oh my house,' said Brenda. 'My home.'

'We'll have to clean it up,' said Marged.

She was trembling now, she could hardly stand. Dimly she saw Martin and Philip, Bren's friend, bringing the bedding down, laying it on the floor in the front room and the kitchen. She had another drink of tea then, exhausted, lay down and slept.

*

The whole world was shocked by the Coventry bombing, for no effort was made to black out the news as in other areas. The German radio proudly announced its new policy of 'Coventration'. The King and Queen visited the shattered ruins where, amid the desolation, the spire of the burnt-out cathedral still miraculously stood. In the city there was no defeatest talk, just anger.

Marged never remembered the next few days very clearly. There were the notices in the street saying BOIL ALL WATER in great black letters, but she didn't know where she walked. Council workers put a tarpaulin on the roof, for it was raining now, and they all, Brenda, Philip, and the two women, Nancy and Edna, cleaned up the house. Buckets of soot from the downstairs floor, pieces of tiles from the roof, shattered glass, plaster from the ceiling. Martin went to find out how the rest of the family fared, to see if they could offer accommodation, but all their houses were damaged too, Aunt Mary was in hospital, Grandma was dead. Grandma had always refused to go in the shelter; now she died as she had lived, defying the world.

Brenda said nothing about her ordeal. She was plainly in shock, and it was Philip who looked after her in those first awful days. But on the Tuesday, four days after the raid, she went back to work, as did four-fifths of the Coventry workforce. In greatcoats, oilskins and gumboots, with tin hats in case of falling masonry, they carried on with the job beneath an open sky. Marged wanted to start back too, but Martin told her: 'Mordant's has been hit. Don't know any more yet.'

He was on duty again on Saturday night, and when he returned he enlarged on his news. 'Mr Mordant was killed.'

Marged stared, horrified. 'I said I wish he'd been bombed. Did I wish it on him?'

' 'Course you didn't,' said Martin, robustly.

'Was he at work then?'

'Well, he was in the office, with his secretary by all accounts. She's been hurt, I think, though not badly.'

'Is Roberta all right?'

'Yes. Park Manor wasn't hit. I took the car back and told her I'd borrowed it. She was OK then.'

'Oh yes, of course,' and Martin looked at her worriedly. Why didn't she cry or something, instead of walking round like a zombie. Why didn't she shout and scream and curse? Because she was Marged, of course.

The day before the mass funerals there came a knock at the door. Marged opened it. Mrs West stood there, a large bunch of flowers in her hand, chrysanthemums, Michaelmas daisies, and two late roses.

She said: 'I brought these, Marged. For your mam and dad.'

Marged stared at the little woman, dressed as always in an overall, though now it was clean. 'Oh thank you, Mrs West. Come in.'

'I won't stop. But I was sorry for you. I always used to see you when you were a kid and your dad had that trouble. You used to go marching along with your head up ... and your mam was so nice. Did you know that she used to bring me some of her cakes when Joe— when we had no money, which was regular in them days.'

'No,' said Marged. 'I didn't know.'

'Things are better now,' said Mrs West. 'Joe got a job. And our Eileen's working in an office in Coventry, getting on ever so well—' She was obviously proud of this step up for the no-good Wests. 'Our Maud's not so clever, she's in a factory. And Vera's courting.'

'I thought I hadn't seen her at the dance.'

'No, she goes out with a soldier, nice chap. He's away now, but Vera don't go out, sits in home waiting for him. Well, I won't stop. I just thought I'd bring these to show

186

my respect. Your mam was so nice. And John an' all . . .'

And when she'd gone, Marged sat and cried, the flowers beside her.

Chapter 9

Chilverton was damaged, though not beyond repair. One of the fine old buildings was burnt out, and several shops demolished, while a cinema showing *Gone With The Wind* had a direct hit. Houses with their fronts blown off stood pathetically, like dolls' houses, open to the air, the little rooms inside still holding furniture, the homes of little people.

It was raining when Marged stood before the ruins of her home. Piles of bricks, no more. She bent to pick up a piece of varnished wood and saw it was her dad's broken chair. Tears gushed to her eyes. Did he deserve no better than this? He had had so little. She saw a brick with coloured wallpaper on it. Mam and Dad used to paper the rooms together before Dad had his accident, Mam mixing the paste, flour and water, Dad cutting and sticking the paper. Pretty little borders round the top.

Someone said to her, passing by, 'You'll get compensation, you know,' and she stared, frozen. *Compensation*? For a home lovingly built over the years, Mam working and working, washing and ironing, cleaning, *loving*. Now rage rushed in. What had her dad said? 'I wanted to buy a nice little semi – I could have ...' if it hadn't been for Mordant.

She went back to work. Mr Mordant's office, at the rear of the main block, was down, but the general offices were in working order, more or less, once they had tidied up all the files, thrown on the floor by the blast, and had found their own chairs, their typewriters ... But before she could do anything Miss Sansome was before her. 'Miss Hampden wants to see you,' she informed her. 'In Mr Brian's office.'

'Miss Hampden? Oh, Mr Mordant's secretary. What does she want me for?'

'If you go along, no doubt she'll tell you,' said Miss Sansome, and Marged pulled a face at her retreating back. 'Some things don't change,' she muttered.

Miss Hampden was waiting in Brian's outer office. A beautiful girl with red-gold hair and green eyes, who always dressed well, more like a model than a secretary, but today her face was white, her hands shaking. 'Sit down,' she said.

Marged sat, and waited. It was obvious that Miss Hampden was under stress; she repeatedly held a handkerchief to her face. She said at last, 'Mr Brian will be taking over now.'

'Yes,' Marged agreed. 'I suppose so.'

'And he wants you to be his secretary.'

Marged stared. 'Me?' The world was mad; Miss Hampden was mad. She was a junior typist, not even a junior secretary. 'But—' she stammered. 'My speeds aren't all that good.'

'That doesn't matter. His usual secretary will be here as well, and I shall be here to help – until he can take over fully.' Again she put the handkerchief to her face. 'I shall be going away as soon as I can—' Her hands shook so much Marged could hardly bear to watch. 'My doctor's orders,' she ended. It was obvious that she wasn't fit to be working now.

'But won't one of the other managers take over?' Marged asked.

Miss Hampden drew a breath. 'They're all at each others' throats,' she said. 'Mr Mordant's genius lay in playing one off against the other. If you put one of them in here he'd soon take over the whole firm.'

'From Mr Brian?'

'From Mr Brian.'

'So Mr Brian will have to do this playing one off ...' Marged paused as she considered what this meant. Could Mr Brian do it, was he capable? He'd need a good secretary ... 'What about one of the senior secretaries?' she asked.

'They're all old maids who've been working for their own boss for twenty years or so. They're married to them, or wish they were, silly bitches. Give them the job and they'd soon be creeping back to their particular boss with all the secrets.'

'Secrets?'

'That the Buying shouldn't know just what deals the Sales is getting and so on.'

'But I don't see what I can do that others can't.'

'Candidly, neither do I, but Mr Brian asked specifically for you. He did say you helped him with the work.'

Marged remembered the reading. That's all she had done for him, read to him because for some reason he found reading difficult. And no one else knew? Well, naturally, he wouldn't want to sit at a meeting with all those other snooty managers laughing behind their hands because he couldn't understand something they showed him. She said slowly, 'Yes, I did help him. And I – persuaded him to work.'

'I see. Well, that apart, you seem to be a bright girl, and one who is fairly shrewd, I'd say. And—' She hesitated.

'And?'

'Shall we say, sharp enough not to let things slide, or people take advantage of you. And not too well-mannered to speak up if they do.'

Marged grinned. 'You may say that,' she replied. 'And as we are plain speaking, I can understand your concern for Mordant's, you being the boss's friend. But Mordant's haven't been very good to me, so why should I bother?'

Miss Hampden shrugged. 'Please yourself. But your family worked here, didn't they, some of them?'

'Oh yes, they worked here all right. And if you think we feel any loyalty towards them then think again. Oh, some people do to some firms, I know. Rolls Royce, Morris, they're good places, names you can be proud to work for. People there are paid well, so they work well. But Mordant's ...'

'Mordant's are making aircraft parts.'

'So they are. And we need aircraft to do a bit of bombing ourselves. So it looks as though I'll have to be on Mordant's side for the duration. Though I still think there are many far better qualified than me.'

Miss Hampden stood up, her calm disintegrating. 'Maybe there are, and maybe they're all dead, or like me, shattered. For God's sake, we're just at the end of an air raid that's killed thousands!'

'I know. My parents were killed in it.'

The other woman sat down. 'I'm sorry. We're all edgy.'

Marged refused to admit she was working for the war effort. 'I suppose I shall get a rise?' she asked.

Miss Hampden smiled fleetingly. 'A good one,' she said.

Marged thought afterwards that if she hadn't been bomb-shocked herself, she'd never have had the courage to take this position on. She had so much to think about – her parents, the house, the raid. Mordant's and revenge came a long way behind.

But they were there, even so. She accepted.

Martin whistled when she told him of her promotion. 'So you've gone over to the bosses,' he said. 'But why did they pick you?'

'I'd be daft not to take this job, all the money I'll have,' she retorted. 'And I've not gone over to the bosses. They picked me because Brian can't read.'

'*What?*'

'It's funny. It's as though he can't *grasp* the words, somehow,' and she went on to explain how she read to him, and how this was the reason behind him choosing her.

'Don't tell anyone about this, Mart, certainly not anyone in the factory—'

'Doesn't surprise me to know that Mordant's is run by a lot of dumb-bells,' he snorted. 'Just watch it, Marged. No telling tales to the boss.'

'Who do you think I am, Roberta?' she asked, and he was silent. But as she turned away he was thoughtful.

It was some weeks before the ceilings were repaired in Brenda's house, and during that time they all slept on mattresses on the floors downstairs, except when the sirens went, for the raids kept on. Not with the fury of the first onslaught, but bombs were still being dropped. Life at home was uncomfortable, and Marged hated to walk down Victoria Street past the rubble where once she had lived. It made working so much easier; she wanted nothing else. She sat in home talking to Brenda – when she was on days – in the silence of the night, for Bren and she were in the front room, the other two women in the kitchen, and Martin and Philip in the back-kitchen.

'I wish I'd been better to Mam,' Marged said, sombrely. 'I was always a trouble to her. Bren, do you remember when we used to go to bed in the summer nights, and I lit a candle to read, and Mam said I was burning daylight? I never knew what she meant.'

'And her fancy hats. She loved her hats.'

'And do you remember when she took us to Birmingham Art Gallery? I wonder why. She never said.'

Intuitively they went back to their childhood, the days before the accident, when days were golden, and the memories brought them some measure of comfort.

But the present intervened soon enough. 'We're so crowded here,' Marged grumbled.

'I know, but Nancy and Edna are looking for somewhere else.'

'And Philip?'

'He's got nowhere, he's not a local man.'

'Who is he, Bren? What does he do? I mean, he's different, isn't he, from us? Talks posh.'

'He went to a public school, and to Cambridge. Rejected from the Army because he's slightly lame, as I suppose you've noticed. So he was sent to work here.'

'He looks like Leslie Howard,' said Marged dreamily.

'Go to sleep,' said Brenda repressively, and Marged turned away.

But Brenda lay silent in the darkness. She never talked about her night in the blitz; even to think of it gave her the shivers. The minute the sirens had sounded planes were overhead. She left her machine, but there wasn't even time to get to the big shelter outside, she and several other women ran to the small warden's shelter under the factory floor.

They could hear the incendiary bombs crashing through the roof, hitting the machines ... hear the ack-ack guns ... then the roof went with a terrific bang, and part of the roof of their shelter with it.

And Brenda knew fear. Nancy was praying, 'Oh God, help us ...'

It was like day outside, with the moon and the fires. They could see the black shadows of the planes like great hovering spiders. The bombs kept screaming down ... she never thought they'd get out alive. There was noise and there were bangs, black shadows and fires, and they were trapped inside the factory ... when something fell over their opening she lost consciousness ... She heard men digging above them, and someone pulled her out ... it was Philip Higham, a man she'd seen occasionally, who lifted her and held her steady as she looked round at the burning and the desolation. She couldn't recognise anything. She was in a lost world, and she was lost, not knowing which way to turn in this maze of horror and destruction. And Philip said, 'It's all right, you're all right. We'll get you home.'

He had such a lovely voice. In the days that followed she liked to listen to him speaking, not that he said much, he was a quiet fellow, but he seemed to enjoy talking to her, or maybe that was her imagination ... She too wished Edna and Nancy would find somewhere else to live, but not Philip ...

Martin had seen Roberta after the night of the raid, when he took her car back. 'You shouldn't have left it unlocked, with the keys inside,' he reproved her. 'You know what they tell us about immobilising cars.'

She ignored this. 'I'm so glad you're all right,' she sighed. 'So very glad, Martin,' and as he hesitated, 'you will see me again, won't you?'

And he looked at her, a calculating stare. 'I'll see you,' he promised. 'Wait till—'

'I know. When it's all over.'

Ten days later, when the funerals were over and the dust had settled, she was waiting for him outside the factory, smart as always in a green suit with a white blouse, and high-heeled shoes. 'Martin,' she breathed.

He halted, and the men poured out around them, along with the women in turbans and coats over their overalls. 'Come on,' he said.

He pushed his bike and they started walking.

'Mother says I have to leave Park Manor,' she said, without preamble. 'And I don't want to.'

'Why? Doesn't it belong to her?'

'No, it's Brian's now, and so is the business. Daddy's left Mother well provided for, and me too, but the house is Brian's.'

'So what's the problem?'

'Mother hates it here, you know that. She says we have to go away. Both of us. She's not been living here during the war. She's been all over the place. Anywhere she can have a good time.' Roberta's voice held bitterness.

He studied her by the light of the waning moon. 'I don't understand. Your mother doesn't seem to care two hoots for you, so why should she bother where you are?'

'I don't know.'

'And you don't want to live with her, so stay here.'

A car approached slowly, its tiny masked lights twinkling in the blackness. He held her arm as it passed. She turned to look at him. 'S-should I?'

'I don't understand you,' he repeated. 'Are you frightened of your mother?'

'I suppose – well, yes, I am. But I'm under age, Martin, that's what she told me.'

'Well, she's wrong. You're old enough to leave home without permission. Especially with a war on. You're on war work, aren't you?'

She pulled a face. 'If you could call it that. So I'm old enough to leave home. But not to get married.'

He was startled, but didn't show it. 'No,' he said levelly. 'Not to get married. Not till you're twenty-one. When are you twenty-one, Roberta?'

'Not for two years.' She smiled suddenly. 'I'll stay here,' she said. 'With you.'

He walked her all the way to Park Manor, then mounted his bike for the short ride home, whistling as he rode. It was going to be easier than he thought. Everything was falling into place. Everything.

A cold east wind blew flurries of snow over the street as Marged battled home through the blackout. It was going to be another bad winter. She ran up the entry and burst into the kitchen. 'Lord, some of these shopkeepers are like little Hitlers,' she groaned. 'I went – oh, it's you, Philip. Brenda in bed?'

'She'll be down in a minute. So what happened with the shopkeepers, then?'

Marged shrugged off her coat and moved to the fire.

'Brr, it's cold outside. Well, I spent all my dinner-hour at the shops. I heard there was a consignment of cosmetics coming in, and I went to every one. "Sorry, not here," they said, and we all know what *that* means. Under the counter. Honestly, the shops get emptier. No sweets, no cigs, no chocolates. There was a notice on one door: "No oranges, no bananas, no onions ..."'

'Then you've had nothing to eat all day?' Philip asked.

Marged looked up. He was considerate, this lodger of Bren's. Catch Martin asking if she'd had anything to eat. 'As a matter of fact, no,' she said. 'And all for nothing.'

'What didn't you get?' Brenda asked, entering. 'Face powder? What for, you don't go out now?'

'No, but we have to look decent at work. We in the office. Not like you scruffs in the factory. Bet you're warmer than we are, though. Honestly, it's so cold in those offices you wouldn't believe. Even ours isn't much better now. You know my idea of heaven is to be *warm*. P'raps I'd be better off in the other place. Not heaven.'

'Take the oven-shelf to bed,' said Brenda, unfeelingly.

'That's a bit hard,' smiled Philip. 'You need electric fires here.'

'We need electricians first to fit plugs,' said Brenda, getting the round stewpot out of the oven. 'Here you are, Marged. I cooked plenty for you and Martin. The butcher actually let me have a bit of stewing meat, though I'm not sure which animal it came from.'

Philip was standing by the table. 'I wondered—' he began. 'Now that Edna and Nancy have gone and the roof's mended, if I could stay? You have three bedrooms.'

Marged looked at Brenda. Her face was pink. 'I don't see why not,' she murmured. 'Though I've only got two beds.'

'Don't worry, I'll get another.'

As they ate, Marged wondered why Philip wanted to stop here – he was so obviously used to a better way of life. Not that he grumbled; he didn't grumble as much as she did.

But it showed in his reactions. He hadn't been able to understand why people didn't use their front room, didn't realise they couldn't afford to keep two fires going. Though now they, like most people, had more money, ironically coal was getting scarce. She wondered what he made of heating kettles of water every time you wanted to wash, lighting the fire under the copper in the back-kitchen for a bath – that's if you could find a place to bath in, if you didn't want to lug the tin bath upstairs. Why didn't he go to a hotel like the Colonel at the office? 'I know I'd be out if I could,' she murmured. 'A nice little semi, like Miss Anson's, with net curtains, fine net, chintz-covered chairs ...'

Dinner over, Marged settled down by the fire. 'I like it when you two are on nights,' she commented. 'Coming home to a warm house, with no fires to light.'

'Make yourself comfortable,' Brenda said. '*We're* just going out in the cold.' And I've seen the time when cold didn't keep you in either, Brenda thought.

'I'll be up with the fire lit when you get back in the morning,' Marged called.

It was twenty past seven when they left to get the bus to Coventry to start their twelve-hour shift, and just an hour later Martin walked in from the day shift. Marged reached the stew-pot out of the oven and poured the remains of the stew on to a plate. 'Going out tonight?' she asked. 'It's not ARP, is it?'

'No, and yes, I am going out.'

'All right, don't tell me,' she said. 'Only don't—'

'Don't get in trouble,' he finished. 'What do you think I'm going to do, flash lights for the Jerries?'

'Well, why can't you tell me? I know there's something.'

'Wait a minute, let me eat this.'

The stew was brown and filling, with dumplings, potatoes and a few parsnips from the allotment, which Martin saw to when he could; whether he'd have time to do much in the spring was in doubt, and Marged wondered if Philip was any good at digging. 'Philip wants to stop on here,' she offered, and Martin grunted.

'Sissy,' he said scornfully. Marged sighed. Stew finished, Martin leaned back. Then: 'Look, Marg, when I talked about taking over Mordant's I meant it, you know.' She said nothing.

'So, now's our chance.'

'You mean – me?'

'Of course. You keep it going till I'm ready to take over. It's a piece of cake.'

'Are you serious?'

'''Course I am.'

'Martin. My dear lad. You can't just walk into a factory and take it over like that. You do have to know *something* about it.'

'Like Brian does?'

'Well, he owns the place. The managers run it.'

'But he's supposed to know all about it, and he doesn't. Because you cover for him.'

'Yes, and it isn't easy.'

He was leaning over the table, staring into her eyes with an intensity that made her uneasy, and she looked away into the fire, reaching for the poker, stabbing at the coal, making sparks fly up the chimney.

'You can do it,' he said. 'You always did stick up for me, Marg.'

'Yeah, just a big softy, me.'

Yet she knew it was true. She had, when they were children, always shielded him from Dad's anger; when they were older, as he said, stuck up for him against the others. And hadn't he done the same for her? Lied unblushingly when she came in late, took her under his wing during the period of wildness when she was running with the lads? She said, 'I'll do what I can, though what . . .?'

'Just learn all you can – and keep me informed.'

He pushed his chair back and went upstairs, whistling.

Marged sat with Brian in his office, while Miss Hampden and Mrs Jennings, his former secretary, were in the outer office. They struggled through, but it was Miss Hampden who carried them.

Marged had to read aloud every letter, every report that came in. She would not have minded if Brian had admitted his disability so they could discuss the best way of organising things, but this he refused to do, pretending every day that he was too busy to sit down and read them for himself.

Marged knew she had to put things right with Mrs Jennings, or there'd be trouble from the word go. Daphne Jennings was a small, dark-haired girl, well qualified and understandably mystified about her apparent demotion. Marged sat with her when Miss Hampden had gone, and tried to explain.

'He's only taken me on because he thinks I can help him,' she said. It's not that I'm a better secretary – we all know I'm not as good as you – and I can't manage on my own. You're an important member of the team. In fact, you'll be doing the same work as you always did.'

'Which was practically nil,' said Daphne.

'No, but we'll have Mr Mordant's work now. The trouble is, Mr Brian was thrown in at the deep end. He –' how to explain without giving the game away? '– was brought in, and stuck in that office with no explanations ... He's not really unintelligent,' she finished.

'You could've fooled me,' said Daphne. 'When I was with him he never tried to learn anything, never read a single letter!'

'I've managed to get him to do that,' Marged said. 'That's why he wants me here.'

'But he knows nothing about engineering,' protested Daphne.

That was a problem. How could the owner of an

engineering factory not know engineering? How could he manage the place if he couldn't read and understand blue-prints, as the merest apprentice could? What on earth was Mr Mordant planning for Brian? Had he hoped his son would improve? Of course, he hadn't expected the raid, thought he'd be here for a long time yet ... As for the engineering side, Martin would have to help. It was the only way.

She told Martin about her problem, and he was quite willing. 'What do you want to know?' he asked.

'Well, there's the Board meetings. How can we control them if we don't know what we're talking about?'

'Don't worry, they don't know either. It's true,' as she raised her eyebrows. 'This work is new to them, we all know it. We've got these new extensions, lots more workers, all from Government training centres – who's to deal with all them? Then we had some sub-contracting work sent to us – the Ministry of Production controls all that, you know – and they sent us the wrong drawings. We made a whole new set of tools –' Martin's job was tool-maker '– then, when work started, found they were all wrong. It's all muddle these days.'

'But you can't blame the managers for that.'

'They should know.'

'What about the Works Manager, Mr Norris, doesn't he know?'

'Of course he does, but he doesn't go to Board meetings, does he? He just has to report to his boss, Mr Walters, and what he knows about jigs and tools could be put on a pinhead.'

'Mr Norris should be at the Board meetings.'

'Course he should. You see, we were making car compo-nents before, not aircraft. This is all new, as I said.'

Marged was silent. Outside she could hear rain beating against the window. It was still cold. She said: 'Mart, why don't we make you an Assistant Works Manager? We need one, surely?'

He brushed his hair back from his forehead, thinking. Then: 'No. Not at the moment.'

'Why not? Surely it would be a step in the right direction? It would help me, and help you—'

'No, Marged. Wait.'

She looked at him suspiciously, and the anger in him that was never far below the surface entered his voice. 'Assistant Works Manager, you think that's good enough for me? That's all I'm capable of? No, when I said I'd take over, I meant it.'

Now she was angry too, and she began: 'I was only trying to help—'

'Yes, I know.' His anger had gone, he was placating now. 'Listen, Marg. You've got the chance now to change how the place is run. *Now* it's all government-controlled. They give the orders, you can't dismiss people – in theory. When the war's over it'll be different.'

'You think I'll be thrown out?' she asked sharply.

'Well, won't you?'

She shrugged. You didn't really plan for the future these days.

'Just carry on for the time being,' he said persuasively. 'Then we'll see ...'

And when he'd gone she sat, listening to the rain. Martin was right in one sense: if she could change the way the place was run, that would be fine. As for him taking over ... well, as he saw it, Mordant's had ruined his life, ruined their father's life ... if Dad had been earning all those years they might have moved away from Victoria Street as he'd wanted, then he wouldn't have been killed. Still, no use thinking that way.

She knew she would help Martin, as ever. *When you pair of devils get together*, Mam used to say, but she wished he would tell her what was in his mind. He always had ...

Shrugging, she began to wash up.

Mordant's carried on. Marged knew the whole firm was

agog at Brian's choice of secretary; there were whispers that she was his favourite, and there was no way of scotching these rumours except to say she had worked with him before. Daphne Jennings seemed grudgingly placated although she had lost status, but then new managers often took new secretaries, so even that was explained. Daphne Jennings was a nice girl, but only human, so if the talk was that Brian had brought in his fancy piece while she, Daphne, did all the donkey work, she did not contradict it very convincingly.

Miss Hampden left after six weeks and Marged knew that the managers thought that now Brian would be a pushover, and that he had to surprise them. So at the first Board meeting, Marged attended, ostensibly to take the minutes, and Brian, primed by Marged, said: 'My father ran this place efficiently, and I intend to do the same. I want all your reports exactly as before placed on my desk every month.'

The managers looked their surprise. But Marged had made her point clear. 'As long as each manager runs his department well, you'll only have to supervise them,' she had told him.

'And make the decisions,' Brian said.

'Yes. But as long as they all keep their departments in order while you pick up the threads, you'll be OK. We're all government-controlled now, Buying, Selling, the lot. You must make the managers toe the line. Remember you're the boss.' And again: 'I know you don't care about the firm, but you can't sell it now, and if you could, you'd be called up immediately. You must carry on.'

She went to the first meeting with some trepidation and faced the men who had been Mr Mordant's aides, who thought as he did, and she studied them covertly. Mr Walters she knew. The aptly-named Mr Byers of Buying was similar in type; where Mr Walters was portly with dark greying hair, Mr Byers was portly with fair greying hair. He liked people to defer to him, and when Marged showed no signs of doing so, he eyed her disapprovingly as though wondering how on earth she'd got there. (You and me both, thought Marged irrepressibly.) Mr James of Sales was younger, and looked more promising. Mr Arnold the Finance Manager, and most senior of them all, was tall and thin with a buttoned-up face, not easy to read. Marged filed him away in her head, to think about when she had time.

The Board did not quite know what to do about her, that she could see. At first she was patronised, the little girl whom Brian Mordant had picked up, a nobody who should have no opinions and know her place. She took the minutes, and at the first meeting said nothing, as befitted the secretary. But at subsequent meetings she found herself saying what she thought. And because she had a sharp brain and some of the things she said made sense, they began to look wary. Brian was the boss, after all.

Marged wondered if they suspected Brian's trouble; they weren't fools. If they did they said nothing, but they were watchful. She thought mirthfully it was like a huge game of poker; they all sat straight-faced, suspecting and trying to outplay the other. As for herself, she felt she played the biggest bluff of all. If anyone lived on her wits it was Marguerite Fennel at the Board meetings, trying to pretend she knew everything when in fact she knew damn-all.

Yet she had to speak her mind. They were so hidebound, so entrenched in their beliefs. We shall never see eye to eye, she thought at the end of one meeting. They are bosses, I'm the worker. You can take the girl from the back streets, but you can't take the back streets from the girl.

'If I ever stopped to think what I was doing I'd shoot myself,' she confided to Martin.

'And then what?' he said seriously.

'And then what what?'

'Brian Mordant would have to get another secretary and she'd probably tell everyone his guilty secret and he'd be squashed by the others.'

'They can't really sack him when he owns the place.'

'No, but they could make things so uncomfortable for him that he'd resign – or just lose confidence and give in to them.'

'You mean I'm the saviour of Mordant's?'

'What else?' he asked, grinning. 'Don't give it away, Marged. Save it for me.'

She managed to deal with the engineering problems. As Martin had said, the shop floor difficulties were dealt with by Mr Walters and he, knowing Brian had no engineering experience, did explain the facts to him, which Marged wrote down, presented them to Martin, and came back with an answer the next meeting. Usually she passed the information on to Brian, for him to speak about it, though his trouble was, of course, that he could not refer to notes, but she primed him well beforehand, prompting him when necessary by reading out details from her own notes.

She asked Mr Norris to take Brian and herself on a tour of the factory, so that at least they would know which machine was doing what. Back in the office she would pore over blueprints, taking them to Martin for him to explain. It was, of course, very much against the rules to take work home, but she knew Martin well enough to believe that whatever plans he had, they were for his own benefit, and not to help the enemy.

She did not tell Brian that it was her brother who was supplying the information which – if it dealt with payments, naturally fell on the workers' side. She was beginning to understand Miss Hampden's dictum that you kept the right hand from knowing what the left was doing. Had Mr Walters known that his scheme for time and motion study was circumvented by a shop-floor worker, Martin would have been out quickly, war or no war. I'm getting as crooked as the rest of them, Marged thought, and wished sometimes she were back with honest-dealing Grant's. Yet she knew how the rate-fixer was hated for his method of timing – and pricing – by the fastest worker, so felt she was justified in preventing what might have been a strike. If the management would talk to the shop floor a little more there'd be far less trouble, she thought.

She learned a lot about Brian Mordant, from his many phone calls, usually to girls, for he was not, and would never be, wholehearted in the business. She discovered that Brian liked a good time, and liked good-time girls. He took them out, dancing and dining ... some of the things he said might have made her blush, had she been a blushing type of girl. He was not out for marriage, that was for sure.

She would have respected him more had he acknowledged his reading difficulty – at least to her. But he still kept up the pretence that he was too busy to deal with the papers and reports, but when something went well – something instigated by Marged – he would boast and swagger to her, and she did find this hard to bear.

Roberta had admired her father, but she had seen too little of him to bear him any great love. She mourned his death, wishing it could have been her mother, but did not think that her life would be much changed.

When she heard of Marged's promotion to Brian's secretary, the old envy reasserted itself. Why should Marged get everything that was going? But after thinking things over she realised that she could turn even this to her own advantage.

She and Brian had, on growing up, become if not close, certainly far more friendly than before. She did not need his escort now her mother was away, yet he had always been willing to oblige, and for this she was grateful. She knew nothing of his reading problems, for in Park Manor the family saw so little of each other that the fact that he never read books went entirely unnoticed. She did think him slow, and knew he was weak, in contrast to her father; she came to regard him as a younger brother rather than an elder.

They were alone in the house now, at the tender mercies of the housekeeper Mrs Stanway, who watched them like a hawk, and whom they both detested. It was fear of the formidable Mrs Stanway – who no doubt would report back to his mother – which kept Brian from holding the sort of wild parties he loved, and sister and brother were united in their dislike of the woman.

With the onset of war, and more and better paid work in the factories, the many servants had disappeared like snow in summer, and Mrs Stanway had to search the highways and byways for replacements. All she could find was a slatternly woman who worked daily, and who refused to do more than the minimum of chores. She served breakfast – the cook, who was elderly, still stayed – in one corner of the dining-room as it was nearest to the kitchen, and here Roberta and Brian sat eating the bacon and eggs that Mordant's had always been able to obtain, at least while their father was alive.

Roberta, who never forgot the eavesdropping of childhood, made sure the door was closed when she said: 'I hear you've made Marged Fennel your secretary.'

'Yes.' Brian was uncommunicative.

'Well.' Roberta drank her tea. 'I do admire you, I really do.'

And Brian, who had never been admired for anything, looked startled. 'You do?'

'Of course. They say in the offices that she's your fancy piece. So I respect your courage.' Brian preened himself at being thought courageous, as she knew he would. 'You have the courage of your convictions,' Roberta went on. 'You like Marged, so you put her in your office. I admire that.'

Brian, unable to tell of the real reason for Marged's promotion, said nothing. And Roberta ploughed on.

'So many men of our class, when they take out their social inferiors, go out of town, to places where they are not known –' *as I do* '– I think you're so brave to be honest. Marged's a nice girl. I used to know her well when we were young—'

'Yes,' Brian interrupted sarcastically. 'You liked her so much you let Mother turn her out of the house.'

'I know, and I was wrong. Though, as I remember, it was your fault. But I told Marged I was sorry. Anyway, you know Mummy. Still, I think you could do worse.'

'Do worse?' Brian asked, bemused. 'She's only my secretary, Roberta. And Father had Miss Hampden. People said—'

'Brian, she is not a top-class secretary as Miss Hampden was, and you know it. We all know it. You are obviously keen on her, and I'd like nothing better than to see you settled.'

'Settled?' Brian asked, astonished. 'Settled?'

'Of course. Married to her.'

'My dear girl, I have no intention of marrying anyone, and certainly not Marged Fennel.'

'I don't see why not. Think about it. More tea?'

As the secretary of the Managing Director, Marged did become important, to her surprise. She knew that, as Miss Hampden had told her, there was intense rivalry among the managers; they were still watchful, waiting for Brian to make such a mess of things that he'd have to be replaced, and she was determined this should not happen. The two she feared most were Mr Byers, who was almost openly antagonistic, and Mr Arnold the Finance Manager. The latter worried her for he had a sharp brain, but was an enigma; he said little, so she could not find out whose side he was on. On the other hand she quite liked Mr James of Sales. Younger than the others, he was a go-getter, the type of man who could sell ice-cream to Eskimos; he had a sense of humour, too, and could sometimes see the other side of a problem, whereas the rest were hidebound in their beliefs.

They hated change and seemed to think the rules of the firm were written in stone.

But when, as Christmas neared, Mr Walters came into the office during Brian's absence and asked her if she'd like a piece of pork, she was surprised.

'I have a friend, you know. He is a farmer . . .' he said.

Marged knew. Farmers had to report each killing, but so many found their animals accident prone, especially at Christmas, and friends benefited.

'So we get the pork,' Marged told Brenda.

'And what does he get in return?' asked Brenda caustically.

'Nothing,' said Marged. 'He might hope he will, but he won't. It's what's known as crawling, Bren, and I'm on the other end of it now.' For the present, she muttered to herself. If she were out, Mr Walters would be the first to ignore her. He was an old rogue and this she understood.

'I'm the boss's right-hand woman,' she grinned. 'The power is going to my head,' she chortled.

They hadn't planned on celebrating Christmas; none of them felt in the mood for merrymaking. Philip had bought a bed and bedding and was ensconced in the small back room, with Martin in the other back, and Marged and Brenda in the front. Philip had also persuaded one of the electricians at the factory to do the necessary rewiring one Sunday, for a fee of course, and now they had electric fires in most rooms. Marged watched all this with interest. Goods might be in short supply, but it was always possible to find them if you had the money.

And it was Philip who changed their Christmas by buying presents. They had intended to give gifts, of course, but token ones only, whatever could be obtained, scarves, handkerchiefs, ties. So when Philip came in on the Saturday before Christmas laden with boxes, they stared. Martin was at work, the girls doing housework.

'Whatever have you been buying now?' asked Brenda.

'Wait a minute,' he said mysteriously, and took them into the front room, where they could see a big van lumbering towards the house and as they stared, two men staggered inside with a huge crate.

'An electric cooker?' gasped Brenda. 'For me?'

'I eat here too, remember,' smiled Philip. 'And you work such long hours, you don't want to come home to wrestle with that coal oven.'

Brenda looked bemused, as well she might, thought Marged sardonically. But Philip hadn't finished. He handed round his parcels, a pretty brooch for Marged – not from Woolworths either, she thought – and an exquisite necklace for Brenda.

Brenda sat down. 'It's lovely,' she said. 'But—'

'No buts. It's an antique.'

'But why?'

'I like buying presents, that's all. You see – about Christmas – I was hoping you'd let me stay here.'

'But don't you want to go home?'

'It's hardly worth it for a couple or days. Over-crowded trains, posters asking you is your journey really necessary ...'

'We hadn't planned on doing anything,' Brenda murmured.

'That's fine. We'll just do nothing.'

That night in bed, Marged said, 'He fancies you, Bren.'

And Brenda didn't scoff as she'd expected. She didn't say anything. Marged raised herself on one elbow, but Brenda said, 'Go to sleep.'

Marged wondered if she were imagining things. Yet ... there had been so many times when she'd wondered about Brenda and Philip, or would have if she hadn't been so preoccupied with her job. The way they walked to the bus together and came back – *well, they would, wouldn't they, being on the same shift* – the way she'd come in to find them sitting close together, talking earnestly – *well, people have to talk, don't they?* And other women might have another man, but not Brenda ...

Christmas Day passed quietly, and on Boxing Day Philip asked them if they'd like to go to the theatre in Birmingham – 'If you want to risk the bombs.' For the raids kept on, not with the furious onslaught of the Coventry blitz, but they were there, even so. Marged declined, but Brenda accepted.

Martin was out, as always, and Marged was quite content to sit in alone listening to the wireless. She went to bed at midnight. Brenda and Philip hadn't returned. And when she awoke, Brenda's side of the bed was empty.

Marged went to work, and when she returned Brenda was in and getting ready to go on her night shift. Marged waited, but her sister said nothing. And the next night she was at home, Marged woke to find she'd left the room. She sat up. Had the sirens gone? No, Brenda would have wakened her. She must be in the lavatory, or gone to get a drink. Then she heard a door closing softly, and Brenda returned.

Still Marged said nothing. They had never been confidantes, the difference in age made this difficult; to Marged, Brenda was always the big sister, the one who, next to Mother, was in charge. She could not, even now, think of her as a fallible woman. She was, like Caesar's wife, above suspicion – or had been.

It was in February when for once they were alone together. Philip was upstairs, Martin out. Marged sat toasting bread on the fire, and Brenda came to sit beside her. The days were lengthening; the first snowdrops showed in the gardens, but it was still cold. The kitchen, with its glowing fire, its kettle on the hob, was cosy.

Brenda said, 'Why don't you go out, Marged? Go to the dance again?'

'I don't know. I can't ... not after ...'

'It won't bring them back, Marged. Nothing will.'

'I know.' Marged took the toast off the fork. And as they sat in companionable silence, she ventured, 'Bren—'

'Mm?'

'No, it's nothing to do with me.'

Brenda paused. 'You mean Philip?' she asked.

'Then it is – you do—'

'Yes.' Brenda's voice was barely audible.

'But Bren. Jack – you—' She wanted to say *love* him, but words like love didn't come easy to Victoria Street. 'You are in love with him,' she ended bravely.

'I know. I can't help it, Marg. I was in love with Jack, but I love Philip too. I didn't know I was going to meet Philip.' Her face creased with worry and bewilderment. 'I didn't know,' she repeated.

'Then you're serious?'

'What's serious?'

'Oh Bren, you know. What about Jack?'

'I don't know, Marged. I just don't know. I can't think about that . . . I never dreamed this would happen. Not to me.'

We were in a mad world where there was only the present.

'But what ab—'

'Leave it now, Marged.'

Marged stood up to butter her toast, but Brenda still sat staring into the fire. And when Marged went upstairs she sat on while the coals dropped slowly in the grate, and disintegrated into ash.

Brenda felt herself far from fallible. Yet she had been as amazed as Marged at the thought of her doing the unforgivable thing – making love to another man while her husband was away in the forces. What had happened to her? She tried to think of Jack, but it was difficult. Jack belonged to the days of pre-war. But she loved him, didn't she? All those years together?

It had been such a long time before she'd had any letters from him, though she'd been given an address at a Stalag ... Germany ... and had written the one single sheet she was allowed. But she'd heard nothing, not till after the Coventry Blitz, and by then her life had changed.

She had seen Philip around, had talked to him before the blitz when he'd pulled her from the ruins of Passmore's, and when he came home with her there seemed nothing to do but ask him to stay. When you were bombed out you slept anywhere and were glad to do so.

She'd known little about him except that he was different from the usual factory worker. The son of a barrister, he was a bit of an odd man out, he told her with his diffident smile. He hadn't wanted to study law and his father thought him effeminate.

Brenda had never met anyone quite like him before. She loved to listen to his voice as he told of his life, the family home in Cambridge, the flat in London, his interior-decorating business. His lifestyle was so out of her ken he could have been from another planet.

The first time they made love she told herself she was sex-starved or words to that effect, and was duly ashamed. It didn't mean anything, it was just an interlude, sweet as new wine ... delicate as a butterfly's wing.

But it went on – and on – and she knew it did mean something.

Brenda, the good girl. Was there some resentment in that? Brenda, who always did the right thing. She'd wanted to take up the scholarship too, but there'd been no question of it. She was the eldest ... the younger ones had to be considered.

Perhaps she wouldn't have minded. John hadn't gone either, but when the twins couldn't go there was such a fuss ... Yet Brenda had to keep working to support the family ... couldn't get married, and when she did couldn't have children because she was paying for the furniture and helping her mother ... Perhaps if she'd had children, things might have been different.

She hadn't visited Jack's mother since the blitz. No doubt old Mrs Morris thought she'd been too uspet ... though she'd find out the truth soon enough. Perhaps she already had, and that's why *she* didn't come to see her. Brenda knew her own mother wouldn't have approved. But now she was no longer Brenda the good girl, she was Philip's lover. And no one would ever understand how good it was, after being the support of her family, to have someone looking after you, to let go, to live for today. 'After the war' seemed light years away.

One short year of war had changed Victoria Street irrevocably and they'd never go back. You couldn't see into the future; you lived for the present because tomorrow you might be dead.

Had that night of the raid changed her? She didn't know. She only knew that pre-war she was able to sacrifice her life because there seemed to be years stretching ahead, she couldn't see an end to them. There was time, lots of time ...

Not now. Death stalked round every corner, hung in the air with those black spiders on the night of the raid. Her parents were dead, John was dead, tomorrow it could be Brenda herself.

Stanislaw Kowalski wondered vaguely how long he had been in the camp; but he could not remember. He did know he was weaker – he could hardly stand. He, with the others, had been working for twelve hours as usual. Now, back in their hut, he collapsed on to the plank that was his bed. He knew that if he didn't hide his weakness he would be finished. Slaves were expendable. Weakness wasn't to be tolerated in the master race.

His thoughts were chaotic, shooting in and out of his brain; he couldn't catch them before they disappeared. Polish culture was to be eliminated ... no weakness ... but what of the great ones of the past? Chopin, tubercular; Dostoevsky, epileptic; Byron, club-footed; Milton, blind; Van Gogh, mad; Toulouse-Lautrec, deformed; their own Beethoven, deaf ... eliminated all? They were talking now about a new pilot plant at Kulm with a new form of elimination, something to do with gas-cylinders ...

So what culture would they put in place of the old one, these brawny giants? Raucous military bands ...? It didn't make sense. Nothing made sense any more.

Not that he was one of the great, but what about Stefan, with his musical talent? Where was Stefan ...?

No, he was pretty unimportant, really. His life had been in Cracow. Cracow with its glories of the past, its palaces, its castles, churches, cathedral ... was the old Cloth Hall still standing, where the flower-sellers stood in the open square? He used to sit there in the summer with his books – he missed his books so much, he'd never really wanted anything else, never really wanted to marry. Just his books and his religion. Perhaps he should have been a monk. He'd have ended up in the same place ...

The prisoners were kept abreast of the news by the incomers, brought in to replace those who died or were killed. They said the Jews were being herded into ghettos, so crowded that there was much disease and death, so the Germans were getting worried about what to do with them all. Surely this new idea of gas cylinders wouldn't be for *that* ... would it? They were building a new camp at Treblinka, be ready in 1942 ... Push the Jews in there? ... Dear God! ... He was back in the farmhouse. His mother was teaching them history: Kings of Poland. Casimir the Great in the fourteenth century, who had given the first written laws and welcomed into Poland thousands of Jews fleeing persecution in the Rhineland ... Couldn't they get out now? Wouldn't any other country take them?

Who else for the gas chambers? All the other unwanted peoples, gipsies, the remaining Poles ... Some fair-haired Poles had been taken to Germany to breed. Why had the Germans decided to define the master race on the basis of fair hair? What was so special about fair hair? But maybe we were all to blame, all the countries that had persecuted

Jews and gipsies in the past, that had made slaves of black people ... yet what about those British slaves taken to Rome, when Pope Gregory said 'Not angles but angels' ... they were fair-haired ... How was England faring now ... How was Stefan ...?

At his side Tomasz looked at him uneasily as Stanislaw's head sank on to his breast.

He was back on the farm, Stefan was playing, his mother standing smiling ... Stefan was to be a concert pianist ... the music echoed down the years, Chopin's *Revolutionary Étude* written for the 1831 uprising against the Czar of Russia ... little Tadeusz was singing ...

A guard entered. 'Stand!' he shouted.

Stanislaw did not stand. He could not. Tomasz bent to help him but the guard yelled, 'Stop!'

Silence. Stanislaw raised his head. He was beating time to the music in his head, singing the Polish National Anthem. *Poland has not perished yet* ...

There was the rattle of a machine gun and he fell, face forward.

Martin was seeing Roberta on the one day a week he wasn't working, sleeping or on ARP duty. They went to the cottage and as before, they made love. And she clung to him and said: 'Martin, Mother's talking again about moving.'

'Then you must tell her you're staying here.'

'Martin, what are we going to do in the future?'

He drew a breath as he looked at her in the firelight, her clothes rumpled, her hair tousled. 'What do you want to do? Get married?'

'Oh yes. Oh yes, Martin.'

He said slowly, 'You'll have to get your mother's permission.'

'Maybe she will agree,' she said. 'Maybe ...' and she was silent. 'I used to think I'd ask Daddy to find you a better job. Then I messed it up when I told about – about your dad. But maybe Brian would help. Would you take a better job, if I asked him?'

'Not yet.'

'What do you mean, not yet?'

'You say get a better job. Doing what? I don't want some little office job that everyone knows has been provided for me. Not unless we *were* married.' He drew a breath. 'It would be different then.'

'I don't see why.'

Because, he thought, as your husband I could take over from Brian. I know his weakness, you don't ... And I'm tougher than him.

It was quite true that Roberta was afraid of her mother: she always had been. These days Adela drank more and more, and when drunk – not that she would ever use such a word – she could be quite frightening. Adela was now in her forties and she hadn't worn well. Men didn't want her so much now. Roberta, like Martin, had been puzzled by her mother's newfound need of her and she asked why she wanted her daughter to live with her.

'Oh,' Adela said carelessly, 'we could go out together, find some nice men.'

Roberta blinked, not quite understanding. But when in February Adela suggested they go out together, she agreed, thinking her only hope of winning her mother's approval for her marriage was to placate her in every way. She put on a quiet dress of dark green – Roberta's clothes were never ostentatious – and went downstairs.

Her mother came in, and Roberta saw her for the first time as a woman. Her hair was jet black, and somehow it looked too black, almost as if it had been dyed. Her face was caked with make-up, her cheeks an unbecoming red, and Roberta was fleetingly reminded of the women in the Red Cow. Adela said, 'You're not going dressed like that, are you? You look like a nun.'

'But where are we going?' Roberta asked, feeling, as she always did with her mother, inadequate.

'To the Gainsborough Club. Come on, Roberta, I need you to be attractive.' And even then Roberta didn't understand, not even when her mother had forced her into another dress with a low neck and back, and had insisted that she put on more make-up. She didn't understand when they arrived at the Club, on the outskirts of Birmingham, and filled with officers, Army and RAF. And women, over-made-up, scantily-dressed women, in short skirts and high heels, flowing hair and flashing jewels, real or fake, heavily perfumed; really, Roberta thought, remembering Melbourne, not very ladylike.

They sat at a little table and Adela ordered two Martinis; Roberta sipped hers without enjoyment. Two Army officers approached both around forty, and both looked first at Roberta as they said good evening. Roberta turned her head away – they didn't know them, did they? But Adela replied, invited them to her table, and chatted while they bought more drinks.

The men introduced themselves as Ian and Keith. Keith sat beside Roberta and Ian, a little hesitantly, next to Adela. And Roberta froze, embarrassed while her mother screamed with laughter at the risqué jokes she told – Roberta didn't understand half of them – and laughed even louder as the men riposted with more jokes. She sipped her cocktail and wished she were with Martin.

When Keith said, 'Let's go, little girl,' she rose thankfully.

He led her to another door which she took to be a second exit. But now they were in a lift, being taken upstairs. Bewildered, she followed him to a small room. A peculiar room with lots of mirrors and pictures of women – not very nice, some of them, Roberta thought hazily. A table, chairs, and in the corner . . . was that a bed?

Keith closed the door, turned, and took her in his arms.

She pulled away. 'What are you doing?'

He fondled her hair. 'Come on, sweetheart, take off your dress.' He tried to pull down the shoulder-strap.

She wrenched away. 'No – no! Please. I want to go home.'

'Don't be silly. Come on, little girl, I like you. I have a present – here—' he took a packet from his pocket, and opened it. A bracelet flashed before her eyes. He held it out, again tried to hold her in his other arm.

Again she pulled away. 'No! No – I shall scream . . .'

He stared, puzzled, as she backed to the door. 'Then why did you come here?' he asked brutally. 'You know the sort of place it is.'

'No,' she whispered. 'No.'

'Oh come on.' Keith had been drinking too. He had come to the Gainsborough for 'sport', a bit of fun, as he was moving on next week. Confused, he lost his temper. 'You sit there, in that dress, pulling in the men for you and your raddled friend—'

Then she understood.

'Let me go!' she screamed. 'Let me go!' She unlocked the door and fled while he watched, as bewildered as she. Downstairs, past two waiters, staring . . . through the big room, more people staring, girls laughing . . . you know what sort of place it is – a glorified Red Cow.

Outside she said imperiously to the doorman: 'Get me a taxi,' summoning all Melbourne's teaching to her aid. Would anyone follow her? . . . No, into the taxi . . . home. Upstairs to the bathroom, shivering. *Your raddled friend.* Her mother. Her mother, who wouldn't let her play with the local girls because they weren't good enough, weren't little ladies . . . Roberta's world splintered.

She was in bed when her mother came in drunk. 'What were you playing at, you little fool?' Adela shouted, pulling the bedclothes away.

Roberta sat up. 'Mother, I – I can't. I'm sorry.' Why did she have to apologise?

'Little fool. We'd have been all right together, you and me. You and me ...' When her mother had gone Roberta was sick.

The next evening she was waiting for Martin when he left the factory at eight. 'Martin, I have to talk to you.'

He stared at her, her white face, her big staring eyes. 'All right, let's go somewhere. Here, in this little park. It's cold, though.'

Shivering, she told him.

He put his arms around her. 'Christ,' he said.

'I couldn't do that, Martin. I didn't know—' She broke off.

His arms tightened. What a mixture of innocence and passion she was. She really shouldn't be allowed out alone. She ought to have lived in Victoria Street next to Mrs Wilton, though not all *her* children approved of what she did, they said. But it was a bit thick her mother using her like that when she hadn't a clue ... But God, you'd only got to look at the woman to understand that's what she was. Aristocrat's daughter, was she? Oh well, they were often the worst.

Roberta was speaking. 'Mummy will never give her permission now,' she said.

'Don't worry,' he answered. 'There are other ways.'

Chapter 10

In Victoria Street, fragments of bombed buildings jutted out like jagged teeth. But on the ground, grass was already creeping gently over the wounds, healing, as it had healed other man-made scars. In the little gardens daffodils took the winds of March with beauty, forsythia flamed, primroses opened. Marged still grieved for her parents and brother, but she was only nineteen, and the burgeoning spring stirred a restlessness within her. Moreover, sitting with Brenda and Philip, so obviously engrossed with each other, made her feel uncomfortable – and lonely. Martin was always out, and there was nothing for her to do but sit alone listening to *It's That Man Again*, or Vera Lynn, the Forces' Sweetheart. She decided to go back to the dance.

The sound of music drifted out on the still air as she approached the Hall, and she hummed along with *Getting Sentimental Over You*, a trumpet solo, one of her favourite slow foxtrots that she used to dance with Ken Phillips. She wondered where he was now. She'd had one letter from France, then a card, and that was all.

She went up the stairs and into the cloakroom, where she took off her coat and looked critically at her reflection in the mirror. She'd bought a new dress, for clothes were not yet on points, and money was no problem now. She liked the flowered pattern, the way it fell to just below the knee, swirling in a flair, with a tie belt round the waist. She'd had her hair shampooed and set; it was drawn softly back from her face to fall in waves on her neck. She touched up her lips and walked into the hall.

And it was completely changed. There were two new girls in the centre now, different soldiers, different airmen; her old partners had disappeared. She saw two girls from Victoria Street, Betty Brown and Gladys Farmer, but they barely nodded to her. She knew why. Her status had changed. She was no longer one of them; she was the boss's secretary. Now they were in awe of her, even while they wondered how she'd got the job – 'She were only a factory worker.' She didn't mind the gossip, but her job set her apart even so. She went to sit on one of the chairs which ran round the hall, feeling, for the first time at the Co-op Hall, lonely.

And a voice said: 'Would you like to dance?'

She looked up and saw the Polish eagle pilot's badge even before she saw the name *Poland* on his Air Force uniform. She hesitated. It was bad form to refuse a partner; she and Corrie, with the arrogance of the top dancers, had done this against the rules. But she was no longer in the centre. She nodded and went on the floor.

It was a waltz, and to her surprise he was first-rate. She said, 'You're a good dancer.'

'Yes, I learned when I was a little boy.'

'You must have been a right little pansy,' she said mischievously, thinking he wouldn't understand, but he replied: 'It was part of my course in music.'

'I see.'

The first dance ended and she took a quick glance at him, noting the high cheekbones, the firm mouth, the clear grey eyes. The music started again and they waltzed in silence till he said: 'You're good, too. But you know that, don't you?'

She sighed. 'I used to dance a lot.'

When the waltz ended they walked to the side together, and she was quite content to stay with him. The music restarted, *Jealousy*, a tango. And it was grand to be dancing again with an accomplished partner, to slide slowly across the floor, to halt to the sound of clapping.

Then it was the interval and he asked: 'Do you want to go out? Have a drink?'

She hesitated. 'I'm not much for drinking.'

'Then let's go upstairs to the balcony and sit down.'

He offered her a cigarette and she said, 'So you're a musician.'

'I was.'

'Of course. What did you play?'

'Piano. I was planning to be a concert pianist.'

'Like Anton Walbrook in *Dangerous Moonlight*, where he plays the *Warsaw Concerto*.'

'And escapes from Warsaw to Rumania, then goes to America. My own experience was similar, up to the America bit. All the Poles I know who got away came to England to fight on.'

'I know, and most of them came to Chilverton.'

He smiled and she said idly, 'Tell me about your escape.'

He told her, about the flight to Rumania, the internment camp, the second escape in the train, then the journey to the Black Sea, on to Malta, Marseilles and Lyon, Cherbourg and finally, Plymouth.

When he stopped she was silent, and he looked down at her. 'I'm sorry,' she said.

'No need,' he said lightly.

Sorry for not knowing, for seeing all these strange faces and thinking of them in terms of how they could dance, when they'd all been through hell just to get here.

'What's your name?' she asked.

'Stefan Kowalski.'

'And you're an officer.'

'Flying Officer.'

So it was true, Polish officers did mix with the men. It made her think and wonder about other places. He was asking her name and when she told him he said, 'That's a nice name.'

He spoke English well, with an accent, of course. He tended to pronounce words like mother to rhyme with moth, and his gender had no neuter; tables and chairs became he or she, yet he was easy to understand. She asked: 'Did you learn English when you were a boy?'

'Yes. I always hoped to come to England. But not this way.'

'And your family?'

'I don't know. I wrote to them the minute I got to England, but I've had no reply. They were living where now Russia occupies.'

'And you don't think the Russians will go away'

'Poland was divided up before, you know,' he said. 'Between Russia, Austria and Germany. Your poet Tennyson wrote a poem about it. The Austrians weren't too bad, but in Poland we hate the Germans but we fear the Russians more. They are more deadly. They will not give way. You should remember that, your Mr Churchill. Stalin is so crafty.'

She shivered. 'Tell me about your home,' she invited. 'That's if you don't mind talking about your family.'

'I don't mind. We lived in a village, on a farm.' He looked down on the heads of the musicians just filing back. 'I can see it now, the river shining in the sun, the storks on the roof—'

'Storks?' she asked, amused.

'They built a nest on our barn; they used to come every year. Nearly all the houses had a couple. They'd arrive in about the middle of March – about now – and stay all summer. We never hurt them.'

'That must've been nice.'

'When they went away, there was a sight. They all

mustered together in a field, like an army, and then the next day off they'd go. It was lovely to see those storks flying. They got in perfect formation, in a great triangle, like it takes our chaps weeks to practise.'

She laughed, and he went on.

'There they'd go, big wings a-flapping, all off together, and the sun shining on the river, though we knew it wouldn't shine much longer. It was the end of summer when the storks went. My mother used to stand by the door ... we played down near the river when we were little, Stanislaw, Tadeusz, Janina and me. In the winter it would freeze over and we'd skate.'

'Were the winters very cold?' she asked.

'Yes, but we were prepared, you see. I feel the cold more here, in England. It is more—' He hesitated.

'Raw?' she asked. 'Damp? I've heard Scottish fellows say they're surprised how cold it is in the Midlands. They always think it's going to be warm down here.'

He said. 'My mother ... she was a good woman, never hurt a living soul.'

'I know,' Marged said. 'Mine too.'

'And?'

'My parents were killed in the Coventry blitz,' and now his hand was pressing hers. 'That's why I haven't been dancing for some time. We quarrelled, you see, and I left home. I was just a silly kid, and now my mother will never know how much I—really thought of her. It was all my fault. I'd been stopping out late—' She wondered fleetingly why she was telling him all this. 'We made it up. I went to see them – but I wasn't there when it happened. Maybe I could have saved them ...'

'You know it isn't your fault,' he told her. 'Any more than it's my fault that I left my mother and my family. Come,' he said. 'Let's dance again,' and they danced to the end, when he took her home.

When did she fall in love? Was it when he touched her,

put his arm around her? Did she feel his love for her, for he told her later that he'd loved her from the moment he first saw her. Or was it when he kissed her hand, and she was moved almost to tears. Because when he did that it made her feel like a woman, and no other man had ever made her feel quite like that.

You came, when the stars were gleaming. You came, after all my dreaming . . .

She met him again, and soon they were going together regularly. He kissed her, and she knew he wanted her, but he never tried to go any further. He took her home, kissed her goodnight, and left. He was so different from the others; she was puzzled.

Till the night they stood in the entry and it was quite dark. They were pressed together and she could feel his arousal. His hand moved beneath her coat, and she didn't stop him.

Then he pushed her away. 'No,' he said. 'We don't want to get too serious, do we?'

'No,' she said, tossing her head. 'We're just dancing partners.'

In May the daffodils had been replaced by pansies and tulips, the blackbirds were nesting in trees in the back gardens. She went to the dance with Stefan, and when she came home both Brenda and Philip were in bed. She made a cup of tea and Martin came in.

'Hallo, stranger,' she said.

'I'm not stopping, the sirens have gone.'

'Yes, I heard.'

'Well, get to the shelter. There's a lot coming over tonight. Call Brenda.' Martin dealt with Philip by ignoring him as much as possible.

Marged could hear the planes now, recognise the *gr-gr* of enemy engines, and she ran to the stairs. 'Brenda!' she called. 'Philip! Come on. Martin says it's bad tonight.'

They came down, yawning, just as a bomb dropped some distance away.

'Get Mrs Travers,' said Brenda, and Marged ran to their neighbour's door.

The old lady called her in. 'I can't come,' she quavered. 'I can't leave Spot.'

'What? The little dog?'

'He's so frightened, you see. As soon as he hears the sirens and the bangs. Look at him.' And she pointed to the poor animal, lying half under the sofa, trembling and whining. 'I can't leave him.'

Psss ... ooon ... crump. The familiar sound. 'You must, Mrs Travers. Won't he let you pick him up?'

But at her approach the little dog slid back underneath the sofa. Marged tried to get hold of his collar, but he was too far back.

Another crash. 'You must come, Mrs Travers. You'll have to leave him. He'll be all right.' And she pulled the protesting old lady to the shelter.

The night was almost a repetition of the Coventry blitz, almost but not quite, not so long, not so bad, but bad enough.

'What do they want here?' Marged wondered. 'There's nothing—'

'There's the aerodrome and the army camp,' said Brenda. 'And Mordant's.'

They crouched in the shelter, one hour, two hours, three ... Towards morning there was the familiar whine, the familiar explosion, the sound of falling masonry. 'Where's that?' asked Brenda. 'It was near.'

Philip looked out of the shelter. 'Farther up the road,' he told them. 'And I think our windows are broken.'

'Damn Hitler to hell,' said Marged. 'Just as we got the house straight.'

The All Clear went, and they stumbled out. 'I'll take you home,' Marged told Mrs Travers.

'Oh,' gasped the old lady. 'My windows – my doors!' The doors had been blown off. 'Spot,' she called. 'Where are you, Spot?'

They moved round the house, calling, upstairs and in the garden, but there was no sign of the dog.

Mrs Travers was crying. 'He's run away. Oh, where is he?'

'Hush, sit down,' said Marged. 'I'll make a cup of tea. Don't cry.'

'He's all I have, you see. No children, nobody . . .'

'He'll come back,' comforted Marged. 'Here's Bren. Ask Philip to look for Spot, will you, Bren? He's run away. Now, have this tea while I clean up the broken glass.'

'You want to get some sleep,' said Brenda.

'When we've found the dog.'

Philip and Brenda searched, but with no luck. In the end Marged had to leave the old lady to get ready for work. She walked down the road, past more damage, more casualties, and was glad there was nothing important going on at Mordant's. Yet there were few absentees; the factory was untouched, though the canteen lights failed at lunch-time and it wasn't easy eating in the dark, until someone brought hurricane lamps. Brian ordered extra tea for the whole factory in the afternoon and Marged was surprised and pleased at this touch of human sympathy. But she was glad when the day ended, for she was tired and depressed.

As she walked along Victoria Street she wondered if Mrs Travers' pet had turned up and went into her yard before entering her own. She saw a man standing in the kitchen, a dog in his arms, and she ran inside. 'He's back?' she asked.

'Yes, this kind man found him—' began Mrs Travers.

'I live over Canvey way, and he ran to my house. Poor little animal. Must have been terrified.'

Mrs Travers took the dog from him. 'My lovey,' she crooned, and Marged and the man went to the door.

'She won't do much good with him,' he said.

'What do you mean? He'll be all right when he's calmed down.'

'No, I've seen it happen before. I'm a farmer, so I know about animals. He won't recover. He's been shell-shocked, like the blokes in the army in the last war. It's better to have him put down.'

Mrs Travers was quietly weeping, the little dog in her arms, all she had to love ...

Marged, drained, returned home. She heard the knock on the front door, went to open it, saw the uniform ... 'Stefan!'

'Oh my love, are you all right? I came as soon as I could.'

She was in his arms, there on the doorway. 'I'm all right,' she said. 'Come in.'

She drew him into the front room. He was still holding her. 'Marged, I love you. I love you ... Nothing can keep us apart ... nothing ...'

Now they danced together every night and the world changed; it was softer, sweeter, colours rarer, music more poignant. *Deep in your eyes there is rapture*, sang the negro boy. *All the loveliness I have longed for*, and Marged felt that all the loveliness she had longed for was within her grasp. Marged and Stefan, dancing in a shabby hall surrounded by mean streets, with sirens wailing and guns booming, reached out to the stars and clasped them in both hands. It blotted out everything – the recent tragedy, Bren's boyfriend, Mordant's ... They danced. Sometimes the crowd, recognising perfection when they saw it, stood back and left them to dance alone, applauding at the end, moved by the artistry of the negro singer of sentimental ballads and the movement of the dancers.

Vera Lynn sang *Yours. Yours* ...

She took him on the bus to Coventry, proudly marked *City*, as always, and it was a brave sight seeing the big red bus driving to a city that wasn't there. They drove through streets and streets of rubble, fine shops smashed, in ruins, churches, hospitals, schools, hotels, houses, all splintered and battered. A shell of a shop with a sign outside: 'Come in at the back, we're more open than ever at the front.' A large van, all that was left of a multiple tailor's, an assistant inside, immaculate in morning suit, fitting a new overcoat on a man ... Stones lying upon stones and a robin singing in the rubble. They went to see the skeleton of the once beautiful cathedral, with the spire still pointing to the sky, and the two pieces of burnt wood making a cross, with the words *Father Forgive* ... And Stefan said sombrely: 'It reminds me of Warsaw.'

They walked over the fields and he laid her on the grass. He kissed her and she shivered with ecstasy. He said, 'You know I love you. I want us to be together for always.'

'You want me to go back to Poland with you?'

'Of course. We shall be free again. Churchill will see to that. He promised.'

'So what will you do? Go back to the farm?'

He hesitated. 'Oh no, I was studying music, I told you, in Warsaw before I joined the Air Force. You should see the wonderful Philharmonic Concert Hall ...'

Had he forgotten the bombing? She said, 'Tell me about Warsaw.'

'It was so elegant, with cavalry officers driving by in horse-drawn cabs, Paris fashions. Gipsy bands in the night-clubs. Then the Old City with cobbled alleys, the statue of Chopin in Lazienki Gardens, Chopin's music ...' His voice was wistful.

She knew she could never lose him. He kissed her again and she wound her arms round his neck. The trees rustled and she opened to him like one of the flowers in the garden, and then there was nothing but love in the silence of the dusk. Stefan knew how to make love, she thought fleetingly, how to arouse a girl. As his head sank on her breast, spent, she stroked his hair and kissed his cheek.

229

'We'll go back,' she said.

The raids continued ... still they loved and danced, and now the dancing fused into her love, giving her a double joy. Stefan was all around her and in her; she had no other being.

She took him home to meet the family; an important step, for when you took a chap to tea you were committed. And when he had gone Brenda asked, 'A foreigner? You're not serious, are you?'

'Foreigners are the same as us, you know. They don't have two heads or anything.'

'But if you marry him you'll lose your nationality. And what about religion? I suppose he's a Roman Catholic?'

Marged shrugged. These things were unimportant when you were young and in love.

'And what about when the war's over?' Brenda fussed. 'You won't go back there, will you? No,' she answered her own question. ''Course you won't. He'll stay here with you.'

''Course you won't go to Poland,' Martin echoed when she told him. 'You've got to stop for Mordant's.'

'Have I?' Marged asked. 'You said yourself I'll be thrown out when the war's over.'

'Yes, but by then—' Martin broke off.

'By then what?'

He didn't answer, and Marged was suddenly angry. It wasn't enough just to say he'd take over. He had to say how. Surely the best way would have been to take the Assistant Works Manager's job, and go on from there. But he didn't tell her his plans these days, and she was hurt at his defection. They had been such pals. And as always, hurt was assuaged by recalcitrance. Why should she tell him *her* plans?

But that would mean not telling anyone. Perhaps better so. Better they didn't know in the office – there were raised eyebrows there too at her affair. 'A foreigner?' they asked, delicately. Isn't an English boy good enough, they meant. 'And what about Brian Mordant?' the office whispered. As always Marged tossed her head. Let them think what they liked. All of them! And when Aunt Mary came down and asked what was all this about her going with a foreigner, she knew she wouldn't tell.

But what explanation would she give to Stefan?

With the advent of their electric fires it was possible to be alone, to sit in the front room without getting goose pimples. So when May brought blossoms and blue skies, but was still cold, she led Stefan through from the kitchen to the front, where she pointed him to the settee, the only furniture apart from one armchair and a bookcase in the corner. Yet it was a nice room, she thought, with its bay window, even if the view was only of the council houses opposite, council-built houses rather, of the same design, but built for sale not to rent, so the inhabitants were a little different.

'Come,' Stefan interrupted her reverie. 'Sit down beside me.'

She sat. 'Do you know, this settee was my mother's,' she began. 'When the bomb dropped at the back of the house, this was in the front – and it was blown right out, into a neighbour's garden. The men brought it here. Look, it's undamaged.'

He put his arm round her, drew her to him. 'Never mind,' he whispered. 'When the war's over . . .'

She drew away. 'Stefan, you won't mind if I don't tell the others yet that I'm going to Poland, will you?'

'No?' he asked uncertainly.

'You see, I thought it better to wait.'

She couldn't see his face, as her head was resting on his shoulder. He held her hand in his. 'You don't want to hurt them,' he said. 'Oh Marged, you are so good.'

'Good?' She almost jumped off the settee. 'What do you mean, good?'

'Good, kind, honourable.'

'Honourable? Oh Stefan, I'm not. Don't idealise me.'

'Idealise?' he asked, puzzled.

'Yes.' She sought to explain. 'You should be more cynical.'

'I don't know these words.' He took the little dictionary out of his pocket and began to turn the pages while she stood up and went to the window. The nights were drawing out now, more so with double summertime, but it would soon be time for the blackout, even so. Stefan looked up from his dictionary. 'You want me to be cynical?' he asked.

'*I* am,' she said. 'I have been since I was born, I think. You know, never really trusting anyone. Oh Stefan, never mind. Just don't think—' She broke off. *Think I am better than I am* ... She wanted to explain about her plans, Martin's plans, the whole story of Mordant's, and knew she couldn't. She wasn't sure that he'd approve.

Brenda popped her head round the door to say that she and Philip were leaving for work. Marged heard Martin come in, and went into the kitchen.

'Hallo,' she greeted him. 'I'll put your tea out. There's a bit of sausage in the oven – Brenda's well-in with the butcher. Stefan's here.'

'Is he?'

'Well, you might come and say hallo.'

'Might I?' He made no move, and Marged was annoyed. OK, so Martin was offhand, he was with Philip too, but it wasn't good enough. 'You make me mad,' she cried. 'Get your own meal then,' and she flounced away.

Yet Martin did talk to Stefan about planes. Stefan flew a Lancaster, though he never told them where he went, nor did Marged ever ask. She never discussed his flying; none of the girls talked about the war with the fellows they met. They joked with the Scottish regiments and asked what they wore under the kilt; when they saw a couple of soldiers in creased uniforms they laughingly told them they looked

232

as if they'd slept in them, and the soldiers said they had. That was all.

She heard the back door slam. So Martin had gone without his meal. Awkward so and so. She drew the black-out curtains and watched him walk down the street, then she moved away. 'Shall we go in the kitchen?' she asked. 'It's cosier somehow,' and she was filled with a terrible longing to be back in her old home kitchen, even though they had only one fire and they were all huddled in one room.

And when Stefan began kissing her, and would have gone further she pushed him away. 'No,' she said. 'Not here.'

'Why not here?' he asked, surprised.

'My mother wouldn't like it.'

'Your mother? But—'

'She's dead, I know. And if she were alive I'd be saying all the things I know you're thinking. What's the difference between making love outside and in the home.' She paused, trying to explain the thought of her mother's disapproval hanging over her. It would be like making love in church. 'No,' she resumed. 'It's not what the neighbours would say. It's just that – there are plenty of women taking men home to their beds. I expect many of your chaps are taking up the offers. The good-time women. I don't want to be called one of them. I mean, I wouldn't mind if I *were*, but with you – it's not like that.'

He looked uncomprehending and she muttered, 'It meant a lot to be respectable in Victoria Street. If you weren't respectable you got nowhere – you didn't get far if you were ...' And she ended to herself ... there's Brenda ... this house'll be like a knocking shop ... and she laughed, as she always laughed at the world.

In June 1941, Germany invaded Russia.

'I don't believe it,' Marged said at breakfast. 'First they

sign a pact, now this. I never know from one day to the next who's fighting who.'

'But it's saved us,' Martin put in sombrely. 'There'll be no invasion now.'

'No more bombing,' said Philip.

'Too late to save Mrs Travers' little dog,' Marged muttered bitterly. And Mam and Dad and all the others . . .

The press became pro-Russian, and Poland was forgotten. There were no more films with Anton Walbrook playing the *Warsaw Concerto*. Britain immediately declared support for the Soviet Union, and General Sikorski, the Polish Prime Minister, was forced to concur. And, thinking of the million Poles in prison camps in Siberia, he went to see Stalin to ask for their release. Stalin now needed the Poles on his side, so he agreed.

Many – not all – were released. The Polish Embassy was swamped with enquiries, the NKVD could not cope, so hundreds of thousands of released prisoners, undernourished, ragged and exhausted, began the long trek to try to get home. The worst sufferers were the children, living little skeletons, dying on the way.

Stefan confided to Marged. 'I am worried about my family. I asked the International Red Cross if they could trace them, but they tell me they cannot. There is no sign of them in the village where we lived.'

'Oh, Stefan—'

He sat, his face still, his eyes bleak, and she was filled with pity. 'If only I *knew*,' he whispered. 'We do hear tales of terrible things happening. They were good people. I can't bear to think . . .'

She put her arms around him, cradling him to her body. There was no sound in the room but for the occasional footfall in the street outside; the other three were all at work. Her pity strengthened, and her love, as she stroked his hair. She dismissed her resolve never to make love here. It was Brenda's home, after all, not her mother's, and

Stefan was so unhappy. She whispered, 'Let's go upstairs.' She stood up and held out her hand.

In her bedroom he turned to her almost desperately. 'My family must be dead,' he said.

'You'll find them after the war,' she comforted. 'We'll find them together.'

At first the underground in Warsaw consisted of large and small military organisations. But in 1941 they joined together to become the *Armia Krajowa*, the AK, of which Tadeusz was an active member. They held secret meetings, organised attacks on high-ranking German officers, and ran guerilla training centres for young boys and men. Tadeusz learned that those Poles who had been conscripted to work in German factories had carried out many successful acts of sabotage.

He himself was on radio transmitter duties, together with Bill Hale, a British sergeant who had been captured by the Germans, escaped, and fled to Warsaw, where he promptly joined the Home Army, and was – together with several other British men with similar stories – invaluable as a wireless operator. A radio apparatus had been smuggled into Warsaw in suitcases, Bill and Tadeusz put it together, and now from the top floor of his aunt's apartment, they broadcast to London and the world.

'You know what's funny?' asked Bill, in his heavily-accented Polish. 'How you get used to things.'

'You mean being in an occupied country?'

'Yeah. Or – no, the way we live. Underground. In more ways than one. Living in cellars – yet somehow it seems normal.' For below the apartment was a cellar, and a hole had been knocked through into the next cellar and so on. They endeavoured to continue life in this manner. Politicians held meetings in the cellars, underground tribunals passed sentence and meted out punishment – Poles who might be thought to betray them were killed – and underground universities and schools awarded degrees.

'It's a crazy way to live,' Bill went on. 'Yet it gets to seem normal. Or maybe I'm crazy.'

'You're not crazy.' Tadeusz liked the stocky, usually taciturn sergeant who said he came from Northumberland.

'Where is Northumberland?' Tadeusz had asked politely.

'It's on the north-east coast of England. We build ships there.'

'You worked in the shipyards?'

'I didn't have any work. That's why I joined the Army. Been in since 1935. Was in India before the war.'

'Oh.' Tadeusz, who had never travelled farther than Warsaw, was impressed. But he was impressed by England altogether. The country lived by faith in the Allies, in Churchill, Roosevelt and Sikorski. It rejoiced in Hitler's first defeats in the east and in Africa, and tried to forget the daily reality of arrests and executions, of death camps at Auschwitz and Majanek. Perhaps you had to forget, he ruminated. That's why you had to accept things as normal. Or you might really go crazy.

The Germans tried to force the hostile population to submit through the use of total terror, but this simply created the perfect underground movement. The Germans knew, of course, about the radio transmissions, the arms' drops, the sabotage and diversion. Occasionally they caught individuals and shot them, but the cause carried on, leaving the Gestapo helpless to stop it.

Already they were planning an uprising. 'I look forward to that,' said Bill.

'We're used to uprisings in Poland,' said Tadeusz a little bitterly.

'Yeah. There's something to be said for living on a little island in a rough sea,' said Bill. 'Though we were expecting Hitler to try to invade before he decided to go to Russia instead. Think he made a mistake there.'

Tadeusz was looking through the tiny window to the

street below. A patrol of German soldiers was marching. 'What's that?' he asked.

For the patrol had stopped before two Jews who were walking along the street. All Jews had been ordered by the Gestapo to wear white armbands, and now the patrol had grabbed the pair and were beating them with rubber truncheons.

'Christ,' muttered Bill, leaning over Tadeusz's shoulder. The Germans marched away, the men ran for cover. The Germans shouted, 'Get back to the ghetto.'

The Gestapo had recently put all the Jews in the ghetto and closed off the surrounding streets, building a wall around them with checkpoints and SS soldiers guarding them. Food was scarce and smugglers made fortunes. Tadeusz, appalled, reported this treatment of the Jews in his broadcasts to London, but he said to Bill, 'They don't seem to believe me.'

'No, well, who would?' asked Bill.

Now all they could do was to wait for their uprising, when the underground army would come to the fore, surging up from the cellars and sewers to fight the oppressor.

Stefan's mood changed from depression to an almost feverish gaiety. He was restless, and from dancing at the Co-op Hall every free night, he began to look farther afield. 'How about if we go to the Majestic?' he asked.

Marged grinned to herself. The place Roberta had once told her was exclusive. 'I'm going up in the world,' she chuckled to herself. 'Going out with an officer.' She wondered why Martin didn't hand out a few sarcastic jibes as he did with Philip. Was it because he didn't take her affair seriously? Or was it that he was full of his own problems?

She dressed with care. Clothes were put on points in June, but she had bought several dresses in the previous months, and when Brenda raised her eyebrows she retorted: 'Making up for the time when I didn't have any.' The time of free boots. Even now, the thought made her shudder.

Her dress tonight was aquamarine, plain, with a cowl neckline and flared skirt falling to just below the knee. It fitted her to perfection. She had her hair permed for the occasion and wore a short swagger coat.

Marged was curious about the Majestic, and she had to admit it was elegant, with a luxurious foyer. Though inside it wasn't a dance hall as she understood it, but little tables where people sat with drinks, and a small space in the centre. Social dancing this, no room for anything better. They were mostly officers there, including Polish officers. One of the Poles came over to them with his English girlfriend, and Stefan introduced him as Antoni Dabski, who had escaped with him from Rumania. They sat and he ordered drinks. 'I'll have a Martini,' said Marged; this was what they always drank in films.

They danced, and when they resumed their seats Stefan's gaiety seemed to have left him. She wondered if he were just tired. How long had he been flying? Too long, surely. She lived just two miles from the aerodrome, but the civilians knew nothing about what went on there. If there were any casualties they did not hear about them, nor did they particularly want to know. In wartime you accepted everything. Bombs, deaths became the way of life; sometimes she felt she'd known no other.

Then, as a couple entered the room, she sat up. A girl in a pale green dress that seemed to *flow* as she walked; a civilian with angry eyes. 'Look,' she hissed. 'Martin!'

'Your brother?'

'Yes.'

Stefan smiled. 'Why so surprised? You know he likes to dance, too.'

'Yes.' I'm surprised because he's with Roberta.

But if Martin saw them he didn't come over, and soon the pair left. Antoni and his girlfriend Denise came back. Marged danced with Antoni. Then they all sat and talked. There was an Anglo-Polish society starting up in Chilverton.

Denise told them. Would Marged like to join? Marged nodded abstractedly; all the time she was wondering about Martin. What was going on now? She wasn't sorry when they went home.

The next day, Sunday, she was working. The following week Martin was on nights, and somehow he managed to be either in bed or out when she was home. It wasn't till the Saturday, after she had finished work at half-past five, that she caught him alone. Brenda and Philip had gone shopping.'Quite a couple, aren't they?' Martin asked sarcastically.

'Well, we all have someone, don't we? You have Roberta.'

Martin was sitting at the table. Marged joined him and poured herself a cup of tea from the brown teapot. 'You are seeing her, aren't you?' she pursued.

His face assumed that shut-in look. 'So?'

'I saw you at the Majestic.'

'I know.'

'But Martin – Roberta Mordant.'

'I don't want to talk about it, Marged.'

'I know she always fancied you, but you're wasting your time if you think anything's going to come of it.' When he didn't speak she rushed on, 'You *don't* think so, do you? You don't think you're going to marry her, like in all the best stories? If you do, you're a bigger fool than I'd thought.'

'I said I don't want to talk about it.'

'I believe you do! Mart, her mother 'ud never let her marry you. Why, when we were kids she wouldn't let her play with the middle-class children in the town, let alone you. And remember when she turned us out of the house?'

'When she's twenty-one, Roberta can please herself.'

'Can she? That's what you think! I'll bet you a pound to a penny her mother'll stop it. Anyway, it's time you did talk about your plans. You're asking me to keep on at

239

Mordant's till you're ready to take over – well, maybe I will and maybe I won't. Maybe I won't hang around waiting for something that's not going to happen anyway. Maybe I'll go back to Poland.'

Too angry to stay, she left the table and went upstairs, even though she hadn't had her tea. And she didn't come down till she heard the back door slam.

Yet even in her anger the old feeling of pity resurfaced. Martin's father had refused to marry his mother because she wasn't good enough. Did he have to put himself in the same humiliating position? With the snobbiest family in Chilverton? What was the point? He'd only get hurt. She knew this as surely as she knew what day it was. Mama Mordant would never accept Martin in the family.

The summer passed into autumn, and gales blew the leaves from the trees. The Germans were advancing into Russia, but Stefan said coldly: 'They haven't encountered the Russian winter yet.' Now they stayed in more often, sitting in Brenda's warm kitchen, and Marged loved these evenings with Stefan, whether alone or not, knowing she belonged to him utterly, that the future was theirs.

In October, Stefan told her he was being posted. 'I'm grounded,' he said. 'They're not doing so much flying now.'

'And it's time you stood down. I'm glad. Though I wish you weren't going away. Where will you be, do you know?'

'On one of those windswept airfields in Scotland, miles away from anywhere,' he told her.

'Good. Miles away from all those pretty Scottish girls,' she smiled.

They were alone. Brenda and Philip were at work and Martin was out, as usual. Marged's face clouded as she thought of her brother. He said little to her these days.

Stefan drew her to him. 'It's the first time we've been apart,' he said.

'I know. How often shall I see you?'

'I'll get a forty-eight hour pass whenever I can.' He was kissing her.

'It's so far away,' she mourned.

His hands were holding her breasts, beneath her dress. 'Come,' she said. 'Let's go to my room.'

They made love slowly, lingeringly, then lay together, and she could feel the beating of his heart. 'Oh Stefan, I'll miss you,' she said.

'Me, too.'

He left at the end of October, and all the colour went out of life.

Now there was nothing but work. And the war had made things surprisingly easy for Marged. They just had to obey orders. In 1940, Lord Beaverbrook, Minister of Production, decreed that every manager of every plant should report in full at the end of each day on whatever shortages of materials and components were holding up production. Marged suggested to Brian that they really should put one man on this job.

'Yeah? But who?'

Mr Walters of Efficiency was the man who reported the factory doings, but it wasn't his full-time job as he dealt with Personnel, too. On the other hand, Mr James of Sales had little to do these days, as their sales were assured. Marged liked and trusted Mr James and wished she felt the same about the rest of the Board. Mr James was given the job – temporarily.

Now he was often in the office to report on shortages, if any, and she wondered sometimes how much he guessed about Brian, for his eyes held a knowing look.

In December there was a full Board meeting, just after the cheering news that British and Dominion troops, under General Wavell, had totally destroyed an Italian army in Egypt. There was cheering news all round. Mr James reported that they had done so well last week that production was up, and they had received a telegram of congratulation from Lord Beaverbrook which was to be pinned on the noticeboard in the works. 'To spur them on to greater efforts, I presume,' Mr Byers said sardonically.

'And I presume that's what we want,' snapped Marged.

Mr Byers mentioned the objectionable fact of a Communist holding a meeting outside the gate. 'He should be stopped,' he said.

'I don't think we have the power,' began Mr James.

'Do many attend the meetings?' asked Marged. 'They're in the dinner-hour, aren't they?'

'In the lunch-break, yes,' said Mr Byers pointedly, and at this Mr James raised his eyebrows comically so that Marged almost laughed. 'But very few attend the meetings, I'm glad to say.'

'Then let them get on with it,' Marged rejoined. 'Anyway, we're friends with Russia now, aren't we?'

'But Communists—'

'We don't know what will happen after the war—'

'Nothing, if we're careful,' retorted Marged. 'If we all play our part.' And now they'll think I'm a commie, she thought. Oh, why do they make me so mad? They're so hidebound, so conventional. She knew they thought she was taking too much on herself, and she suspected they'd like nothing better than to see her go. Indeed, Mr James almost warned her of this fact.

He came in with the production figures, saw she was alone, and hesitated: 'You know,' he began, 'some of the other managers don't always agree with you.'

'I do know. They're not likely to, are they? I'm on the other side.'

'Yes.' Again he hesitated. 'I know you mean well,' he went on, 'but perhaps it is better to be careful.'

'If I want to hang on to my job, you mean. But Bevan's made it illegal to sack anyone in war-work, you know, except for a very serious reason. Incidentally, I heard that some man was dismissed last week from the staff, supposedly because he was a bad worker, when this was not true. I'd like you to look into it. But quite apart from that, they have no power to sack me, Mr James.'

'No, but—'

'But there are other ways! All I'm trying to do is make this a decent place to work in, and yes, this means change.'

'I know: They know, too. And they'll fight you every way.'

'I'll watch my back,' she said with a grin. And, as he went to the door, 'I'm the girl from the back streets, remember? I know all about skulduggery. And about fighting. I'm used to it.'

Mr Walters was the next to call on her, and as he advanced, all smiles, she wondered what he was thinking. This man she didn't trust, and for no better reason than her own intuition. Most people, even the workers, thought him an extraordinarily nice bloke. If he tried to get rid of her it would never be openly. Now he told her that they could not get any ENSA concerts before Christmas for the canteen, and what did Mr Brian advise?

Brian said, 'Can't you get someone locally?'

'I can get someone,' Marged said. 'He was a pianist in Poland, and is serving with the Polish Air Force in the RAF. I'll write to him immediately.'

And Brian said, when Mr Walters had gone: 'So he's away, your friend?'

'You know he is.' It was impossible to work closely with one person and not talk to them, if only a little, about your private life. Not unless you hated them utterly, in which case there'd be no option but to leave. She did not hate Brian Mordant; she regarded him with a mixture of amused tolerance and dislike of his drinking, his weaknesses. Yet he had shown some good qualities, the time when he ordered tea for the workers after the raid, and the time when she'd been upset and he'd offered to take her home, not for his own ends but out of sympathy. But he still refused to admit his disability, and this irritated her.

He said now, 'You'll have to come out with me,' and she sighed. If only he'd stop pestering her.

'No,' she retorted.

'My father used to entertain quite a lot,' he told her. 'Maybe we should do that, too.'

'Not in wartime,' she said firmly, and he turned away.

She wrote to Stefan and he wrote back: *Of course I'd love to come. I think I can get leave for Christmas, so I'll write you as soon as I know.*

The occasion was a great success. These ENSA concerts were held in the works canteen, where a stage had been erected, and though the piano was hardly up to concert standards, under Stefan's skilful fingers it managed to give out wonderful ripples of sound. He finished with a medly of popular songs. *We'll Meet Again, Roll Out The Barrel, Bless 'Em All, Yours . . .*

Then they were back in Brenda's, for what Marged felt was the best Christmas she'd ever had. Philip had managed to get a small tree from somewhere, they had put up decorations left over from pre-war days. They all, Philip, Brenda, Stefan and Marged, listened to the wireless, hearing the King's speech. They had a good Christmas dinner, they toasted all those who were far away from home on this day, they listened to the Forces' Sweetheart, Vera Lynn, singing their favourite tunes. Martin was home for dinner, then he went out again, and Marged's eyes clouded as she watched him go. He was off to meet Roberta, she supposed. Couldn't he see that it would end in trouble?

Yet she was pleased when Martin offered Stefan his room, saying he'd sleep downstairs on the sofa, and wouldn't listen to Stefan's protests. 'I'll be out a lot, and coming in late, so I'd only disturb you. Take it and be thankful.' Was this an olive branch? You never knew with Martin.

But when she thanked him privately he grinned and said, 'I just didn't want him slipping into your bed—'

'Martin Fennel!'

'There's enough of that goes on with the other two,' he ended.

'You don't like Philip, do you?' she asked curiously.

'Thinks he's everybody. Raises the tone of the establishment, does he?'

'You're only jealous,' she taunted, 'cos he went to university and has his own business, interior decorator.'

'Interior decorator,' Martin scoffed. 'That's a sissyish job.'

'And that's a typical working-class remark,' Marged retorted. 'We'll never have a classless society while you look down on interior decorators.'

'Hark at Miss Fennel in the boss's office,' said Martin, who had an answer for everything. 'Who wants a classless society anyway?'

'Put some coal on the fire,' Marged ordered. 'I'll mash some tea.'

But Martin was brooding. 'What's he think he's doing, carrying on with our sister when he knows her husband's a prisoner? I never thought our Brenda'ud let herself be used like that.'

'But Martin,' Marged held up the big brown teapot, 'Brenda isn't *letting* herself be anything. Brenda is doing what she does of her own free will.'

Martin grunted.

'You sound so old-fashioned,' Marged went on. 'You fellows have your fun, why shouldn't we?'

'You know why.' Martin was grinning again, and Marged banged the teapot on the table, wishing it were his head.

But Martin seldom spoke to Brenda either, and although they had never been particularly friendly, Bren noticed his disapproval. Really, she thought, piqued, being a bad girl wasn't so easy after all, and she half-regretted her lost status. You had to go around telling lies, pretending at work that it was just for convenience that Philip lived at your house, knowing the neighbours gossiped, almost hearing the words. 'Them Fennels. Thought such a lot of themselves, and look at 'em now. Good job their mother's out of it.'

Brenda tried not to think of the future. Until the day after Boxing Day, when Marged had gone to the station with Stefan, and she was in the kitchen, peeling potatoes, and Philip came to stand beside her.

'Brenda,' he said. 'I have something to say.' Even in that he was different, *announcing* when he wanted to talk to you.

'Yes, Philip?' she asked.

'When we started this – thing – it didn't really mean anything, or so I told myself. I knew you were married, that you were a decent girl—' He broke off, turned, seemingly embarrassed, but the kitchen was too small and too narrow to take more than three steps, so he stood at her other side. 'But now it's changed, hasn't it, Brenda? I'm falling in love with you. I am in love with you. And I shouldn't. I keep telling myself that. But you see ... before ... it wouldn't have meant much. I played around a lot.' He faced her again. 'But *you* didn't, did you, Brenda? You're different.'

She still peeled the potatoes, letting them drop one by one into the pan. Outside, the Virginia creeper shivered in a breeze.

'Yes,' she said. 'I'm the sensible type.'

'Brenda. I love you.'

She did stop then, let the knife fall from her fingers.

'What are we going to do?' he asked.

'Oh, Philip. We're so different. I don't belong in your world.'

'The only reason you say that is because you never saw my world before – as I never saw yours. It's happening all over England, Brenda. Things'll change after the war, they'll have to.'

'Leave it now, Philip. Let's wait and see.'

'But you'll think about it, won't you?' and she nodded.

She hadn't wanted to tell Marged any of it, for even now the big sister attitude intruded. But on the Sunday afternoon when for once none of them was working, and Philip was in the back-kitchen using the long tin bath, she sat brooding by the fire. And Marged, her antennae picking up the many cross-currents swirling through the small house, asked: 'What's the matter, Bren?' So Brenda, looking into the fire, haltingly told her.

Marged sat down beside her. 'What are you going to do?'

'I've thought all along I'd go back to Jack when he comes home. That I'd have to go back, it's only right.'

'As if nothing had happened?'

'Well – yes, I suppose so.'

'But?' Marged prompted.

'But now I don't know. I thought this – this would be over, but it goes on ... The way he reads poetry to me ... I always liked poetry. Jack would never do that.'

'He really wants you to marry him?' Marged asked.

'Don't sound so surprised,' Brenda said, nettled. 'Yes, he does.'

'Well,' Marged nodded towards the back-kitchen, covering the uncomfortable moment with humour, 'he must love you to have a bath in there. Bet he has a bathroom at home. But Bren, what would you do? Stop here?'

'Oh no, of course not. We'd go back to Cambridge. Jack could have this house.'

'And you think you might do that?' Marged was incredulous.

'It would be an upheaval.' Brenda was still the big sister. 'What would you do – and Martin? Not that I worry about Martin. If he fell in the canal he wouldn't get wet.'

'You always had a down on Martin.'

'And you two were always thick as thieves.'

'Well, we're twins.'

Brenda snorted. But she said no more about the future.

The Germans advanced in Russia, had reached Moscow in October. The Japanese bombed Pearl Harbour, forcing America into the war. Britain and the US declared war on Japan, and the Japs invaded Burma and North Borneo; the British in Singapore surrendered. Thousands of GIs came to Britain, though few were in Chilverton, and the Co-op Hall hastily banned jitter-bugging which would ruin the floor. Not that that worried Marged, for she did not dance any more. She had found the perfect partner in Stefan, and until he came back she sat in home. Again there was a cold winter, with snow and ice, and with single summertime on the clocks, mornings were dark, and the buses were late.

Now there was nothing but work, and waiting for Stefan's leaves. *We'll meet again . . .*

February 1942 was cold. Patches of snow lay on the ground, frozen, dirty: spring seemed far away. An icy wind blew the gaunt trees into wavering skeletons and the office was chilly, even with the second electric fire Brian had purloined. Outside in the main office the staff wrapped themselves in woollies and found it difficult to type with numb fingers. Marged made her way to the Boardroom thankfully. This room was small and always warm.

The senior managers took their places, and Marged said: 'You remember that Mr Bevan made an order that firms with more than two hundred and fifty workers were to appoint Welfare Officers? We haven't so far.'

'Don't see the need,' grumbled Mr Byers. 'This fellow Bevan seems to want to mollycoddle the workers, all this talk of welfare and music while you work. Don't know what the country's coming to.'

'Well, we didn't comply with the order, so this morning we received a letter reminding us of the fact,' said Marged briskly. 'The letter also informs us that there are courses for these new Personnel Managers to attend – three months they run.' She looked up.

'What do we need a course for? To learn how to employ and dismiss workers? Waste of money!'

Marged privately thought that Mr Walters would do well to take a course on how to treat people, and how to treat workers as people. And he thought that once the war was over they'd go back to the old ways. If these new provisions were kept on, they would certainly not go back. 'I think we have no choice,' she said. 'Have you any suggestions for this post?'

No one did, and she knew why. At present Mr Walters combined dealing with workers with his other duties; employing another man would mean another salary. Mr Mordant certainly wouldn't have sanctioned it in the old days.

She thought again of Martin. This would be ideal for him, as a jumping-off post ... she'd tell him tonight. Aloud she said: 'Shall we think it over, and discuss the matter again? Now, is there any other business?'

They returned to their own offices. Brian yawned: 'God, these meetings bore me to death.'

'I had noticed,' she said drily.

'Well, I'm going out for an hour. I expect you'll manage without me for a time. You can sign the letters.'

'Yes.' M. Fennel, per pro Brian Mordant, Managing Director. The power behind the throne.

He moved to the door, then turned. 'When are you coming out with me?'

'Brian—'

'Well, I only asked. You haven't got anyone now.'

'I don't need anyone.'

'Oh come on, an attractive girl like you. Don't tell me you don't like it.'

'Oh go away,' she said. 'Leave me alone.'

He left, in no way abashed, and she looked down at her desk. Mrs Jennings brought in the letters, perfectly typed as always. Marged signed them, then opened her drawer where a book was concealed: *How Green Was My Valley*, the new bestseller.

She heard the commotion outside, closed the drawer. The office door burst open. 'I'm sorry, Miss Fennel,' apologised Mrs Jennings. 'She would come in.'

'She' was the factory nurse, from her surgery at the rear of the offices, where she tended to accidents and women who were taken ill. 'Where's Mr Brian?' she gasped.

'He had to go out. What's wrong? What is it?' Marged was on her feet, staring at the usually immaculate nurse, now dishevelled, her spotless overall covered with – was it blood?

'A girl – in the women's toilets. We've sent for an ambulance. She's dying.'

'*Dying*? What's the matter with her?'

'One of the women tried to do an abortion – with a knitting needle.'

They were outside now. 'In the toilet? My God! And who is the girl? One of the factory women?'

'No. It's—' The nurse stopped walking.

Marged stopped too, and a cold fear snaked round her heart. 'Well. Go on.'

'It's Miss Mordant.'

'Miss Mordant ... Roberta? In the women's toilets?'

'Yes.' They both started walking again. 'We had heard a rumour that one of the women did this. We didn't know it was in there, of course – so many girls with their husbands away get caught.'

Marged was running now, out into the yard, past clusters of men staring ... inside the factory, men and women talking in shocked groups, their faces alarmed ... into the factory women's toilets. ...

Roberta lay on the floor in a pool of blood. Marged wouldn't have thought it possible that one person could lose so much blood. Her clothes were disarranged, her skirts pulled high, her legs stretched below as though they belonged to someone else. Roberta, who always looked so well-groomed!

Marged knelt down beside her. 'Roberta,' she gasped.

Her eyes were staring. Then she said in a clear voice: 'I was always afraid of Mrs Stanway.'

'It's all right, Roberta. Don't try to talk—' She was elbowed aside as two ambulance workers knelt too.

'Roberta!' Marged cried. 'Roberta!'

One of the men stood up. 'She's dead,' he said.

She couldn't be dead, it was a nightmare, like the bombing of Mam's house. Marged stood in a corner as they carried her out and there was nothing now but the blood and the smell ... Marged breathed deeply. She wanted to be sick. Smelling salts were pressed to her nose, and a voice said: 'All right, Miss Fennel, come on now. Come outside.'

When she went back to the office she was fairly composed – outwardly, at least. And when Brian came in she was able to tell him. He was shocked, for though he hadn't been very close to his sister, he hadn't disliked her. 'But I didn't know she was expecting,' he said, stupidly.

'No.'

'I'm going home, Marged. Will you carry on?'

'Of course.' Marged had to carry on, though she was upset, too.

She said coldly to Mrs Jennings: 'Find the woman responsible if you can, and dismiss her immediately. I expect the police will be involved.'

'Yes, Miss Fennel.'

What a boss I'm getting to be, she thought drearily. But Roberta ... why? Why had she done this with a woman in the factory? Surely she could have found someone better if she had to have an abortion. Yet Roberta was so naïve in some ways – always had been. Not that she was much wiser herself. She'd always known that some women tried to 'get rid' of unwanted babies, usually married women with other boyfriends. She'd heard of them getting pills from the chemist, of drinking gin – but this? And what had Roberta meant, by saying she was afraid of Mrs Stanway? Who was Mrs Stanway? Wasn't she the housekeeper at Park Manor?

And there was another fear niggling at her. She had to get home, had to wait for Martin. Thank God Bren and Philip were on nights, so they'd be alone.

The wind was rising as she walked home; it blew flurries of sleet through the icy air, yet she didn't hurry. She wanted Bren and Philip to be gone when she arrived. She walked straight up to her room; waited for Martin. And when she heard him put his bike away she went down.

'Martin.'

He stood, wet and bedraggled before the electric fire, his hair falling over his forehead.

'You heard about Roberta?' she asked.

'Yes.'

Suddenly all her frozen calm left her, and she felt half-hysterical. 'It was yours, wasn't it?'

'Yes.'

'For God's sake, Martin, why didn't you marry her?'

He said nothing, and they stood there in the kitchen, like two actors in a bad play, blackout in place, no sound but for the wind. 'Is this the revenge you wanted? That she's dead? Oh God, it makes me heartsick,' a favourite phrase of her mother's came unbidden to her mind. Heartsick. *Heartsick*. Sick to the heart.

'Listen, Marged.' He moved at last. 'Shut up a minute, will you? I did want to marry her, but her mother wouldn't allow it.'

'What?' She was clasping the back of a chair. 'You mean you asked her?'

'Of course I asked her. I went to see that bloody woman who should never have been a mother. She refused point blank. I wasn't good enough. Roberta would have to go away and have the baby then get it adopted. I didn't know she was going to do this.'

'Oh Martin, I knew Mrs Mordant wouldn't let her marry you, whatever you might have planned—'

'Oh yes, I had it all planned. Right from the start. I was going to marry her and take over the factory. And the only way I could marry her was to get her pregnant. So I did.'

She was staring at him, little cold knots of fear coiling inside her.

'So you could say I killed her, couldn't you?'

'*Martin.*'

'Only you see, it's backfired on me. I loved her.'

'Oh my God.'

He sat down, but Marged couldn't rest. She looked at the empty fireplace. The electric fire was burning, and while they used this for convenience, they still liked to have a fire occasionally, though coal was rationed. She picked up the coal-scuttle to fetch coal – usually Martin's job – took a torch and went outside. The wind banged the door behind her and she walked across the yard, opened the coalhouse door, and again the wind took it and banged it shut so she had to prop it open. She shone the torch. The coal was in large lumps. She took the hammer and cracked them, filled the scuttle, then staggered back through the howling wind.

Martin hadn't moved. She lit the fire, watched it burn redly, then sat back on her heels. 'Martin, you didn't want her to die, of course you didn't. You didn't know she was going to do that. You wanted to marry her, you couldn't do any more.'

'I got her pregnant.'

'It takes two, Martin. She'd been going out with you for a long time. You didn't rape her.'

''Course I bloody didn't.' He sat unmoving, and there came a knock at the front door.

'I'll go,' Marged said.

She pulled the blackout curtain – a dyed blanket – over the door and opened it. And could smell the strong scent before she made out the figure of a woman in the darkness.

Adela Mordant. She saw the shape of a car in the background.

'Is this where Martin Fennel lives?'

'Yes.'

'I want to speak to him,' she said, imperiously.

'You'd better come in.' Marged led the way through to the kitchen. Martin turned, but he didn't stand up. Nor did Marged ask Mrs Mordant to sit down. Not yet. They waited.

'I've just come to tell you the police have been at my house,' she said. 'About my poor daughter. I told them that you were to blame.'

'What?'

'I wanted you to marry Roberta but you refused. You wanted this abortion. You know I'm against abortion.'

'You – *what?*' Martin was standing now.

'You're to blame for the whole business. I expect you arranged it all. You do work at the same place.

'But that's not true! You know it's not true! I wanted to marry her. We asked you—'

'I've never seen you before,' said Adela Mordant.

'Why, you lying—'

'Hush,' put in Marged. 'Don't make things worse.' She turned to Adela. 'Martin's telling the truth. He did want to marry her. Roberta was always running after him.'

'Well,' said Adela, 'it's his word against mine, isn't it? And I know who'll be believed.'

'You'd better go,' said Marged, and even in her pain and worry she found pleasure in saying this. 'Go on, out of my house.' She marched her to the front door, then returned. 'She can't do anything,' she said to Martin.

Except make things very unpleasant . . .

'I'm going to bed,' he said.

Marged made more tea; she didn't want to eat. She took Martin a cup but he refused to say any more. She went to bed, but she couldn't sleep; she lay awake listening to the howling wind, shivering, trying to warm the awful coldness deep inside her. Martin didn't carry out the abortion, so they couldn't do anything to him – could they? Never trust a Mordant, he'd said once. Why did they always have to make trouble for the Fennels? Why did Roberta have to do this stupid thing? Why?

She was down early in the morning before Brenda and Philip were back. The fire was out; nothing remained of the brightness but grey ash and an empty grate. She switched on the electric fire and Martin came in. He was dressed, but not in his overalls.

'Aren't you ready for work?' she asked him.

'I'm not going.'

'Well – all right. I'll tell them you're ill.' But she was worried. Martin was more upset about this than she'd thought possible.

He said, 'I'm not ill. I'm not going back.'

She stared.

'I'm going to join up.'

'But you're reserved.'

'Well, you can de-reserve me, can't you? It shouldn't be difficult, not at Mordant's.'

'But, Martin, wait! Don't go rushing off like this.'

He brushed her aside. 'Why not?'

'You didn't do what – what that woman said. So there's no need to run away.'

'I'm not running away,' he said. 'I've just had enough. Enough of Mordant's. I'm going to do my bit for King and Country.'

The door slammed, and there was nothing but the wind whistling in the chimney.

Chapter 11

When in 1944, Marged looked back at the preceding two years, she saw nothing but railways and trains. Meeting Stefan at the station, waiting on a platform filled with servicemen with their bags and their girls and their wives saying goodbye, or waiting, as she was, to welcome them on leave. Clouds of steam and hooting whistles as the train drew in, then the visit home ... Stefan sleeping in Martin's room, she creeping out every night, preserving the proprieties but everyone knowing now that he was her fiancé.

Then the return to the station, the waiting for the train, jam-packed with soldiers and servicemen huddled in corridors, asking, 'Have you got a light?' for matches were scarce, someone singing *That Lovely Weekend*.

Home again, and tears.

She heard occasionally from Martin, but he was a poor correspondent in the sense that he wrote only when he felt in the mood. He had been in Africa with the Desert Rats, and had written: *Did you hear about the victory at El Alamein? We're winning the war together, Monty and me. He's a great general. Even I like him, so you can imagine!!! He won't have any bullshit (spit and polish to you), walks round in a beret and tries to act as if he were a human being, one of the lads instead of a brass hat. But he doesn't wear a brass hat, just a beret.*

He never mentioned Roberta. Marged missed Martin, and sometimes she visited Roberta's grave. She had attended the funeral, representing the firm, and saw Adela Mordant there in black, stony-faced. No one could possibly know what she was feeling. Was there no guilt? The whole town had been shocked by the affair, but in the end little had been said about Martin. Nobody seemed to think he was in any way connected.

Nothing appeared in the papers, naturally, except a brief report about a woman being charged with carrying out an illegal abortion. Marged wondered why Adela Mordant had come to see them. Had she panicked? Thinking she'd be in trouble herself, and wanting to shift the blame to Martin?

Brian had seemed more bewildered than anything; unable to believe it. Marged wondered if she should tell him Martin was involved, but he didn't show any sign of wanting to know who the man was – as Martin would in his shoes – so she let well alone. The fact that Martin had joined up went practically unnoticed, especially on the managerial side, who knew little about the doings of the workers. Even Brenda hadn't guessed.

Marged thought she would miss his advice about the work, but this was easier now. Both she and Brian knew more than before; she had managed to get Mr Norris to the Board meetings – 'a temporary measure to help us'. Mr Norris had no particular axe to grind and he was willing to discuss and explain what was being done, with Brian, as the others were not. They guarded their own pieces of knowledge as if they were Secret Service men facing the Gestapo, Marged thought angrily, terrified of letting their colleagues know as much as they. Trying to keep Brian in the dark – oh, she rumbled their little game, though it was new to her and she thought nostalgically of Grant's, where everyone had been willing to help the others. But they managed without Martin, and gradually the scandal of Roberta died down.

Yet Marged felt a simmering anger that Martin had been banished – for that's how she saw it. If Adela Mordant hadn't called on them just when he was upset, he'd never have gone, of that she was sure. And had he finished with Mordant's now? Was that all over? And where did it leave her? She wished she knew more about why Roberta had done that terrible thing: there must be something they still didn't know.

She found some comfort in attending the funeral. At a proper burial like this, you could say goodbye, feel the person was gone, not like with poor John, missing believed killed, so you never really believed it. You wanted to *know*, to see his grave . . .

And ironically, she was to find out about John quite soon.

Joanie Farmer was one of the Victoria Street girls who did not treat Marged any differently whether she was the boss's Secretary or a factory worker, but then they said Joanie was not quite all there. She had worked at Grant's on the button machine, and now Grant's had gone she was, she said, 'on munitions' in Coventry, where she made the tea.

Joanie caught up with Marged one day as she walked home. 'I know somebody who knows about your John,' she told her.

Marged stopped dead. 'Who?'

'Well, our Gladys goes out with a soldier, an' his pal said he was with your John, in France. He was in a shed.'

This garbled tale set Marged's heart racing. 'Who is he?' she asked.

'Dunno his name. He just said.'

'Tell him to come and see me,' Marged commanded. 'You know where I live.'

'All right, I will, Marged. I'll tell him.'

A week went by and nothing happened. Marged thought

Joanie had got it wrong; she wasn't an exactly reliable source of information, and she tried to put it out of her mind. Till a knock came on the door and the young soldier stood there in the uniform of the Royal Warwicks.

He said: 'You are John Fennel's sister?'

'I am. Come in.'

He stepped inside, and she noticed how ill he looked. He took off his forage cap. 'It's bad news, I'm afraid.'

'He's – dead?'

'Yes.'

'You were there?'

'It was at Dunkirk. There were six of us, trying to get to the coast. The Germans got us. They didn't attempt to take us prisoner . . . took us to a shed, put us inside—' He broke off, shivering, and she said, 'Don't go on if it upsets you.'

'I'm all right. They put us in there and shot us, then set the shed on fire – it was brutal – we were prisoners. I – I escaped. I lay there with those dead men, pretending to be dead, till the Germans had gone.

And John was one of the dead. Well, at least they knew.

'Maybe I shouldn't have told you,' he said.

'No, it's better that we know.' And she felt a sudden upsurge of hate, that the Germans should do such a thing. 'They were responsible for so many deaths . . . Yes, let's bomb them hard. Let's get our own back!'

She told Brenda when she came home; Philip, tactfully, left them alone. 'I'm glad Mam didn't know,' Marged finished. 'Not about how he died.'

'Poor old John,' said Brenda. 'He was such a nice lad.'

Oh God, we often wonder why the best are the first to die . . . People put that in the newspaper, in the *Memoriam* notices.

They brooded awhile. 'I hope Mart will be all right,' Marged said. 'I wish he hadn't joined up.'

'Why did he?' asked Brenda.

Marged shrugged, saying nothing.

'So much for him going to take over Mordant's,' said Brenda caustically. 'He's left that to you, Marged.'

'I do try to persuade Brian to improve conditions,' Marged answered. 'I do try, Bren.'

'Yes, well, things will alter after the war, they'll have to. People won't go back to the old ways. And now there's this Beveridge Report on changes we'll be having. A free health service, allowances for children, no more poverty—'

'I didn't know you were interested in these things,' said Marged, astonished.

'Oh, I talk it over with Philip.'

'Philip? Is he interested in poverty, then?'

'Why shouldn't he be?'

'He's well off—'

'Lots of well-off people want a better deal for the poor.'

'Not the ones I know,' snorted Marged.

'Because you only know this little world. There's another world out there, and I—' she broke off.

'Yes, you?' Marged asked, suddenly alert. 'You're planning to enter that other world, aren't you, Bren? You're going with Philip.'

'I think I am.'

Marged said no more. She went into the front room and gazed out of the window at the ruins of her former home. Before the war they'd all have stayed here, living up the road, near to Mam, she and Brenda and John, all married locally, while Martin wouldn't have had a chance in hell of getting revenge on Mordant, and she wouldn't have been Brian's secretary. She saw that this was not only the end of the old ways, it was the end of an era.

As the weeks passed, she read the papers. The Germans had reached El Alamein, advanced in Russia, there was fierce fighting round Stalingrad. The Germans and Italians retreated in Egypt, still fierce fighting around Stalingrad. The Germans surrendered in Tunisia; the Red Army counter-attacked in Russia, Mussolini resigned. Italy surrendered, the Russians retook Smolensk. Italy declared war on Germany, the Eighth and Fifth Armies linked up in Italy. The Russians retook Kiev ...

But the press took little heed of the event that was to shape the world in the future. The Germans had dug up the bodies of ten thousand Polish officers at Katyn; these men had been taken prisoner by the Soviets, then shot through the head and thrown into pits. General Sikorski, head of the London Polish Government, asked the International Red Cross to investigate. Russia broke off diplomatic relations with Poland. Two months later, General Sikorski was killed in a plane crash, and things were in place for Stalin to set up his puppet Polish Government.

Britain was preparing for the second front; everyone knew it. And then the war would be over.

In February 1944, on a cold wet day, Stefan came on leave. 'I've been posted,' he told Marged. 'To the south of England.'

'Stefan – aren't they preparing for invasion down there?'

'Are they?'

'You know they are. They say it's like a vast armed camp. You're not going abroad, are you?'

'Yes, Marged, I hope to.'

'But Stefan, you're not flying now—'

'I am.'

'But I thought you didn't have to!'

'I volunteered.' And, as she made to protest: 'Of course I did. I can't just sit back *now*. The underground army in Warsaw is preparing for their uprising. They're waiting for the word to start. I have to be in at the finish.'

'Yes, I suppose so.' She hid her doubts. He was so excited about the coming liberation of Poland that she hadn't the heart to voice her misgivings.

'We'll soon be free,' he said excitedly. 'And then we can start our life together.'

Marged tried not to worry, yet she felt she had to see

Stefan again before he left. She wrote: *Remember when you asked if I'd go away with you for a weekend? Well, I'd like to. Can you find me a place to stay and I'll come down?*

He wrote that he could, and did. And on a summer-like day in May, Marged set off with a small suitcase for Sussex.

Stefan met her at the station and took her to a little olde-worlde pub. The sun shone on green lawns and massed flowers; their room had a pretty patterned wallpaper and latticed windows. 'It's beautiful here,' she murmured.

They went to bed early and as darkness fell, the scent of honeysuckle drifted through the open windows.

'Take your clothes off,' Stefan said softly. 'I've never seen you naked.'

No, even when she went to his room it had been a hurried affair, she thought, as she took off her clothes, and soon they'd be free to make love as and when they liked. She stood proud and unashamed. 'Take yours off then,' she commanded. 'Stefan – you have a lovely body.' *His legs are as pillars of marble, set upon sockets of fine gold. This is my beloved* . . .

Their love was daring, their passion deep. And for the first time they slept in each other's arms.

The landlady woke them with tea which she left outside the door. She knew they weren't married, but people were tolerant in wartime, especially with members of the forces.

Marged opened the curtains. 'It's a beautiful day,' she cried. 'Let's go to the seaside.'

He watched her lazily. 'The where?'

'The sea. It must be near here. Where's the nearest place?'

'There's Brighton.'

'Yes. Let's go to Brighton! Come on, Stefan, I've never been down south before.'

They ate breakfast alone in the small dining-room, and stepped into the sunshine to catch the bus. They chugged through the green lanes and pretty villages until the bus halted and a policeman boarded.

'All identity cards, please,' he ordered.

The passengers complied; they were used to this. Stefan showed his Air Force pass, Marged drew out her identity card. The policeman picked it up, studied it, and stared at her.

'*Warwickshire?*' he asked incredulously. 'How did you get here?'

'By train,' said Marged, flushing as the passengers craned round to see what was going on.

'And nobody stopped you?' The policeman was still incredulous.

'No.'

'You shouldn't be here. No civilians are allowed here now, except the ones who live in the area. Where were you going?'

'Brighton,' and Stefan added: 'She just came to see me for the weekend.'

'When are you going back?'

'Tomorrow.'

'Then my advice is to go back to where you're staying and lie low tonight. Tomorrow, first thing, get back home. If you'd been picked up in Brighton, they'd have likely put you in prison.'

They were put off the bus to the stares of the passengers, and had to walk all the way back to the pub. Stefan said, 'You hear that? Getting me put in prison. Leading me into bad ways,' and then they were laughing.

'They shouldn't have let me through,' Marged said finally. 'Nobody told me.' And they trudged on through the heat.

But that night was worth all the discomfort and embarrassment. They parted in the morning, and she left, waving bravely.

That lovely weekend ... She cried all the way home.

*

263

On 6 June, D-Day was announced on the wireless, and Marged trembled. She felt Stefan had been flying for too long. His luck was bound to run out.

On 23 June, the Russians, after their successes in the Crimea and entry into Rumania, now started an offensive on the Central Front, into Poland. Stefan wrote from France: *I am fine, but I wonder how they are getting on in Warsaw.*

Tadeusz and Bill Hale sat in the little room of the apartment in the road branching off Nowy Świat Street, where they'd moved when their organisation had enlarged.

There was a different atmosphere in Warsaw these days, an excitement in the air. People talked freely about the approaching Russian front, now advancing towards Warsaw. No one, as yet, worried about what would happen when the Russians came. The nightmare of Nazi terror and occupation would soon be over. Even Tadeusz did not think past a German retreat, and if his mother did, she kept silent. Every night Russian planes bombed the city. The Germans were leaving; a crisis was approaching.

The Soviet radio sent out messages to the Poles. 'Soon you must start fighting,' it said.

On 27 July, the mobilisation of thousands was proceeding almost openly under the eyes of the Germans. And they did nothing.

The Soviet radio repeated its message. 'Soon you must start fighting.'

'Hear that?' Bill Hale asked. 'They'll soon be here to liberate us.'

'Yes,' Tadeusz said.

'I know you don't like the Russkies, but if they get rid of the Germans—'

'Yes,' Tadeusz repeated. For five years they'd endured the nightmare of Nazi terror. 'I suppose Churchill will see we're all right.'

'You've got a touching faith in Churchill, old lad.'

'Of course – haven't you?'

'Oh aye, up to a point. He's won the war for us, but we didn't like him too much in peacetime, some of us, that is. But hey, forget that now. Your shift's over. Go and see your girl.'

'I am waiting for her.'

She entered as he spoke. Nina, the liaison girl who carried messages round the city from one cell to another. It was dangerous work, and all the more so because Nina was a Jew. To be out on the Warsaw streets in daylight took courage indeed. Tadeusz didn't know what had happened to her family; she didn't say and he didn't ask. You didn't ask questions like that in Warsaw, 1944. His aunt was a staunch member of the AK, his mother sheltered refugees. She had been asked to take in a young Jewish girl and had agreed, knowing that if the Nazis found out they would all be shot – probably tortured as well. Nina took off her white armband and slept in a cupboard.

Now on this sweltering day of 27 July, they stepped outside to see a German patrol in the street. Neither hesitated. To do so would be fatal. Both had forged papers – the AK specialised in forged documents; Nina did not wear the white armband of the Jew. The pair moved on slowly, and the patrol passed.

They entered the apartment, where Pani Kowalska was in the kitchen, cooking. She smiled and they went into the bedroom adjoining Nina's hiding place.

In the distance, Soviet guns were firing. Nearer to them, an exploding grenade shattered deafeningly. Tadeusz stood before the girl and said: 'I love you, Nina.'

She looked up at him, her dark eyes glowing. 'I love you too.'

'Let's get married.'

She smiled slowly. 'By a priest or a rabbi?'

He shrugged impatiently. 'What's it matter? We are

people, Nina, we are in love. The rising will start any day now. We've been lucky –' *lucky to stay alive* '– I know a chaplain who will marry us.' He took her in his arms. 'You are so beautiful. It will be legal,' he added.

She let her hand touch his face. 'Do you think I care about that?' she asked. 'You have brought me the only happiness I've known for four years.'

'Little love,' he whispered. 'Little sweetheart.'

They couldn't get married in church, as the priests would have to write a detailed report for the German authorities. Tadeusz felt God would understand.

The next day they were married by the field chaplain. The witnesses were Bill Hale and Maria Bilska. They spent their honeymoon in Tadeusz's little room, while the Russian planes bombarded the city and the Germans fired anti-aircraft guns.

The Soviet Army had reached the Vistula, and the next day, 28 July, the order was given for the mobilisation of the Home Army, and it was taking place almost openly. The Germans did nothing, and Tadeusz wondered why.

The city was like a barrel of dynamite. Waiting for the order to begin. Nina said, 'The British will help us when we start.'

'We have our own bomber squadrons in England,' Tadeusz told her. 'Stefan is there. Wouldn't it be wonderful if he flew here?'

Sunday, 30 July, and the Russian radio broadcast the appeal to start the fighting. *Our guns are firing*, the announcer said. *Take action now. Attacks on Germans are the duty of every Pole. Your sufferings will be over in a few days. Listen carefully and obediently to our authorities.*

Machine guns and rifles began to fire. Insurgents poured out of courtyards, running along the walls. Tadeusz put on his armband with the white and red letters, WP for *Wojsko Polskie*, the Polish Army, an eagle underneath.

Little flags sprouted from many windows. In the street

266

below, a captured armoured car appeared with the emblem of the Polish forces painted on it. People in the street stopped what they were doing and began to sing the hymn of the 1831 Polish rising against the Czar: *This is the day of blood and glory, May it be the day of victory*. And Tadeusz was filled with joy.

In the street German tanks turned into the narrow side streets and were trapped. Bottles filled with petrol and grenades were thrown down on them. In the next street the battle for the Hotel Victoria was being fought, the headquarters of Colonel Menter and his staff. From there he would command the rising all over the city. On top of the Prudential Building a huge red and white flag waved proudly.

Tadeusz tuned into London on the radio, and heard of the successful offensive in Normandy. Too soon to hear about us, he thought. Now in the streets barricades were erected, preventing German tanks from entering.

By 3 August, those spontaneously erected barricades had effectively blocked German tanks and armoured cars from penetrating into the city and operating there. Inside the area held by the Home Army there were pockets of resistance from which the Germans shelled the nearby streets and barricades. The rising had achieved its goal, two-thirds of the city was now in their hands. The Polish administration began functioning in the liberated areas and the main German communication lines had been cut. The Russians must hurry now.

German planes flew over, dropping incendiary bombs. The streets were crowded with people running from their burning buildings. The German artillery was trying to shoot down the Polish flag but did not succeed.

It was on 4 August that Tadeusz said: 'Listen!'

Bill asked, 'What is it?'

And Tadeusz said uneasily. 'The Russian artillery fire has stopped.'

He sat by the radio all day listening for London to

broadcast the news of the rising. In the afternoon he heard: 'This is the Polish radio in London,' and a brief announcement of the fighting in Warsaw. Nothing more, but he felt happier. Now the world knew. Now they would help them to freedom.

During the following days Tadeusz met another Britisher, called John, who transmitted dispatches to London. He reported that on the night of 13 August, a British drop of arms was to be expected. Signals on the roof were prepared. Suddenly searchlights cut the sky. 'Halifaxes!' Bill Hale exclaimed. The planes flew low over the city, lit up by the searchlights. One of them flew so low they could clearly see the Polish insignia on the fuselage and wings, and saw the dark oblong bundles drop out on to the roofs, and into the streets. They watched it go; it disappeared into the darkness, then suddenly there was an explosion, and they could see wings and fuselage scattering in all directions. Tadeusz crossed himself and murmured a prayer for the unknown airmen. But there were no more losses, and the boost to morale was powerful.

'Why the bloody hell don't the Soviets help them?' asked Bill. 'Why didn't they let the British planes land there? And why can't Soviet fighters take off from where they are, so close?' They could shell the German batteries that were reducing the city to ruins.

And John came in and said, 'I heard that the *London News Chronicle* wrote that the Russians had refused permission for British aircraft to land with supplies.'

Now doubts crept in. They could clearly see the Soviets, established on the left bank of the River Vistula. What were they waiting for? Why didn't they carry on, as they'd promised?

The Soviet armies sat on the bank of the river and waited.

And now the Soviet radio poured out abuse and invective towards them. Bill Hale put down his receiver. 'I don't like it,' he said. 'I don't like it at all.'

Radio London broadcast the news that Paris was liberated, and the Home Army sent them a message. *Honneur aux vaillants soldats de l'Armée de l'Intérieur de la France. Honneur aux héros de Paris. Vive la France! Vive la Pologne! Vive la Liberté.* It was recorded by the BBC and went out on Radio London to Paris, while Poland struggled for freedom, and wished the Polish squadrons in England could fly to help them as well as France. The Soviets still did nothing. They could see them clearly. So could the Germans.

'They're not going to come, are they?' Nina said heavily. 'The Soviets are not going to help us.'

'No,' Tadeusz replied. 'They are not. Not until the Germans have finished.' He took her hand. 'Nina . . .'

'I know, love,' she whispered. 'We stay together now.'

In the middle of August the Germans returned and positioned the heaviest guns in the world outside Warsaw and directed them on the city. Buildings hit by the 24-inch shells collapsed immediately, burying all the inhabitants. The Power Station was bombed, and fires raged all over the city. One huge shell from the monster guns hit the Philharmonic Concert Hall, burying a whole detachment of people in its cellars, all young, singing a song of the rising: *My Heart's in a Knapsack.* Tadeusz and Bill helped to dig them out; the corpses were naked, their clothes blown off by the blast.

In the last week of August the agony of the city began in earnest. The Commander was forced to move his headquarters to the centre, making his way there through the sewers, while all experienced forces were withdrawn from the centre to concentrate on attacking the German corridor from Saski Gardens across Iron Gate Square, which separated the old city from the main part of town. Women sappers blew a hole in the wall, but they could not get through it; German howitzer shells were falling on the hole and the courtyard beyond. Then grenades exploded amidst the waiting men

269

and women, and girls' voices cried out in fear. The scene was horribly floodlit by the flames showing a tangle of burning and wounded people.

A shell landed close to their apartment; the one next door was ablaze. 'We've got to move,' said Bill. 'Dismantle the apparatus.'

'Back to my aunt's,' said Tadeusz. 'Through the cellars.'

Feverishly they worked, for the flames were spreading. They ran down to the cellars, through the openings. Coughing, gasping, dragging the equipment, they finally reached their aunt's apartment, and Barbara Kowalska pulled them inside.

They worked all night, and in the morning they were finished.

And the Russians waited by the river.

Now incendiaries and high-explosive bombs rained down incessantly; fires started all around. A steady stream of refugees and wounded tried to move away and were shot by German snipers. Young girls carried reports or guided people through the sewers, Nina one of them. In the last weeks of Warsaw's agony they were the only channels of communication; highways for transport of ammunition, arms and food, evacuation of wounded, armed units. Manholes were always strongly guarded and people were pulled out exhausted, covered in black stinking mud.

Now every apartment house that had not been entirely ruined or burned out had to be ready to defend itself from fire or from enemy attack. Guards were posted in relays. Contact with the outside world was made through cellars and holes in the walls.

So the Poles in Warsaw fought and died at their barricades and cursed the Russians for doing nothing while the Germans crucified them. As the Germans advanced they methodically drove civilians into the courtyards, machine-gunned them and set fire to the buildings.

Tadeusz, Bill and Nina had fought in the streets with the

Army. Now, exhausted, they returned to their little room. Fires were raging all along the street; the Germans were approaching.

Tadeusz said: 'It's no use, Bill. The Soviets aren't coming. No one is coming. Why don't you go through the sewers? Escape?'

'Me?' asked Bill. 'No, I like it here.'

'Bill, we shall have to surrender. The city's in flames, we're being massacred.'

'I stay to the end,' said Bill stubbornly. 'What's our latest report?'

Hitler had ordered a complete razing of Warsaw, so that no settlement would rise there again. Systematically his troops crept along each street, driving people out, pouring petrol round the houses, burning them ...

The little apartment was a world on its own. Outside the blacked window, flashes of explosions lit up the room, shells shattered their eardrums. They knew the Germans were close, but in the din none of them heard the steps creeping up the stairs. Tadeusz tapped the radio. 'Help us,' he cried to the world. 'In the name of the four freedoms, help us.'

The German entered. Nina placed her arm round Tadeusz, and in a final gesture of defiance, put her white band back on her other arm. '*Jude*,' spat the German, and the machine gun rattled. Tadeusz and Nina lay in pools of blood before Bill Hale shot the German. 'Bugger off,' he said, and sank to his knees.

The world would not hear them again.

The Allied forces landed in Greece, the British entered Athens, the Americans disembarked in the Philippines, and on 17 January 1945, the Russians finally entered the ruin of Warsaw.

Mr Churchill paid tribute to the heroism of the Poles who suffered in the battle of Warsaw. *When the final*

*Allied victory is achieved the epic of Warsaw will not be
forgotten. It will remain a deathless memory for Poland
and for the friends of freedom all over the world.*

On 4 February, Churchill, Roosevelt and Stalin met at
Yalta, sat together and rearranged the frontiers of Poland,
giving a large slice in the east to Russia. Stalin smiled.
Marged read the news in dismay. That was where Stefan's
home was ... She decided to ask Philip what he thought.

Philip might have raised the tone of the establishment as
Martin had mocked; he certainly educated them. The
family were introduced to *The Times* in place of the *Daily
Express*, and would discuss matters of the day. Marged
found herself sympathising a little with Philip's father: he
had too good a brain to be an interior decorator, she
thought.

'What does this mean?' she asked him now, about
this 'partition' of Poland. 'The papers seem to think it's a
victory.'

'Except Michael Foot in the *Daily Herald*,' responded
Philip immediately. 'But what they've not told you is that
in the debate in the House of Commons, there were doubts
on all sides. Labour's Arthur Greenwood, for example said,
and I quote: "It is foreign to the principles of British
justice for the fate of a nation to be decided in its absence
and behind its back." Conservative Captain Graham said we
should stand up for juster treatment for our first and
martyred ally in the war.'

'But how do you know all this?' Marged asked, mystified.

'I have a friend who's a Member of Parliament. He has a
local constituency near here, and I meet him sometimes.
That's how I know,' and Marged was suitably impressed.

'America protested too,' Philip went on. 'There's a lot of
Polish Americans in Wisconsin, and their representative,
named Konski, said Roosevelt had talked about a free and
independent Poland, yet a hundred thousand Polish boys
could not go home without being sent to Siberia.'

'Stefan said Stalin would be too clever for us,' mused Marged.

'But what can we do?' asked Brenda. 'We can't fight the whole of Russia alone.'

'We stood alone once before,' Marged retorted.

'Not quite,' Philip told her gently. 'We had the Dominions, Australia, Canada, India, the Europeans who'd escaped, the Free French, Poles, Czechs, Dutch – all the rest.'

She understood. They couldn't take on the might of the Soviet Union. Not now. They were too war-weary, battle-scarred, tired. She wondered what Stefan would say.

He wrote in February, telling her he was being posted to England. The letter was brief, as were many of the others she'd received in the past months. No doubt he was too busy to write properly, Marged thought. But she worried.

Now he was coming on leave, and she desperately wanted to see him alone. Luckily Brenda and Philip would be on nights when he came. The train arrived at six in the evening, so they would have the house to themselves.

It had been another bitter, frozen winter, and there was still snow on the ground in March when she went to the station. She waited, as always, then when he alighted, ran to his arms. He was thinner, she thought. He looked white, strained. It was a long way to their house but they usually walked, arms entwined, enjoying each other's company. This time Stefan suggested the bus, where they both had to stand.

Once in the house, they were greeted by Brenda and Philip. 'We're just leaving,' said Brenda tactfully. 'There's a stew in the oven,' and she guided Philip out of the house.

'Are you all right, Stefan?' Marged asked. 'It's been so long.'

'Yes, I'm fine.' But as he took off his overcoat he winced and she said, alarmed: 'You're not all right, are you?'

'Just a little strain on my shoulder, that's all.' And she had to prise the story out of him, how they'd been shot

273

down, and how he'd managed to get the plane back to base, but the crash landing had wrenched his shoulder. His gunner had been killed.

He sat by the fire, the coal fire which she'd lit specially for him though fuel was very scarce, but he seemed remote, so she went to the back-kitchen and dished up the stew. He only toyed with his food, however. 'I ate before I came,' he said.

The nights were lighter now, the blackout lifted, and it was pleasant to sit in the darkening room without fear of angry shouts of 'Put that light out.' The fire burned bravely and she sat beside him, stroking his hand. 'What is it, Stefan?' she asked. 'You must tell me. Is it Warsaw?'

'You heard?'

'It was in the papers. Some of it, anyway. I expect you know more—'

He shrugged. 'It's over now. Warsaw has been massacred.'

Again she moved to take his hand, but he pulled it away. 'No, that's not all. It's this Yalta agreement! Have you heard about that?'

'Yes. The meeting of Churchill, Stalin and Roosevelt.'

'They decided to give Poland to Russia. Without asking us.'

'Not all of it—'

'Not all, just a good slice, the slice where my home is. That makes me a Soviet citizen! And do you think Stalin will leave it there? Oh no, you'll see. Already he's setting up his puppet governments, made up of men who were taken to Russia and forced to fight in the Soviet Army – or be shot like the officers at Katyn. And I know he's promised free elections, but there won't *be* any free elections. Not there. I warned you,' he ended savagely. 'I warned you about Stalin.'

She said timidly, 'I understand you'll be given a part of Germany in replacement—'

'But we don't want a part of Germany. We've had enough of Germans.'

Now she was silent. The fire burned redly; outside some children ran up the entry to see Mrs Travers.

'I didn't come before,' he went on, 'because we were talking about what to do.'

'So what do the other men say?'

'They're broken-hearted,' he said simply. 'All these years we've been fighting for freedom. We never collaborated, nor had any quislings ... Now we have nothing.'

There was a silence. 'What are we going to do?' she asked.

'Do?'

'About going to Warsaw.'

'I told you, Warsaw no longer exists. Hitler systematically destroyed it. Deliberately. Anyway, we can't go back or we shall be shot like those officers in Katyn.'

'Oh no.'

'Oh yes, Marged.'

She said, timid again: 'You can stay here, Stefan. In England.'

He did not speak, and they sat in silence. She had never seen him in this mood; she could not reach him. She tried, she talked, but he barely answered. Defeated, she took the dishes into the back-kitchen, washed up. 'I'm going to bed,' she said wearily.

He didn't answer, but as she was undressing the door opened and he came in. Without a word he took off his clothes, led her to the bed. He pulled her to him, and still in silence, began to make love, roughly, so that she almost cried out. And when it was over he turned away from her, as he never had before, and she lay awake in the darkness, dry-eyed, feeling his hurt, his pain. 'But you could have been more gentle, Stefan,' she whispered, and turned her face into the pillow.

He tried in the next few days, tried to be his old self, but his eyes were bleak and he didn't even attempt to make love to her again.

He went back to camp and she wondered about their future in England. What would he do? He'd find work – men said they weren't going to come back to dole queues as after the last war – but – as what? He had no training except as a musician, and of course his Air Force experience. But Marged, brought up in a hard school, knew that pilots would be ten a penny after the war ...

Mordant's!

What a blessing she hadn't said she was going to leave. For now she wasn't. And she still had her dream of making Mordant's an ideal place to work in. No doubt she could get him a job there.

She wished Martin would come back. She needed his help.

In April Marged knew she was pregnant: she felt sick in the mornings; she couldn't drink tea or smoke. It must have happened on that last leave, that last unhappy leave when he was so despondent. She knew he hadn't been careful as he'd always been, but she hadn't the heart to say anything. Once wouldn't matter, she told herself, and anyway, if it did, they could get married.

She hadn't told him yet, not wanting to write the news. She'd wait till she saw him. But she was pleased. This would settle all her problems; she didn't know how, but it would. Stefan would be happy about it. It might take away some of his sadness – he'd have something to look forward to. They'd find a house somewhere ... *where?* ... she had saved most of her pay, but she doubted if Stefan had very much, and they'd need such a lot. There was a terrific housing shortage, for apart from the bombing no new houses had been built for six years. That meant prices would go sky-high. And she'd have to stop work.

But she desperately wanted this baby, a son, a little Stefan. She'd work for as long as she could.

No, she wouldn't write, but she begged him to try to get leave for Victory Day, when it came. Everyone knew now it wouldn't be long. She visualised their meeting, her breaking the news, the double celebration . . .

Stefan wrote saying he'd come, but again the letter was lacklustre.

Victory in Europe Day was taken fairly quietly at first by the citizens of Victoria Street. They had had a long war; they were tired, they had to take stock, but at least they'd give the children a do. The blackouts were pulled down – then put back again as housewives realised they had no more curtains. By the late afternoon faces had lightened as the news really sank in, and people were laughing and singing.

Stefan was arriving on the five forty-five, and Marged was at the station an hour before the train was due. Of course it was late, trains were always late in wartime. She bought a platform ticket, and waited among the crowds of soldiers and happy wives and girlfriends and mothers all throwing their arms around Johnny and Jimmy and Bill, home at last. Some people had painted great WELCOME signs on their houses.

So many people coming and going, so many happy faces, children shouting, the shrieking whistles and escaping steam from the trains . . . where was Stefan?

The train chugged in, slowed, doors opened, bags were thrown on the ground . . . and there he was. She ran to his arms.

'Oh my love.' For a long moment he held her, and it was as if he couldn't let her go. Then he said: 'Come, let's have a cup of tea.'

'Oh Stefan, I have food waiting!' But he was already leading the way to the crowded little room with the buffet at one end, where she found a table, littered with used cups and plates, while he fetched tea.

He sat down and she said, 'Stefan, I have something to tell you. But I'll wait till we get home.'

277

'I have something to tell you too,' he said, and now his face was sombre.

She waited, sipping the tea in the thick white cup, trying not to grimace, not wanting to tell him yet the reason for her dislike. 'Well, go on,' she prompted.

He fingered his cup, and she noticed he wasn't drinking either. He said, 'I had a letter from my mother.'

'You did? You heard? They've traced her, then? How is she?'

He looked away, through the tiny window, then said, 'She moved to Warsaw, then had to move again. My brother Tadeusz was killed in the rising, my brother Stanislaw died in a German concentration camp. Janina was taken to Russia.'

'Oh Stefan, I'm so sorry.' How inadequate were words. *Sorry* ... for the death of a family.

He said, 'I can't stay here.'

'Well, let's go home.'

'No. Here in England. I have to go back.'

Now she just echoed his words, stupidly. 'Back ... but why?'

He didn't answer.

'Why?' she pressed. 'You want to see your mother?'

'I have to find Janina.'

'Janina? Your sister?'

'Janina is my wife.'

'Your—' She couldn't say the word. The tea she'd swallowed was making her feel physically sick, the noise deafened her. She just stared. He'd said Janina was his sister, hadn't he? No, he hadn't. He'd just talked about Stanislaw, Tadeusz and Janina ...

He was continuing in a dull flat voice. 'It wasn't a real marriage. We lived next door, and it seems my father had set his heart on joining the two farms – they should have picked Tadeusz really, he was the farmer, but he was too young, and my mother sent for me. It was 1939, we were

waiting for the Germans to invade, my father was dying ...
We didn't know the Soviets were going to invade, too, or we
needn't have bothered.'

He paused. The little café was getting more crowded,
more noisy, her head was throbbing.

'It was my father's dying wish,' he went on, knowing he
wasn't explaining how he felt the deep need to repay his
parents for their sacrifices, the way events were sweeping
their lives out of control, the Germans on the borders, soon
he might be killed ... 'We agreed,' he ended. 'But we also
agreed between ourselves that later we'd part if we met
someone else.'

'You mean – divorce? But you're a Catholic.'

'If I had to choose between the Church and you, I'd
choose you,' he said simply. 'If it makes you feel better, the
marriage was never consummated. It could have been
annulled.'

'So that's why you never wanted to marry here.' So many
girls had married Poles.

'They would have traced the marriage,' he said. The bit
of paper that meant nothing.

'But you said we were going back together?'

'Yes. I would have written to Janina, explained ... But
now, she's been taken to Siberia or somewhere. The Soviets
took one million Poles to Russia in 1939, then all those who
fought in Warsaw were sent to Siberia.'

'But, Stefan—'

He wasn't listening. 'I have to find her. You see, they
only took her because of me. She had a letter from me when
I reached England, so they took her away because she was
my wife.'

'But that wasn't your fault—'

'If she hadn't been married to me, they wouldn't have
taken her. I have to go back, have to find her.'

All around her people were laughing while in her head
thunder claps were banging so that she felt dizzy and sick.

All the songs about hearts breaking were true. Now the thunder claps had sunk to her heart and she was dying of it. Now all the crowds were distorted, laughing at her with crazy eyes and she had to escape ... she pushed the table back and ran to the door.

Railway stations. This is where dramas are carried out. Not in drawing-rooms or even bedrooms, but on draughty stations with the five forty-five coming in and people milling around with suitcases and bags.

She couldn't stand the crowds. She went to the ticket office, handed in her ticket. Stefan had to search for his warrant, so he was held up. She walked outside to the piece of waste ground which led to a bombed area, where grass and ragged robin already covered the rubble. Here she stood, drawing great, shuddering breaths. Here it was quiet.

When he rejoined her she had reached some measure of calm. She asked: 'Why didn't you tell me? Were you like all the others, just after one thing?'

'You know I wasn't. I love you. At first I tried not to be serious. Then I thought, it will be all right, Janina will divorce me ... I suppose I was mad.'

We were all mad in the war.

'I wouldn't go back now, I want to stay with you, but I can't leave her there.'

'But you'll never find her, Stefan. How can you?'

'I can try. I can't leave her, Marged. She's such a gentle, simple girl. I can't betray her.'

'No, there have been enough betrayals. But what about me?'

'You'll come through, Marged, you're strong. And you have your country.' He leaned forward. 'I'm sorry, I shouldn't sound so bitter.'

'Why not? You have a right.' *Only I get caught up in it, too.* She saw couples hurrying from the station, arm in arm. They were happy now, they had a lifetime before them ...

most of them, not all . . . some would never come back . . .
some came back to find their wives had left them . . . some
wives had been killed in the bombing . . . some came back
to other men's babies . . .

Babies.

If she told him, would he stay? Yes, perhaps. And regret
it? Would he always be thinking of that other girl, alone
somewhere, suffering . . . In the distance a firework exploded. VE Day. Who would think of Janina if Stefan
didn't?

And yet. 'She might be dead.' Her voice was calm.

'I know.'

She said, wretchedly, feeling ill: 'Let's go home,
Stefan. Brenda and Philip won't be in.' We arranged it
especially . . .

'No, Marged. I'm not coming with you.'

'Stefan.' She was pleading now and he put his hand out
to touch her face, held out both arms, then drew back. 'No,
I can't. I daren't. If I come . . . No, I must go.'

'*Now?*' It had to end here, on this railway station?

His voice was ragged. 'I can't stay with you. If I did—' If
I did I'd never go back. The words were unspoken but she
heard them, they hung on the air like great bells that have
tolled their doom. She thought, Why don't I persuade
him? Tell him . . . if he goes back, he's wasting his life.

As his brothers did . . . and his wife?

She walked back with him on to the platform. She didn't
get a platform ticket, she never thought of it, and the ticket
collector, who had seen many tragedies over the last few
years, saw her face and let her through.

'Six forty-five,' he said to Stefan. 'Train's coming in.'

Six forty-five. How many hours she'd waited for trains,
and now this one was on time, this one that would take Stefan
away from her for ever. They walked to the train; he got in.

She made one last, despairing cry. 'What about these
rumours that returning Poles will be shot?'

281

'That is a risk I'll have to take.'

She wanted to shout, to scream, 'Don't be so quixotic, don't be so high-minded,' and she knew this was the one thing she'd never quite understood about him, this quixotism, tilting at windmills – was it a Polish trait ...? Fighting, over the centuries, big bad giants to the east and west. She wanted to persuade him to stay with her and the baby.

She knew she couldn't.

He lifted her hand, kissed it. The train moved away. It was six forty-five. They'd been one hour together. One hour for her life to fall apart.

She didn't go straight home, but walked ... through the bomb damage, past the crowds still celebrating ... What was she going to do?

Get rid of it, like Roberta? Oh, God forbid! She wanted his baby.

Have the baby then ... How? Brenda was leaving. Jack would take over the house. There'd be no place for her, and things would be difficult enough for Brenda without the added problems of an illegitimate baby foisted on her and Philip. She mentally ran through her relatives. Aunt Mary, eldest daughter and child in back bedroom (turned out of their digs when baby expected, a legitimate baby), cousins Jack and Tom, when on leave sleeping in front room downstairs. Uncle Harry, house similarly full; Aunt Ann, still in the sanatorium. Overcrowding everywhere, housing shortage ... one councillor saying if you hear the tales I hear ... cases of incest because families are forced to sleep together, we need a massive building programme ... If only Martin were here, they could find somewhere together ...

What was she going to do?

Yes, she had some money saved, but even if she could find lodgings, could she afford to keep on paying for – how long? If she could find a room and someone to look after the baby, would Mordant's take her back? Or use this

282

chance to be rid of her ... oh yes, there'd be some rejoicing in the Boardroom when she left. They'd be able to get rid of Brian then. So where to work? Grant's had gone. Everywhere men were coming back; women wouldn't be needed. She was a partly-trained tailoress, a partly-trained secretary, with no home ... Where did girls go to have babies when they had no home?

There was only the workhouse. *They call it the institution now.*

It was nine o'clock when she returned to Victoria Street, having no idea of where she'd walked. Getting dark now, but still children were shouting in the street, people singing; somewhere a band was playing. Front doors were open, light streaming on to the road as it hadn't for years. The war was over. She reached the house, Brenda and Philip still out. She went straight up to her room, took off her clothes and lay down.

She didn't sleep. Her thoughts milled around in her head; shooting, darting, she couldn't control them ... What to do? ... Corrie. 'It's a battle ... it's us or them.' ... Mordant's had sacked her father for being ill. Remember the poverty? Mordant's ... Now the old fear rose in strength and the desire to be revenged. If Mordant's hadn't ruined their lives, she wouldn't be here now ... If Mordant's hadn't sent Martin away ... Mordant's were to blame, always Mordant's ... It's a battle ... What would I do with a baby? What would I live on?

She fell into an uneasy doze, and when she woke in the morning everything was clear in her mind as if she'd never struggled. Corrie could do it, so why shouldn't she? She needed a husband. Brian Mordant was waiting ... waiting for someone to take him over. The Fall of the House of Mordant.

She went down to breakfast and Brenda said, 'What's the matter, Marged? You do look ill.' Marged felt sick and was thankful that the lavatory was outside. She replied, 'Stefan's gone back. Don't say anything, Bren—' and was glad she hadn't told them of her plans.

They had two days' holiday. Brenda and Philip went into the front room, as much, Marged guessed, to talk over their own future as to show solicitude for her. She spent most of the day in her room and the next day she went to the office.

She began to look through the reports. Brian came in, late as usual, and greeted her. 'You look tired, like I feel.'

'Yes, I am tired,' she said.

He looked at her keenly. 'You need a holiday.'

'Yes, I think I do.'

He leaned forward. 'I say, how about coming away with me for a weekend?' His tone was light; he had asked her so many times, hadn't a hope of her accepting. He was surprised when she said, 'Maybe I will.'

'What?' He turned. 'Do you mean that?'

'Oh—' don't appear too eager, 'I don't know.'

He came to her desk. 'What about what's-his-name? The Pole.'

'He's gone back.'

'Ah, I told you he would. Never trust a foreigner. They're all the same.'

She said nothing.

'Hey. You're not upset, are you?'

'I shall miss him.' And that's an understatement, if you like. I don't know how I can go on living. Except for his baby. And for that I'd cheat and lie and steal, if necessary.

'I say, would you come with me to Scarborough?'

'Why not?' Try to be casual. All her life would be casual from now on. Nothing mattered any more.

She told Brenda she was going away with a friend from the office. Brenda looked sceptical, but was worrying too much about Jack to think about it. Jack would soon be coming home. 'Be careful,' she warned, big-sisterly, and Marged grimaced. Bit late for that.

She went with Brian to Scarborough, in the train, and

they stayed in a large hotel on the front, as Mr and Mrs Mordant. 'You don't need ration-books here,' he said. And he was quite pleasant. If only he didn't drink so much. At dinner he drank both before, during and after the meal, finishing off with a number of whiskies.

Their first night was merely something to be endured. He didn't take too long, that was one good thing. Her main memory was of his drink-laden breath, which made her feel sick. 'Hey,' he said. 'You're not very responsive. Don't tell me you never slept with that Pole. I thought those foreigners were supposed to be good at this sort of thing. If nothing else.'

She didn't answer, and he rolled away and in seconds was snoring. She lay beside him, patting her stomach. 'It's to protect you,' she whispered.

She slept towards morning then woke feeling quite dreadful. She ran to the little toilet and was violently sick. She sat for a moment, hardly able to breathe. Then the worry and fear and desperation overcame her and she began to cry and she couldn't stop. Long tearing sobs that shook her body.

She didn't see Brian in the doorway until he said, 'I say, whatever's the matter?' He sounded alarmed.

Still she couldn't stop; her body was racked with sobs. He put one hand on her arm and guided her back to the bedroom. 'You're ill,' he said. 'I heard you. Shall I get a doctor?'

'A doctor? No.' And because she felt so ill, the words that she had not meant to say burst out: 'I'm pregnant.'

He stared at her aghast, speechless. At last he managed feebly, 'Don't worry. You'll be all right.'

'All right? With nowhere to live? Do you hear me? I've got nowhere. My home was bombed, my sister's going away, my brother's in the Army, thanks to—' she caught herself in time. 'I'll have to go away, and they'll never have me back, all those snooty managers of yours. They'll be glad I've gone, then they'll get you out too.'

He was startled. He had never thought of Marged leaving. What would he do without her? If he let Marged go he'd have no one to help him in the office and things would get tough now the war was over. Brian knew he had the reading problem, the way the letters jumbled on the page so he couldn't understand them. His mother had called him a fool; his father hadn't had time to bother, was too impatient. His school had tried, but hadn't understood either. They thought he was backward. His schoolfellows laughed at him. He had to hand it to Marged, she had kept it to herself. If he let her go he'd have to find someone else, and he'd be worrying all the time she'd spread it around. Then he'd be at the mercy of the managers. Of course, he could sell the factory, but even that would mean reading documents ... and it wasn't the best time to sell, not now ... He'd be better to hang on to Marged.

But how? There was one way, of course. But did he want to marry her? She wasn't bad. And he had no one else in mind. Marrying was a problem he'd never quite faced up to because he was never quite honest with himself ... If he married one of the middle-class girls, he knew she'd find out about his – difficulty, then her parents would know and all their friends. They were all friends together ... the Round Table, Mordant's managers too ... Even now he skimmed over the problem, covering it with the thought that he was being noble.

He said, 'I could marry you.'

She stared at him, almost laughing hysterically at this twist to her plan. She said perversely: 'What would your mother say? Marrying a girl from the back streets?'

He frowned. No, Mamma wouldn't like it, but he didn't doubt Marged could stand up to her. She could be a hard little nut at times. And he couldn't afford to let her go.

He said loftily: 'You're not from the back streets now, you're my secretary. And a big help to me.'

I should be, I do all the bloody work.

He said: 'Roberta thought I should marry you.'

'*Roberta?*' A voice from the grave. And a feeling of inevitability came over her, that for better or worse she was tied to Mordant's, that all the other was a dream ... except for the baby. She asked: 'Don't you want to know whose child it is?'

'The child will be mine. That is one stipulation I make. No one must know any different. No one.'

She understood that, too. Brian was weak, lacking in confidence. He, above all men, could not stand being thought a cuckold. She said, 'All right, Brian, thank you. We will be married.'

She closed her eyes. She should be grateful, and she felt resentful that she had to feel grateful.

Chapter 12

Peace brought as many problems as war had. Britain had survived, but had sold her foreign assets and took on a crippling load of debt to the United States. Rationing grew more austere, and the spiv came into his own. There had been a black market during the war, but now 'spivvery' ranged from small fiddles by builders carrying out repairs without a licence, to the sales of practically any scarce commodity. Amazing bargains could be found by some people, including items looted from European battlefields. For necessities, queues grew longer. Meat, bacon, butter, cheese, tea, sugar and sweets rations were less than during the war, while the egg allowance was one a month.

Marged moved through the weeks feeling as though she were in a glass bowl, detached from reality. Just as happiness had painted the world in vivid colours, so now did unhappiness surround her with a sheet of dark glass, perhaps mercifully blocking out the jagged edges of life. Pain was submerged; she swam above it. Trouble either makes or breaks you, Grandma used to say, omitting to add that it didn't leave you untouched either way. Marged had changed. Something inside had hardened; her sense of fun became a sharper mockery. She pushed the pain away as she had with the bombing tragedy, trying not to think of Stefan, but only of his son to come. As for love, she'd have no more of it. She'd devote her life to good works like a Victorian heroine; in her case, improving the conditions at the factory. Faces from her childhood came back to her ... Mrs Jackson, with eleven children under sixteen ... Mrs West – 'Your mother gave me cakes.' ... Hungry faces. Well, they wouldn't go hungry again. She'd see to that.

The sense of unreality persisted all through the wedding ceremony, which took place within ten days. 'Better arrange it as quickly as possible,' she'd said when Brian asked her, on their return to the office. 'Quietly, no fuss. Isn't there such a thing as a special licence?'

'Yes. I'll get one. So, what day?'

'Oh – Tuesday week?'

'I'll see the vicar.'

Outside the office she could hear the rattle of Mrs Jennings's typewriter. There wouldn't be any rejoicing for Daphne Jennings; her husband had been drowned at sea. General rejoicing was so much worse for people who'd lost loved ones. Quickly, Marged switched her thoughts back to the wedding.

'Have you told your mother?' she asked Brian curiously.

'Er – no. Not yet.'

She turned to look at him. Fair hair, loose mouth, round face with typical English pink and white skin. Stefan's hair had been fair but his skin was darker ... *don't think about that.*

'You're not asking her to the wedding then?' she asked.

'Good Lord, no.'

He was scared, she decided. There would be a rumpus, no doubt. Well, she could deal with it, she supposed. If only she didn't feel so sick all the time ... surely morning sickness should be over at three months, and she was nearly that. She'd have to see a doctor. But get the wedding over first. And she still had to tell Brenda. She'd do that tonight.

It was drizzling with rain as she walked home, nodding to Mrs Littleton her neighbour on the left as she passed.

The Littleton family had recently been increased by the addition of a married daughter, her demobbed husband, a baby, and a gramophone, and the strains of *Lily Marlene* filtered through the walls. Marged switched on the electric fire, but pondered whether to make a cup of tea or wait till Brenda arrived. Their tea ration wouldn't go far now there were only two of them, and they liked to offer Mrs Travers a cup when they mashed. Heaven knew how she managed, an old lady alone.

Marged knew that all she had to do was ask the canteen supervisor to send her a couple of packets of tea 'for the office', but she hesitated. Not from any sense of moral superiority – everyone fiddled what they could in wartime – but she did feel that, as a boss, she could hardly stop workers from fiddling if she did the same thing. The boss had to be incorruptible. 'Incorruptible,' she said aloud, liking the sound of the word.

'What are you muttering about?' Brenda asked, bustling in.

'Just congratulating myself on being incorruptible,' Marged replied. 'As a boss should be.'

Brenda snorted. 'Not many bosses are,' she said tartly.

'I know, but if you are, then nothing can touch you. You're impregnable.'

'Here endeth the first lesson,' scoffed Brenda. 'Have you mashed the tea?'

'Making it now. Anyway, you're early.'

'Yes, well, I'm finishing this week. Gave my notice in.'

Marged put the kettle on. 'Glad?'

'Of course. No more nights. No more long days.'

'I thought you'd carry on a bit longer—'

'Till Jack came? No. I'll wait till I've seen him – won't be long now – then I can go to Philip.' She paused, as Marged poured water into the teapot. 'You can stay on here, you know, Marged.' Her brow creased into a worried frown. 'I haven't given enough thought to you – I mean, I expected you'd be with Stefan.'

'You don't have to worry about me,' Marged told her. 'I'm getting married.'

'You – *what?*'

Marged carried the teapot into the kitchen. 'I'm marrying Brian Mordant.'

She took the cups out of the cupboard, then returned to the pantry for the sugar. Brenda followed her into the back-kitchen. 'You can't be serious.'

'Yes, I am.' She took the sugar, went for the milk, and now Brenda waited in the kitchen. 'It's a week on Tuesday. And I'd like you to be my bridesmaid. Or witness, whatever it's called when there's no one else there.'

'Marged—' Brenda had taken the proffered cup, but she did not drink. 'Are you sure about this? I know Brian Mordant's been hanging after you, but you were so keen on Stefan. Supposing he came back? Or sent for you or something?'

'He's married, Bren.'

'Oh my God.'

'Look, it's not like you think. It was an arrangement to please their parents—' and as Brenda looked sceptical, 'he wouldn't have gone back but she, Janina's been taken to Russia, probably to Siberia.'

'Oh, the poor girl,' Brenda interrupted. 'How come we don't hear about these things?'

'Because Russia is our ally, so we have to love her,' said Marged drily. 'Anyway, Stefan wants to find her. He feels responsible.'

'And he thinks he *will?*'

'Leave it, Bren, I don't want to talk about it.' She walked to the window. The drizzle had turned to a heavy shower. The leaves of the Virginia creeper glistened in the gloom. A bird cheeped hopefully. The gramophone played *The White Cliffs of Dover*. 'Come on,' said Bren. 'Sit down. Drink your tea. I won't say any more.'

But that night, as Marged lay in bed, Brenda came in and

sat beside her. 'Look, Marged, you don't have to marry Brian Mordant. You can come and live with us. Philip isn't poor, he'll help you.'

'Bren, you've enough to cope with, with Jack, and Philip's parents, who don't sound as if they're over-fond of him as it is, without bringing poor relations into it. I'll be all right. Besides, I want Mordant's. I'm going to save it for Martin.'

'You should look out for yourself, never mind Martin.'

I am looking out for myself, and my baby. 'I'll be all right,' she repeated aloud. 'Why, I'll be rich, wearing fur coats and riding in cars—'

'Stop it, Marged.'

Marged turned her head away. *Don't say any more, Bren, please...*

Brenda stood up. 'Well, if your mind's made up. Goodnight.' She closed the door quietly, and Marged stuffed the blanket into her mouth.

The wedding was to take place at ten o'clock, and Marged dressed in one of her office suits, not even bothering to buy a new blouse. Brenda hovered in the background, looking as though she wanted to say more; only Marged's white, set face and forbidding expression prevented her. Brian's car drew up outside – taxis were unobtainable – and there was no crowd of well-wishers round the doorway. That would be another mark against her, she knew. You were expected to tell all your business in Victoria Street, or you were stuck-up. Well, let them think that. There'd be plenty of twitching curtains as they drove off, no doubt.

She put a suitcase in the car and it slid away. Two women walking by with empty baskets stopped to stare. Just fancy, they'd say when they knew, Marguerite Fennel marrying a rich man! Bet they had to get married. She read in the paper the other day how many illegitimate babies were being born now – and that war-workers in billets could be kicked out if they were pregnant. As if it were something new. There'd always been illegitimate babies –

look at Martin. She wished Martin were here now. She missed him, hadn't told him yet about Brian – or Stefan . . .

They were at the little church. Brian's best man was waiting – Marged didn't even know him. Inside, and the short ceremony passed in a blur. *Will you take this man to be your lawful wedded husband*? Why not?

Outside again, and now the sun was shining. No crowds, no confetti. She said to Brenda, 'We're going back to Park Manor, to get settled in. Do you want to come?'

'No, love, not now.'

'Then I'll say goodbye.'

And Brenda put her arms around her and for a moment the sheet of glass almost cracked as she held her big sister, the one who'd always been there . . . till now. 'What do you mean, goodbye?' Brenda asked robustly. 'I shall come over to see you, and you must come to see me.'

They clung together, then Marged pulled away. Brenda stood back, waved, tears in her eyes.

Brian drove them to Park Manor, and as she stepped out of the car, Marged took a good look at the place which, incredibly, would now be her home. A large square building, of no particular period, surrounded by trees which came right up to the path. Not a pretty house.

They entered the large hall where a figure stood waiting to greet them, a figure dressed in black, with iron-grey hair and a grim face. Mrs Stanway. What was it Roberta had said? 'I was always afraid of Mrs Stanway.' Marged could understand that: there was something about the woman she disliked, even at the first meeting, some malice in the narrowed eyes, the air of watchfulness which did not denote a pleasant character.

'Ah, Mrs Stanway,' Brian was saying. 'This is my wife.'

Mrs Stanway nodded. 'Lunch is waiting,' she said. 'Then afterwards I can show you round.' She looked at Marged but did not use her name.

Well, that figures, Marged thought irrepressibly. The housekeeper never does like the new wife in all the best fiction. The thought helped her. Gentleness she could not deal with at the moment; hostility she could fight.

The meal was served in the dining-room by an untidy young woman in a loose overall. Brian said little, and when it was over they went upstairs to the bedroom, which had been prepared for them. They both looked round uncomfortably, then Brian said in a would-be hearty tone: 'I say, I think I'll go out for a while. Got some fellows to see. One of the girls will unpack your things. You go down and tell Mrs Stanway.'

She looked round the room. Like the dining-room, it was furnished expensively but without taste, as if someone had ordered a suite of furniture, stuck it in the room and left it at that. As if they didn't care. Brian saw her gaze and said: 'Mother took away the furniture. It was hers.' And he went out, not attempting to kiss her.

Alone, she stood doubtfully, then went to the window. The trees were close, darkening the room, giving it an almost claustrophobic feel. She shivered.

Her wedding day. She thought of the girls in the factory, at the dances, in the office, how they'd all talked about their wedding day, every girl's dream, wearing white, having bridesmaids, then living happily ever after ... She'd dreamed it, too. Her knuckles turned white as she gripped the windowsill until pain forced her to stop and draw a breath.

She went down to speak to Mrs Stanway,

'You've seen the dining-room,' Mrs Stanway said. 'On this side is the ballroom—' and she opened another door leading off the hall.

'I've been here,' Marged said. It was smaller than she remembered. That was the door that led to the garden where Roberta had been with Martin, where she had stood while her mother ordered Marged out of the house. Now, sofas and chairs were scattered round the room. 'We use it as a drawing-room,' said Mrs Stanway.

They walked on. 'The library.' The housekeeper pointed but made no attempt to open the door, so Marged did, and looked over the books, many of them new, untouched. Fancy buying books and not reading them. Were they only for show? How her family had cherished the books they had, the Sunday-school prizes, the Christmas presents . . .

'And this,' said Mrs Stanway, 'is the morning-room.'

This was at the back of the house, on a bend, a little away from overhanging trees, and thus much lighter. In one corner was a window-seat. Marged thought it was the nicest room she'd seen so far. 'I think I'll have it for a sitting-room,' she said.

'Oh no,' Mrs Stanway contradicted. 'This is the morning-room.'

Marged raised her eyebrows. There was going to be a battle here and no mistake. 'From now on it's the sitting-room,' she said.

'Houses like this don't have sitting-rooms,' Mrs Stanway objected patronisingly.

'Then it's time they did,' returned Marged.

'Mrs Mordant always calls it the morning-room,' persisted Mrs Stanway.

Marged turned to survey her. 'You've been reading *Rebecca*, Mrs Stanway. *I* am Mrs Mordant, and if I want to call a room a sitting-room then I shall do just that. Now, show me the kitchen.'

The kitchen was large and old-fashioned, but contained a modern cooker and fridge. Marged took in these wonders then turned. 'And where's the staff?' she asked.

'We have a cook, Mrs Bannerman, who lives in. No doubt she's in her room now. The others—' Mrs Stanway sniffed. 'You can't get staff these days, they're all off to the factories. We have a woman comes in to clean and two other helpers who turn up when they feel like it.'

295

'How much do you pay them?'

'The cleaners? Half a crown an hour.'

'Double it. And get good workers.'

Mrs Stanway was aghast. 'Double it? But—'

'People earn more money now, Mrs Stanway. They won't work for peanuts any longer. Now, what do you do?'

'I? I am the housekeeper.'

'Yes, I know. But what do you do? Help the cleaners or what?'

'I do not clean,' said Mrs Stanway, affronted. 'I manage the staff.'

'But if you don't have many staff there's not much to manage, is there?' Marged asked. 'Now the bedrooms, please.'

They walked up the plain varnished stairs. Funny, in Victoria Street no stair-carpet meant you were poverty-stricken. Obviously there were different rules in Park Manor. Mrs Stanway's face was set in rigid disapproving lines – she'd have been ideal for the Gestapo, Marged thought as she was shown the six bedrooms and two bathrooms.

'Bit of a waste for two people,' she muttered. 'What's this room?'

'This was Miss Roberta's,' said Mrs Stanway.

Marged entered. Dark again, almost gloomy, with the usual set of furniture – bed, wardrobe, chest of drawers. A somehow colourless room as though all traces of its occupant had been erased. Nothing personal remained, no photographs, no pictures on the walls. There was a bureau under the window and Marged walked over to it. Was this where she'd made the awful decision that killed her? Poor Roberta.

She hadn't realised she'd spoken the last two words aloud until Mrs Stanway said disparagingly, 'Miss Roberta was always a silly girl.'

And Marged knew a sudden anger, and her dislike of this woman grew. 'You can go now,' she dismissed her.

Alone, she moved round the little room, remembering the child Roberta. 'Excuse me, where am I?' the words that had started it all. Dimly she recognised now, from her own pain, Roberta's loneliness. Even when she seemed to get so snobby, no doubt it was a form of compensation. Was that why she'd fallen for Martin, because she wanted someone to love her? She could understand her now, living in this dreary house with the awful Mrs Stanway.

She moved away, into the nearest bathroom. This was better. The white bath on squat legs, the clean towels. First thing I'll do is have a bath, she thought, and turned on the tap. The water was hot. Oh, bliss. Real hot water coming out of a tap. You could have a bath every night, not wait till Friday to put the copper on ...

Along the passage she saw stairs going to the attics, plain unvarnished stairs these, and she walked up. There were a number of doors along the landing, all open, showing tiny rooms with small beds having iron bedsteads. Only one door was closed; no doubt Mrs Bannerman the cook lived here. Marged knocked, anticipating her reception. Either it would be 'Oh, I know where you come from, don't expect me to bow and scrape to you,' or a fawning obsequiousness. A voice called, 'Come in.'

Mrs Bannerman chose the first option. She was sitting on the bed, reading a magazine, and she didn't rise. Marged grinned to herself. Mrs Bannerman knew her value. Cooks were worth their weight in gold these days.

Marged said, 'I'm just looking round. This room's a bit small. Like the ones I've been living in—' taking the wind out of Mrs Bannerman's sails.

'It's all right,' the woman said grudgingly.

Marged sat down on the one chair. The only other furniture was a chest of drawers with a mirror hanging by it. A strip of gaudy matting on the unpainted wooden floor. 'Are you alone in the world?' she asked. 'Is that why you live in?'

'Yes. Widow, no children.'

'So this is your home.' Marged was appalled. No wonder girls didn't like being in service. 'How would you like one of the rooms on the floor below? They're much bigger.' And they have carpets and are well furnished . . .

Mrs Bannerman was plainly startled. 'But they're guest-rooms.'

'I know. And empty.'

'But Mrs Mordant wouldn't allow it—' Mrs Bannerman broke off.

'I am Mrs Mordant,' said Marged. 'We could make an arrangement that if ever we fill the house with guests – which is unlikely – you could move back temporarily. But it seems such a waste to have all those empty rooms. How do you wash? Carry water upstairs?'

'Yes. Well – thank you, Mrs Mordant.'

'Where does Mrs Stanway sleep?' Marged asked curiously.

'Room off the kitchen.' Mrs Bannerman paused, then added as Marged went to the door, 'She won't like it, you know.'

'Like what?'

'Well, Mrs Mordant always let her run the house – gave her a free hand, you see. Let her do the arranging, an' all.'

'Well, if she doesn't like it she'll just have to lump it, won't she?' Marged asked pleasantly.

'Next thing,' Mrs Stanway was heard to mutter when she heard, 'she'll be bringing loads of people from Victoria Street to fill the empty rooms. It's not going to be like the old days with *her*.'

'She'll have to go,' Marged told Brian when they lay in the big bed.

He looked alarmed. 'Who? Mrs Stanway? Oh no, she's Mother's choice.'

'Well, your mother will have to take her then, won't she? I don't want her here.'

'But Marged, you can't sack a woman of her age! What would she do?'

'Oh come on, Brian, don't talk as if you're an aristocrat looking after his old retainers. You don't apply this rule to the factory, do you? If you want to look after her, shouldn't you provide her with a pension?'

'But Mother—'

'Don't be scared of your mother, Brian, she won't bite you.'

This annoyed him and he made a grab for her, kissing her wetly, so that she could smell his whisky-laden breath. She tried to turn away but he pulled her closer with a strength he didn't normally possess. His hands moved over her body, thrusting inside her, and she found herself – to her amazement – responding.

'That's better,' he said as he felt her move with him and, as she released her breath in a shuddering sigh. 'I always knew you were a hot little number.' Then he turned away and went to sleep and she thought how Stefan used to hold her close afterwards.

She lay awake in the darkness. What sort of girl was she? She didn't even like Brian very much, much less love him ... Still, this is what the magazines told you, wasn't it? Be nice to your husband, make sure you please him. *And in return you'll have a big house and plenty of money and a factory* ...

She wondered drearily why she felt more degraded than if she couldn't bear him to touch her.

On Sunday morning she wondered what to do. How did people occupy their time in a house where servants did all the work? She had another bath, luxuriating in the pleasure of getting hot water from turning on a tap. She didn't even have to arrange meals. Mrs Bannerman and, no doubt, Mrs Stanway saw to all that.

She had asked Brian after breakfast if he'd run her over

to Brenda's to fetch the rest of her clothes. 'When I come back,' he'd said. 'Just going to visit a friend.' She longed to see Brenda, but waited dutifully. He didn't return till twelve, so once Marged got to Victoria Street, she and Brenda had no time to talk. Brian was in a hurry now to get home to lunch.

On the way back he said, 'I'm going to have a party tonight.'

'Party? Who's coming?'

'Oh, friends of mine. I've just invited them.'

'Have you told Mrs Bannerman?'

'No. You can tell her now. That's your job.'

'But what sort of meal do you want? And can we get it without rations?'

'No, we can't,' Mrs Bannerman said flatly. 'Not at such short notice, though old Mr Mordant always got plenty of stuff from his friends. But I know Mr Brian's parties—' She sniffed. 'I'll prepare a few snacks if you like. I expect Mr Brian will have plenty of booze stashed away. He allus does.'

Marged didn't know any of the visitors, and as the evening progressed and she watched them, wasn't sure she wanted to. Some were still in uniform, some not, and as they drank more and more and their dancing grew more boisterous, she watched in amazement. One young man she recognised; he was a doctor. Fancy a doctor acting about like that! They were shouting, 'War's over. Now we can have fun.' One of the girls was taking off her blouse; another removed her stockings. Marged hadn't imagined the middle classes behaved like that. She'd thought they were all like Roberta, quiet, well-behaved. It just went to show . . .

Nor did they ignore her, but pressed her to join in the fun. 'Are you really married to Brian?' one girl asked. 'Fancy old Brian being married. Come on, have a drink.'

She didn't want to drink, she was pregnant, and she

watched in dismay as Brian drank more and more. 'Come on,' he shouted to her. 'Let yourself go.'

She felt ill and tired and slipping out, walked up to Roberta's room.

She felt she could be private here. She sat at the bureau and saw there was writing paper in the little shelves, so she pulled a sheet towards her and began to write to Martin.

She wondered what to say. *Dear Martin . . .* She hesitated. If only he were here she could confide in him as she always had – but could she write about Stefan? . . . She couldn't; the pain must not be allowed to surface. So what to say?

She began again. *Dear Martin.*

First she wrote a few lines asking how he was and when he would be demobbed, and giving the latest news. Brenda was waiting for Jack to come home; some of the prisoners had arrived already. Then Brenda would leave for Cambridge.

She paused again, looking out of the window at the heavy trees. Why didn't they have a real garden with lawns and flowers? Could she arrange it, find a gardener? If only she felt well . . .

She wrote: *This will surprise you. I married Brian Mordant yesterday. Stefan has gone back to Poland.*

Another pause. Should she tell him about the baby? In a letter read by censors? Or weren't they censored now the war was over? Even so she couldn't do it, couldn't put it all down on paper, couldn't find the words . . .

She ended: *Hope you are well. Love, Marged.*

Martin sat on his bunk with the Army in Germany. He quite liked the Army. You didn't have to think or worry, just do as you were told; it was a relief.

He hadn't left Chilverton because he was afraid of what Mrs Mordant would do or say as Marged thought, but for two quite different reasons. First, he was so shocked at what had happened – why hadn't Roberta told him? There was no need for her to do what she did. They could have found a solution, got permission from the Court, run away – though they'd have had to come back, it being wartime. Was she so afraid of her mother? What had Mrs Mordant said to her to make her do *that*?

And the second reason was that he was so angry with Mordant's – this time with Adela Mordant – he had to get away. He was afraid he'd do something violent to her if he stayed. But it all fuelled his hatred of Mordant's to an even greater pitch.

Once in the Army he simmered down somewhat as time passed. In the desert, fighting Rommel, private worries got left behind, or perhaps put into perspective. By the time he was in Italy, he wasn't even sure whether he loved Roberta, or whether it had just been a passionate affair.

So why hadn't he gone home for leave when he returned to England in 1943? His violent feelings had burned themselves out in the desert sands, leaving an emptiness he didn't know how to fill. What was there to go home for now? Brenda would be with Philip, and he didn't approve of that affair. Marged would be with Stefan. What was the point?

His letters to Marged were few and far between now. He supposed he was a bit tired of hearing about Stefan. Not that he begrudged Marged her happiness. They had always been so close. No, it was just that he wasn't much good at writing letters.

So he spent his leave in London, never telling the family he'd been back. He thought sometimes that Brenda suspected, but Marged said nothing. Well, as he said, she was so taken up with Stefan. D-Day, and they went through France . . .

Now he was in Germany, among the ruins. The Germans had surrendered and all he had to look forward to was going back to the ruins of his home. Then they'd all have to start rebuilding.

He lay back on his bunk on this pleasant evening in June, watching one of his mates slicking back his hair. 'Where you off?' Martin asked.

'To that dance hall. Coming with us?'

'It's out of bounds, no fraternising,' called another soldier from the bunk at the end.

'Pooh, nobody takes any notice of that. Anyway, it's not a dance hall, it's a brothel. Mart?'

'Can't be bothered.'

'Hey, look here lads, here's the post. What a time to come. Here, Mart, one for you, Pete, Jack ...'

Martin took the letter. It was from Marged. Suddenly a wave of homesickness swept over him. He'd give anything to be back with the family – with Marged. He wished he could talk to Marged, he missed her. Still, letters were the next best thing. He hoped it was nice and long. He'd settle down to a quiet read when these louts had gone out ...

He opened the letter. Quite short. Oh, well ...

He read: *I married Brian Mordant.*

He couldn't believe it! Brian Mordant ... and Marged. *Stefan's gone back* ... So the minute he'd gone she married Brian Mordant. That dumbo, that idiot, that ignorant lout who'd insulted her at his home ... how *could* she? His anger reasserted itself, and why shouldn't it? His sister, his confidante, marrying Brian Mordant ... God ...

He shouted: 'Hey, Pete, Bill, wait for me!' He crumpled the letter and threw it away, then ran to join his friends.

Brenda was informed that as soon as Jack landed he could come home for leave, then go back to be officially demobbed. She had written: *I shan't come to the station, Jack, I'll wait in home. Please – don't bring your mother. I want to see you first. And I won't pretend, Jack, it isn't going to be good news for us.*

She waited in the front room, looking out of the window, behind the green curtains that she and Marged had sewn and put up together. She glanced round the room. She had never managed to furnish it as she'd planned in those far-off days before the war, when the summit of her ambition was a three-piece suite in uncut moquette in beige or brown, serviceable colours to wear for years ... another world, another life.

Jack was coming. She watched him walk up the street, still in uniform, saw people stopping him with little cries: 'Jack, you're back ...' He reached the house and without a glance at the window, went round the back. He looked older; he was thinner, his face a yellowish-brown, and her heart was wrenched with pity as she walked into the kitchen. It was a hot day, doors and windows were open, the Little-tons' gramophone was playing *Goodnight Sweetheart* – some-one had sung that in a film she'd seen with Jack years ago. It had been very popular. He came in, took off his cap and battledress, but did not move to take her in his arms. He sat down.

'Do you want a cup of tea?' She asked evenly. 'I have the kettle boiling.'

'I see you've got an electric cooker.'

'Yes, I was earning good money in Coventry,' she evaded.

She poured the tea, placed his cup on the table close to him, then began, 'Jack—' but he forestalled her, putting his own hand over hers. 'Bren,' he muttered. 'Oh, Bren.'

'Jack,' she said. 'I have something to tell you.' Better get it over.

He sat back, releasing her hand. 'Go on.'

She stood up, closed the door, turned and said: 'I've – . met someone else.'

He was still, and she thought, Oh God, why do I have to hurt him when he's been a prisoner?

She forced herself to go on, and now the words came in a rush. 'I didn't know what to do, Jack. I went over it so many times. Lay awake, thinking ... At first I thought I'd give him up, try to carry on as before. Then I knew it would be wrong. He'd be unhappy, I'd be unhappy, and because of that I'd make you unhappy. I'd be thinking all the time I should have gone. I couldn't settle here now, so I'd come to resent you. Do you understand? Jack, I'm so sorry.'

He said dully, 'I knew.'

'You *knew*?' And she took a step towards him, no longer wanting to keep the distance between them. 'How?'

'Someone wrote and told me.'

'Your mother?'

'No. It was anonymous.'

'Oh, Jack. One of our friendly neighbours. Why didn't you tell me?'

'I dunno. Lots of chaps got letters like that. I thought maybe they were wrong, just trying to make trouble ... thought I'd wait and see ... It isn't like you, Bren.'

She moved away a little. 'I know. But what is like me? People don't always act the way you think they will, I've seen that. But why shouldn't I have a beautiful life too?'

The question hung in the air. A fly buzzed in the window. The gramophone was playing incongruously *The Umbrella Song*. Brenda sighed. She hated noise, always had, hated the clang and clatter of the factory, the coming home to more noise. She did not even like Victoria Street, though she never told anyone, but thought sometimes her mother had felt the same way. She wondered if it would be quiet in Cambridge. She expected it would. If you had money you could buy peace and quiet.

Jack was lighting a cigarette with shaking hands. 'He was a civvy, I suppose,' he said bitterly.

'It wasn't his fault. He's lame.'

Jack breathed out the smoke. 'Well, go on, tell me about him.'

'Jack you won't do anything—?' She sat at the table, leaned towards him.

'Like those blokes who come home and find their wives in bed with another man and shoot the two of them? No, I won't do that, Bren. At least you've told me to my face.'

'I felt I owed you that. And I know what you're asking, why did I fall for him? I can't tell you. He's an interior decorator and his family live in Cambridge.'

'You've met them?'

'Not yet.'

'Will they accept you?' His voice was harsh now.

'They're very tolerant.'

'I suppose,' Jack was bitter again, 'he can give you more than I can.'

Brenda's mood changed and she said sharply: 'Why must men always think that women can be bought? Yes, he had money, but that isn't why I fell for him. You know me better than that, Jack. He – opened a new world to me.'

He looked a little ashamed and for a moment didn't speak. He got to his feet and looked over the garden while she watched him. 'What's happened to the back field, all ploughed up?' he asked. 'And the bomb damage! God, I didn't know the place—' He broke off. 'I'm sorry about your parents, just when things were going right for them.'

He turned. 'It was waiting so long to get married that did it,' he stated. 'You had to support your family when you should have been having a family of your own. If you'd had several kids when I went things might have been different.' He looked at her. 'You haven't—'

'No, Jack.' She wondered if he might have felt better if she'd told him she'd had a child, forced the issue . . .

'So what do you want me to do?' he asked. 'Divorce you, I expect.'

'That would be best. Then you can marry again.'

'Huh!'

'You can have the house, of course.'

'I don't want the bloody house, I want you.' She saw to her horror that he was crying. 'Bren. I've been in that bloody prison for years, never seen a woman. Stay with me tonight, now. Just once more, Bren. Just once.' He dropped to his knees; his arms were around her, his face near, pleading. She stayed motionless and he pressed his head to her breast. 'It's not much to ask, is it?'

She paused, hesitated. It wasn't much, just once, but ... She asked. 'Would it be just once? Would you let me go, then?'

'I promise, Bren. Just once.'

'Will you be careful?'

'I'll be careful, Bren. Please.'

They went upstairs together, and he fell upon her like the starving man he was. And she realised sadly that it really was over between them. She wondered if he felt it too? Perhaps not this time, not yet. And afterwards he said dully: 'You can go now.'

'Jack – are you all right?'

'Yes. And I promise not to use this to cock up the divorce.'

Divorce, she thought, derisively. Men's definition of divorce: who a woman sleeps with. When will they learn that it means nothing? That's why she could do this now. It's who you *love* that counts, who you live with. And some of the guilt fell away.

She said, 'Goodbye, Jack, and thanks.' No use prolonging the agony. 'Will you go to your mother's now, she'll want to see you?' And he nodded.

She went downstairs with her cases, let herself out of the house, walked down to the station, past the twitching curtains, the neighbours who came to the gate in pretext of looking for someone, wanting to ask her about it, not daring, wondering why there hadn't been a big row that the whole street could enjoy ...

Next door, the gramophone ground to a halt.

Marged learned, even in the first few weeks, that marriage

to Brian was not going to be easy, that he did not regard
her as an equal partner, but a sort of mother figure with sex
thrown in. In any problem with the house, when she tried
to discuss a matter with him, it was either, 'Oh, you deal
with it,' or a stubborn argument, as about Mrs Stanway.
He brought his friends home regularly for drinking parties,
and he liked her to be there. If she made excuses that she
was tired, and went to bed, he would start an argument
when he came up later.

She did not feel well. The morning sickness persisted
but, having no one to talk to about it, she thought it was
normal. She had not visited a doctor yet. Brian insisted that
she book in at a private nursing home – no wife of his could
be seen in a public hospital, much less with a midwife.

But the hardest thing was dealing with the factory. She
had hoped that they might get closer after marriage, that
she could broach the subject of his 'problem', perhaps get
something done about it. But to her tentative approach he
merely said, 'What are you talking about?' and they carried
on as before.

He had asked, 'When do we tell the directors about us?'
and this irritated her too, that he left all the decisions to
her, yet pretended to be the big man.

And she'd replied, 'Wait till the next Board meeting,
then we can say – truthfully – that we've been married for
some time.'

The meeting went slowly at first. There were discussions
about government plans for manpower. 'Demob begins six
weeks after D-day. First out will be those in Class A.' Mr
Walters shuffled his papers. 'The Essential Works Order
remains.'

There was discussion about returning to car components,
when this could be done. And Mr James would have to
have his old job back on Sales. They would need a new
Personnel Manager.

Marged felt waves of nausea sweep over her. 'I think,'

she said, 'we can discuss this at a later meeting,' knowing full well it should be dealt with now, but wanting to pick her own man.

'We need a good man,' said Mr Byers. 'Personally, I think these ten-minute breaks for tea, morning and afternoons, should be dropped.'

'There was an article in a newspaper,' said Marged, blessing the fact that she'd seen this almost accidentally, 'saying that a worker could not do a job continuously for five hours without a falling-off in output.'

Mr Walters said meaningfully: 'I think, with all due respect Miss Fennel, we have been running the factory longer than you have – er – been a secretary.'

'That,' said Marged smoothly, 'leads me to the next point, not on the agenda. Brian?'

'Oh, ah, yes. We are married. This is Mrs Mordant.'

There was a silence. Marged studied the faces around the table. Mr Arnold impassive as ever. Mr James, broadly smiling. Mr Byers, chagrined, then covering with a smile. Mr Walters, the smile coming first, but not reaching his eyes, which did not meet hers.

'When did this happy event take place?' asked Mr Walters.

'Weeks ago,' replied Marged sweetly. 'We thought we'd wait for a full meeting before making the announcement.'

'A quiet wedding,' murmured Mr Byers significantly.

'Very quiet,' agreed Marged. 'There is – or was – a war on, you know. Food is still rationed. We might have a celebration later.'

'Why not at lunch-time?' asked Mr James. 'We can run over to the Golden Hind. I'm sure they'll find us a bottle of champagne under the counter.'

'What a good idea,' said the silent Mr Arnold, and Marged blessed Mr James for getting them over an awkward moment.

It made it easier too for her to announce to Mrs Jennings:

'Mr Mordant and I are married. Do get some cakes for the staff – if you can. Yes, we kept it a secret till now.'

There'd be talk, she knew. And the managers wouldn't be happy at all.

Brian's mother descended on them the next weekend with no warning. It was Sunday, lunch was over, Brian getting ready to go out. Marged was in her sitting-room, writing a few questions she intended to put to the applicants for the job of Personnel Manager, when one of the two maids knocked and entered. 'Lady to see you,' she said.

This was one of the aspects of life with servants that Marged could not get used to. It seemed such a waste for her to sit here, having heard the doorbell, while the girls had to walk from the kitchen to open the door. Marged could not shake off the habit of doing things for herself.

Her musings were interrupted. Mrs Mordant stood in the doorway. She wore a new coat, not utility, but smart blue edge-to-edge, showing a paler blue dress beneath. With her high heels and cigarette in a holder, she looked across between a fashionable modern and a throwback to the twenties. Her face was, as always, heavily made-up. Cosmetics might be scarce, but not for Adela Mordant.

She did not greet Marged, but turned. 'Girl,' she commanded, 'tell Mr Brian to come down at once. We'll go into the drawing-room,' and she swept out.

Marged pressed her lips together angrily, half-inclined to stay where she was. Then she stood up. Some people have to show good manners, she told herself, and walked towards the drawing-room.

When she entered, Brian and his mother were sitting together. Brian looked up uncomfortably but Mrs Mordant ignored her completely. She was talking about people she and Brian knew, but Marged didn't, and Marged recognised it as the old ploy to shut her out.

She sat on an armchair opposite the two of them and

waited, studying the large ornate fireplace, partially hidden by a black japanned screen, the red and white carpet square on the polished wooden floor, the heavy curtains. Then she said loudly, 'Brian, aren't you going to introduce me?'

'Why – why, yes. Mother, this is Marguerite – my wife.'

Mrs Mordant gave her a hard stare. 'We have met.'

'Why, so we have,' said Marged. 'It's a small world, isn't it? Would you like tea?'

'No thank you,' snapped Mrs Mordant. 'Not served by one of your maids if they're all like that slatternly person who opened the door—'

'And was hired by your housekeeper.' Marged had no intention of being browbeaten by this woman.

Mrs Mordant turned to Brian. 'Of course you know you've made a great mistake. But then you always were a fool.'

'He hasn't done me any favours in marrying me, Mrs Mordant,' Marged said cuttingly. 'If he didn't have my help to run the factory he'd have to close it down and get a job.'

'Pah.' Mrs Mordant stubbed out her cigarette on a gold-plated ashtray. 'You were determined to get the factory, weren't you? You and your conniving brother.'

'Your family ruined mine when I was a child,' Marged said. 'My brother and I swore we'd be revenged.' She stared coldly at the woman before her.

'So that's why you married my son. Some pathetic revenge from a pathetic little family in Victoria Street.'

'People in Victoria Street have long memories,' said Marged. 'You and yours would do well to remember it.'

Adela lit another cigarette and stared at her daughter-in-law through narrowed eyes. 'And is this part of your revenge, to change this house and the way we've lived for generations?'

'This house?'

'I hear you're already moving servants to guest-rooms.

What are you, a Communist? And what's all this about a *sitting*-room. These houses have morning-rooms. We all,' she declaimed, 'have certain standards, certain ways of doing things.'

'Who's we?' asked Marged.

'The aristocracy, of course.'

'Oh I see. I always thought the rich led funny lives,' said Marged. 'Now I know. They can't do as they please in their own houses. They have these rigid rules written on tablets of stone and they all have to obey. Well, I'm *nouveau* rich so I shall do as I please.'

Surprisingly, Adela Mordant smiled. She stood up, walked to the sideboard and stood surveying Marged. 'You've got spirit, I'll say that for you,' she said. 'Unlike my daughter. She was a poor thing. Took after her bourgeois father's family.'

Marged's mouth hardened. 'Don't talk about Roberta like that.'

'Why not? It's true.'

'You should have treated her better.'

'She should have stuck up for herself. People who don't, get trampled on.'

Marged's lip curled. 'You pride yourself on being an aristocrat,' she cried, 'and you call me conniving. You're conniving if you like, and a bully. A conniving bully.'

Mrs Mordant drew on the cigarette in the holder and smiled again through the smoke. 'Of course,' she said lazily. 'How do you think we got here in the first place?' She moved to go. 'You'd do well to remember that,' she ended.

'Me?' Marged echoed in surprise.

'You. You're on the up and up, aren't you? Don't try any of those Quaker ideals about doing good to your work-people – or anyone. Use your friends and then stamp on them—' and she went out with a little wave of her hand, leaving Marged fuming. She was absolutely impervious to any insult.

But of course she could be. Her position was unassailable. Adela Mordant could afford to be as rude as she liked.

But Adela's words started the biggest row she and Brian had had so far. There had been arguments, but this was more serious.

When she had gone Marged said, 'Well, now you know it's true what I said about Mrs Stanway.'

'What?' He didn't appear to be listening.

'Obviously someone told your mother about all my doings in the house, and who else could it be?'

Brian said, 'What about the factory?'

'The factory?'

'Is that why you married me, to get your revenge?'

She hesitated. Brian didn't know about Roberta and Martin and she saw no point in raising the matter now. She said lamely, 'You know why I married you, Brian. But yes, it was true about my father, you know that too. As for revenge, all I want to do is make things better, so that sort of thing never happens again. I told you—'

He said angrily, 'You didn't tell me that was why you wanted to marry me!'

'But Brian it wasn't, exactly.'

'I feel I can't believe anything you say any more.'

'But I didn't lie to you, what do you mean? It's true about the baby—'

'All your talk,' he said. 'About making a home, about love—'

She stared, trying to think what she had said about making a home, or about love, and could remember nothing. He was talking as if the baby were his, as if she had pretended she loved him . . .

He carried on in the same vein, and she did not know how to answer. Did he really believe that she'd said she loved him? Did Brian just believe what he wanted to believe, and if so, how could she argue with him when he never kept to the point?

313

He carried on until she was exhausted, and even when he finally went out the matter was never dropped. It was brought up in every future argument. 'You only married me for the factory,' he would shout, and what was worse, he began staying away from the office.

She tried to see his point of view. It was true in one sense; the factory was part of the reason she'd married him. But to play the role of the injured husband finding out his wife no longer loved him seemed to her absurd. Her direct way of thinking could not fathom Brian's self-deceit; they could not even argue and make sense.

Marged tried not to think about Stefan as she had promised herself, but it wasn't easy as she lay in bed beside Brian. It was quiet in Park Manor and she liked that. Liked walking along the tree-lined Park Manor Road with its neat houses set well back, but she missed the street, having no one to chat to, not so much over the garden fence but coming home from work, walking to the shop, stopping to hear the latest gossip. She supposed wryly that she was the latest subject of gossip now.

But if she didn't think about Stefan she did think about the baby. She knew it would be a boy, the image of his father, and she would name him either Frank or John – she dared not use Stephen. She furnished the end bedroom – the one over her sitting-room – as a nursery, with a blue cot, pale blue washed walls, and pretty curtains. It was a large room with a fireplace, and though there was an electric fire she thought a coal fire would be more cheery.

One advantage of being well off was that they had a phone, as did Brenda, so they could talk to each other whenever they desired.

'Tell me about your life,' Marged commanded. 'How is Cambridge? How are the parents?'

'Cambridge is wonderful, I love it here. And the parents like me. They're very liberal. You see, what they had against Philip was that they thought him airy-fairy. They think I'm not.'

'I see. Down-to-earth Bren.'

Brenda chuckled. 'Yes, the sturdy peasant, the salt of the earth. It's a bit patronising, but if it makes them happy . . .'

'And do you live with them?'

'Oh no, we have an apartment. Philip's work's a bit scarce at the moment, can't get materials yet, but it will improve. There'll be a big housing programme starting soon, and everyone will want decorators. When the election's over. But how are things with you?'

'Oh, so so. I don't like Mrs Stanway.'

'Then sack her.'

'Brian doesn't want to. And she is over fifty. But there's something about her . . . I don't know, she gives me the creeps.'

'Then she'll have to go,' Brenda said decisively. 'If it's making you miserable, you can't afford to keep her on, can you?'

It was true that Mrs Stanway did make Marged miserable. There was something about the woman, her watchfulness, that was disconcerting, even, if you were fanciful, frightening. As if she were waiting for her to make some big mistake, then she would pounce.

Or, Marged ruminated, she would report to Adela, and Adela would pounce. Marged didn't fool herself that she and Brian would ever make a love match, but she had hoped they could get along together, work together – but his mother wouldn't want that. She'd wreck the marriage out of spite, aided by Mrs Stanway.

Marged did think Adela had been right on one point: the maids they had were useless. She had increased their pay, but still they came in late and did as little work as possible. The rooms were seldom dusted; even the dishes never appeared quite clean. Knowing Mrs Stanway's standards, Marged came to the conclusion that either she did not try to get the best out of these workers, or attempt to get others. Having slovenly maids would be another nail in Marged's coffin. *The place is getting like a slum*, Adela would say. On the morning Marged went into the dining-room to find last night's dishes still on the table she decided to take matters into her own hands. When she left the office she went to Victoria Street.

It was a clear evening. The children were congregating round the corner shop, younger ones running and shouting. She pushed open the rickety gate of the Wests' house and Mrs West herself came out of the back door. 'Why, Marged Fennel,' she cried. 'Have you come to see me?'

'Yes.'

'Come round the back – the lads keep their bikes in the hall.'

The council houses were smaller than the private ones. They had a tiny kitchen leading off a passage which held coalhouse and lavatory, an even tinier room with bath but no hot water, a front room with the minute hall leading to the front door and the stairs. As Marged entered, the whole house seemed crammed to bursting point with Wests of all ages and sizes.

She looked round bemused as Mrs West fluttered about the room, wiping a chair with her overall for Marged to sit down.

'It's awful to be so crowded,' she confided, brushing two toddlers off a sagging armchair where they stood, trouser-less, holding pieces of bread and jam which was slowly dripping down their jerseys. 'These are Maud's kids,' she said. 'And the other one – pick her up, Doris, do – Doris is Tom's wife. Tom's in the Army.'

Perhaps as well, Marged thought. Where did they all sleep? Aloud she said, 'I'm looking for someone to work for me in the house, cleaning. I'm willing to pay well, but I must have good workers.'

'Mm.' Mrs West bit her lip and Marged tried not to look

round the room. It was dirty and there was a smell she didn't like. Was it not stupid to ask for cleaners in a house where, obviously, little cleaning was done? Yet they had seemed to improve with the war and more money. She supposed the newfound cleanliness had gone because they were so appallingly overcrowded.

'I don't know that my lot would want cleaning,' Mrs West said dubiously. 'Our Vera's working – she's married now, but they don't live here, Eileen's in an office—' proudly. 'Maud's married.'

'What about Joanie Farmer?' asked Doris.

'Yes. 'Course. You know Joanie Farmer up the road. Oh, I know she ain't all there, but she's a good worker. She cleans for a woman along Park Manor Road and she takes advantage of the gel summat awful. Only pays her one and six an hour. She's got no mam, you know, Joanie, and her dad's not got much light in his lantern either. She'd jump at it.'

'I'll go and see her,' said Marged, and rose.

'There's our Renie,' piped up one of the younger Wests.

'Yes, she's just leaving school, fourteen, ain't got a job yet,' said her mother.

'Maybe she'd prefer a factory,' Marged wondered. 'I mean, there aren't many prospects in cleaning.'

'Oh, she's courtin',' said Mrs West. 'Nice lad he is an' all. Here she comes now. Renie, would you like to work for Marged Fennel at that big house?'

Renie looked an intelligent enough girl, Marged thought. Thin, with a peaky face and straight mousy hair. Would cleaning satisfy her?

'Could I live in?' Renie asked.

'Why yes, if you wanted to.'

'And just work days? Nights off?'

'Oh yes.'

'What's the pay?'

'Well, I've been paying five shillings an hour, but of course if you lived in you'd have your meals . . .'

317

Renie did a quick calculation in her head. 'I'll take it then,' she said.

This one was sharp enough, Marged thought. An attic in Park Manor – for she couldn't spare another guest-room – would be an improvement on an overcrowded council house in Victoria Street.

Marged arranged for her to start when she left school, and went up the road to see Joanie Farmer, who also jumped at the chance. Then she went home to start the biggest rumpus she'd yet encountered.

She entered the hall, noting the dust on the stairs, and into the dining-room where the table was not laid. There was, as always, no sign of Brian. Into the kitchen where the two girls were sitting, giggling. Marged said: 'I'm giving you both a week's notice.'

The girls jumped up. 'You – *what*?'

'I'm not satisfied with your work. I want you to go.'

'Mrs Stanway never said anything—'

'I can't help that.'

They stood open-mouthed as she left the kitchen 'Fine thing,' one muttered, and didn't try to keep her voice down.

'Who does she think she is?' sneered the other. 'Mrs Stanway'll put her right.'

Marged turned back. 'Where is Mrs Stanway?' she asked.

'In her room.'

'Tell her I want to see her in the drawing-room, please.'

She walked away and in about five minutes Mrs Stanway joined her. The woman was obviously angry. 'What's the meaning of this?' she asked.

'Of what?'

'Usurping my authority. I hire the staff, and I hired those girls.'

'And I'm dismissing them. I'm not satisfied with their work. Look at this—' Marged pointed to the dust. 'Tell me,

Mrs Stanway, what exactly are their duties?' I should have asked all this before, she thought.

'They light the fires—'

'But we have electric fires except for one room seldom used. Go on.'

'One does the bedrooms, the downstairs rooms and the stairs. The other answers the door, waits at table, cleans the kitchen.'

'And we have another woman to do the heavy cleaning. We also have a cook. We have a window-cleaner for the windows, we send the laundry out, the shopping is delivered – I don't think that is too much work for two people. Anyway, I've hired another two.'

Mrs Stanway bristled. 'It is my place to hire the staff. Mrs Mordant wouldn't have done it.'

'If Mrs Mordant is satisfied with poor work that's her lookout. I'm not.'

Mrs Stanway seemed to swell with anger. 'How dare you talk to me like that!'

'How dare I? Because I'm the mistress here, Mrs Stanway, though you can't seem to get that into your head.'

'Well, you do all the wrong things—'

'I shall do as I please, and the sooner you realise that the better. Now excuse me,' and she left the woman gasping.

Fuming, Marged went to the place she had made into a refuge – Roberta's room.

She was breathless, as if she had been running, and she threw her bag down on the bed, then took off her coat.

She sat at the little bureau, wondering what to do about Mrs Stanway. Were they going to have these confrontations every day?

Angrily she tapped her fingers on the side of the little drawer at the front of the bureau. And her anger made her careless. One finger caught in the side between two little knobs. She pulled it away, wincing as the skin tore. There was a clatter and the whole section at the side of the drawer opened.

'Well, I'll be damned,' she gasped seeing the papers inside. 'What's this? The secret drawer that reveals the family will?' She leaned forward, though it was not a will she drew out but a book. She looked at it. *Roberta Mordant: Diary*.

Roberta's diary, which she'd cleverly hidden in this secret place, to keep from Mrs Stanway's prying eyes, no doubt. Well, she wouldn't open it ... and yet ... Roberta was dead. Would it possibly throw any light on the reason she wanted the abortion?

Tentatively, Marged opened the little book. The handwriting was clear but childish, and she realised that the diary had started when Roberta was quite young. She obviously just entered important events. She flipped through the pages. *I love Martin so much ... Making love with him is so wonderful ...*

And then: *I can hardly bear to write about this. Mummy took me to this awful place and we talked to these two officers. Then one took me to a room – I didn't know what he wanted ... I was so ashamed that Mummy ... how could she? I felt degraded. I told Martin. He was comforting.*

'My God,' muttered Marged.

She closed the diary and stood up, taking a pace backwards, hardly wanting to read any more sordid details. Yet she had to know. She opened the journal again at the last pages, almost fearfully. *I am having a baby, but I don't mind, as we can get married. Martin wants to marry me. I am so happy.*

There was a gap, and when the writing began again it was uneven, jagged, as though the writer were under great strain, as if she could hardly hold the pen. Then the last stark desolate words:

Today Mrs Stanway told me that my father met a young girl years ago. She had his child. Her name was Grace Lewis, and the baby was Martin Fennel.

'Oh my God! Oh God!' Marged jumped up as though

something had bitten her fingers and the diary dropped to the floor. She was gasping as if she'd been punched. She whirled around, unable to stand still. No, it couldn't be ... could it ... ? *Could it ... ?*

No. Yet why not? Grace Lewis had been out with a rich man, they said, and there weren't many rich men in Chilverton in the twenties. *Mrs Stanway told me.* Even if it were true, the housekeeper shouldn't have told her ... should she?

Yes, she had to be told. But not that way. Not in a bald statement made by a grim-faced woman to shatter a young girl's life. Had she done it off her own bat? How did she know? From Mrs Mordant, of course. She'd told her to tell Roberta ... And Mrs Stanway would take pleasure in the telling. *Miss Roberta was always a silly girl.*

That woman. Now anger seemed to burn inside Marged as the rage against Mrs Stanway mounted. She opened the door, ran down the stairs. The two maids, still in the kitchen, jumped back in alarm as the wild, white-faced figure passed them and banged on Mrs Stanway's door, hardly waiting for it to open before pushing her way in. And even the housekeeper took a step back at the sight of this avenging angel before her.

Marged was breathing heavily. 'You are dismissed, Mrs Stanway.'

'What are you talking about?'

'Dismissed. Now. Just go.'

'How dare you? Mrs Mordant would never see me dismissed. And certainly there should be a settlement after my years of service.'

'Not from me, there won't. Not after what you did. I've found out, Mrs Stanway. About Miss Roberta.'

Mrs Stanway's mouth opened and closed like a fish, but she did not speak.

'I think you know what I mean. You will leave tomorrow.'

Mrs Stanway rallied. 'I suppose I couldn't expect any better from a jumped-up gutter brat from Victoria Street—'

'No, you couldn't,' shouted Marged. 'We're not soft like Roberta. You drove Miss Roberta to her death, so get out before I forget all the ladylike manners I picked up along the way and let you have a mouthful I learned from other gutter brats.'

Mrs Stanway said no more, and Marged went out, banging the door. 'That's for you, Roberta,' she said.

She went back upstairs. She couldn't eat. Now she was shivering as though with an ague. She knew she was suffering from shock and would have loved a cup of tea, but couldn't face going in the kitchen again. She ran a warm bath, and the shivering subsided, but she still felt shattered. Her head seemed to have sharp needles digging in from all sides. She went to bed and lay on the very edge, hoping Brian wouldn't want to make love to her, for this she could not bear. She pretended to sleep when he came in.

But she couldn't sleep. Thoughts jangled round in her head. Poor Roberta ... if only she'd told me. Everybody treated Roberta badly ... and now guilt crept in ... If only I'd been nicer to her. If only I hadn't let Corrie persuade me to take her to the Red Cow. How thoughtless were the young, Marged reflected from her maturity. Maturity arising not so much from her twenty-five years, but from death and loss and bitter sorrow. She felt old now, immeasurably older than Roberta had ever been or ever would have been ...

If only she herself could talk to someone. Brenda was too far away, and Martin, her confidant, couldn't be told about this, could he? Would it not hurt him too much? Was there no comfort anywhere?

She fell asleep and dreamed of Stefan.

Chapter 13

In Poland after 1945, everyone seemed to be on the move. From Germany came emaciated thousands freed from the concentration camps, factories and farms of the Third Reich. From the east there were still people from the lost lands appropriated by the Soviet Union making their way by train, cart, or on foot. On the railways, Soviet trains crawled eastwards carrying personal booty and machinery and stock of German factories in the new Western territories which were by rights Polish property.

All over the land people were building what was almost a new country, pulling ploughs themselves where there were no horses, taking over factories and starting production without waiting for managers. By 1946 basic industries had been nationalised. The country wanted a strong egalitarian nation; they would probably have voted for a Labour Party, as in England, given the chance. They did not want Soviet communism.

Soviet 'advisers' had taken command of the security police. And all was not peace. Some Home Army units carried on the struggle, ambushing Soviet convoys on the roads, and were in turn repressed.

Danzig had been smashed to rubble, Gdansk was to rise from its ashes. There was no defeatism in the air, but energy. Men, women, even young children were clearing

323

away the stones, some with their bare hands; there was a faintly sweet smell coming from some of the ruins, the smell of rotting bodies.

The street where Barbara Kowalska lived was part of the rubble. It contained a small burnt-out shop with window-frames but no glass, and no stock inside the shell, just a bench outside holding a few odds and ends. After the shop came a gap, and finally one apartment block, the only one left standing, its neighbours' struts emerging drunkenly amid a pile of bricks and ashes.

There was nothing in her apartment but a table and two rickety chairs, at one end a tap and sink, and an old gas cooker. The windows were broken, but on the sill was a vase of flowers.

It was the spirit of Poland: flowers in broken windows, shops with nothing to sell but a few oddments, yet flowers, gaiety hiding the tragedy. It was said that the first shop to re-open in Warsaw was a boutique for ladies' hats!

As Barbara filled a kettle she heard a knock on the door. 'I'm coming,' she called. 'Why, it's the lady from the Red Cross.'

'That's right. Are you Barbara Kowalska?'

'Yes.'

'There is a phone call for you, in our office. It is from England, from your son.'

'From Stefan? Oh – one moment—'

And a few minutes later she was hurrying down the street to the corner where the Red Cross office was.

'Stefan,' she said. 'How are you?'

'I'm well, *Matka*. I must be quick. I'm coming back.'

Barbara looked hastily round the little office, which was empty. 'You must not,' she hissed. 'You will be interrogated, very likely put in prison. Stefan – why?'

'I have to find Janina, *Matka*. Have you heard from her?'

'No. No. When we first went to Warsaw, Tadeusz and I, the Lenskis refused to come with us. I think they hoped

324

Janina would come back. I wrote to them when I got here, and they answered. They said they had had a letter from her, and she was in a camp near Magadan.'

'Where's that?'

'Siberia. In the Soviet Far East.'

'And is she still there?'

'The Lenskis stopped writing. I don't know where they are, if they are alive or dead.'

There was a little silence. Then, 'I must go and find her,' he said.

'Stefan, how can you? Maybe she won't be there now. Maybe she was released, some were in 1941, when General Sikorski went to see Stalin and he agreed an amnesty. We heard about them coming back, it was pitiful. There were so many of them, hundreds of thousands trying to get home at all costs, travelling by train, in carts, on foot, carrying each other, ragged, exhausted ...'

'But she is not home—'

'Stefan. So many didn't come back. So many died. They were starving. Especially the children died.' Barbara drew a breath. 'Anyway, she wouldn't be in the old home, that is Soviet territory now. The people were sent away over here, those who weren't deported to Russia.'

'I must find out.'

Barbara whispered, 'Don't, Stefan.'

'We can't leave her there, what would she do? She wasn't hard, she was innocent.'

'People get hard with the years, Stefan. I did.'

'We should never have married, *Matka*. We didn't want it, either of us.'

She drew a breath. 'You blame me?'

'You wanted it, *Matka*.'

'It was for your father, to let him die happy.'

'So you sacrificed us. And in the end it's Janina who's been sacrificed. Because she was married to me, an officer serving in the West, she had to pay ...'

It was the first real quarrel they'd ever had. Neither spoke, and in the silence Stefan heard a new sound. '*Matka*,' he said. 'What is that? It sounds like a baby crying.'

'Yes,' she replied. 'He is in my arms. It is Tadeusz.'

He was startled. 'Mama,' he said softly, fearfully, 'Tadeusz is dead.'

'This is his son.'

'Tadeusz's son? I didn't know he was married.'

'You don't have to be married to have a son, but he was. I didn't tell you before because I didn't want to persuade you to come back. I wish now I hadn't told you about Janina.'

She made a hushing sound and the baby was quiet. 'It was a miracle,' Barbara said softly. 'How we got away. How I found milk to feed him. But I prayed ... He is a little miracle, God's little miracle. He is the spirit of Poland, Stefan. We are not defeated, we shall rise again, as we did before. This little one proves it. You will never believe how he was born, never. He was determined to be born, Stefan. He is special.'

'Oh, Mama.' And all his resentment fell away. How could he resent her, who had done so much, endured so much? 'I must go now,' he said. 'Take care of yourself, Mama.'

'Write to me,' she said. 'And God go with you.'

The phone went dead, and Barbara returned to her apartment. The shadows were creeping round the little room as she lit a candle, and as the shouts and cries from the street gradually died away, she sat rocking the baby, reliving her experience.

Barbara had heard the gunshots even above the din outside, the crackle of the flames as the Germans systematically fired Warsaw. She ran up the stairs to see all four lying on the floor like rag dolls, puppets whose strings had broken, the Englishman, Tadeusz, Nina and the German. She ran

326

to Tadeusz. He was lying across Nina, and she pulled him away. His head lolled at an angle. He was dead. They were all dead. She bent down to touch him, hearing the crackle of the flames growing nearer, coughing in the acrid smoke, and as she knelt she thought she heard a sigh.

Nina lay in a pool of blood, she felt cold to the touch. But Barbara ran to the stairs. 'Jan!' she called. 'Jan. Josef. Quick, quick!' And they came running.

Jan was not a doctor, but he was trained in medical care, and as he bent over Nina he said, 'Yes, she's alive. Take her down, we must get out of here, the flames'll be up any minute. Come, Pani Kowalska, you must go down.'

Barbara was still kneeling beside Nina. 'Is she seriously hurt?'

'I don't know yet. One bullet went clean through her arm – look. The blood—' He paused, puzzled.

'Could have been Tadeusz's—' and Barbara reflected that her son must have deliberately shielded Nina rather than go for his gun and save his own life. Jan and Josef carefully lifted her, and as she moved she opened her eyes. She said, clearly. 'Baby.'

'Baby?' asked Barbara. 'There's no baby here.'

'She's delirious,' said Jan. 'Come down now.'

Barbara had moved to her son. 'We'll have to leave him,' Jan said. The first flames were licking round the door. 'We must get Nina to safety.'

'Goodbye, my son,' Barbara said, and she laid him flat on the floor, putting the Englishman beside him. Somehow it looked more fitting that way. 'Goodbye, Englishman. We can't bury you,' she said, 'but you will go out like the old Vikings on a funeral pyre.'

Dry-eyed she moved to the door, stopping by the German. 'You killed my son,' she spat. 'If you weren't dead I'd shoot you.' She kicked him, then bent to take the machine gun from the floor. She moved to go then had a thought. Coughing hard now, her eyes smarting from the smoke, she opened his pocket. Inside was money, Polish money; she put this in her pocket, together with a small pistol. Then she went down to the cellar.

It was dark and cold in the cellar; the air was being poisoned from the tiny grating that opened on to the street. Jan was dressing Nina's wound, and she was coming round, staring in bewilderment at the faces above her. Then recollection came. 'Tadeusz?' she asked in a whisper.

Barbara put her hand on the girl's. 'I'm sorry,' she said.

Nina sighed, and closed her eyes again.

Barbara lowered her face to the girl's. 'What did you say about a baby?' she asked.

Nina's eyes flickered open. 'I am having a baby,' she said.

For a moment no one spoke; even the crackles above seemed to stop. Then, 'Can we get her out?' Barbara asked.

For answer, Jan took her to the cellar opening. The sky was lit by flares, but they could see a column of people marching towards the nearest manhole leading to the sewers. The whole street was under fire from mortars and snipers. A stream of refugees and wounded were trying to get across, one by one near a high barricade. As they peered through the cellar opening, mortar fire smashed into the barricade and those trying to cross at that moment lay dead.

'She isn't fit to travel,' said Jan.

'Can we get her to hospital?'

'The hospital was bombed,' Jan told her gently. 'All were killed, including the doctors and nurses. Her arm should be stitched, but we have nothing ... We'll do what we can, and hope there's no internal injury. She should not be moved any more than is necessary, but we must get her into the next cellar.'

As the fire raged above them they tied wet cloths round their faces and lifted Nina into the next apartment through holes knocked in each cellar wall. The air was clearer here; there was no opening, and it turned into the next street. Formerly, each apartment block held a community of people, living in the cellar, with guards on the doorway. In each hallway stood an altar where Barbara had often knelt in prayer. Soldiers had moved through here; liaison girls like Nina had carried important reports through the sewers. Now the cellar was empty. Outside, the Germans were driving unarmed Polish civilians before their troops as they advanced, to screen them from fire. Hungry, filthy, exhausted, almost without ammunition, the defenders fell back from cellar to cellar, women and children attacking German tanks with home-made petrol bombs.

'The passages are blocked now by refugees,' Jan told them. 'There's no order now. The way through the sewers to Mokotow is closed.'

'Let me go and help,' Nina said. 'I know the way through the sewers.'

'You are not fit,' Barbara replied. 'We'll wait a few more days.'

The cease-fire came on 1 October 1944 and on the second, sixty-two days after the beginning of the rising, Warsaw surrendered to the Germans.

The third of October saw a silent city. Their cellar was empty now but for the two women and Jan. Josef had been killed by a sniper. 'The Germans say all inhabitants are to leave,' reported Jan. 'And there will be no reprisals.'

'Ha!' snorted Barbara.

'Members of the Home Army will be treated as prisoners of war. Civilians will be marched to internment camps.'

'I was working for the Home Army,' said Barbara. 'So was Nina.'

'They won't know that.'

'And,' Barbara added, 'Nina is a Jew.'

There was a heavy silence.

'We can't risk it,' said Barbara.

'You must go,' Nina urged. 'Don't stop because of me.'

'And leave you?' Barbara asked. 'You, who have done so much for Poland? You, who have my son's baby?'

The doors of the cellars were opening now, and the remaining few people, men, women and children, made their way to where they were to walk to the German prison camps, ten miles away.

'There's no way out,' Jan told them. 'The sewers' exits are blocked by Germans.'

Then Nina said: 'If you are determined, I know a way, but it might not work.'

They stared. 'What is it?' asked Jan.

'Remember I know the sewers inside out. There is one tunnel that leads to the river. But – it has bars over the entrance. We would need a hacksaw.'

'I have a hacksaw,' said Jan. 'But once in the river, what then? Swim to shore?'

'There is a boat nearby, hidden in the reeds,' Nina explained. 'If it is still there. One of the men, Pietr Janski, put it there, for anyone who might escape that way. Not for himself – anyway, he was killed.'

'It's worth a try,' Jan said. 'We can always come back.'

They packed what was left of their meagre rations, along with cans of water which Barbara used to fetch from the nearest well under cover of darkness. Jan took the machine gun, Barbara still had the small pistol in her bag, and they had a torch. They waited till dark, then slipped into the street to the nearest manhole, climbed down the iron-rung ladder.

The sewers were round, brick-built, high enough for them to stand, and the water level was low. But it was pitch dark except for the tiny light from their torch, the air was foul and the stench appalling.

They slipped and slithered through, relying entirely on Nina, who had, as she said, spent her war delivering messages through these sewers. How she found her way baffled her companions, as they left the main tunnel and turned to the right.

Dawn was breaking before they saw the chink of light. 'This is it,' said Nina.

They reached the end of the tunnel and gulped in great breaths of fresh air. And now they could see the river, the wide expanse of water, a ship on the far bank.

'Careful,' said Barbara. 'Don't let anyone see us.'

Jan crouched down with the hacksaw, loosened one bar, then another. The bars were wide, and now they could squeeze through. Barbara found herself praying again. Let the boat be there ... They must not get Nina, the girl's strength was ebbing.

Jan slipped out. The boat was there!

And when they'd all left, the Germans, on Hitler's orders, razed every last building in Warsaw to the ground.

On 17 January 1945, the Russians finally crossed the Vistula and in a dead city they held a victory parade.

But by then Barbara and her companions were miles away.

'We travelled all the way by river,' Barbara murmured to herself. 'Rowing at night, hiding by day. We got what food we could. Sometimes farmers would let us have what they had; sometimes we found potatoes left in the fields to rot, their owners dead or driven away. Desolation everywhere. But I had the money from the German, so we came to Danzig and found this place.'

This place, where the occupants had all died. And where Nina caught typhus.

Barbara nursed her day and night, so dreadfully ill, missing Tadeusz, crying for her love. She lived just long enough to see her son. 'He is like Tadeusz,' she said, and then she died.

'So I have little Tadeusz,' Barbara concluded. 'The little one who was born out of chaos and destruction.'

Tadeusz. The hope for the future.

Mordant's was in turmoil. The demobbed men started coming back, their jobs held for them by law, so the women in their places had to go. Some went gladly, others would have liked to stay on for the money. A few even liked engineering, and where possible, jobs for these few were found. But most of the women wanted to stay at home and start a family.

The staff were shaken up, too. Those who had come to 'do their bit for the war effort' now left. Married women whose husbands were coming home also wanted to leave. It looked as though there was going to be a staff shortage, a situation so unusual to those brought up in the thirties, that they hardly knew how to deal with it.

The factory was changing back to car production, and orders were secure for the present. Everyone wanted cars – there were long waiting lists. The problem was obtaining the materials to manufacture them. Mr James was very busy now, and Marged had to move quickly to find a new Personnel Manager.

She knew, too, that with the war ending, there would be renewed difficulties in the Boardroom, battles between the Old Guard and the Moderates, and she mentioned this to Mr James, still her ally. 'Mr Walters won't have so much to do now,' she commented. 'I hoped he and Mr Byers might find other situations.'

Mr James quickly disillusioned her. 'No chance,' he said. 'They'll never go, they have shares in the place, didn't you know?'

'I thought the Mordants owned it outright.'

'So they do, except for ten per cent each for Byers and Walters.'

'And not you or Mr Arnold?'

'Oh no, we came in later. You see, what happened was that when Maurice Mordant's father died, he'd owned half of the business with his brother. Maurice wanted the whole of it, and so he got his uncle out, with the aid of Byers and Walters, who were there at the time. He needed their help, but had to agree to their terms.'

'I see. I didn't know that. So we can't get rid of them?'

'Not easily.'

'And they try to block every improvement I make.'

'Yes. The only thing is to get new men on your side. I'm with you and so, in his odd little way, is Arnold.'

'I wish Mr Arnold would make it more plain.'

'Yes, well, some people don't like to go against the Big Guns.'

Marged wondered if she would ever be regarded as a big gun. She doubted it. Not only was she from Victoria Street, but she was a woman, and women didn't sit on the boards of engineering factories. It was laughable, to their way of thinking. They patronised her and talked down to her simply because she wore a skirt and not trousers. And now there was the fact that she was pregnant. Pregnant women didn't work, at least not ladylike women. As June opened she was beginning to show and wore a smock-like blouse, for she wanted to carry on as long as possible. No one said anything, of course. It was another unmentionable thing . . . There was also the problem of who would deputise when she was absent.

She must get a Personnel Manager who'd be on her side, for the knives would be out in the Boardroom now and no mistake. If Byers and Walters held shares, this meant they had a stake in the profits, and they'd want to do things their way – the *old* way – profits first, workers last.

If only she felt well. She'd booked into the private nursing home, but this did not run ante-natal classes as the public hospital did, trusting her to visit her own doctor. And this she kept putting off till she had more time.

Over the next few weeks, she interviewed several men for the post, and was not happy with any of them. Some were do-gooders, with no knowledge of factory life, while others were, as she termed it, 'soft', and to handle factory men you didn't have to be soft. Then, when she had almost despaired of finding the right man, Colin Jackson turned up.

As he walked into the office she read his notes and

thought he was the last type of person she wanted. A former Captain in the Army, he had a patrician face, and looked every inch an aristocrat. When he spoke it was with a cut-glass accent. She was immediately hostile.

'Colin Jackson,' she said, deliberately omitting the Captain. 'You are thirty, and before the war you used to be a teacher. What did you teach?'

'Engineering at a technical school.'

This surprised her. Aristocrats didn't usually go in for engineering nor, for that matter, teaching. 'Did you like teaching?' she asked.

'Not a lot.'

'Oh. So then you joined the Army. As Captain?'

'As Second Lieutenant. My college training saw to that. Then I got promoted.'

'I see. I'm afraid I don't know much about Army officers.'

'No, I didn't. None of my family was ever an officer before.'

Now she looked her surprise, and he grinned, which made his face look more youthful. 'My father worked in a factory.'

Instantly she warmed to him. So many men in this position tried to hide their humble beginnings; so many were forced to do so in the climate of the time. 'So did mine,' she said. 'But I didn't think you—' She broke off.

'My accent? I learned it in the Army. It still goes down well with certain people – and certain employers.'

'Well, you needn't put it on with me. But you really had me fooled. I thought you were—'

'Out of the top drawer?'

'Frankly, yes. You look like—' and again she broke off.

He grinned. 'There was one aristo in our lot, a duke's son. He looked like a farmer. It's only in novels that people look like who they are, if you follow my meaning.'

'Well,' she said. 'You would be used to dealing with

334

men! I'll explain what I want. When my father worked here, the conditions were dreadful.'

'My dad was at the Morris factory, in Cowley,' he said. 'Wasn't bad there at all. He was an intelligent man so he determined to let me take the scholarship to the grammar school.'

'I want to improve things,' Marged told him.

'Things will change now,' he said. 'The men won't stand for going back to the old ways. I know, I've heard 'em talking. And of course, there's plenty of work now.'

'I hope you're right.'

'Oh yes, things are changing. You can see it already, can't you? This war is the big divide. On one side the people who still want the old ways, on the other the New People. And you're one of the New People.'

'Naturally,' she said drily. 'I didn't have much out of the old world.'

'No, but it's more than that, isn't it? A vision of the future, a brighter future, a caring society.'

Suddenly, inexplicably, a picture of Martin flashed into her mind. She said, 'I'm not idealistic, just practical.'

'I wonder,' Colin was musing, 'if the Old Guard realised, when they put on their uniforms, that they were fighting to defend a way of life that would vanish with victory? Stands the church clock at ten to three? Not any more, it passed with the big houses and servants. It'll take some adjusting to.'

'There are still plenty of big houses,' she said, astonished.

'Yes, but who's going to run them without an army of servants? They'll all have to go.'

Marged hadn't thought England would change quite so much. Then she recalled her own efforts to find someone to clean Park Manor, and wondered what on earth they wanted such a big place for? A small house wouldn't need servants. She'd have to see about that, too, when she had time.

But meanwhile she had to fill this post. She was satisfied

that Colin Jackson wouldn't be a soft touch, that he'd be able to sort out the malingerers from the good workers. She gave him the job.

'One word of warning,' she concluded. 'You'll have to drop that accent.'

'Eh, I will an' all,' he smiled.

The Board weren't very impressed with his ideas.

'New ideas,' scoffed Mr Byers. 'What's wrong with the old ways, I'd like to know.'

And now the election was looming, and the Labour Party promised a New Jerusalem. Free healthcare for everyone, pensions, unemployment pay with no Means Test, education for all . . .

Everyone listened on the radio to the results as they came through in that July. And when the Labour Party was swept to power, the Board was horrified.

'I don't believe in all this Jack's as good as his master talk,' said Mr Byers. 'Communist, that's what it is.'

At Park Manor, things had greatly improved with the departure of Mrs Stanway. Joanie Farmer proved to be an excellent worker, so eager to please in return for her better wages that she had to be forcibly stopped from cleaning and polishing. Renie West arrived when she left school, looking quite smart in a new cotton frock. Marged supposed coupons were not in short supply at the Wests' home. She took her to the attic, which she'd improved with the aid of a spare piece of carpet and a large mirror hung over the chest of drawers.

'I couldn't get anything else because of the shortages,' Marged apologised.

'Why, it's luvly,' Renie answered. 'I never had a room to myself before.'

'Well, if you have anything of your own to brighten it up, do bring it,' Marged told her. 'Or if you want to hang pictures on the walls. I used to have Gary Cooper, Tyrone Power, and Dick Powell.' She smiled reminiscently.

'I like Clark Gable,' answered Renie. 'He was luvly in *Gone With The Wind*. I suppose I've got to call you Mrs Mordant now.'

'I'm afraid so,' said Marged. Soon everyone would be calling each other by their Christian names, but that was not yet.

Renie settled in, and Marged finally found time to visit the doctor. It didn't occur to her that she need not be a panel patient any longer, having to sit in a dreary waiting-room filled with coughing miners and runny-nosed children where you waited up to two hours to be summoned by a bell to the august presence. She was going round to this back entrance when a maid opened the front door. 'It's Mrs Mordant, isn't it?' she called.

Marged halted. 'Yes.'

'I thought I recognised you. You should have made an appointment. But come in, you don't have to wait.'

And Marged was led into a waiting-room that was more like her own drawing-room, and she hadn't been there two minutes when she was called into the surgery, wondering guiltily how many poor patients were having to wait longer while she had her consultation. She felt she should apologise to them.

The doctor examined her and frowned. 'Blood pressure is high,' he told her jerkily. 'Baby isn't in quite the right position. May right itself. But you must rest, Mrs Mordant. If not—'

'If not?'

'Nothing to worry about if you rest and take care,' he evaded.

She went home. 'Fat chance of resting,' she scoffed to herself, and struggled on. Strange how this baby, so wanted in the beginning, was now becoming a liability. She still looked forward to Stefan's son, but resented feeling ill. She had so little time to do everything.

If she stayed at home now, Mr Byers and Mr Walters

would override Mr Jackson in his new job – or try to. And such men were at a premium these days. That Mr Jackson could stick up for himself she had no doubt, but he had no passionate interest in Mordant's as she had. If they were too brutal with him, why should he stay?

There was only one way out. She made him her deputy.

August Bank Holiday week came and, thanks to holidays with pay, everyone went away to have a glorious peacetime break by the sea. Shortages and rationing were forgotten as the sun shone and people crowded the beaches, paddled, and sunbathed in deckchairs. And in the same week, the atom bomb was dropped on Hiroshima.

Marged spent the holiday trying to catch up on a few things. She mulled over the facts she had learned recently, about Byers and Walters holding shares that she had known nothing about, and this brought her to the whole question of finances.

She worried about money. Brian was so extravagant. Marged couldn't quite get used to spending. True, she had earned more during the war and had spent when necessary and enjoyed the novelty. But she never wasted money. Whereas Brian seemed to have no idea of its value. He spent prodigally – on his drinking, his parties – she suspected he must have to pay over the odds for the whisky he consumed so lavishly. He was not mean with her, rather the reverse; she could spend what she liked. She had no settled allowance, they had accounts at all the big shops, and as for spending money, she had her own pay, the secretary's pay, for officially she was still a secretary.

Marged had no desire for money for herself, but she did not want to see the firm go bankrupt, or worse perhaps, fall into the hands of Byers and Walters. She resolved to talk to Brian, but he was so difficult to pin down. She decided there was only one way to get him to listen, the tried and trusted woman's way.

338

Opportunity came sooner than she imagined. When they went to bed on the August Bank Holiday Monday – Brian early for once – he said: 'By the way, I've ordered twin beds instead of this double.' And, as she looked her surprise: 'I thought it would be easier for you, you don't always sleep well.'

'I'm sorry if I've kept you awake,' she said, and wondered if she dare suggest separate rooms. She decided to wait.

He began to get undressed, and she studied him for a moment. His face was getting plumper now – or should it be bloated? Not really a healthy face. His hair was limp and his body, too, was fatter than formerly. Surely it would be good for him to stop drinking?

As he got into bed beside her and put an arm around her she let it rest for a moment then pushed it away. 'Brian,' she began. 'I've been wondering about our finances. Can we really afford to spend so much?'

'So much? A couple of beds? We don't spend much.'

'There's the upkeep of this big house, the servants' wages—'

'We don't have many servants, not like we used to when Mother was here. What have you got now? A girl who isn't right in the head, and a young kid from Victoria Street. If that's the best you can do—'

'It is today—'

'You shouldn't have got rid of Mrs Stanway. Just because you didn't like her—'

She had never told him about Roberta. 'I don't see that she did any better. But that's my point, Brian. Women won't come into service now, they say all that's finished.'

'All what? Servants? Don't be ridiculous. There have always been servants in England, and there always will. It's just that you don't know how to pick them.'

She sighed. 'They do say that people will be selling these big houses, and I think that would be a good idea. We could sell this, get a smaller place.'

'Sell Park Manor? You must be mad. This is my home.'

And I have the bother of it, she thought tartly. She went on: 'Brian, about money. I just pay the bills, the servants' wages and so on, but I don't know how much is coming in.'

'If you mean my money, then you aren't going to know. Now come on, old girl—' and his hands moved again. This was the only time he ever used any endearments, or indeed spoke to her in any but a disparaging tone, and she had to take advantage of it. So she moved his hand and they carried on fencing.

'Wait a minute, we must talk first,' she persisted. 'Does Mr Arnold send you statements? Do you get an allowance?'

'Yes, to both.'

But, she thought, he can't read . . .

'Did you know that Byers and Walters hold shares in the firm?' she asked.

He hesitated. 'I think I heard something about it.'

'But how much do they get? Brian, we must get things sorted out. We can't run the place this way. Shouldn't we put part, or most, of the profits back into the factory? Or do you just spend what you want of it?'

'Oh, don't bother about that,' he said sulkily, and tightened his hold on her.

She held him off. 'I must know,' she said.

'I tell you it's all right. Arnold will tell me if I'm overdrawn.'

'No, it isn't all right,' she persisted. 'I know Arnold's a good man, but whose orders does he take? Byers' and Walters'? You're never at the Board meetings now. Don't you see, Brian, they'd jump at the chance to get hold of the whole factory! They'd get you out if they could. Brian, I'm on your side.'

Now he moved uncomfortably; his hand was still – for a moment.

'I'm just a secretary,' she said. 'As I act on your behalf I think I should be made a director.'

His hand had resumed its movements.

'Brian—'

'Oh, all right,' he said, and pulled her to him. 'Do what you like.'

'Then you'll have to come to the next meeting and agree to it.'

'All right,' he repeated. 'Now come on, Marged ...'

On 14 August, the day before Parliament met to inaugurate the New Britain, Mr Attlee announced the surrender of Japan. Next day was to be celebrated as VJ-Day. And the men who had been slogging in the jungles of the Far East, contending with malaria and tropical diseases, the men in Japanese prison camps, living skeletons, would – those who were still alive – be able to come home. The USA announced that all Lend Lease aid had been terminated; Britain was practically bankrupt. And Marged was made a director of Mordant's.

At the beginning of October, in London, the Soviet Foreign Minister took off his velvet glove and showed the iron fist beneath, astonishing his British and American colleagues by putting forward a number of unyielding demands, till the conference collapsed in a welter of recriminations. Stefan Kowalski was in Warsaw – in prison.

He had, with some others, been flown back in a Dakota, tired, worried, wondering what he'd find when he reached Poland, thinking of Marged.

He loved Marged, wanted to stay with her for ever. Should he have stayed ...? Thoughts jostled inside his brain. Disappointment, disillusion, yes, and anger ... He'd had such high hopes ...

He supposed he was lucky to have survived the war; so many pilots hadn't, Polish and English. He'd flown on far more ops than his quota, yet it hadn't affected him ... had it ...? He'd always loved flying, loved to be up in the great wide sky. Even when on the lookout for enemy fighters part of his mind had still rejoiced in the freedom of the skies, the other part being the fighting man, waiting for attack, geared up ready to go, then coming back to earth – and Marged.

Marged's love had sustained him; all through the tragedies Poland had faced – the siege of Warsaw, not hearing from his family – she had been there right to the end. And the end was bitter.

They'd be celebrating in England now, but Poland wasn't celebrating. Was there not some resentment inside him, some anger that had been taken out on Marged ...?

Should he have stayed ...?

He tried to marshal his thoughts in some semblance of order. He could have married Marged, no one would have known about Janina once he was demobbed. But *he* would know. It was really a matter of honour. And there was little enough honour in war, for all they pretended there was. He was disillusioned with war. He'd started out with such strong convictions, all shattered. Perhaps that was why he had to keep his own honour, no matter what. Because once you let honour go you started to rot inside. You'd just take, take for yourself and never mind a lonely girl in a Siberian prison. Yes, they'd be celebrating, but Janina wouldn't be celebrating.

The plane was over Poland now and he was able to crane his neck and see below. He was appalled. He could hardly believe what he saw. So much destruction! He thought he'd witnessed destruction, in England – hadn't he seen Coventry? In Germany, when he carried out the raids, he'd even felt a little unhappy about those last attacks on Cologne and Dresden. Not now. They had done this. They had reduced his country to devastation.

The cities were rubble, the lovely old churches, the fine old houses, the little cottages, the hospitals ... And in the country, crops had rotted in the earth, storehouses cared for and built up over many years were burst open and destroyed. The fields were full of rusting iron; even the last hayricks had been pulled down and trampled on, fired.

The plane was on the outskirts of Warsaw now, was circling, landing. They were taken out.

But not to freedom. They were bundled into trucks and driven to a building, told to wait in a room guarded by soldiers answering to the NKVD, the secret police.

'What's all this?' Stefan asked one of the guards.

'First you must come for interrogation,' he was told.

Interrogation? For coming back to his own country?

He looked round at the others. There weren't many of them, for the majority had stayed in Britain. Only the ones who had families returned. The young single men, the flower of the country, refused to go back into servitude. Stalin had promised free elections, but the Poles didn't believe him. Foreigners thought they were being awkward; the Poles knew better.

Stefan waited. He had heard all the talk about what would happen if he came back. Fears of prison, of being shot ... And yet, in a mixture of grief and duty and anger, he had come. And now he realised what he had done. The Iron Curtain that Churchill was to speak about had fallen behind him; he could hear the clang. He would never be able to get out.

On the same day in Chilverton, Marged came home from the office to find Renie West waiting for her.

'Can I see you, Mrs Mordant?' she asked.

They went into the sitting-room where Marged sank into the armchair with relief. She did not go to the office every day now, as much for the not-so-oblique glances she received for even daring to be seen in such a public place, as the fact that some days she did not feel well enough to go. She had not visited the doctor again, knowing she should but repeatedly putting it off. After all, she reasoned, you didn't feel well when you were pregnant. All you had to do was rest, and she did – at least, occasionally. And if her ankles swelled, that was just because of her condition.

Renie stood before her, looking quite smart. Her hair had been permed, and it suited her. She and Joanie wore dark green coat overalls instead of the former cap and apron, and both were happy with the change. 'Well?' Marged smiled. 'Don't tell me you want to leave already. You seem to be getting on fine.'

'Oh no,' Renie said. 'It's just – when we were at school we did some first aid, because of the bombing, you know. Well, I'd like to carry on with that, go to St John Ambulance classes once a week.'

'Why, of course, you don't have to ask my permission for that,' Marged said. 'Are you interested in nursing, then?'

'I just thought – when your baby's born I could pr'aps look after it while you're at work. I suppose you'll have to go to work again?'

Marged noted the 'have to'. Renie knew Brian seldom went to the office. She said, 'Well, to be truthful, I hadn't thought about who'd look after the baby.' *It's enough now to get through to the birth itself.* 'But yes, I shall go back to work.' She studied the girl. 'I suppose you know a lot about babies?'

'I should think so. There's two younger than me, and now there's Maud's and Doris's kids. I nursed them through measles and whooping cough.'

'So—' Marged sought to find a key to this offer. 'You like babies?'

Renie shrugged. 'Not partic. I mean, I wouldn't want none of my own. But I don't mind looking after other people's – if the money's good.'

'Ah.' Marged hid a smile. There were no flies on Renie. 'You don't want any of your own?'

'No fear. I've had enough with our lot. I'm not having a life like my mam.'

'I'm surprised your dad lets you go courting so young.'

'He don't bother about me so much. The youngest allus get on better. When our Vera was my age she had to be in early or he'd knock her through the window. Then when the lads got older he daren't say much to them else they'd hit him back. So he don't bother so much wi' me. Anyway, he knows I'd leave home, as I have done.'

'But you won't stay here for too long?'

'Well, if I do decide to get married I want a house of my own, when they start building 'em. Not a council house either. So I should get a job in a factory then, save up. But that won't be yet. I ain't getting married till I'm twenty-two or three.'

'But you'd have to live in, Renie, be here most evenings.'

'I know. But that nursery you've prepared, it's luvly. And I suppose the nurse would sleep next door.'

'Yes.'

'That's a luvly room,' Renie said reverently.

'What about your boyfriend?' Marged asked. 'If you didn't go out so much?'

'Oh, he won't mind.' Renie dismissed her swain. 'He'll just have to wait.'

'I see. Well, I'll think about it, Renie. I don't see why you shouldn't take over. I'd have to get someone in your place though.'

'Don't worry, Mrs Mordant. I'll find somebody for you.'

Four weeks before the child was due Marged woke to strange cramps that were not exactly pains, but not normal aches either. She couldn't sleep, so got out of bed and walked round the room. It was the end of October, a chilly dark morning with strong winds beating against the side of the house.

She dressed and went downstairs, switching on the electric fire in the sitting-room. Light strengthened, the wind blew the last remaining leaves from the trees, they swirled round the house in a brown and orange storm. She stood by the window, then a sudden pain wrenched her and she knew she'd have to go to the nursing home.

She woke Brian, and he drove her there in the car. It was a large building surrounded by trees blowing in the wind, not unlike Park Manor. She was taken to the Labour Ward, a room with one bed, high and hard, and told to lie down flat.

There followed two days of sheer torture. It was a long and protracted birth; the nursing home was not in the forefront of expert care, and Marged was left alone for long periods on the hard bed, where every time a severe pain started, she jumped off and crouched over the radiator to try to alleviate it. She would be found there by a nurse and put back on the hard bed. 'I can't lie here,' she protested feebly.

'No such word as can't,' replied the nurse.

'How would you know?' muttered Marged to the retreating back. But she was too ill to complain. Only to reflect that when you are ill you need to fight back and can't.

Then they came back. They tried to bring the baby, as day and night merged and the wind screeched and the leaves swirled past the windows. The doctor came with forceps and there were more examinations while Marged writhed in agony. And through mists of pain she heard him say: 'We're going to send you to hospital.'

'Why?' she managed to gasp.

He didn't answer, but left the room to telephone, and the nurse murmured: 'We haven't the facilities here, Mrs Mordant. I'm afraid you'll have to sink your pride and go into a public ward.' And Marged wanted to say that it wasn't her pride, but Brian's. She just wanted someone to help her – she wouldn't have cared if it were a chimney sweep!

At the local hospital she was wheeled straight into their labour ward and there was much shaking of heads and frowning. And she was told that there would have to be a Caesarean operation.

*

346

Marged came round to find herself in a ward with the curtains drawn about her bed. But this did not cut out the sounds – of women talking, of the clatter of cups, each clatter piercing her brain. She tried to call out but no sound emerged, and she slid back into unconsciousness. The next time she surfaced a nurse was entering, followed by a doctor.

'Well now,' the nurse said briskly. 'And how are we feeling?'

'Am I dying?' Marged asked. 'Having the curtains drawn?'

'No, you're not dying.' The doctor was quite young and he looked efficient. 'You had a Caesarean, and everything's fine now, including the baby. But you didn't take care of yourself, did you? Letting things get to that state! Now, let me look at you.'

She felt bruised all over. She asked: 'The baby – what is it?'

'Why,' the nurse said, 'it's a little girl. She's very tiny, so Doctor thinks it best she should be kept in the special section. You'll be able to see her soon, but for the meantime we are feeding her.'

A girl. After all this, a girl. It couldn't be ... 'Are you sure?' she asked. 'That it's a girl?'

'I do know the difference,' the nurse said tartly, and Marged turned her face away.

Brian came to see her and sat by the bed. 'Why ever didn't you see the doctor earlier?' he asked. 'Leaving it so late and having to come *here*. Why, you might have di—' He broke off, and she wasn't sure which was the greater sin, being in the public ward or dying.

'Have you seen the baby?' Brian asked. 'She's a funny little thing, isn't she?' and she stared in amazement that Brian should take an interest in a new baby.

He said, 'They think she should be christened. What name do you want?'

347

'Christened, why? Is she not going to live?'

'They always christen them when they're so small.'

'I haven't thought of a girl's name,' she said. 'You decide.'

Marged didn't see the baby for over a week, when they wheeled her to the nursery, for babies were only brought to their mothers when they were fed, and there was no feeding for Marged's child. She was taken past the rows of babies to the end cot, where she bent over the tiny red face and searched for some resemblance to Stefan, but there was none. None at all.

She sighed and turned away.

Marged was discharged after two weeks, but the baby stayed in hospital. And once home Marged lay dispirited, depressed. Brian asked if he should hire a nurse for her, but a nurse to look after one sick person was so out of her experience that she answered, amazed: 'Good God, no! Whatever for?'

'Well then,' he said. 'Shall I send for Brenda?'

Brenda would be busy with her new life – and she didn't want her to know that this wasn't Brian's child; she couldn't bear to talk about Stefan now ... But longing overcame scruples and she agreed.

Brenda came and sat beside her sister, saying tentatively: 'Marged?' but Marged replied, 'I don't want to talk about it.' So Brenda asked no questions, worrying inwardly over what had happened in those last weeks when Stefan went away, blaming herself for being too wrapped up in her own affairs to look after her younger sister, feeling guilty that she was happy while poor Marged was not. But to Marged her very presence was reassuring. It was the next best thing to having her mother there.

Brenda saw the doctor, who was vague, understandably, as he had seen little of her. 'She had a difficult time,' he barked in his usual short sharp bursts. 'Been very ill.

348

Neglected herself beforehand. Had high blood pressure. Baby in wrong position.'

What none of them realised was that all the grief and shock of Stefan's leaving was now surfacing. For months Marged had kept herself going with the thought of Stefan's son who would be a miniature Stefan, who would replace him, almost as if he had come back to her. Now there was no son, and she was devastated.

The baby came home after four weeks and was installed in the nursery with a nurse hired by Brian. Marged showed no interest.

'I must say he's proving to be good dealing with illness,' Brenda remarked. 'And he's really keen on the baby.'

Brian was surprised himself at his interest. When he first saw the baby soon after the birth he was amazed that anything so tiny could live. 'Will it be all right?' he asked.

'Oh, I've seen smaller than this one survive,' said the nurse robustly. 'She's a little weak still. Doctor thinks it might be a good idea to have her christened. We always like to – you know ...'

Brian named her Marie. He was at the christening, indeed, he fetched the vicar himself. And after that he still visited the baby in hospital even when Marged was discharged.

And two days after the baby came home Brian crept a little sheepishly into the nursery.

The nurse sat by the window, reading. The baby lay in the cot, crying.

'I say,' Brian said. 'Is anything the matter with her?'

'No, of course not.'

'Then why is she crying?'

'Babies do cry,' said the nurse shortly.

'But shouldn't we do something?'

'She is not hungry, her nappy is clean, there is nothing wrong, Mr Mordant. We don't have to pick babies up every time they cry, you know. We just leave them.'

'But that's a bit hard—' He had been about to say heartless.

The nurse did not answer.

'I say, how about if I hold her for a minute?' Brian offered.

The nurse frowned. But Mr Mordant was her employer and Park Manor wasn't a bad place to be. Grudgingly she picked up the baby and placed her in Brian's arms.

And Marie stopped crying.

'I say.' Brian was delighted. 'Look at that!'

The nurse sniffed, but Brian sat down and the baby slept.

He let the nurse put her back in the cot, but he sneaked in again the following day and insisted on holding the baby.

The nurse complained to the doctor. 'I have had the latest up-to-date training,' she told him resentfully. 'We have our routine, but Mr Mordant insists on picking the child up whenever it cries. It will ruin her.'

The doctor didn't altogether agree with modern methods. 'Babies need love,' he said. 'And he is the father.'

Brian completely forgot he wasn't the baby's father. Or to be correct, the thought did cross his mind as he held her. And another, stranger thought came to him: that the baby didn't know or even care whether he was her biological father or not. She came to him trustingly, as if seeking for the love the doctor had spoken of, needing love to survive. And it was true she did not cry when he held her.

Sometimes she would open her eyes – dark blue – and gaze at him consideringly. And he'd talk to her, and it was as though she was listening carefully to each word. Brian had never in his life felt protective towards anyone before; no one had ever come to him for protection, rather the reverse. He'd been the derided one, the last person to be asked for protection. Now he was, and he liked the feeling.

He thought of his own father who had spent all his life working, never having time for his children. He couldn't remember ever having a proper conversation with his father.

Well, this little one *would* have a father.

Marged was so slow in recovering that it was decided she needed a holiday, and where better to go than to stay with Brenda for a few weeks? 'You won't mind leaving the baby?' Brenda asked.

Marged shook her head. By the time the baby came home, she was a stranger. Marged had gazed down into the tiny face, trying to summon up some vestige of mother love. She felt nothing. She felt nothing for anyone these days, excepting Brenda, and she clung to her as to a lifeline.

They travelled to Cambridge by train, for though Philip had a car, petrol was still rationed. The trains were dirty, packed, and always late, still full of returning servicemen, with long queues on platforms for tea or coffee. Taxis were scarce too, but Philip met them in Cambridge and drove them to their flat.

Marged looked round the apartment at this example of modern décor – the pale washed walls, large plain windows, plain furniture. 'Ye-es,' she said hesitantly, and Brenda laughed. 'I know it's different from the hugger-mugger of Victoria Street, takes some getting used to,' she said. 'And it's not much like your new home, either.' She turned to Philip. 'I'd like to give you a free hand at Park Manor, see what you could do with it.'

'No,' Marged said. 'You can't do much with that house at all, except raze it to the ground.'

Philip and Brenda exchanged glances, but Marged was thinking of the dream home she'd had for so many years. The chintz-covered chairs, the net at the window. Funny, they had the money now, but Brian wouldn't move from that old mausoleum, not to a semi-detached, anyway. Houses were still a mark of class in post-war Britain; it would be *infra dig* to move to a semi.

Yet Marged enjoyed her stay in Cambridge. They took her sightseeing round the lovely old city, and the cool crisp air of East Anglia helped her to recover. 'I must go back for Christmas, Bren,' she said. 'Start the New Year at the factory.'

'Do you have to go back to the factory?' Brenda asked.

Marged stared ahead. All the women were returning to their homes, staying there, having babies ... She said bleakly, 'What would I do all day at Park Manor?'

'You have the baby.'

'Yes.' A baby who's a stranger to me and I can't understand myself. Mothers loved babies, babies loved mothers; such feelings as she had were alien, never mentioned. Unless you were like that Mrs Armitage up the top end of Victoria Street, who went dancing every night during the war and left her children in bed, dirty, verminous, till the neighbours complained. But respectable women loved their babies, respectable women like Mam.

'I've got to keep the factory going,' she said dully.

'What for? To hand it to Martin?'

'Do you hear from Martin?' Marged asked.

'Occasionally. Why?'

'I wondered when he would be demobbed.'

'Not for some months. He wasn't one of the first in. He's in Germany now, in the Army of Occupation.'

'Bren – don't tell him about the baby.'

'Why ever not?'

'Well, I didn't. I told him I was marrying Brian, and he's never written since. Don't know why.'

'Oh well, he always was funny,' Brenda snorted. 'But I won't tell him, if that's what you want.'

'It is. Thanks, Bren.'

Marged started back at the factory in the New Year. Colin Jackson had visited her at home several times to keep her informed about progress, and everything was as it should be. At home, nothing had changed. Brian might be a good father, but it did not turn him into a good husband. The drinking continued, and the absenteeism from work.

Marie was thriving, though still fretful, and as she had been born out of disillusion and tragedy, Marged thought, how could she be anything else? She tried again to find some love for her, but failed.

The nurse left and Renie was installed in her place, causing another row with Brian.

'That kid from Victoria Street?' he asked indignantly. 'What does she know about babies?'

'A lot. She's been looking after them all her life.'

'But she's not *trained*.'

'She's trained in first aid, and she's had years of experience with babies. I can't see that the nurse we had was much better equipped, for all her training.'

'But she'll have to stay in all evening.'

'I know, and she doesn't mind.'

He snorted. 'What? A kid like that not wanting to go out? I know her sort, off gallivanting—'

'No, Brian, she has a young man, and I've told her that he can come in and sit with her.'

'You've *what*? Sit in where? In her bedroom?'

'She's moving her bed into the nursery, says she'll hear the baby better in the night. The other room will be her sitting-room.'

And indeed, Renie had been overjoyed at this arrangement, looking round in awe at the size of the room she was to inhabit.

'But good heavens,' Brian persisted. 'You don't know what they'll get up to!'

'They won't get up to anything. I've told her what I expect. Anyway, I can't see that it would harm a baby of two months, whatever they got up to, as you put it.'

'And who's to take her place? I thought you couldn't get servants?'

'Renie found one. Violet Masters. She's married, but she's willing to work days. Anyway,' Marged ended, a little acidly, 'you're usually at home all day, so you can keep an eye on her, can't you?'

Brian said no more, but he was mollified by the fact that Renie had no objection to his picking the baby up whenever he cared to. As he'd said, Renie had no modern training, and this worked to his advantage. The baby was picked up when she cried and seemed happy with this arrangement.

In the Boardroom, Marged did not find that her new status as Director changed attitudes towards her. There had already been a long battle about holiday and sick pay, with Mr Byers saying they couldn't afford it, and Marged asking Mr Arnold for figures proving they could. 'And if we don't pay, our skilled men will only move to all the other firms who do, and then what will we do?'

And so it went on. Each improvement was fought every inch of the way, and Marged returned home drained, for she had not fully recovered her strength, to find Brian either out at a drinking party or entertaining friends of his own. She had no time to spare for Marie, and was thankful for Renie West.

On one such day in March, she entered the hall to hear the phone ringing. She picked up the receiver. 'Hallo,' came a strident voice. 'Is that Marguerite Fennel?'

'Yes.'

'This is your Aunt Mary.'

'Aunt Mary, how are you?'

A snort came over the phone. 'I didn't think you were interested in us any more. Never a word to us for ages, never a word about your little girl – we had to read it in the paper. And—' the voice was shocked now '—not a word about your wedding!'

'I'm sorry, Aunt, but it was very quiet. We didn't have any guests.'

'That's as maybe, but it is usual to let your relations know at least, then they can come to church if they want to, even if they're not good enough to be invited back to the house. Your mother would never have done such a thing. I'm only glad she isn't here to see you, what with your behaviour and Brenda going off with another man—'

354

Marged closed her eyes. 'I'm sorry I haven't been in touch, Aunt, but I do have a lot to do.'

Aunt Mary snorted again. 'Can't think what.'

'Well, I do go to work.'

'And sit in an office all day messing with bits of paper. Well, I won't interrupt your busy life. All I wanted to say is that your Aunt Ann hasn't got long to live.'

And now Marged was conscience-stricken. 'I am sorry, I really am. I should have visited her. But I've been ill myself.'

'Yes, well, if you can spare the time she is at home now.' The pips sounded; the line went dead.

Aunt Ann lived in a terraced house similar to those in Victoria Street, and Marged went to see her that same evening. It was the other side of town and she had to get a bus, thinking she'd have to learn to drive as soon as petrol became obtainable. She knocked at the door and Uncle Jim opened it.

'Why, Marged,' he said. 'Come in, do,' and he led her into the kitchen and poured a cup of tea from the pot on the hob.

'I should have come sooner,' she said. 'I should have done something for her. How long has she been home?'

'They sent her home to die,' said Uncle Jim simply.

And then he led her upstairs where her aunt lay in the big bed, her face a yellowy-white, her hands plucking at the sheets. There was a faint sweet smell in the room, as if death were already there.

'Oh Aunt,' Marged cried. 'I should have come before this. How are you?'

'Middling, love, middling,' said her aunt, holding one wasted hand up from the bedclothes.

'I've brought a few grapes—'

'My, my, however did you get grapes? Bet you had to pay a fortune. Look, Jim, isn't she kind?'

Marged sat on the chair near the bed and Uncle Jim went downstairs again. Aunt Ann asked, 'How is Martin?'

'Oh, he's fine. He's with the Army in Germany.'

'He was always such a nice lad,' said her aunt. 'In spite of—' She broke off, and a wild thought jumped into Marged's mind. Could she ask ... dare she ...? Yet why not?

She said, 'I don't like to bother you, Aunt, and don't answer if you don't want to, but – I wondered if you knew ... You were next to Aunt Grace, weren't you?'

'Oh yes, only eighteen months between us. Mary was the oldest –' she smiled faintly '– Bossy Mary, then your mother, then us. Oh yes, Grace and me were always pals.'

'And did she – did she ever tell you – who Martin's father was?'

There was a pause, Aunt Ann wiped her lips with her handkerchief. 'Yes, she did tell me, but she made me swear not to tell anyone else. That's why I never did. Anyway, I thought it better not to—'

'Yes, of course. But you see – I've heard that it was—'

She stopped, for her aunt was speaking again. 'Poor Grace,' she said. 'She really thought he loved her. And I think he did. But there was nothing he could do.'

Marged sniffed.

'No, really. His wife wouldn't ever divorce him, and for him to divorce her would have raised such a scandal – people didn't do such things then, you know. It would have ruined the business.'

'And we couldn't have that, could we?' muttered Marged. 'So who are we talking about, Aunt?'

'Why, Maurice Mordant,' said her aunt.

Marged stayed a little longer, though she didn't remember a word that was said afterwards. She asked her uncle downstairs if he needed any help. He replied sadly there was nothing anyone could do.

Aunt Ann died two weeks later and Marged went to the funeral, which mollified Aunt Mary somewhat. As did the fact that she wore a new black coat, which took a number of coupons. 'Don't hold with wearing grey at funerals, war or no war,' Aunt Mary said loudly, as a cousin entered wearing a grey suit. 'You should always keep a black outfit ready for funerals, show respect for the dead.'

Chapter 14

It was April in Victoria Street; washing flapping in the back gardens showed the world it was Monday. Pale sunlight put new heart into the little houses, children ran down to school and Martin walked with a spring in his step. The war was over, now for the peace.

And it was happening, the new world they'd promised. No more dole, no more unhappiness ... they'd fought for this and it was coming. *Bliss was it in that dawn to be alive, But to be young was very heaven*! He'd learned that at school, off by heart. Bet he'd remember it all his life. Not that he went in much for poetry. Some things he liked, though. *Friends, Romans, Countrymen* ... that was a good play, if you like. That was how people were, pretending to be your friend, then stabbing you in the back.

He'd liked school, though he'd die rather than admit it.

And now he had the option of a new future. He could take one of those educational courses open to forces personnel; he could go to a training college and become a teacher – teachers were needed. He hadn't given his final word, yet: he wanted to see Marged first.

Martin didn't really understand why he had been so upset about her marriage to Brian Mordant. He supposed it was just that the letter came when he was thinking about her, about the confidences they had always shared, and to get this bald missive stating only that she was married, somehow shook him. Stupid, it was obvious why she'd married Brian – to get the factory. He'd go and see her in a day or two. They'd have a chat, it would be like the old days. They'd talk about the new world, which already the Labour Party was presenting: free healthcare, sickness benefit, unemployment benefit, old age pensions, maternity benefit, and a separate act insuring workers against injury at work. These measures would all but eliminate poverty. Victoria Street would be transformed. A new world. A dream come true.

He stopped at number forty, and a neighbour called: 'Why, it's Martin. Are you all right, my duck?'

'Fine, thanks, Mrs Littleton.'

'Brenda's away, you know.'

'Yes, I know.'

He knocked on the door, and Jack Morris opened it. 'Martin! Brenda's—'

'I know. But all my things are still here.'

'Come in. You just been demobbed?'

'Can't you tell?' Martin looked down at his demob suit.

'Well, sit down. Want a cup of tea? I'm off work today. Start nights tomorrow.'

'Love one.' Martin slung his bag to the floor, sat in the kitchen by the fireplace and waited till Jack returned, noting that the room had been newly colour-washed, wondering who had done it, Jack or Philip.

'You were with Monty, weren't you?' Jack sat opposite. 'How was it?'

Martin shrugged. 'Hot and hellish in the desert. And you?'

They sat chatting of their war experiences, then ate fish and chips for dinner from the shop round the corner, Jack cut thick slices of bread. Martin went upstairs to sort through his clothes, and changed his suit. When the clock struck seven he asked: 'Are you going out or anything?'

'Me? No.'

'Why don't we go and have a pint somewhere?'

'Why not? If we can find a pub that's got beer.'

They went to the Weavers' Arms, but it wasn't the same now they were not in uniform. No girls smiled at them, no one offered to buy them a drink or give a scarce cigarette. The girls looked different these days, wearing trousers and head-scarves. Martin wondered why they didn't dress up any more. Didn't they know the war was over? They sat at a little table with the former occupants' beer spilled over the surface and Jack said, 'I don't go out much now.'

'Well, you should.'

There was a pause. 'I didn't expect it of Brenda,' Jack muttered. 'I know lots of women went off, but not Brenda.'

'She shouldn't have done it,' Martin offered.

'What sort of bloke was he, then? You must've met him.'

'I didn't like him much. Don't know what she saw in him.'

'He was well off,' said Jack bitterly. 'Same as Marged, marrying that Mordant bloke. Oh sorry, I shouldn't go on about your family.'

'It's all right.' But a little of the day's brightness had dimmed. 'I know how you felt about Brenda,' he finished.

'I thought the world of her,' said Jack simply. 'I know one thing. Next war I'll stop at home.'

'Talking of home,' Martin said, 'I was wondering if I could stay on with you for a few days till I get something sorted?'

'Sure, if you want. But I thought you'd be going to Marged's.'

'Oh, I'll see her in a day or two.'

'Me mother comes over weekends, gives the place a clean,' Jack told him. 'Does a bit of cooking, though I eat at the canteen, of course. I expect she'd cook for you as well.'

'I could give her something.'

'No need.'

The polite but necessary exchanges over, they left the pub. Martin knew he would offer Mrs Morris 'something', and she'd refuse, when he'd insist, and she'd finally give in. It was all part of the ritual.

Marged liked Sundays; she could really have a day of leisure. Though too often problems from the factory would need resolving, or there'd be some manoeuvre to be puzzled out. Once lunch was over, Brian would be out till late, coming home the worse for drink, as usual. But although he still spent royally, she was not quite so worried about their finances.

When she became a director she was able to talk to Mr Arnold about the money situation. She would now be paid a director's salary and Mr Arnold asked her if she wanted a joint account with Brian.

'Oh no,' she said quickly, and then felt her face reddening. He would think she was after the firm's money. She had to make her motives plain. 'Don't you think it should be put back into the business?' she asked.

'But this is your salary,' replied Mr Arnold. 'You earn it.' Was there a slight emphasis on the *you*?

She said, stammering a little: 'We seem to spend an awful lot of money, that is ... I mean ... is Brian ever overdrawn?'

'He gets his statements,' replied Mr Arnold.

'Yes, but—' How could she explain? 'Supposing he takes no notice of them?'

'Oh, then I have a word with him.' Mr Arnold was as impassive as ever, but he avoided her eyes and Marged thought, He knows. Of course he knows, and she put her head in her hands.

'It's all right, Mrs Mordant,' Mr Arnold said. 'I shan't let Mr Brian get in the red.'

She wanted to ask him if the others knew, but could not. Mr Arnold was so unapproachable. Yet this very quality was a help to them. He would not, or so she believed, talk about Brian.

But she was relieved. Even so, their combined salaries seemed exorbitant to a girl brought up to think that two pounds a week was a princely sum. She banked her salary, and this gave her an added sense of security. If Brian did overspend then she could help out, or if Mordant's ever needed money, she would have some. For, like all the workers, she could not get used to full employment, could not believe that it would last.

The doorbell interrupted her musings, and she waited as Violet came to the sitting-room to say there was a gentleman at the door. 'Then show him in,' Marged said.

'I'm already in,' said a voice. 'I've called to see Lady Muck. Good-morning, Madam. Would you like to buy a vacuum cleaner?'

'Martin, you fool!' She jumped up, ran towards him. 'You're back. Why didn't you tell me you were coming? Why haven't you written?'

He reached her side, took her hands, swung her round. He did not kiss her; they were not a demonstrative family. He stood back.

They eyed each other uncertainly and Martin looked round. 'So you're living here, maids and all. Can't you afford caps and aprons?'

'Maids don't wear those things now. And you know I'm living here. Where are you staying?'

'At Jack Morris's. And she was hurt that he hadn't come straight to her. 'Let's sit down,' she said. And now I can tell him everything, about Stefan, why I married Brian but first:

'How about you?' she asked. 'Have you – got over Roberta?'

'I suppose so.'

She eyed him keenly. 'Nothing happened, you know Martin. Your name wasn't mentioned. You needn't have gone.'

He shrugged. 'I suppose I was to blame for it really. Though I still can't understand why she should have tried to get rid of it—'

Marged hesitated. She knew why, and she had pondered long and hard about when to tell Martin – or whether to tell him at all. Yet maybe he should know. Apart from absolving him from any guilt, if he was Maurice Mordant's son he had a right to the factory ... and if she told him, maybe it would help him to feel better about Roberta. She'll tell him later, when he'd settled in.

He asked: 'Where is he, then?'

'Who, Brian? Out somewhere.' And was ashamed that she didn't know where, or who with. There were other women, she guessed.

Martin noted her hesitation, and wondered at the reason for it. Didn't she want him to meet Brian Mordant, then? Had he got to be kept hidden like the black sheep of the family he supposed he was? He stood up, looked round the cosy sitting-room, out to the gardens, the trees, felt the size of the great house behind them. And for all his good intentions he was unable to keep the bitterness out of his voice, even though he hardly understood why he should feel that way. 'You've done all right then, haven't you?'

'What? Marrying Brian?'

'You certainly didn't wait long to get your hands on the factory.'

'Well, it's what you were doing, isn't it? That's why you were marrying Roberta. You weren't in love with her at all, so don't fool yourself.'

He looked at her, already in a temper. How pretty she was. No, pretty wasn't the right word – attractive, that was it. She'd always been attractive. Yet there was a difference about her that he couldn't pin down. A sadness in her eyes, a low-spirited air. And she didn't look well. Not really well. 'No,' he said slowly, calming down, regretting his outburst. 'I wasn't in love with Roberta.'

'Well then, I'm not in love with Brian.'

He took this to mean that she wasn't sleeping with him, and was pleased. Didn't want to think of his sister with that dumb cluck. And he was angry with himself for starting an argument when he'd promised himself he wouldn't.

'There's a new world beginning,' he said enthusiastically, and she nodded.

'I know, I want to change the factory. That's what I want to do. And maybe you can help me.'

He pursed his lips but did not reply. They sat in companionable silence looking out at the trees. Maybe I should stay here and help, he pondered, and was suddenly filled with eagerness at the thought of this new world they could bring into being together.

Into the silence came the thin wail of a baby's cry. Martin's head jerked up. 'What's that?'

He was answered by Renie, carrying Marie. 'I'm just going to take her for her nap, Mrs Mordant,' and she brought the child to her mother, who kissed the little cheek gently. Immediately Marie started to cry again.

'Better put her to bed,' Marged said with a sigh.

Martin stared. Like most men he had no idea of a baby's age. He said harshly: 'Well, quite the happy family then. You and Brian and the baby. You didn't tell me that.'

'I was going to—'

'You said you didn't care for him. What is it with you? You couldn't wait five minutes, could you? You had this big love affair with Stefan. You were going to marry him, as I remember—'

'Stefan went back, alone.'

'Oh, did he? And as I said, you couldn't wait. Off with the old love, on with the new. First Brenda, then you—'

She frowned, thinking she understood. He was old-fashioned about women as she'd told him, especially women of his own family. She began: 'It wasn't quite like that, Martin.'

'But it is like that, isn't it?'

Now she was angry too. They had always struck sparks off each other. 'That coming from you!' she cried. 'How many girls did you go with? Why is it different for men?'

'But you said you didn't care for him—'

'If you'd just listen—'

'I've heard everything I want to hear. Anyway, I'm going away. That's what I came to tell you.'

He turned, and she stood up, her lips pressed together, obstinate and obdurate, as always when faced by his anger, hiding the hurt that he had planned to leave, that this was just a quick call, hello and goodbye. 'Where are you going?' she asked.

'I'm taking one of those educational courses, training to be a teacher. I shan't come back.'

And she was filled with panic that he was leaving, all the family were going, had gone. Brenda ... she couldn't lose him, too ... She wanted to beg him, to plead. You're all I've got, stay with me. My baby doesn't want me, Brian doesn't want me. I'm just here to run the factory. But it wasn't her way, especially when she was angry. She said, 'You can't go like that. You can have a good job at Mordant's.'

Again he stopped. 'Courtesy of my sister and Brian Mordant? No thank you.'

'Don't be so stiff-necked, Martin.' And then it all came out, in her anger, the words she hadn't meant to say till there was a propitious moment. 'You must stay, you have a right. Martin—' he was walking away. 'I know why Roberta did what she did. She found out that—'

'Yes?' He waited.

Now there was no turning back. 'That Mordant was your father,' she whispered.

'You – *what?*' *He came to her then, grasped her arm and shook her.* She thought he was going to hit her. 'What are you saying?'

365

'It's true,' she said dully. 'I read it in her diary. And I went to see Aunt Ann. She told me it was true. So you see, you're entitled to a good job.' Now she was holding his arm, begging him to understand.

He wrenched away and walked to the door.

'Martin,' she called, despairingly. 'Stay here with me!'

There was no answer. The outer door slammed.

Martin had never wondered too much who his real father was. Families in Victoria Street before the war were never the small, tidy nuclear-family units they were to become in later years. They were made up of so many oddments, cousins, older sisters' babies, orphans brought up by relatives, all jumbled together. After the first shock of hearing the conversation in his childhood, his anger had been turned against the unknown man who had hurt little Grace, the girl in the photograph, and this remained, anger against an unknown man. That in due course this anger was turned on Maurice Mordant seemed a natural progression, but he had always thought of Frank and Eva as his parents. He still did. There was a sort of inevitability about the unknown man being Mordant, as if he'd always known.

He thought of Roberta with revulsion. Incest was a word never used in Victoria Street but it was there; it hovered over the small houses like a shadow waiting to pounce, and they all knew it. It was the reason their mothers never let boys go in the girls' bedrooms and vice versa, why they went to inordinate lengths to take separate baths, why, when one man up the road had 'touched' his daughter, the shocked whispers echoed round the street for years. It was regarded as far worse than anything Mrs Wilton did. And this shadow killed any feelings Martin had for Roberta. Only the anger remained.

He walked back to number forty, nodded to Jack, went straight up to his bedroom, gazing unseeingly at the former back field. He'd go away as he'd said, leave Mordant's to rot. It didn't matter now. Leave Marged to it.

He paced round the room. So why was he hesitating? He didn't want to stay now, did he? With Marged? Why should he?

He stopped pacing, stood if as struck. He knew why he didn't want to leave, not even for the education he'd always craved. He was in love with Marged. That was why he was so upset when he heard she'd married Brian Mordant – why the thought of them sleeping together made him squirm.

Why hadn't he realised it before? He hadn't been jealous of Stefan. Had he ...? Marged used to complain that he was offhand with him, and there was the time he'd offered Stefan his own bed because he didn't want him slipping into Marged's. Not that he'd really believed they were having that sort of relationship, nor did he really believe they'd stay together. Wishful thinking? Or was it because he wasn't in love with Marged then; he was having that mad affair with Roberta. So when had he stopped thinking of Marged as a sister? Was it not true that he'd loved her for a long time – had known in his heart, though refusing to admit it with his head. Somehow he'd always thought Marged would be there – for him. Typically masculine, she would say.

So now what to do? Other men would be little gentlemen and go away. He grinned. He was no gentleman. He'd stay and get her away from Brian Mordant. Why should Brian Mordant have everything and he nothing? *Even Marged.*

Jack Morris said incredulously, 'You're going back to Mordant's, to your old job? I thought you were taking one of those courses—'

'I've changed my mind.'

'But why?'

No answer.

'Surely, if you want to stop, your sister could get you a better job.'

'She's not my sister.'

'Well, your cousin, then.'

Martin went to the wireless set on the sideboard, turned it on, and the strains of a dance band filled the room. He switched off and stood, moodily.

'She's not my sister, and if you must know, I've just learned something about my family. I don't suppose it's a secret any longer—'

'What are you talking about?'

'You know I was illegitimate?'

'Yes.'

'I've just learned who my father was. Mordant.'

'Mordant?' Jack whistled.

'Funny, en't it? The man I've always hated.'

'Oh come on, I don't suppose he was all that bad. Just an employer.'

Martin threw himself into the armchair and sat sullenly, hands in pockets, legs outstretched. 'Maybe not.' He snorted a half-laugh. 'Do you know, when I was a kid listening to my dad I thought of Mordant as an evil-looking man like a Dickens character, stumping around with a big stick. I was quite surprised when his daughter said she liked him. Even more surprised to see he was a smart, good-looking man. My first lesson in how not to judge by appearances.'

'Oh well.' Jack moved to the window where a few spots of rain began to slide down the panes. 'I don't suppose it's any worse having him for a dad than somebody like old man West who drinks and knocks his family about.'

'Not now he don't. They've grown up,'

'But you think this is a reason to work in the factory? You're off your rocker.'

'I used to want to ruin Mordant,' Martin said.

'And Mordant's dead.'

'But his son's still alive, and Marged seems to have gone over to the enemy.'

'Martin – don't make trouble.'

Martin, unable to settle, jumped to his feet again as the Littletons' gramophone began to play. He banged on the wall. 'Bloody racket,' he shouted. He turned to Jack. 'People have always been telling me that. Why shouldn't I make trouble? I seem to get hold of the raw end of the stick every time.'

'So what about the new world you were so keen on?'

'Oh, there'll be a new world all right. I'll see to that.'

'So what do you plan to do?'

The Littletons turned the gramophone up louder. Martin shrugged. 'For the start I'll go back to my old job.'

'You know,' Jack moved to the fireplace and took a spill from the shelf to light his cigarette as matches were scarce, 'if there's to be a new world, we've got to forget, as well as the bosses.'

'Yes, thank you, Patience Strong. But some things can't be forgotten, can they? Like who your father was.'

In June 1946, the Communists proposed a referendum in Poland. The results were faked and everyone knew it. The 'free' elections promised at Yalta to Churchill were not to take place until 1947. In Gdansk, Barbara Kowalska waited for news of her son. But Stefan was no longer in Poland.

The interrogation had been long, and in between he had been taken to a cell with nine other inmates. There were four planks in the room, a table, a bucket of water. They were given a little bread and water and a portion of soup, were taken to the lavatory twice a day, though not allowed to stop too long. As night fell he lay on the floor and tried to sleep. Once he thought he heard cries and he shivered. The prisoners talked in low tones, said how even if they were released they would not be free. They would not be allowed to work unless with one of the working parties. They'd have nothing . . . 'We should not have come,' they said. 'We should have stayed in England.'

The next night, he had just managed to doze off when

there was a clang, and a bright light shone into the cell. He woke with a start to see two guards. 'Stefan Kowalski!' they shouted, waking everyone in the cell, and presumably in the whole prison. And when he staggered to his feet they pulled him roughly through the door.

They took him to the interrogation room, with bare table and chairs, behind which sat two NKVD officers, tall, stern men. The questions he had already answered were repeated. What was he doing in England? Why did he go to the West? Why not join with the Soviet forces?

And be shot like those officers in Katyn? Aloud, Stefan said: 'The Germans were behind me. I had no choice.'

And in England you did what? Were stationed where? All the time? Which towns did you visit?

'I wasn't on holiday,' Stefan returned, shortly.

'You went to London?'

'Only to get trains . . .' What was all this about? Why was he being interrogated? For going away or coming back?

The questions went on. Were you influenced by the decadent West?

The what? The bombed cities and the people in queues, the women in the factories, the men in the forces? He said loudly. 'What on earth are you talking about?'

The NKVD officer nodded to the guard at the door. 'Take this man back to the cell,' he ordered. And he went back, and was fetched for questioning again the next night and the next, until he could hardly think straight.

'Why did you come back?' they asked. 'Do you still have any communication with London?'

'No. And why did I come? I wanted to find my wife.'

This was met with astonishment. 'Where is your wife?'

'You took her to the Soviet Far East for no reason except that she was my wife.'

'She must have committed a crime against the State.'

Stefan said nothing. The thought of Janina committing any sort of crime was laughable.

The other man said, 'Come now, confess the whole of your activities and those of your wife.'

Stefan blinked. 'I've got nothing to confess,' he said, astonished in his turn. It was like talking to people from another planet. Nothing they said made sense.

'Come now,' repeated the second man 'Confess everything counter-revolutionary that you have done in the whole of your life against the cause of the working people.'

Stefan stared. Were they serious? 'I haven't done anything against the workers,' he replied. 'I am a worker myself. My father was a farmer. We all worked hard. My mother is living in a tumbledown apartment.'

'You were born near Pinsk, yes?'

'Yes.'

'Then you are a Soviet citizen. That area belongs to the Soviet Union.'

'It didn't when I lived there,' muttered Stefan.

'Were you a farmer?' asked the second officer.

'No!' defiantly. 'I was a musician.' He wondered if he'd get on better if he said he was a labourer. But the world needed musicians just as it needed labourers, doctors as well as dockers.

'A musician. Where did you study?'

Defiant again he replied, 'Warsaw.'

'And during the war you went to England.'

This, of course, put him beyond the pale. He was a Western sympathiser. Probably a spy. Again he was asked to confess, again and again. In the end he was silent; there seemed no point in talking. He supposed he was lucky he wasn't tortured. . He was marched back to the cell. Fetched out again. Asked to confess. Again and again.

Time no longer meant anything. Some of his cellmates disappeared – no one knew where they went. Stefan was taken before the NKVD again.

They kept him waiting as they deliberated together. Then the first officer spoke. 'You will have to go to prison.'

'But why?'

This seemed to flummox them. You didn't ask Soviet secret police why. 'What am I accused of?' he asked.

'You are a socially dangerous person and can be sentenced without trial.'

And then – perhaps they did have a sense of humour after all: 'You want to find your wife in Siberia? You will go to Siberia for six years. To Magadan.'

And he was led away.

The journey to Magadan took four weeks in winter weather. There was still deep snow when he arrived at the penal camp. He saw hundreds of prisoners, living in huts, one hundred to each hut. The other inmates looked a rough lot, to put it mildly. They were not merely political prisoners but violent murderers and cut-throat thieves.

He was thrust into a hut and a hundred pairs of eyes stared at him. One man said, 'Got anything?'

Stefan eyed him warily and said cautiously, 'I have a cigarette.'

He held out a packet and it was snatched from him. He was allocated a bed. It was bitterly cold, so no one undressed. Stefan looked with distaste at the 'bed' of planks, covered by a dirty blanket. 'Who was in this last?' he asked.

'He died,' said a voice.

He saw the man in the next bed was winding wire round his body. This man looked approachable so Stefan whispered, 'Why are you doing that?'

'So nobody will steal my clothes,' he replied, and Stefan was thankful that someone had warned him to wear all his clothes and to hide all his valuables. Even so, he did not sleep that night, and in the morning he mentioned casually and untruthfully that he had been a boxer.

Life in penal çamps was no Sunday-School picnic, he reflected ruefully. The first law was to survive.

Reveille was at five o'clock, and the prisoners were given

a piece of bread and a portion of gruel, neither enough to feed a man. Then they were marched under escort to the mines. Stefan was given work on the surface, digging the frozen earth with picks and chisels. They stopped for half an hour's break for dinner – five ounces of bread and sometimes a piece of fish. He found himself near the man from the next bed, and joined him.

'You're Polish too,' he said. 'How did you come to be here?'

'Yes, I'm Jacek. Well, I was in the AK during the Warsaw siege. I didn't give myself up to the Germans, I carried on with the resistance.' He paused as a guard approached. 'Those who gave themselves up were persecuted; more persons were arrested then than during the entire German occupation. Then the leaders of our new movement were enticed to Warsaw on 29 March, 1945 – by assurances of safe conduct – and were taken to Moscow and condemned to long terms of imprisonment. One of them was Wojciech Jaruzelski. Fifty thousand of us were deported to the Soviet Union – and here we are.'

'How long are you here for?'

'Once here, it's for life. They give you five years, and when that's finished you get another five – if you're not dead first.'

'Come on, up!' shouted the guard.

They worked until eight p.m., then, if they had done their stint, they could return to camp. Stefan had not, so he had to work another two hours.

For the first few days he was too exhausted even to think. The savage cold bit into him though, unlike the others, he was wearing good clothes. The cold was agonising. The air burned, sounds were brittle, frost seeped everywhere, clung to them, attacked them, froze their breath as it escaped from their tortured lungs. The convicts had no way to dry their clothing, disease was rife, and if a prisoner died in the night his body was concealed for as long as possible so as to receive his ration of bread. Sunday was not recognised. They worked every day; all mention of religion was forbidden.

There were all nationalities and classes. As well as the Soviet criminals and political prisoners, there were Poles, Czechs, Jews who had fled eastwards to get away from the Germans ...

It was on the coldest day of the winter that he trudged over the frozen snow with Jacek. He thought the man seemed exhausted, near to breaking point. Once the digging had started and their breath froze on the air it was first Leon, an elderly Jew, who collapsed. The guard dragged him to a nearby hut. Stefan thought he was giving the man a rest when he heard a shot.

He stood, appalled. Jacek threw down his spade. 'This bloody place is hell,' he cried. 'Hell, it's hell! It shouldn't be allowed.'

'Steady,' whispered Stefan, but it was too late. The guards ordered Jacek to the hut. They heard another shot. Then the two bodies were thrown into the snow.

'Any more?' asked the guard. Stefan carried on working.

He was seething, furious, angry at his own helplessness. And back at the hut he looked round at his fellow prisoners. They had all seen what had happened, but had carried on as if it were normal procedure. Perhaps it was. He wanted to shout, to protest, to hit out ... He knew he could not, or he too would be shot, and that wouldn't help anybody. He had to survive. He would survive.

He set himself to study survival methods.

He learned about life in the camps as he trudged through the frozen snow, the water and mud when the snow melted; when his boots began to wear out and he should have had a new pair but didn't; when the sun shone and swarms of mosquitoes began to bite, causing sores that would not heal, and diarrhoea and dysentery were common; when the men fought among themselves for the least thing and the weakest were beaten to death and no one cared, and he thought, I must get out. I must get out, must . . .

He learned that survival was obtained through '*blat*', graft, putting someone under an obligation to you, so he survived by bartering his goods. Even the NKVD were eager to buy his clasp-knife – he had another one concealed – and his compass. Then he started to study the work methods.

The work-gangs were split into brigades, each with a leader drawn from the prisoners themselves and chosen by them to be their mouthpiece. The executive posts were held by the NKVD, but the clerical work was done by prisoners; the overseers, chosen from convicts. Yet it was the brigade leaders who were the most important. They needed to keep up maximum output or they'd lose their privileges. The NKVD had to keep up output or they, too, would be in trouble. So to this extent the NKVD were dependent on the brigade leaders. And it was, naturally, the roughest of the criminals who got this power.

Their own brigade leader was Boris, a criminal-looking type if ever there was one, and Stefan kept an eye on him. For some time Stefan had been surviving by bartering his possessions and by making himself indispensable, writing and reading the few letters for those Soviets who could not do either. And when Boris came in with written orders from the NKVD and sat with a puzzled frown, Stefan offered to help. Boris accepted and he was in business.

Now Boris owed him a favour and one humid day when the mosquitoes were particularly virulent, he mentioned to the leader that he knew another man was needed in the office, and if he could get the job he could help Boris by favouring him with work allocations and so on.

'Political prisoners are not allowed to take those jobs,' Boris told him.

'No, but surely, in this out-of-the-way camp, who's to know? I could perhaps change the way the prison's run.'

'We like it this way,' Boris told him. 'We want to pick our own brigade leaders,' and for the moment Stefan was nonplussed.

Boris was not a particularly bright individual. Brawn rather than brain, he had already killed one man in the camp. But favours he understood, and as the NKVD were getting desperate for help, before the winter set in Stefan was moved into the office where his life became much easier.

Though not *too* easy. He had to write out false reports of the work that was done, knowing that the gang leaders cheated on this, just as the NKVD sent out false reports in their turn, to both their superiors and to the brigades. So Stefan had to ride this merry-go-round, trying to please both sides, giving favours to Boris who had got him the job, and keeping the NKVD sweet, as his bosses. It was like walking a tightrope that threatened to break every day.

Yet he managed to talk and even joke with the NKVD at times – at least the ones who owed him favours and who were less rigid in their attitudes. He needed their help to find Janina. He had to find the weakest link, and he was genuinely curious as to what made them tick.

They all repeated the Communist dogma parrot-fashion, and he wondered if they believed it. Sometimes they'd give talks to the hapless prisoners, and when they returned Stefan would indulge in a little mild teasing. So when they said, 'No one suffered as we did in the war,' Stefan replied: 'What about Poland? We lost one in five people and all our country, which was the most devastated in Europe.'

They were astonished. They had never been to Poland.

'Why did you take Poland?' Stefan persisted.

'We didn't take it – your people wanted us to come. You were a capitalist country, like the West. Now you must suffer for the greater glory of the Idea. You will all be citizens of the great Soviet Union.'

'That's what we were afraid of,' muttered Stefan.

376

'We were invaded by Germany,' said another officer. 'Now we must have a buffer state between us and them.'

'And what about our buffer state?' asked Stefan.

'What?' They were puzzled.

'Why shouldn't Poland have a buffer state to protect us? Why shouldn't every country?'

This was beyond them and the subject was changed. But when the two went out and Stefan was left with a quiet officer named Vladimir Primakov, the man said: 'You should be careful. You could be shot for talking like that.'

Stefan knew he was right. But he also knew that he had to say these things, had to insist on his individuality to prevent himself from becoming an unthinking zombie – even if he were shot.

Vladimir was watching him, seeing the conflicting emotions chasing over his face, for Stefan had not yet learned the poker-faced immobility that the NKVD wore to hide their thoughts. 'I'm used to freedom,' Stefan said shortly.

'What is freedom?' asked Vladimir. Then: 'Just be careful who you say these things to.'

Stefan stared. Was this an invitation to talk to him, or merely a trap? He'd have to watch this man.

But he survived. And he managed to send a card to Marged.

Chapter 15

It was Colin Jackson who told Marged that Martin was back in his old job. 'I wondered if you knew?' he asked.

She looked up. 'No. No, I didn't.'

'You see, I thought maybe you would want him to have something better—'

'Yes, I did,' she said shortly. 'He obviously didn't.'

Colin looked uncomfortable. 'Perhaps he thinks the others would see it as favouritism. If so, I'm sure he's mistaken. Martin is a skilled worker. He is above average intelligence, the men like him, and he would make a good leader. In short, he deserves something better. I thought maybe we could do more of that in the future, move people upwards instead of bringing in outsiders.'

'Yes, I agree. And no, Martin wouldn't think it was favouritism. In any case, there is another reason for him deserving a better job which has nothing to do with our being related. Maybe I'll tell you about it some time.'

'I take it you have quarrelled?'

'Yes, and that's not new, we always did. So I'm afraid there's not much we can do.'

'You wouldn't want me to have a word with him?'

'I think you'd be wasting your time. No, leave it for now.' She hesitated. 'I never believed in tale-bearing, as you know, and I don't listen to gossip. But I would like to

378

know how he goes on – as he won't tell me.'

'He's joined the union.'

'Well, yes, I suppose he would. He believes in that sort of thing, and Mordant wouldn't allow them before the war.' She broke off. 'Just a minute, I have a better idea. Will you be meeting the union leaders?'

'I suppose they'll come to us if they have a dispute.'

'Would it not be better if we had regular meetings? Get to know each other, work together—'

'That's pretty revolutionary.'

'Still, I think it would work. Say, with you and perhaps Mr Norris, the Works Manager. Then I could come to the first meeting, and to others where there is a dispute.'

'You're expecting disputes?'

'Knowing Martin, yes.'

The first meeting took place in the staff canteen after hours, and as Marged and Colin Jackson walked across the yard she remembered the first time she had entered the canteen as a new little shorthand-typist, scared of the senior staff. How much had changed since then. Miss Sansome, Mr Walters acid-faced secretary, had retired, and he had taken on a much younger, much prettier girl. Still, she supposed Miss Sansome had been young once.

'We'll have to improve this,' Marged said as they entered the canteen. 'Bare tables, it's like the workhouse.'

'At some firms they have mixed staff canteens, with little tables set out like a restaurant,' he told her.

'But not mixed with the works?'

'No.'

'Same as the lavatories, one for works, one for staff. It's like apartheid in South Africa.'

He chuckled.

The union men were waiting as they entered, sitting at one of the tables, and they did not stand. Martin was there, with two other men she did not recognise. So the cousins met for the first time since their quarrel, seated at opposite sides of the long table, introducing themselves, Martin Fennel, Les Morton, Norman Wells. Marged welcomed them to the first meeting, said she hoped it would be the first of many, and if they had any grievance, they must put it before the meeting when she would endeavour to set things right. She wanted them all to work together. She'd be pleased to receive any suggestions etc ...

Martin gave a colourless response, without making any promises, and there followed other short speeches from Colin Jackson and Mr Norris, who was reputed to be strict but fair and was in no way disliked.

When the meeting broke up, Marged waited for some sign from Martin, but there was none. He simply walked away. She left, feeling let down.

The Board, as always, gave a mixed reaction to the meetings, with sniffs and scepticism from Walters and Byers. 'This fellow Norman Wells is a Communist,' said Mr Byers.

'How do you know that?' asked Marged.

'I heard it on the grapevine,' he retorted smugly.

'Is this true?' she asked Colin Jackson.

'I believe so. But I don't think there is any need to worry. The Communists have been working with the government during the war, and still do. And anyway, he is not the chief shop steward. That is Martin Fennel. Voted in by the men.'

Mr Byers sniffed. 'There'll be trouble,' he warned. 'You mark my words.'

'I see no point in looking for trouble,' Marged said firmly. 'We have a full order book, though cars are to be mainly for export to help the money situation—'

'Poor old Britons. We won the war, now can't have cars,' said Mr Byers.

'We have a lot to do if British industry is to recover its pre-war trading position,' Marged continued. 'We must work with all those involved in making the components—'

'But not let them get the upper hand,' interrupted Byers again. 'Or we'll soon be losing money.'

'I have noticed,' Marged ignored him, 'that firms are using more road transport these days. Whether this will go on, I don't know, but it would mean more work for us. Mr James, will you look into this?'

'I already have, Mrs Mordant. I have the promise of a large order from one lorry-making firm, and possibly another.'

'Good,' said Marged.

1946 was not the best of years. A world wheat shortage forced the government to ration bread in May; normal consumers were allowed nine ounces daily, male manual workers fifteen. But Labour went ahead and nationalised the ailing coal industry. Railways and road transport were added, then gas and electricity. The British love affair with the Soviet Union was cooling as it became clear that the Russians were determined that all the Eastern European countries should be under Communist control. Britain, France and the US found themselves supplying goods to the Russians, and as the Germans could not support themselves, they were helped by the British taxpayer, which meant rising taxes, and made Marged wear a worried frown. Mordant's had a full order book, but could not afford to let up. Wages had risen, and she wanted to make so many improvements. To do this she had to keep things on an even keel, and this depended on unpredictable outside factors – the world situation, prices, costs, and the hope that the car factories wouldn't have any problems or they'd be in trouble, too.

And Martin began to show his hand.

'I think you'd better come to this next union meeting,' Colin told Marged. 'We've been officially informed that the men have a grievance.'

'Oh dear. Do you know what it is?'

'Not yet.'

They walked to the canteen together, and the meeting opened without much of a welcome. 'What is the trouble?' Marged asked.

Martin stood up, his dark hair falling over his forehead, making Marged long to push it away – and him with it. He said: 'Every time a man wants another tool he has to walk right down to the end of the shop, back again, use it, return it, instead of having them all to hand.'

'Well?'

'We want new methods.'

She turned to Mr Norris. 'This would save time, I suppose. Can it be arranged?'

'This is the way we've always worked. Yes, the system could be changed, but it would take a lot of reorganisation.'

'But it would save time in the long run?'

'Certainly.'

'Then get it done.' She turned away from Martin's look of triumph. She knew the Old Guard would say she was giving in, but as she told Colin Jackson later, 'The trouble with Martin is that he's always right. That was time-wasting.'

'I agree. But if he'd just mention it first at a meeting instead of waiting and making a big grievance out of it, getting the men all worked up.'

'Does he do that?'

'Yes.'

Outwardly, number forty Victoria Street looked pretty much the same as when Brenda had lived there. The garden was tidier though, as Jack Morris was fond of gardening, or perhaps it would be truer to say that like most men of his class, he had grown up with it, regarded it as a duty. So now, as autumn approached, the back garden still produced potatoes, runner beans, a few cabbages.

Inside, the furniture was exactly the same. It was kept clean by Jack's mother on her twice-weekly visits, but there was a general air of untidiness, of coats slung over chairs, of pots in the sink waiting to be washed up, of dust allowed to settle on the sideboard. The photographs that had once stood there, of Brenda and Jack's wedding, of the Fennel family taken in their back garden, had disappeared, as had the embroidered runner, leaving more space for caps and scarves to be abandoned on the once-neat top.

Martin lounged at the table, watching Jack comb his hair before the mirror. The teapot stood on the bare table – tablecloths were a refinement not considered necessary by two men alone – and he poured another cup of tea, as a knock came at the back door.

'Here's your mate,' said Jack. 'Come in, Bob. I'm just off. I'll leave you to your night-shift,'

'Where's he going, all dressed up?' Bob Simmons asked, as Jack strode away.

'He's found himself another woman.'

'Has he now? Serious?'

Martin shrugged. 'Who knows?'

'I hear you're taking out one of the office tarts.' Bob turned back to Martin.

'Yes. Ann Waring.'

'All right, is she?'

'She passes the time.'

'Well, en't you ready? Come on, get moving.'

Martin gulped the rest of his tea, jumped up, combed back his own hair, for he always looked neat even when going to work, ushered Bob out, locked the door, and walked round the entry.

Children were playing in the street as they always had; the only signs of war here were in the odd tiles on the roofs, replaced in a hurry, showing up now in different colours. Even the bombed houses had been completely cleared. It was rumoured that someone wanted to build posh semis in the space when they could get permission.

The desperate housing shortage was being alleviated by council pre-fabricated and steel houses built on estates instead of being part of the ordinary street, and the most overcrowded of the citizens had already been installed there, including two of the Wests, who loved their new bathrooms and mod. cons. Though it was said that the owners of the nearby semis didn't fancy having all the town's riff-raff placed next to them. The back streets of the future? Martin wondered. Or perhaps there wouldn't be any back streets in the future. The council were building good houses now, made of brick, with big gardens.

Bob interrupted his reverie. 'I wanted a word with you,' he said.

'Um?'

'About this meeting you're calling. Is it really necessary?'

'I think so.'

'Well, I don't see it. I mean, I don't understand what you're doing. I know you always hated Mordant since we were at school, but he's dead now.'

'Brian's not dead.'

'So what are you trying to do? Get rid of Brian?'

'He's a Mordant.'

'But he's never at the place! He doesn't run it now, and you know that. Your sister runs it.'

'So?'

'So if you get rid of Brian, you'll get rid of her an' all.'

'Well, if she will take up with the likes of Brian Mordant—'

They had reached the corner and waited as a council dust truck passed them. 'Well, I think you're daft, and I'm not the only one. I'm not coming to your meeting, and neither will some of the others. You'll only have Norman Wells and the likes of him.'

They walked past the canal, on down the hill. 'I don't understand what you're doing,' Bob repeated.

They had reached the bus stop, and inside the bus they

separated. As Martin alighted at the factory and walked through the gates he brooded on Bob's words. He liked Bob, they had been pals since childhood.

You can't get rid of Brian Mordant, they said. Why not? Maybe when you'd been in the war you didn't think in the same way when you came back. You had been trained to kill out there, that's why so many kept on doing it. And you came home to find your girl had married someone else ...

So he was seeing Ann Waring. She was all right, as girls went. Trouble was, he *had* changed. He no longer wanted to go hell-raising, taking out as many girls as he could for what he could get. As a man got older he wanted to settle down. Like Jack Morris.

So you came back and had different hopes, and found them thrown back in your face. So you had no hopes now, and that left only the anger.

In Poland the Communists did not seize power. They were installed, protected and directed by the Soviet Union. The NKVD had searched through the prison camps to find Polish men and women who would be loyal to Marxism, to the Soviet Union and to Stalin. Barbara Kowalska heard of it and snorted: 'Bribing them with freedom if they join the Party – what's it called? – the Polish Workers' Party. Ha!'

But as the 'free' elections approached in January 1947, Barbara was worried, as were they all, at what was happening to the candidates of the Peasant (Non-Communist) Party. Mr Mikolajczyk, leader of the London Poles, protested from Warsaw that scores of the candidates had been terrorised or murdered. Britain and the US sent notes of protest, which the Soviet Union rejected. They tried to send independent observers to the elections, but all such attempts were blocked.

Barbara had a job now, helping in a small shop. It kept body and soul together, and she could take little Tadeusz with her. The child was thriving. Now a year old, he stumbled around the apartment, a bright boy, resembling his father in looks but with his mother's dark eyes. Barbara searched the shops, queueing for food, for clothing, and came home triumphantly one day with a huge knitted garment which she proceeded to unravel and knit a little suit from it for the child. There was so much wool she was able to knit four, and she laughingly called it *Babcia*'s everlasting wool.

She had received a letter from Stefan some months earlier, from the prison camp, and her heart was heavy as she read it. *Don't worry about me, Matka,* he wrote, *it will only be for a few years. And maybe I'll find Janina here – if only I knew where she was.*

Barbara thought of her favourite son in a prison camp. 'I was wrong to arrange that marriage,' she told herself. 'I was crazy – but we were all crazy at the time. With German tanks rolling through Czechoslovakia, I knew it was only a matter of time before they came into Poland. It was Jan's dream to join the two farms ... and I thought, "If Stefan doesn't come back, maybe there will be a son to carry on." I was selfish. God forgive me.'

She went to Mass every Sunday, praying for her son, asking forgiveness for her part in the tragedy. But she did not spend too much time in repining, nor, when she heard from Stefan, in tears. It was not her way. She did her penance, but saying a few Hail Marys was not enough for this indomitable woman. She would work for the future. She pestered the offices of the International Red Cross for news of Janina, then went home and waited.

She would sit with little Tadeusz in the evenings, telling him of their old home where the storks flew, the river shining in the sun, the cows grazing in the meadows, the children, now lost to her ... She turned it into a fairy tale, the happy family, the big bad giant who threw them out, the handsome prince who would one day save them. And little Tadeusz would stare at her, round-eyed.

Then one hot day in July a couple turned up on her doorstep, the man thin, emaciated, the woman supporting him. He said: 'You have been enquiring about Janina Kowalska? I think I can help you.'

'Come in, come in.' And they went into the room with the table and chairs and Barbara asked, 'My poor boy, where have you come from?'

'Siberia.' And a little shiver went through her.

'And you live here now, in Gdansk?'

'We have no home,' the woman said. 'I found him on the station. The Red Cross told us about you looking for information.'

Their names were Jerzy and Ewa, they explained, as she bustled around finding food. 'First eat,' she commanded, and they all sat at the rickety table, with Tadeusz on Barbara's lap.

And Ewa said dully, 'I've just got in from Warsaw, looking for my parents who were taken to Germany. I cannot find any trace of them. They must be dead.' And they thought sorrowfully of the thousands of people searching hopelessly for their loved ones, of crowds waiting on railway stations, holding up names, wondering if anyone had news of Jan or Josef or Maria . . .

'And you have nowhere to stay?'

'Not yet,' Ewa said apologetically.

'Then you must stay here.' And Barbara placed the mattress on the kitchen floor, while she and Ewa slept on blankets on the bed. Tadeusz, of course, had his cot.

'That's a fine cot,' said Ewa admiringly.

'Yes, I found it,' Barbara answered complacently. 'There was this big house, it had been bombed – naturally. The people were dead, God rest their souls, and this cot stood there, on the pavement. I knew they would wish Tadeusz to have it.' She beamed.

It was three days before Jerzy was well enough to tell her his story, and she waited patiently. So they sat, in the evening after their meal, looking out through the open doorway to the setting sun.

'I lived on the eastern side,' Jerzy began. 'with my family, parents, brothers and sisters, six of us. I was fifteen, the eldest. We were all taken to Russia, but I was separated from my family – I never saw them again.' He drew a breath. 'I was taken to Vladivostok, in the Far East. It was a sort of clearing house for prisoners. There were about twenty-five thousand people camping in the open—' He broke off and Barbara said, 'Go slowly now, Jerzy.'

'Yes.' He paused a moment, and from above came the sound of hammering. 'I was taken across the Sea of Japan to Magadan, then to another centre farther north. Another boat up-river – sleeping on the deck. Oh—' Again he broke off. 'The horrors – the people who died, were just thrown off the ship—' He began to tremble, and Barbara said, 'Wait now, Ewa, a drink for Jerzy.'

He drank a little of the weak tea, then continued: 'The river became unnavigable from ice, and we ran out of drinking water.' He took another gulp of tea at the memory. 'It was thirty-five degrees below zero – many were frostbitten, had to have legs amputated—' He stood up, shaking.

'That's enough now. You stay here with us, we will take care of you,' Barbara said, and much as she wanted to hear about Janina, she would not let him say any more.

But he wanted to talk, wanted to relive the horrors and perhaps then be able to forget all that now hung at the back of his mind like a black shadow threatening to creep over the whole of his brain, to paralyse him completely. Gradually his strength returned, and dressed in a suit of clothes given by the Red Cross, he began to look more like a human being. Ewa found a job in a new hospital, tending to people like Jerzy, while he helped with Tadeusz and slowly recovered. He liked Tadeusz, and said once: 'I had a little brother like him,' and he sat him on his lap as he told them the rest of his story.

'I was in Maldiak in 1941, when the Germans invaded

Russia and General Sikorski went to see Stalin about the release of the prisoners. I couldn't believe I'd be freed, but I was. I was given a document to say I could take up residence anywhere within the Soviet Union – with a few exceptions. I didn't want to stay. I wanted to go home, so I tried to get to Khabarovsk because I thought I'd get a train from there. We had to wait days on the railway station, hordes of us, trying to get food, queues everywhere, ex-prisoners begging for food ... We were ill, starving. The Russians were afraid of epidemics, so they refused to let us on the train. And indeed –' he gave a weak smile '– we were covered in lice. So I got a work permit and that's where I heard about Janina. She worked on a farm but she got her release.'

'And?' Barbara asked eagerly.

'She was ill. Helen, her friend, told me. Helen was with her but was re-arrested when she went for help. Later she heard that Janina was living with a family nearby.'

'Living with a family?'

'That's what she told me. She said Janina was afraid to go any further – she had been badly treated in the farm camp.' Again he was shivering uncontrollably.

'Enough now,' said Barbara. 'You're home'.

He said, 'I was working and I couldn't get my visa again. I had to wait ... wait ... Now I am free, caught a train part of the way. The rest I walked.'

Barbara was silent.

But later, as Jerzy, working now, and Ewa made their home with Barbara, she wrote to Stefan, telling him all she had learned, about Janina. She said that everything was fine with her, with Jerzy and Ewa helping, they shared expenses. But some things she did not tell him: how the NKVD went round to all the families of those servicemen who had stayed in England, interrogating, questioning ...

The time will soon pass, she wrote. *Then, please God, you will find Janina, and be able to come home, to me.*

★

When Janina had arrived at Vladivostok she was put on another truck and driven through green grass and fields. On they drove, and now the country was grey and flat. At last they came to a settlement of small dirty huts; no trees here. They were dragged down from the lorries, were told nothing. They simply lay on their bundles, too tired even for hunger. They waited for hours till at length several men approached them, not Russians, but local natives. They were very poor, and took them to an empty hut with four small rooms inside, earthen floors and open spaces for windows. The rooms were alive with bugs. There was one big kettle, but the nearest water was half a mile away.

The women had to collect dung for fuel. The men, mostly aged over seventy and including university professors, had to dig latrines and plough with oxen while the natives jeered. The women tried to make a stove with clay and old tins, but were sent out to work the next day. Only those who went to work were allowed to buy bread when available, though they bought some eggs from the natives, who didn't want money, just goods; they eyed the new-comers with envy, for the few possessions they had left were of much better quality than anything they themselves could obtain. After some time, they did get letters from home, and when food parcels started arriving they did well – for a time, anyway, since as in the penal camps, a good deal could be done by bribery and barter. Tea was especially coveted, and once Helen exchanged a packet of cigarettes for a whole bucket of scraps.

Helen was a lively girl who, seeing Janina's dejection, tried to make her laugh. 'Come, sing,' she'd say, and they'd begin some of the old Polish songs they loved so well.

The snow was deep, and they had to keep digging them-selves out; the hut was cold and dirty. Helen asked about Janina's life in Poland. 'You're married?' and she pointed to the ring.

'I don't remember.'

'Can't you think of his name?' Helen coaxed.

Janina tried. Strange how her memory seemed to play tricks these days, and she couldn't think clearly. Yet she remembered the day she'd fallen in the river because they were all so happy together, before any of them went away. And that other day when she walked home from church with Tadeusz ... Tadeusz, who'd said: 'I'll always take care of you.' That was the night Pani Kowalska proposed the idea of marriage to Stefan and she hadn't wanted it. She didn't really know Stefan – he'd been away so much. Tadeusz had always been her friend; she wasn't afraid of Tadeusz. And he was a farmer, which she liked, but he was too young, her own mother said. Her parents urged the marriage, it was a step up for them. Had she agreed ...? Was she really married ...?

It was such a critical bewildering time, with Pan Kowalski dying, the war imminent, Stefan waiting for his orders, sent for so hurriedly ... And Stefan had taken her aside and told her gently that he was doing it to please his parents. He owed them so much. Later they could part if they wished, and she asked how, and he said, it will not be a proper marriage. No, she could not remember any marriage. She was not anyone's wife – she was still a virgin.

So why did she wear a ring?

Her mind groped, went blank. There were always these patches of blackness in her mind these days ... Why did she wear a ring? ... Tadeusz had promised, 'I'll always take care of you ...' She said aloud: 'Tadeusz. My husband's name is Tadeusz.'

Helen looked at her in concern. 'Are you sure you're all right?'

'Yes, it was just a dream, the talk of marriage to Stefan. I get these strange dreams, bad dreams about men putting me on a truck and a train. Why would they do that?'

'Don't worry, it's all over now,' Helen soothed her.

'I don't want to go on a train again, Helen.'

'And you shan't. Now, when you get these bad dreams just think of Tadeusz, eh?'

Someone else had said that, who ... Pan Nowak? The schoolmaster? Why would he say that in school? But Janina said 'Yes,' obediently, and if the dream threatened to come again she blotted it out with the memory of Tadeusz saying: 'I'll always take care of you.' Tadeusz would come and find her.

'It will soon be Christmas,' Helen continued.

'Oh yes.' Janina's face lit up. 'I love Christmas, the celebrations, the tree with the angel on the top.'

And Helen said to the other women, 'Look, I'm worried about Janina. Let's give her a nice Christmas, eh?'

So they began to prepare. One brought in a branch of a tree, they decorated it with bits of rag torn from their clothes, and Helen secretly made a tiny doll out of sticks and dressed it in a strip of white cotton ripped from her petticoat. They saved bits of food and just before Christmas one girl received a food parcel from home containing a tin of fruit.

So on Christmas Eve Helen said to Janina: 'Let's go outside for a moment, shall we?'

'If you like.' Janina was always compliant. 'But it's cold.'

'I know, we'll walk,' and she put her arm in Janina's and they crunched over the frozen snow. Then, after ten minutes, Helen said, 'Look, Janina, the evening star.' And she led her back into the hut.

'Merry Christmas,' cried the women and Janina stood, transfixed.

The table was covered with their tin plates; on each was a biscuit and one plum from the tin. In the middle of the table was the little tree, and on the top, the angel.

'Oh,' Janina cried, clasping her hands. 'It's *lovely*!'

'Come, sit down,' invited Helen.

Janina sat, her face shining with joy. At the end of the table was an empty plate. She said, 'That's for Tadeusz.'

But she seemed brighter afterwards and Helen hoped she would be well.

The summer came, and it was hot when they were sent to summer pastures, to another small dirty hut. They had to milk the cows and as Janina began the natives mocked her for washing the udders, and she drew back, afraid of their laughter, their jeering faces.

One of the overseers began to follow her around, and this frightened her. She said nothing, not even to Helen, for what could she do? Janina was in a waking dream these days. She had never experienced anything like this man following her, and she didn't know how to deal with it. She was afraid. The brief bright spell at Christmas had lapsed, fear returned, lived with her the whole time. It was not a specific fear, not now. She was afraid of everything, of the harsh conditions, the men, the overseer, the NKVD, of the future, of what might happen next. Her face grew pinched and thin, but this only made her more desirable to the squat-faced natives.

Helen had no idea that she was suffering in this way. Helen, who would have repulsed any advances with a hearty farm-girl kick, who had no fear herself, could not possibly understand. She did sense Janina's trembling unhappiness, and tried to cheer her up. 'We'll get out,' she said optimistically. 'You'll see.'

Then Janina worried about her parents, for their letters had stopped coming and she wondered why. She, and all of them, were always hungry. Sometimes they stole ears of barley from the fields and made it into a sort of barley bread. It tasted strange, but it was food. For the rest they lived for food parcels, which were shared around.

The overseer was still following her, and she tried to stay close to the other girls. But it only needed one person to milk, and when it was her turn she took the milk to the shed – the nearest the farm came to a dairy – and the man followed her inside. Without a word, he came up beside her, and pushed her back to the wooden wall. Another native stood watching as he pushed himself against her while she made little frightened whimpers. He tore off her clothes. Janina struggled, tried to scream, but the other native came and held her. The overseer pulled down her knickers that were ragged and torn and of which she was ashamed even in her fear. Then he stood and raped her. Grunting like a pig, he forced himself into her, over and over. She could smell him, dirty, unwashed, the native giggling at his side. And when he'd finished and Janina fell to the ground, the native raped her too.

She staggered to her feet, went to the door. 'Tomorrow,' called the overseer.

Back at the hut, Janina collapsed on her bed. She felt unclean. She had lived on a farm and knew what animals did to copulate. She wanted to have children of her own and had no fear when it was Tadeusz in her mind. But this dirty creature forcing himself on her ... she knew she would never get his smell out of her nostrils, never. She lay, moaning.

Helen found her, saw her rumpled clothing, dragged the truth out of her. 'The rat,' she said. 'I'll tell the NKVD man when he comes.'

'Don't put ideas into *his* head,' interposed another woman.

'Well, I'll do something to put the fear of God into him,' Helen said, and went to look for the overseer. 'Hey, you!' she shouted. 'If you touch her again I'll report you to the NKVD.'

Now Janina lived in a dream. The dream took over completely; nothing was real any more. Sometimes she thought about the farm, her home, about Tadeusz, and she tried to keep hold of these thoughts, to blot out reality. Some day she would see Tadeusz again and her mother, her home, see the smoke curling from the chimney, *smell* the wood-smoke, which would take this other smell out of her nose.

394

She heard the others talking, but she herself said little. Sometimes she understood, sometimes not. But when, in 1941, everyone grew excited she, too, was infected by the euphoria. Hitler had attacked the Soviet Union, and General Sikorski was getting Polish prisoners freed from the camps. They were going to be released!

It was June when they heard, the weather hot and sticky. Many remote camps did nothing about the order, so they waited ... Suddenly illness struck. There was typhus in the camp, and the NKVD let them go.

Helen and Janina left together. Helen had set herself up as Janina's guardian since the rape. She knew the girl was hardly able to take care of herself.

They walked through the gates. Janina had a blinding headache, though she said nothing. She so often had headaches these days; she seldom felt well. She had a violent thirst too, but that wasn't so unusual, not in the Far East where you never had enough to drink. Nor did she think her flushed cheeks were anything out of the ordinary. She stumbled along beside Helen, hearing the other girl's excited chatter, not comprehending a word of it. Then, as they walked along she found the road beginning to slip up and down in the strangest way. Without warning she fell to the ground.

Helen, horrified, knelt beside her. 'Janina,' she cried, and now the girl was shaking with spasms. 'Janina! Oh my God. Typhus.'

She looked round wildly. They were on a lonely country lane. They'd been so eager to get away she hadn't taken enough care as to the route to Khabarovsk and the railway station. Now there was no sign of anyone, nor of any building.

Janina had lapsed into unconsciousness. 'I'll go and get help,' Helen said. 'I won't be a minute.'

She ran back to the camp where, in the inexplicable manner of the NKVD, she was re-arrested and taken inside. They had found they now had a shortage of labour.

Janina lay in the hot sun all day, and when night fell she opened her eyes to see a man leaning over her. 'What is the matter?' he asked. 'Who are you?'

'Janina Kowalska.'

'You're Polish?'

'Yes. From the camp.'

'So am I Polish. Or my ancestors were. Shipped out here in 1863. You're ill, aren't you? Come, I'll take you home. My wife will look after you.' And he picked her up and carried her away.

Marged was used to working with men, knew there was always the arm round the waist, the request for a date – and the married men were the worst. But now she had no one to chat with about fellows and homes and children. Corrie had promised to write but never had. That left only Brenda, for their marriages and lack of other women friends had brought them closer, and they would chat over the phone. On this bright day in October, when the leaves in the garden were turning red and brown, Marged sat on the chair in the hall giving Brenda the gossip – how there had been talk because one of the staff, a middle-aged man, had run away with a young typist.

'He used to buy me cups of tea when I was in the general office,' mourned Marged. 'How fickle men are.'

Brenda laughed. 'Poor you. Do you have to buy your own tea now?'

'Well, I don't have any offers from men these days. The ordinary staff wouldn't dare approach the boss, and the Board have different ideas.'

'Don't they like women?'

Now it was Marged's turn to laugh. 'Women wouldn't like Mr Byers – he resembles a fat pig.'

'Marged!'

'Well, he does. And Mr Arnold never looks at anybody, male or female. I sometimes think he's a robot. Then there's Mr Walters. Now he does have a roving eye, and if I were still in the general office he'd very likely offer to take me out, as his little bit on the side. But not now.'

'Now you're the boss.'

'Ye-es. But it's not just that—' Marged sought words to explain. 'He still looks on me as a little typist, not an equal. He can't take me out for a bit of fun, but he still thinks I'm not quite the kind of lady his wife would invite home for tea.'

'Well, you're not, are you?' Brenda chuckled. 'And what about Mr James?'

'Oh, all the girls say he's a bit of a lad, and he is, it's there in his eyes. I reckon he fancies me a little bit. If I just gave the word—'

'But you won't.'

'Won't I?'

'Not even to buy you a cup of tea. You're both married.'

'Yes, unfortunately.'

'It was your own doing, Marged.'

Yes, Brenda was still the big sister. So Marged did not tell her when, a few days later, Mr James came into the office ...

She had been checking the orders, trying to concentrate and finding it difficult because she hadn't had much sleep. Brian had been out most of the night, had come in the worse for drink, had woken her up, demanded his 'rights'.

'Oh, go to sleep,' she'd said.

'My rights,' he muttered thickly. 'You don't do much else for me.'

'Why—' She struggled to sit up. 'What do you mean? You get your meals, you're well looked after—'

He staggered as he fumbled with his coat, throwing it on the floor, pulling at his shirt. 'It's your fault,' he said.

'What is?'

'Always off to work, you won't have any more children.'

'That's not true, Brian.'

397

"Course it is.' He pulled on his pyjama jacket, tried to fasten the buttons, failed, and threw it off again. 'You must *do* something, or why don't you have another baby?'

'Brian, honestly, I don't do anything.' And this was true. She would have been willing to have another baby. Brian did like children, and she felt she owed him that, at least. She wondered sometimes if the operation had affected her in some way, made it more difficult to conceive; she'd have to ask the doctor.

Now she waited passively for his embrace. She no longer responded to his love-making; it filled her with revulsion, perhaps because Brian himself revolted her. She hated these nights when he was drunk, when he merely used her, then turned away and started snoring. And tonight was worse, for he subjected her to new humiliations. When he finally turned away she got up and went to Roberta's room. She often came here, would have liked to sleep here alone. Brian could visit her when he felt so inclined. She knew he went with other women and only came to her when he had no one else; she meant nothing to him.

Now, in the morning, she was heavy-eyed and knew it. So when Mr James leaned over her desk and asked, 'Why don't you get him to help you?' she was surprised.

'Who, Brian?' she asked.

'Of course. He's never here.'

'Oh well – his health isn't too good.'

'Don't pretend, Marged.' It was the first time he'd called her Marged. 'I know.'

She was startled. Had she been stupid, ostrich-like, thinking that only Mr Arnold held the secret? 'Do the others know?' she asked.

He shrugged. 'That I can't tell you. We never discuss it.'

She breathed again, 'Well, you see it is difficult for him.'

'But he could be here. He can talk, can't he? Instead of leaving everything to you.'

She did not answer.

'When was the last time he took you out? He or anybody?'

'I don't want to go out.'

'Then you should.' Now he leaned closer. 'You're an attractive woman, Marged. You coop yourself up in here . . . what for?'

'Because I want to run the firm, Mr James. You know that.'

'Well.' Now he moved away. 'If you ever want to go out, I'm waiting.'

'You're married, Mr James.'

'Don.'

'Don.'

'And my wife and I are separating.'

'Oh, I'm sorry.'

She looked at him fully. She liked Don James, liked his merry eyes, the way he looked at you as if you were a woman, liked his thin face, his laughing mouth. A little of the Frenchman about him; not surprising as many of the locals had French descent from the Huguenot weavers who'd settled here. She knew if she gave the word he would start an affair.

But she did not give the word.

Yet she was tempted. Why not, after all? Stefan was lost to her and Brian was . . . well, Brian. He seemed to dislike her so much these days, endlessly gibing about her working. 'Little Miss Know-all, think you're so clever, don't you?' She no longer answered back, but the constant carping, coupled with the fact that Marie seemed to prefer him to her – a fact he played on and encouraged – undermined her confidence. So it was good to have a man looking at you as though you were a desirable woman again, who could revive those feelings first aroused by Stefan, temporarily stimulated by Brian, and pushed below the surface now, but still there. She thought of those women during the war who went with other men and were castigated for it – it wasn't easy living like a nun. Mr James's work took him abroad a lot these days, but he was in England until after Christmas. So he came in the office, they talked and it was good to have a man interested in what you did, who was protective.

And it was he who suggested reviving the Staff Dance at Christmas.

'I haven't been to the Staff Dance since the year I started,' Marged said. The dances had stopped after the bombing and the death of Mr Mordant; and were never started again – till now.

Now they agreed to hold them again. And she was quite looking forward to it until Brian refused to go.

They were in the drawing-room; it was Renie's night off, so Marie was with them, sitting on Brian's lap, and he tickled her chin as he said, 'I shan't go to any dance.'

'But, Brian, why? You are the boss, after all.'

'Huh! Some boss. You do all the work, don't you? That's what you're always saying. You wanted the factory, that's why you married me—'

'But I did think we could run it together, Brian.'

'Listen to that, Marie. Listen to Mummy pretending. She wanted the factory for herself and her brother. Daddy is left out. Never mind, you love me, don't you? And I have a present for you, here in my pocket.'

The child laughed with glee, and Marged said, 'You buy her too much, Brian,' and then could have bitten her tongue out.

'Hear what Mummy says? I buy you too many presents. I don't, do I?'

'No,' the child cried.

'You love Daddy, don't you?'

'Yes.'

'Who do you love best in all the world?'

'Daddy.'

'Here you are then, here's your present. And play with it now, 'cos Daddy has to go out.'

'Don't go, Daddy.'

'I must. You'll have to stay with Mummy. Play with your present. Oh, and give me a kiss before I go.'

He bent down and kissed her, then, without a word to Marged, was gone. Alone, she looked at Marie, playing on the rug with the doll Brian had bought her. It was true, he did buy too many presents. She had only to ask for a thing and it was hers. And all the time he was turning her against her mother.

The child sat quietly now, and when Marged told her it was time for bed she went without demur. But when Marged asked which bedtime story she wanted, Marie said, 'The one Daddy tells me.'

Long after the child had gone to sleep Marged sat in the nursery, looking down at the little pink bed, bought by Brian, the heap of toys at the foot, the figures painted on the walls, and she felt excluded, as doubtless Brian intended. When she left she had made up her mind. She would go to the dance – alone. After all, Don James would be there.

She decided to buy a new dress; it was years since she had bought any clothes. Would they wear long or short these days? She had a word with her secretary.

'Oh, bound to be short,' said Daphne. 'I don't think we'll ever go back to the days before the war.'

She spent some time looking for the right dress, and finally chose a pale blue, with flared skirt and a small bolero over the bodice lined with flowered material. It suited her, and recklessly she bought new sandals and sheer stockings.

The dance was held in the works canteen which had been decorated with streamers and balloons. Jimmy Foster's band sat on the stage at the end, and a huge ball of coloured light had been fixed in the centre. Marged felt a little embarrassed as she entered alone, but immediately Don James came to her and led her on the floor. And when the dance ended he sat with her.

'Your husband didn't come, then?' he asked.

'No.'

'I'm glad *you* did.'

The band struck up again, a slow foxtrot. Marged said, 'This is the first dance I've been to since – oh, a long time.' *Since Stefan went.*

'Then we must see you enjoy it,' he said. And they danced again and again. But other members of the senior staff were there, and she had to do her duty. Mr Walters asked for a dance, though not Mr Byers. Colin Jackson introduced his wife, a pleasant fair-haired girl. And in the interval they all went out to the nearest pub for a drink.

Back in the canteen Mr James danced with Mrs Walters, and Marged sat idly watching. She gave a start as she saw Martin on the floor. He was partnering a dark-haired girl she had vaguely seen around the office. He was good too. Funny, the only times she'd danced with him was when she was learning. After that they went their own ways. She saw him glance across at her, but he didn't speak.

He seemed to be watching her more and more as the evening wore on. They were playing the war songs now, and she wished they wouldn't, for they brought back too many memories ... *Yours, Starlight Serenade, Lily Marlene* ...

Then there was a Paul Jones, and Don James pulled her to her feet. 'Come on, we must join in,' he said. So she linked hands with the ring of ladies, while he went to the inner ring of men. They walked round, the music stopped, and she found herself facing a gangly youth who looked frightened out of his wits at who he'd picked, and they stumbled around together. Into the ring again, stopping – and she faced Martin.

Without a word he took her in his arms. It was a tango, *Jealousy*, and the lights were dimmed.

He danced well, but angrily, forcefully, like those Apache

dancers they saw on films, she thought, as if he were going to throw her across the room. Even the crooner sounded angry rather than sad as he sang about his crime being blind jealousy.

They were at the end of the room now, near the door, and abruptly he stopped dancing. She was breathless as he pulled her through the door into the yard. 'Hey, wait a minute,' she protested.

'You're enjoying yourself,' he said nastily.

'Yes, I am.'

'So it's Mr James now.'

'What do you mean?'

'We hear about it, even in the factory. How he's always running into your office.'

She gaped at him. 'I never heard such rubbish in my life!'

'You can't deny he fancies you.'

'Well. So what's it got to do with you?' She glanced round the yard anxiously, hoping no one was within earshot. From behind came the clatter of the music as the Paul Jones started up again.

'So you're running round with him now,' Martin hissed. 'You're going to get yourself a name, aren't you? First Brian, now him—'

Suddenly she was furious. 'What's it to you?' she repeated. 'You're not my keeper. I shall go out with Don James if I want to—'

'So you do go out with him?'

'Nothing to do with you. Go away, go back, leave me alone!'

The orchestra was playing a waltz. 'You know what you're getting to be?' he jeered. 'A little no-good, that's what—'

Crack! Her hand dealt him a stinging blow on the cheek. He pulled her hand away, took the other one. She wrenched it free and tried to scratch his face. He shook her till her teeth rattled, then let her go suddenly, so that she almost fell. When she recovered her balance he had gone.

Shaking now, she looked again round the yard, but it was still empty. Thank goodness. Whatever would people say? The boss's wife, fighting. Fighting like a common woman in the back streets...

She almost ran into the cloakroom, tidied her hair, powdered her cheeks, then walked back to Don. The dance was nearly over, and he said nothing as she asked him to take her home.

But the evening had been spoilt and he knew something had happened. And at Park Manor she simply said, 'Goodnight,' and went inside.

There was no sign of Brian, so she went straight up to bed. And as she undressed she shivered again as she thought of the brawl, yes, that's what it was, a brawl. Her mother would have been shocked. So would Brenda. She needed Brenda to watch over her, keep her in order. Brenda, who would never do such a thing. Brenda, every inch a lady, like Mam had been.

And like I'm not, thought Marged, ungrammatically. Yet it was only Martin she fought with. They used to say that, the family. 'When those two get together' ... 'He makes her as bad as he is himself' ...

She got into bed, but she could not sleep.

The next morning she went downstairs to see a card on the hall table. She picked it up, stared at it dully. Just a plain card, redirected from Brenda's old home. She looked more closely. The postmark was a strange name she could not read, but below it the word Siberia. There was no message, just one name. Stefan.

He was safe. He had not been shot. But – Siberia? What was he doing there? Had he found Janina?

She put the card safely away in Roberta's bureau, then went to the office. She knew the affair with Don James would never progress any further. He seemed to sense it too. And after Christmas he left for America on a sales trip for the firm.

Chapter 16

The winter of 1947 was the worst for half a century. Villages were cut off in this Arctic Britain. It was colder than in Iceland. Power cuts stopped trams and electric trains. In February a blizzard with a-mile-a-minute winds swept over a vast area of the north; railway points were frozen solid; miners could not get to the pits. In the homes electricity was off for five hours a day.

Marged got up, had a cold breakfast by candlelight, then ran up to the nursery. This was warm, for so far coal had been delivered locally; they were lucky to live near the pits.

She went out into the dark streets. They had managed to keep the factory working so far, in spite of the power cuts, but there was no heating in the offices.

In the general office typists were muffled in overcoats and rugs; it was the war all over again. Hurricane lamps stood on the tables, but Marged wondered if she would have been wiser to close the offices for a few days. Yet how could she? Work had to be done, wages had to be paid, goods delivered – or would they, with the railways frozen? How long could they carry on?

She sat at her desk, and Mrs Jennings brought in a cup of tea. 'Thank you,' Marged said. 'We're managing to boil kettles, then?'

'With a struggle,' smiled Daphne.

'Well, keep making it as long as you can for the staff, keep them warm.'

The door opened, Colin Jackson stood there, wrapped in an Army greatcoat, muffled with a scarf. 'Not trouble?' Marged asked, looking at his face.

'A union meeting.'

'Now? In this? You mean Martin, I suppose.'

'I'm sorry, Mrs Mordant.'

'What is it now?'

'Does it matter? If we settle one thing he'll only start another. This time it's demarcation.'

'Not that again.'

'Yes. Seems there was a faulty wire on one of the machines. Quite a simple job to fix it so the man repaired it himself. Martin objected. Says it's the electrician's job.'

'As it is.'

'Says that before the war if they learned that a welder, say, could do repair jobs on electricity, they'd sack the electrician and the welder would have to do two jobs.'

'As they did,' she said wearily. 'But not now.'

'Mrs Mordant,' Colin began. 'I know he's your brother—'

'Cousin.'

'What? Oh well, whatever, but that's why I can't understand him.'

'Oh I can,' Marged said. 'I understand only too well. You see – he always hated Mordant, the former owner, for doing all those things, for ruining our father. And then – oh, it's a long story, but I think I made things worse by telling him something I should possibly have kept to myself.'

'Why should you?' he asked surprisingly. 'Why should you bear all the burdens? I'm sorry, Mrs Mordant, but I have no sympathy with your brother – cousin – whatever the reason. And he's egged on by Norman Wells.'

'I don't think Martin allows himself to be egged on by anyone.'

'But he's there, Mrs Mordant. I know I said at first that the Communists were on our side – they were then. But things have changed. Britain isn't so fond of Stalin now we can see what he's doing in Europe. Then there's the atom bomb – all this puts the Communists in a different position.'

'What position is that?'

'Possibly to work against us.'

'And you think Martin—'

'I think that Martin, for whatever reason he has, is playing into their hands.'

'So what do you suggest I do?'

'There's only one way.'

'What's that?'

'Dismiss him.'

Marged sighed. 'And bring the men out on strike?'

'Well, I hate to sound like a boss, but a strike now won't hurt us, will it? We'll probably have to close the factory anyway, as the weather's getting worse.' He paused. 'We can't go on like this, Mrs Mordant. All this disruption—'

Marged knew he was right. She, too, had had enough of Martin. She sat in the cold office when Colin had gone and tried to warm her numb fingers. This cold was worse than during the war, for then they'd always managed to keep one little fire going. Outside, the frozen snow began to get on her nerves, the same old picture, day after day, week after week, and she had a moment's fleeting sympathy with the Russians. Fancy living in these conditions all winter long, wrapped up in rugs and blankets so that you looked like something found in a jumble sale. She would have given a month's salary to be *warm*.

Colin was right. Martin had been given enough rope. And to start today, of all days ... She pulled the blanket tighter around her shoulders and set her lips. This was it. Time to end it all.

She sent for Martin.

He entered. The same old Martin, the same sullen mouth

and angry eyes. And a tiny gleam in those eyes showing he thought he'd got her where he wanted her. He said smoothly: 'You sent for me.'

'Yes.'

'Well, there is another problem.'

'I don't want to hear about it.'

He was a little taken aback and she said angrily, 'All this trouble – from you, who was so eager to welcome the New Jerusalem. And now you're still living in the past.'

'Me and a million others. Don't you read the papers, the sneers about the age of the common man? They won't rest till they've got us out.'

'And you're playing into their hands. I don't know what our dad would have said—' She broke off, wondering if the subject of fathers was a tactless one, but knew he always thought of Frank as his father, so pressed on: 'Yes, I do know. He'd have been delighted about the new world, and he'd have worked all he could to make it a success. Not acted like a big kid just to be awkward – just to get back at me, and for what? What have I done to you? Nothing.'

He did not reply, but the gleam had gone from his eye, and he looked the slightest bit abashed.

The cold stung her cheeks, making them smart. She pulled the blanket around her more tightly and took a breath. She had the words ready: *We can't go on like this any longer. I've tried to see your point of view, but you won't see reason. You'll have to go.*

She opened her mouth, paused. She knew he would never give in. Not Martin. He never had. She could dismiss him, she had the power – and he'd never forgive her. They would be estranged for the rest of their lives. She would have won – at a cost. Was this what she wanted ... power? No, it never had been.

He was waiting. She said: 'I never told you about how I came to marry Brian, did I?'

Now he was definitely taken aback. She went on, 'Stefan

went back—' she could even talk about Stefan now without wincing, without wanting to die inside. 'He was married. I was pregnant. I didn't know what to do. I had no one, nowhere to go. So I married Brian.'

He was staring, wide-eyed. Whatever he'd been expecting, it wasn't this. 'You had me,' he muttered.

'You were in Germany and you didn't write, did you? Brenda was leaving. I had no home, nowhere to go.'

'So it isn't Brian's child?'

'No.'

He suddenly turned, walked up and down the office as if he were practising for a marathon. His hair, that was always so unruly, fell over his forehead, and he brushed it back in the old remembered gesture.

He stopped quite suddenly. 'Why are you telling me this now?'

'Because I know what you're doing. All this – it's just to get back at me, and I'm not sure why. I don't know what you want. I did at first – you wanted revenge on Mordant. Well, Mordant's dead—'

'I know, we've said all that.'

'So why keep on, except to hurt me? What have I done?'

'I suppose I was just jealous.'

'*Jealous?* Why? 'Cos I have the factory, and not you?'

He shrugged.

She had said she wouldn't lose her temper, but she did. 'Why don't you take the bloody factory, then? I don't want it. It's cost me too much. And I only did it because—' She broke off.

'Because what?'

She didn't answer.

'Because of me?'

'Well, it was you who wanted it, you who started it all.'

He said, 'We'll talk about this later. Shall I come and see you?'

'If you like. And will you call this off?'

'Yeah. I suppose.'

She passed the good news on to Colin. 'It'll be all right,' she said. 'I've talked to him. I don't think there'll be any more trouble.'

'Oh good.' He waited, but she didn't enlarge, so he left the office.

Alone, Marged found her hands were trembling. Yet she knew she had done the right thing. Martin needed her, he always had. For underneath the anger, the hell-raising, the conceit, was a loneliness and a hurt that stemmed from a little boy not knowing who his father was.

He came the very next evening, and she led him into the drawing-room as the small sitting-room had no fireplace. Brian was in – the bitter cold made going out very unpleasant – but he was in the nursery with Marie.

They sat, one each side of the fire, and he carried on the conversation as if he'd never stopped, and she was pleased. They always used to do that when they were kids.

'Are you happy with Brian?' he asked.

'No. But I didn't expect to be, so that's no worry.'

'Do you hear from Stefan?'

She told him then, the whole story, and when she'd finished they both sat silent, watching the flames crackling in the chimney. Then he asked, 'Wouldn't you ever like to marry again – someone you could get fond of?'

'No. When Stefan left I said I'd never fall in love again. And I never will.'

'Oh, come on!'

'No. Because I'd never trust anyone again.'

'Not even me?'

'You? After the way you've been acting—'

He turned away from the fire, from her, and there was no sound anywhere; they could have been in a dead world. And he thought: I've made a right cock-up of things, haven't I? I'm in love with Marged and I've been acting like a big kid, as she said. What in hell was I playing at? Just to get back at her ... Except I never would have let it go too far – never really brought the lads out on strike, not that they'd have come, they're not daft. Just posturing, me. Though the things I was protesting about were real, were true ... But ...

Selfish, that's me. I always was. They always told me that, the family. Except Marged. She was the one who always stuck up for me and what do I do? Somebody ought to kick me.

Well, I've blown it now. Anyway, she only thinks of me as a brother ...

Aloud he said, 'I've been a pig.'

'Glad you realise it.'

'All right. Don't push it.'

She stared at him speculatively. 'Did the war upset you? You never said.'

'Well, it wasn't exactly a picnic in the desert. But no, I'm OK. Anyway, I'll be a good little boy now.'

She laughed shortly. 'That'll be the day.'

He brooded, and the firelight cast shadows over his face. 'I've been fighting all my life,' he said simply. 'Not just in the war. It's not easy to stop.'

'No. But you're getting on now. Twenty-seven.'

'Thanks for reminding me that I'll soon be thirty. One foot in the grave.'

'It's time you were getting married,' she said equably. 'You might settle down then.'

He stood up abruptly. 'Marriage isn't for me,' he said. 'Anyway, think I'll get along.'

Now what have I said? she wondered as she rose too. 'You'll come again?'

'I suppose so.'

She went with him to the door, and the snowladen trees dripped icicles. She called, 'Goodnight,' and shut the door on the bitter cold.

Martin walked home in a mixed frame of mind, crunching over the frozen snow where it hadn't been cleared, slipping on the ice where it had. In Victoria Street the bombed area had been turned into an ice rink by the children. They had slides, they used home-made sledges, they shouted with glee. He entered number forty and made up the fire.

It was obvious that Marged had no thought for him as a potential lover, and anyway, she was married, however unhappily. And she still hankered for Stefan, of that he was certain.

So where did he go from here? Visiting as a brother, being a good little boy? That was hardly his line.

The weather grew colder and colder, coal could not get through, no electricity could be supplied to any industrial user in London and the Midlands. Mordant's had to close. Railwaymen laboured long hours to get the trucks moving, miners volunteered for Sunday work, troops were sent to help at the pithead. Two million men and women were thrown out of work by the closing of the factories. The price of food soared.

Marged sat in home, worrying about the loss of work, thinking about Martin. And when in March the thaw came with great floods she felt she had solved his problem.

She genuinely thought that it was right for Martin to inherit. Not for her man-made laws. Martin was Mordant's son and that was that. He hadn't been to see her again, so she waited till the factory resumed work then, after a hectic day of getting things together again, and after deciding to let the men work overtime, she went into the factory to see him.

'Martin, I have a plan. When can I see you?'

'Well, if it's private, come round to our house, Jack's going out.'

'Is he?'

'Yeah. He's courting again.'

'Oh. Hasn't waited long.'

He had been about to say *People don't*, but stopped himself in time. 'Come about eight,' he said. 'I'll make you a cup of tea.'

Victoria Street was awash in the aftermath of the floods, though patches of frozen snow still lingered in some of the gardens. She entered number forty and looked round in distaste at the untidiness, the bare table, with an alarm clock ticking away on the sideboard. Mam would never allow that. 'What happened to the wall clock?' she asked. A wall clock was a mark of respectability.

'It won't go. Sit down, let's hear what you've got to say.'

'Right. Well, I want you to train for management.'

He laughed incredulously. 'Just like that?'

'Listen a minute. You served your apprenticeship, you had a spell in the drawing office. Now, I thought you could deputise for Mr Norris, say for a year, then come on to the Board with me. You could deputise in turn all the other work, Personnel, Buying, Sales ...'

'Hey, wait a minute.' He stopped her. 'Haven't you forgotten one thing?'

'What?'

'Brian.'

'What about Brian?'

'Well, he does own the place.'

'But you have a right to Mordant's.'

'I have no legal right. Bastards don't inherit. But does Brian know about me?'

She paused, idly running her finger over the arm of the chair. 'No. Though –' thoughtfully '– I suppose his mother does.'

'And she won't want the factory to be run by me, will she?'

'I don't see that it's anything to do with her. Or Brian – he never comes near the place.'

'Even so, I can't see him handing the firm over to me. I think you'll have to tell him.'

'Why? You're getting very righteous. I don't want to bring up the subject of illegitimacy.'

'Your case is different. It was wartime. It happened to thousands.'

She sat thoughtfully looking into the fire. The alarm clock ticked loudly. Out in the street children shouted. She asked, 'Have you any money?'

'My pay and my gratuity. You're not suggesting I *buy* Mordant's? With my gratuity?'

'I have some money,' she said. 'I do get paid, and well.' *Now I'm a director.* 'I save my money, and Brian's not mean, I'll say that for him. Then there are banks.' She leaned forward. 'If you trained as I suggested then you would be in a position to borrow.'

'With your help. I'd never have enough collateral myself.'

'All right, with my help you could buy the factory, and that should settle any moral scruples I didn't know you had.'

Now it was his turn to ponder. 'Maybe you're right,' he said. 'Maybe you've got something.'

'You do still want Mordant's, don't you?'

And now the old grin was back. 'Sure. I did say I'd take over one day ... but I didn't believe I ever would.'

'Well, think about it. And now—' she looked round, sniffing. 'I suppose I'd better tidy the place up before I go home.'

Martin knew he would accept. He knew too that he'd be accused of getting round Marged to grab the factory.

He was right. There was talk.

'Just goes to show, if you mek enough trouble you get promoted – especially when your sister's married to the boss.'

Stefan found the office he worked in, though far from ideal, a vast improvement on the appalling conditions outside, as men struggled to work in a temperature of 50° below zero, many dying from frostbite, from gangrenous legs, or who were so weakened they were shot. He tried to speak for them to his NKVD bosses, but they merely shrugged, impervious to his pleas.

Sometimes he would study these officers, asking himself how they could allow such conditions to exist, wondering how they came to be there in the first place. Had they volunteered to work in the Far East or, as he sometimes suspected, had they been sent there for some minor misdemeanour? Were they perhaps not up to Moscow standard – Moscow was the summit of all ambitions – or, most probably of all, didn't they know enough important people? He knew you had to be a member of the Party to get on at all, and the more influential people you knew, the higher you could rise. So much for equality.

Whatever the reason for their being there, they all talked in the same way, mouthing the same platitudes. Only once, after such talk, did Stefan hear Vladimir Primakov mutter to himself: 'I wonder.'

No one else heard, but Stefan did, and he suspected that Vladimir *intended* him to hear. But he marked Vladimir as a man worth cultivating; he needed such a man.

The dreadful winter at last gave way to spring, the ice melted, became floods; men worked now knee-deep in mud and said those in the mines below were the lucky ones. Stefan was at least instrumental in seeing that they got their proper ration of boots. They were entitled to one pair in winter, one other warm jacket, and felted leg coverings. They seldom had any decent boots at all, so what they did was to wrap their feet and legs in plaited straw or rags, plaster the whole thing over with mud and then plunge the limb into water. The coating of ice which instantly formed protected the limb from frostbite.

Stefan did all he could, though he knew it was a losing battle. The convicts had to carry on, working for weeks on end above their knees and up to their waists in snow, mud or water. One man could do little, not in a land where people didn't count, where they were expendable. The whole system was at fault; you just had to try your best to survive yourself, and again Stefan would repeat to himself, I must get out, I will survive.

As the summer sun drove away the worst excesses of the winter he was sharing an office with Vladimir Primakov. He had had several conversations with this man now. Vladimir never said he was not a devout member of the Party, and Stefan never asked him about it, just as Vladimir never asked Stefan outright about Poland or England. However Stefan, getting used to the method of doublespeak, recognised the man's curiosity so described the West in an indirect fashion.

'Life is dreadful in capitalist countries for the poor,' said Vladimir in his soft voice.

'It's not perfect,' conceded Stefan, 'but we can say what we like, criticise—' He broke off, that was enough. 'Churchill was a great leader,' he said another day. 'But the people threw him out. That is the way with free elections.'

The days grew hotter, flies buzzed round the little office. Stefan knew an order had been placed for a screen to cover the doorway, but it never arrived. So they had the choice of closing the door and sweltering in the heat, or being massacred by the flies and mosquitoes. Vladimir Primakov sat silent for the most part, a thin, dark-haired man with brooding eyes. But gradually he talked more about himself.

'My father took part in the Revolution,' he said. 'He was an ardent Party member from the start – it was his life. He was a man of ideals. "Give according to your ability, be given according to your need." Surely that is good?'

'The ideals, yes,' Stefan replied. 'But it's what men have made of it. What about Stalin? The atrocities?' and he wondered if Vladimir even *knew*, or if he knew, did he condone them? What about this camp?

Vladimir looked troubled. 'There have been mistakes,' he admitted. 'As there have been with religious leaders, yes?' and Stefan wryly had to nod.

'We were not free under the Czars; we lived like pigs,' Vladimir said.

'I know,' said Stefan sombrely.

'We had to have a revolution.'

'Yes, I understand that. So where did it go wrong?'

'How can it be wrong?' Vladimir asked. 'Every child is educated, every man and woman has a job.'

'But no freedom,' said Stefan.

'What is freedom?' asked Vladimir. 'Freedom to starve?'

Yet he looked puzzled, as though he were trying to gain insight into Stefan's mind. Stefan frowned. He genuinely believed Vladimir to be an honest man, torn between his beliefs and a nettle he dared not grasp.

Yet, honest or no, he still took bribes. It was a way of life here, and Stefan had come to Siberia for one reason – to find Janina. To do that, he needed help. He inched up his sleeve to show his watch, reflecting he was working his way round the world by the aid of watches. And here, the more you had to offer, the better you got on. It was the only way.

He said, 'I suppose you know – or could find out – who is in the other local camps? You visit them from time to time?' And he wondered if he *could* find out. The whole bureaucratic system of papers for everything, even walking down the street, seemed to collapse when it came to tracing anyone.

Vladimir looked up. 'You are still talking about your wife?'

'Yes.'

'How should I know who is in the other camps?'

Stefan looked at his watch and began to wind it. The other man's eyes followed. This was not such a good watch as the one he'd traded to get out of Rumania. He had bought this in England when jewellery was getting scarce and he had not the money to buy anything too expensive. It was not gold. Even so, it was far better than anything obtainable in the Soviet Union, as were all the goods they bartered.

Vladimir said, 'That's a good watch. You were lucky to keep it so long.'

'Yes. I hid it.' But Stefan did not tell him where; how he'd sewn it into the lining of his coat, how he wore his coat at all times when in the hut with the convicts, even in bed. The only time he took it off was when he was in the office with the NKVD men around, and when he visited the bath house – compulsory for all, though visits had to be taken out of working hours. 'I'm willing to part with it once I know where Janina is,' he said.

'Janina Kowalska,' said Vladimir.

The summer passed all too quickly. Stefan thought the other man had forgotten. But in September, as he sat alone, Vladimir came in and said, 'I have some news about your wife.'

'You have?' Stefan tried to keep his voice calm.

'She was in that camp you told me about, but she left. She is living now—' Vladimir paused and looked at the watch. 'You still have it, I see?'

Stefan took off the watch, placed it on the desk. 'She is living—?' he prompted.

'With a family named Bratkowski. Just outside Khabarovsk.'

'Bratkowski? That is a Polish name. Are they Polish?'

'They were.'

Stefan handed Vladimir the watch. He wondered if it were true. Vladimir was certainly the best of this NKVD bunch, but you couldn't trust anyone. Yet it tied in with what Jerzy had said. He could but hope.

On Monday morning, wrote the *Daily Mail* in July 1948, *you will wake in a new Britain, in a State which takes over its citizens before they are born, providing care and free services for their birth, their early years, their schooling, sickness, workless days, widowhood and retirement. All this, with free doctoring, dentistry and medicine for 4/11d per week insurance.*

The Old Guard were disgusted. 'People sitting in doctors' surgeries to get free cotton wool,' snorted Mr Byers.

'Yes, I read that in the papers too,' said Marged. 'Whatever do they want all that cotton wool for? Sitting for hours in crummy surgeries just to get *cotton wool*?'

'There's too much materialism today,' Mr Walters said gloomily. 'People want too much. Washing machines – even refrigerators. Never heard anything like it. Too many possessions.'

'All this free welfare saps the moral fibre,' intoned Mr Byers, righteously. 'People should stand on their own two feet,' and Marged wondered why Mr Byers worried so much about the effect of welfare on the poor, but didn't think that free benefits would sap his own moral fibre.

She asked innocently: 'I suppose you must be against those who live on inherited wealth, what it must do to them,' and Colin Jackson chuckled.

But when the Conservatives were elected in 1951, to 'set the people free', the Old Guard were delighted.

'About time too,' said Mr Byers.

Clothes rationing had ended two years ago, together with tinned food and soap. Another year would see the end of tea rationing, then chocolate and sweets, eggs and sugar. There were more goods in the shops, and everyone went out to spend their money. Mordant's was doing well, wages were good, yet Marged still wondered how long it would last, and she wore a worried frown as she went to the Board meeting, and told them of her new fear.

'A trickle of foreign cars is coming into Britain,' she told them. 'Mainly from Germany. I hope it doesn't affect our sales.'

'No, no, why should it?' asked Mr Byers. 'We've always been the best.'

'I think you're wrong,' Martin said. 'I think it will affect our sales in time.'

Martin had been training now for three years – one year with the Works Manager, one year with Mr James, now he was with Mr Byers, and sitting with the management. And Mr Byers didn't like it at all.

So when the meeting was ending and Marged asked if there was any other business, Mr Byers asked: 'When are we going to start entertaining again?'

'I beg your pardon.' Marged looked up, surprised.

'Entertaining would-be buyers. Customers. If, as you say, sales will go down then it's time to start entertaining again. Mr Mordant always used to do it. Didn't matter during the war, but it's different now.'

'Ah.' Marged paused. 'You mean at Park Manor?'

'Where else?' What was that gleam in his eye? What was he up to? She talked it over with Colin Jackson, who shrugged.

'I don't suppose it's absolutely necessary,' he said, 'but if it's always been done, I shouldn't think it would do any harm.'

'But couldn't we do it at a hotel? I mean, there are still shortages.'

'Ye-es. I don't know myself how things were done here before the war. Maybe you'd better speak to one of the Old Guard.'

'But that's just what I'm against, Colin. Their attitude that the old ways are written on tablets of stone. Still, I'll have a word with Brian.'

She hoped he'd say no. She didn't want to tackle entertaining on a large scale when she'd already done a hard day's work. When she arrived home Brian was in the drawing-room, playing with Marie, now a schoolgirl of six years, taken and fetched home from the convent school every day by Brian.

'Hallo, Marie,' Marged said. 'Had a good day at school?'

'Yes, thank you.' The child barely looked up, and Marged's heart gave a pang. How quickly she was growing, and she seemed to see so little of her.

'Brian,' she said. 'I want a word with you.'

'What is it? Can't it wait?' he asked rudely.

'I suppose so.' She went upstairs, took off her outdoor clothes, changed her blouse and skirt, went down to dinner. It was always called dinner, though it was more of a supper, for both she and Brian ate a large lunch. They sat at the table and she told him of Mr Byers' request.

'Yes, why not?' Brian asked. 'It'll be like old times, to have entertaining in the house again.'

'But how many people would there be?'

'Oh, all the Board and their wives, plus the people we want to sell to.'

'Brian, I don't know the first thing about entertaining on a large scale. Or a small one, for that matter.'

'My, my,' sneered Brian. 'Miss Know-all doesn't know everything after all. We'd better get Mother down.'

'Oh no,' said Marged. 'I'll manage.'

But alone she pondered. Who would wait at table? Joanie Farmer, who wasn't all there, and would be bound to drop the soup in someone's lap? Violet, who wasn't much better? Perhaps Renie would give a hand, but then, who'd look after Marie? Still, the child would be in bed. She wondered sometimes how much longer Renie would stay. She was still courting her young man, and they didn't really need her so much now. She thought that maybe Renie liked the bed-room too much to want to leave, and houses were still in very short supply.

She spoke to Mrs Bannerman. What did she suggest?

'We-ell,' the cook answered. 'It wouldn't be anything lavish, that I can promise you. Not with the shortages.' Meat's still rationed, so is butter and fats, eggs . . .'

Marged was tired of the word shortages. She wondered

sometimes if Mrs Bannerman used this as an excuse. Maybe she couldn't cook anything too elaborate. 'Couldn't we buy it all from a hotel?' she asked vaguely.

'Not in a little place like this. 'Tisn't London, you know. But I could do soup and chicken, that's always safe.'

'Ye-es. But what about waitresses? Can we hire them?'

'Where from? The days when people were queueing up for jobs are over.'

In the end it was Renie who came to their rescue. If the middle classes always knew someone who could let them have extra food during the war, so did Victoria Street have its own system. Someone's friend/cousin-in-law aunt by marriage always knew someone who worked in the building trade or shops and hotels, and who could help out with odd jobs, cleaning and the like. So did Renie know a man whose sister used to be a waitress and would be willing to offer her services for a remuneration.

Then came the question of guests, and Marged began to see Mr Byers's cunning. There had to be the same number of men and women, but Mr James was in the process of divorce, and Martin had no one to bring. Should she ask Martin? He settled the matter by turning the invitation down flat. That left Mr James, so one extra woman was needed.

She spoke to Brian again. 'We'll ask my mother,' he said.

'Do we have to?'

'I think she has a right.'

Marged was forced to agree. Perhaps the Old Guard would welcome her, an old friend.

Adela arrived in a flurry of vanity cases, cigarette holders, taxi drivers waiting at the door, and expensive perfume, and immediately began to take charge. Marged was half-glad that she was taking over the dinner party, half-annoyed at her assumption that she belonged. And when she made a muted protest Adela said, 'My dear, you don't know anything about entertaining, do you?'

So Marged went to dress, hoping that Adela wouldn't put any poison in the soup.

The guests arrived. Mr Byers' wife, who talked with an accent you could cut with a knife, about her fathah, the Majah. In which war? Marged wondered unkindly. Mrs Walters, quite good-looking, and pleasant with it. The biggest surprise of all was Mr Arnold's wife, slim and beautiful in a long grey sheath.

Adela was in her element, and Mr James paid her extravagant compliments. 'Creeper,' Marged whispered. Adela looked exactly the same as she had ten years ago, hair still jet black, lips a bright red, too black and too red for her fifty years.

The visitors arrived – Mr Turner, the buyer from Austin-Morris, with his wife. Mr James and Marged greeted them.

'This is our MD,' said Mr James.

'Really? How astonishing, a young lady!' marvelled Mr Turner. 'And do you know all about engineering?'

'Everything,' boasted Mr James. 'Down to the last nut and bolt, Mrs Mordant knows it all.'

Marged said, 'Well, I'll try to live up to this fulsome praise. I hear you're doing well at Morris.'

'Ye-es, at the moment. Personally, I'm getting a bit worried about the foreign cars beginning to come here—' he echoed Marged's fears. 'It could be a problem. There's this new Volkswagen from West Germany. It's a good little car.'

'And I suppose Volkswagen would use their own components,' Marged said worriedly to Mr James as they went into the dining-room.

Renie's friend brought in the soup and Marged gave a sigh of relief as she served impeccably. The chicken followed.

'Rather dull,' commented Adela. 'I didn't have time to arrange the menu. Oh, the dinner parties we used to have.' She turned to Marged and fluted, 'You see, in business, it isn't just office work that counts, it's all this—' she waved her hand. 'That's why I was such a help to poor dear Maurice.'

Just when Marged thought everything was going well, a silence fell over the table. And in the silence – as though he'd been waiting for it – Mr Byers said loudly to Marged, three seats away: 'And where's our trainee?'

'Trainee?' asked Adela, and the whole table listened.

'Yes, young Fennel, Mrs Brian's brother,' said Mr Byers.

'And what is he training for?' asked Adela.

'Oh, just—' Colin Jackson tried to help, but Mr Byers said even more loudly, 'For management, what else?'

Colin Jackson interjected firmly, 'Oh, we do a lot of training at Mordant's,' and talk was resumed. Marged sat back. So that was what was behind it all. Get Martin out campaign.

They moved into the drawing-room for coffee, and here Marged could hold her own as she set out to entertain the guests. Men liked talking to her; she knew they liked her sense of humour. So she pulled out all the stops, laughing and joking with the prospective buyers, while Renie's friend hovered in the background with drinks.

Guests began to go, murmuring their thanks. Adela waved her hand with the inevitable cigarette holder. 'A plain meal, not quite up to the Mordant standard. But Mrs Turner as she bade goodbye to Marged said, 'It was a lovely meal, I enjoyed it,' and Marged was grateful for the obvious sympathy.

Then they had all gone and Adela and Brian showed no sign of moving; they were still drinking. Marged yawned. 'I think I'll say goodnight.'

'Wait a minute.' Adela stopped her. 'What was all that about your brother training to be a manager?'

'Can't it wait till morning?'

'No, it can't,' blustered Brian, fortified by his mother's presence. 'I want to know.'

'Very well. Martin is training for management.'

'Why didn't you tell me?' Brian asked truculently.

'If you'd attend the meetings occasionally you'd know what is happening,' Marged told him.

'It's as I said,' Adela cried, waving her cigarette holder. 'These two are planning to take over Mordant's!'

'And he has no right,' Brian interposed. 'Not Martin. He has no right.'

'Oh yes, he has.' Marged was stung now, angry in her turn. 'Since you ask, Martin has every right. He is Mr Mordant's son.'

There was a dead silence. Faintly they could hear sounds of mirth coming from the kitchen, the clatter of dishes. In the drawing-room they all stood like statues.

'His son?' croaked Brian at last. 'Mother, is this true?'

'Of course not,' Adela said witheringly.

Marged drew a breath. 'I didn't really want to tell you, Brian, but now ... it was Martin who had that affair with Roberta, as your mother well knows. Don't you?' and she swung round. 'Didn't you come to our house and threaten Martin with what you'd do? And someone told Roberta that Mr Mordant was Martin's father.'

'What nonsense,' cried Adela, but her face was white under her make-up, two spots of rouge stood out on her cheeks, her hands shook a little.

'It is in Roberta's diary,' Marged said wearily. 'And when I asked my aunt if it were true, she said it was.'

'Well, she would, wouldn't she?' Adela was regaining her composure.

'So.' Marged addressed Brian. 'I think Martin has every right to take a part in management. And, as you are not interested, and as you are always saying you want to sell the firm, what better plan than for Martin to buy it from you?'

'Can he afford to?'

'With my help, yes.'

Brian was staring. Adela said, 'Let's sleep on it. We'll discuss it in the morning.'

Marged went to the kitchen where Joanie Farmer was washing up with a will, saying, 'Weren't it luvly? Didn't they all look nice?' She thanked the helper, paid her, made sure she'd get the last bus, helped Joanie and Violet put the dishes away, went to bed.

The next day when she came home from the office Brian and Adela were waiting for her in the drawing-room.

'We've been talking,' Adela said silkily. 'And we have no opposition to what's going on.'

Marged looked at her suspiciously. 'No?'

'I don't agree with what you say about your brother, of course, or what you've been saying about me. I never saw your brother, much less threatened him. However, we are willing to say nothing if you will do the same.'

'I see.' Keep quiet, Marged.

'And Brian has promised to attend all future Board meetings.'

Marged raised her eyebrows. All this was too good to be true. Far too good. But when the next meeting was held, Brian was there.

And when they came to any other business, Marged said: 'Yes, I want to talk about Martin, and his training for management, since this was brought up in such a public way, a way I deplored, I might add—' she looked at Mr Byers. 'I would have preferred the subject to be introduced in the proper place – here. However, I will now tell you what I propose Martin does next. And this is with my husband's full knowledge and consent.'

There was a silence, and she went on.

'Are you afraid of the talk of favouritism? If so, why? It has always been the custom that fathers take sons to work with them, if the factories are good ones. It is in fact a sign of a good firm. Women take daughters to the tailoring and hosiery. So why can't that apply to us? Why can't I promote my cousin if he is up to standard? If there should be any other reason – Brian?'

426

'No,' he said sullenly.

'Secondly, apart from favouritism, Mr Jackson told me at the start that Martin deserved a better position. Perhaps you will repeat what you told me, Mr Jackson.'

Colin did so, and she went on: 'It is our policy now to promote any man or woman who we feel has the potential for management.'

'Any comments?' she asked. 'No? Good. Then this is what I propose to do next with Martin Fennel. I want to send him on a tour round other manufacturers in European countries, mainly Germany, to study their methods. We need someone to do this, for I am getting concerned at the way they seem to be, if not overtaking us, certainly catching up. None of you can be spared. And Martin speaks German; he was with the Army of Occupation.'

No one spoke, and she ended: 'I worry about the future.'

'Nonsense,' said Mr Walters.

'If they're getting on better it's because their workers work harder,' growled Mr Byers.

'And perhaps the management work harder too,' said Marged drily. 'But you have no opposition to the plan?'

No one had. Martin was to go to Europe.

In the few months he was away, Adela was a frequent visitor to Park Manor, and each time she invited the Byers and the Walters to dinner, which she personally supervised, driving poor Joanie almost into hysterics, and grumbling the whole time about the quality of Marged's staff. And it was Adela who got rid of Renie.

Adela was fond of her 'grandchild', but she thought Renie was not a suitable person to look after the great-granddaughter of a noble line – making Marged long to tell her just who the child was, knowing she could not for Marie's sake. So Adela complained about Renie, her accent, her youth, the fact that her 'follower' was allowed to call at the house, to visit Renie's room. All this was just not done.

So while Martin was still away, Renie came to Marged. 'I'm leaving,' she said. 'I can't stand that old cat any longer, finding fault, can't stand her airs and graces.'

'Oh Renie, I'm sorry. Do you want me to have a word with her?'

'Won't do no good,' said Renie, truthfully. 'Anyway, Marie don't want a nursemaid now – 'scornfully '– now she's at school.'

There had been a shortage of school places after the war: some schools had been bombed, and there had been an increase in births, so Marie had to wait. And the little convent which she attended had had its ranks swelled by the newly affluent lower-middle classes and even some working class - parents, were all clamouring for better education for their offspring. But Marie had been at school now for some months, and there was little for Renie to do; if Marie wanted to go out, Brian was always ready take her.

'What will you do?' Marged asked.

'Oh, I'll go in a factory. Then me and Jim'll get married.'

'And you think you'll get a council house?'

'We don't want a council house, I told you. No, they're building some nice semis now, under licence, so we should get one of them. Price controlled, fourteen hundred pounds. We pay a deposit, then get a loan from the Council. It's only three per cent.'

Marged looked with respect at Renie. She wondered if she'd tried for a scholarship, but knew it would have been hopeless. Her parents couldn't have afforded to let her go to the High School, and in any case, she'd never have been accepted. Not Renie West from the council houses, father a drunkard, mother feckless ... secondary schools pre-war liked nice respectable little girls.

'I hope you get a licence,' she said sincerely.

Yet she knew she would miss Renie. She was her last link with her childhood. And though they couldn't be called friends exactly, Renie did keep her up to date with what was happening in Victoria Street. Mrs Trigger's husband had died but she doubted if she'd miss him. So had Mrs Johnson's; you know, her that was going with the lodger for years – wonder if he'll marry her? Our Maud and our Tom, now out of the Army, had council houses, but our Vera, living with her husband's family, wanted to buy one, like Renie herself.

'So will you go back home till you get a house?' Marged wanted to know.

'Not on your life. I shall go to Jim's. I told me dad when I left that I'd never come back, except to see me mam sometimes. But not him, never. He can rot for all I care.'

So Renie left. Marie didn't seem to mind, and Adela was pleased.

What Adela and Brian talked about when Marged was in the office was never repeated, but it was no secret that she had made up the quarrel with her father, now in his eighties, and was living with him. Adela said nothing about the factory in front of Marged, but Brian carried on attending the Board meetings regularly.

He was there when Martin returned with his findings. Marged remembered the day well. Adela's father had died the previous week, and she and Brian had attended the funeral. They had returned the day before, full of the news that Adela had inherited the estate and there was a legacy for Brian, who was, of course, Adela's heir. So he looked pleased with himself as he joined the directors at the meeting

Martin started by saying that he was impressed by Germany's efforts, but there were certain factors that must be taken into account. 'I have five of them here,' he said, and read them out.

'Firstly, the Germans re-equipped after the war, because their plants had been ruined, so the United States and Britain helped them get back on their feet. Their plants are new, their machines modern. Britain is still using the same old plant and machinery.

'Secondly, management attitudes are flexible and up to date in Germany.

'Thirdly, we have too many different unions. Germany has only three.

'Fourthly, our production is less efficient.

'Finally, our sales, after-service and spare parts need to be overhauled. Foreign firms are more aggressive and effective.'

At this point Martin looked up from his paper, and Marged fleetingly thought how smart he looked in his dark grey suit and white shirt. He said: 'Our production, here at Mordant's, lags behind theirs because we're using the old machinery that's been here since the Flood. We have so many breakdowns, which slow up production time. It's no use our promising better service if we can't rely on our machines. We have a good workforce, and our sales service is good. I think, therefore, to make us competitive in the years ahead, we need to invest in new machinery.'

Marged pursed her lips. She knew this was true. She turned to Mr Arnold. 'Can we afford to replace the machinery?'

He had been scribbling figures on the pad before him. 'Making a rough estimate, I would say no,' he said. 'Not at the moment.'

'But we're making a profit?'

'The government are talking of slashing food subsidies. That will mean higher prices, so less money will be available for luxuries. There might even be a little slump. We can't afford to overspend.'

'Then we'll go to the bank,' said Marged.

Mr Arnold frowned. 'For some of it, perhaps, but I doubt you would find a bank to lend the whole. It would be a tremendous sum, and would put us in their hands.'

'But we must invest for the future,' Marged protested.

'Not necessary,' said Mr Byers. 'Not necessary at all. No other firms are doing so.'

'Then Germany will outdo them in the future,' put in Martin.

Mr Walters looked at him disdainfully, and Marged could read his thoughts. What did this jumped-up shop-floor worker know about management? 'We're all right as we are,' he said.

'It's a short-sighted policy,' argued Martin.

'I agree,' said Mr James. 'I see quite a lot when I travel. We're all right now, but we have think of the future.'

Marged looked round the table. 'Shall we vote on it?' she asked. 'Those in favour of borrowing to get new machinery?'

Three hands were raised, Mr James, Mr Jackson and Marged herself. Martin had no vote.

'Against?' Mr Byers, Mr Walters and Mr Arnold.

Marged looked at Brian. 'You have the casting vote,' she told him. And please, Brian, show some sense ...

'Against,' said Brian.

Marged sat still. What was Brian playing at? Trying to run the factory down now he had money coming from Adela's family? Had all this been plotted in their little sessions together? Or was it just to get back at her?

She glanced round the table. Byers and Walters she understood. It was short-term profits for them every time. But Arnold? Was he being cautious, or just keeping in with the Old Guard? She wondered for the first time if his expensive-looking wife had anything to do with his caution. She didn't know, any more than she understood that gleam in Brian's eye, a gleam of triumph.

She tossed her head. 'We need to invest and we shall,' she said. 'I have some money saved. It won't be enough, but if I am willing to put all I have into new machinery then the banks will help, I am sure.'

There were faint murmurs, but no one disagreed. Why should they, Marged thought cynically, when it wasn't their money? 'Is this agreed?' she asked, and this time the motion was carried.

She looked at Martin, and he knew what this would mean. There'd be no money for him to buy out Mordant's. Brian knew it too, and his gleam of triumph deepened.

Chapter 17

In 1953 Stalin died, and his reign of terror came to an end. Soon Krushchev was to make his famous speech denouncing Stalin's crimes, but this was not released in the Soviet Union, and it was one of the Polish delegates who delivered it to the West.

Stefan heard the news with joy. He knew now the dangers of being sent to prison, when a five-year sentence could mean for life. He was due for release next year and he still had in his coat lining one small gold tie-pin.

But it wasn't necessary – not at first. More men were released on time and when his term expired he was told he would be able to go. As the time drew near Vladimir Primakov came to him.

'Now you're free,' said Vladimir, a little wistfully.

The two men had a strange relationship. Neither could ever quite allow himself to like the other, for race memories were too strong, yet each felt a vague – and surprising – sense of respect. And Stefan had come to know Vladimir's story, how he'd been destined for the Party by an idealistic father, for an official post, but was now questioning the system – even disliking communism, at least as it had become under Stalin. He never breathed a word of this, but Stefan knew, and Vladimir knew that he knew; it was almost a secret bond. Vladimir had never talked to anyone

433

from the West before, and underneath, he envied Stefan his freedom of thought and speech because *he* was afraid to be free. With any other officer, this might have resulted in even more bullying, trying to beat out of the prisoner what he most envied in him, but not with Vladimir.

Yet even in his pity, Stefan knew a moment's impatience. How could the man excuse the camps, the brutality? He and so many others seemed to be able to turn a blind eye to horrors all around them. Stefan felt he would never understand the ordinary Russian people. They did not appear to be blindly obedient as the Germans and Japanese were said to be; instead they were sullen, they turned away.

And it's easy for me to say he's afraid to be free, Stefan mused. What could he do, after all? It took courage to be a dissident in the Soviet Union, and Vladimir had a wife and family to support. Well, he thought, I've done my best.

'You will need a work permit,' Vladimir said now. 'You were a musician, yes?'

'Yes.'

'Mm. Maybe something could be arranged.'

And Stefan produced the tie-pin, and this time it wasn't altogether a bribe.

He was duly informed that there was a school near Khabarovsk where a music teacher was needed. 'You know, we Soviets are very fond of the arts,' said Vladimir, who sometimes relapsed into the official dogma, especially if anyone was within hearing. 'We have fine new buildings—' and he reeled off a list of schools, arts centres and the like. 'We give our artists the finest training.'

'Yes,' agreed Stefan dutifully.

'So if you apply to this school I am sure they will take you.'

'Thank you,' said Stefan, and the tie-pin exchanged hands.

Freedom. The thing that meant so much to him; the cause to fight and die for.

Yet at the start he felt nothing. He even understood how some people could be willing to embrace their chains, to cuddle ever closer in the womb of the known security however appalling; how men not only got used to suffering, they welcomed it. He was horrified at these thoughts, but was not this the basis of totalitarianism of any sort?

He was in a dream as he left the camp, was taken to the station and boarded the train to Khabarovsk. Only when he walked along the main street of the town, among the hurrying passers-by, who at first bewildered him by their very bustle; only then did he think 'I am free.' And suddenly he wanted to run, to jump, to shout: 'I am free, I am free!'

It was August, hot and humid. He was still wearing the coat he'd worn when he went to the camp; now he took it off. His suit was threadbare, but no matter. He was free.

He decided to go first to the address Vladimir had given him, where he hoped Janina was still living. It might take some time to find and it was beginning to get dark. He didn't want to stay in any hotel, even if one would take him in. He would sleep outside if necessary, under the stars. Though – would he be arrested for that? Fears were still with him and would stay for some time; he was ever alert for the hand on the shoulder, the ominous knocking in the night.

Only when he told himself that the KGB could not possibly follow every single person everywhere, did he relax and realise it was all psychological, and that they wanted you to think that way, to keep you afraid.

He pressed on, not thinking about food. He was used to hunger. He walked most of the way, and came at last to a lonely road, with here and there some small wooden houses. And finally, he reached the address he'd been given.

He knocked on the door.

It was raining now, heavy silent rain that soaked him to the skin. The door opened, a man in his fifties stood there.

'Yes?'

Light streamed out from the little house. 'I am looking for my wife,' said Stefan. 'Janina Kowalska. Is she here?'

The man's eyes widened. 'Your wife?'

'I am Stefan Kowalski.'

And then he was ushered inside, into a tiny annexe, beyond which was a room where two women were sitting. The man said, 'I am Jan Bratkowski. Before you see her, I must tell you how she came here—'

'I know she was in a prison camp.'

'A farm, yes. She was released, but she had typhus. I brought her here.'

'You are Polish?'

'My ancestors were. They were exiled to Siberia in the 1863 rising. So they settled here, but they always taught me about Poland.'

Stefan smiled faintly. 'I know. My mother was the same.'

'I think all Poles are. We carry our history around with us. But about your wife . . . She was very ill, and I think she is much changed. She is—' He hesitated. 'Well, you must wonder why she stayed here. It is because she is afraid to move.'

Stefan would not have understood if it had not been for his own recent experiences. 'I know,' he said. 'I've just come from prison myself. But I'm sure I can persuade her to go now.'

Jan nodded. 'First of all I will warn her of your coming. If you will just wait here . . . Hang up your coat, take off your wet jacket.'

When Stefan finally entered the room he saw it was dominated by the big stove above which, he knew, in these old houses, people slept in the winter. The room was sparsely furnished, table, chairs, cupboards – with a door leading off it, presumably to bedrooms and a curtained alcove for the kitchen. One woman, with greying hair, obviously Jan's wife, stood up and came towards him. A second . . . was this Janina? Was this the girl he'd known?

She'd be thirty now, but her fair hair was faded, as if she

were an old woman, her face lined and sad. She looked up, and her eyes were expressionless.

'Janina,' he said gently. 'Do you remember me?'

She stood up slowly, and slowly came towards him. 'Tadeusz,' she said.

'No, not Tadeusz. It's Stefan.'

She did not seem to hear. 'Tadeusz,' she repeated. 'I knew you'd come.'

Stefan looked at Jan, who shrugged expressively. 'That's how she is,' his eyes said. 'That's what they have done to Janina.' He looked at his wife. 'Come, Maria, let us leave them to talk,' and they walked outside, where now the rain had stopped.

'Sit down,' Stefan said to Janina. He sat beside her, then did not know what to say. He had pictured this moment, had thought of her pleasure at seeing him, her delight at being able to go back with him to Poland. He had pushed to the back of his mind any reason she might have for staying. Whatever it was, he had not expected this.

He talked to her of their former home, of his mother, but he did not mention Tadeusz. 'We'll go back to Poland,' he said at last. 'You've had your release papers, and I'm sure I'll be able to get back.'

But Janina shrank against the wall. 'No,' she whimpered.

Maria was preparing supper and Jan returned. 'Come, Stefan, you must be hungry,' he said. 'We have good soup. Eat, then we'll go to bed, and talk again in the morning.'

During supper Stefan asked Janina what she did, for everyone had to work in the Soviet Union. 'I work in a factory,' she said. 'I put things in boxes.'

'We all work in the factory,' Jan said heartily. 'But maybe, Janina, you will have a better life now, eh?'

She did not answer.

Stefan realised just how hungry he was, hungry for good food made by a good cook, instead of the watery gruel he was used to at the camp. And then he was tired, so tired ...

437

Jan led them through to the bedrooms. There were two, one was Janina's, and here he left them.

Stefan looked at Janina. He had no idea what she expected of him. But he was so tired. For years he had slept on planks, now here was a comfortable bed and he merely wanted to sleep. He took off his clothes, ashamed of their sorry state, then, in shirt and pants, got into the one bed where Janina was already lying. He had no thought of touching her; he wanted only to sleep.

He said 'Goodnight,' and held her cheek to kiss her. She drew away sharply. 'No!' she screamed. 'Don't touch me.'

He spent the rest of the night on the floor.

In the morning – Sunday – he said to Jan: 'You must have heard last night. I just went to kiss her goodnight. I would never touch her in any other way – if she did not want it. I never have.' And he explained their marriage.

'I think she had a bad experience at the farm,' Jan told him. 'We had a doctor to her in the beginning and that's what he said.'

'I'll take care of her,' Stefan nodded. 'She is my wife.' But his heart was heavy.

He talked to her – or tried to. 'Janina, we must go home. Don't you agree? Home to Poland.'

'My parents?' she asked.

'I don't know,' he replied sadly.

'Tadeusz?'

He hesitated. 'Tadeusz is dead,' he told her gently.

She said nothing.

He tried again. 'We must apply for visas, Janina. You are a Polish citizen, you were released in 1941. I am released now. Stalin is dead. We must try.'

She shrank away. 'No,' she said. And apart from going to her factory, she would not even venture out of doors.

Stefan went to the school Vladimir had told him of, and made a formal application for the post of music teacher. He knew he stood a good chance – his music skills were high

438

and not everyone wanted to live in the Soviet Far East. It was too hot, too humid in summer; and cold in winter, with bitter winds sweeping from the river.

He looked round the little town when he returned from the school. Bordered by the River Amur, one mile wide, on the other side was China. Just a few miles away was the Sea of Japan. Even in the hot summers there was much monsoon-like rain. No, not everyone wanted to live here. And perhaps Vladimir had used his influence, for Stefan was given the post.

He applied for an apartment and, knowing he might have to wait years, made himself a bed out of planks. 'I'm used to this,' he laughed, and though he had to put it in Janina's room, he placed it as far away as possible from her.

'I'm sorry you're stuck with me as well,' he said to Jan. 'I thought that once I'd found her – well, you know. And you've been so good to her all these years, I can't thank you enough.'

'Think nothing of it,' Jan said. 'As for staying here, we're glad to have you. We have no children – at least, we had one, but he died.' Momentarily his eyes were sad. 'But I like to talk to you about Poland.'

'It isn't the same,' Stefan said. 'They have to build apartments, now, Soviet-style, not houses. They're all grey. Everywhere's grey. But –' his face brightened, 'I can tell you how it used to be when we lived on the farm, when we were children and played by the river, and *Matka* stood by the door calling us in for supper, and we'd hide. The storks flapping over the roof, the scent of wood-smoke . . .' Janina liked to hear about this too, and they'd sit in the evenings, outside when it was warm, indoors when winter came. But she still called him Tadeusz.

But before winter set in he was sent to Irkutsk for three days, for a short course on the teaching of music. He could, he was told, take his wife, and he carefully prepared Janina for the journey.

439

She had been out for several small walks recently, and he thought this a great improvement. So when the time came he packed their clothes, the new suit he'd been able to buy, her new dress, her warm coat, and they set off for the station, Jan and Maria with them to see them off.

Janina walked slowly, turning her head from side to side. He took her arm, and she allowed this. He had gone to the expense of hiring a car, and although she got in, she shrank back into a corner and when they arrived at the station, seemed only too glad to get out.

They walked inside, and the train drew in. And Janina screamed and ran back to the barrier, beating her hands against the wooden partitions until they let her through, when she ran – Jan in hot pursuit.

Maria stopped Stefan from following her. 'You must go,' she said. 'Jan will catch her and we'll take her back. Don't worry, we'll look after her.' Her eyes were full of sympathy.

He had to leave her but he entered the train with a heavy heart.

Irkutsk, on the Trans-Siberian railway route, was on the shores of Lake Baikal, the oldest lake in the world, and Stefan had hoped to be able to take Janina sightseeing. He had been allotted a room in a private house and he found this to be one of the old Siberian wooden homes, with three windows and painted shutters, again no central heating, but the old-fashioned stove as Jan had. He knocked on the door.

Sergei Andropov was also a teacher of music. He welcomed Stefan, led him into the living-room and introduced him to his wife. Stefan tried to show and interest in his surroundings. He was taken on a boat on the lake, but he had no heart for sightseeing. No heart even for the conference.

For the first time in his life he lost confidence. Always before there had been hope. In Rumania he'd hoped for escape. In Siberia he'd hoped to get out somehow, had planned for this, so that he could find Janina and take her home.

440

Now hope had gone. The Iron Curtain that had clanged behind him was being held down now by the girl who was his wife, and by the treatment she'd received for doing absolutely nothing.

He went into the bedroom he'd been given, sat on the bed, and was lost in a depression so deep that he wondered what was the point of going on. Would it not have been better if Jan had left Janina to die, rather than to live this half-life – then he could have stayed with Marged.

He stood up. It was night, and getting cold. But he could not sleep. He paced round the room, careful to take off his shoes so as not to disturb his hosts. What was there for him in life now?

For hours he paced, his mind a blank. And as morning showed a chink of light through the shutters he went to the window to pull them open. With one shutter half-open he stopped. On the wooden wall behind them names were scratched.

He peered closer. Then he went back to the chest of drawers, brought a candle. Was it possible? One of the names was Stefan de Reszke.

Now he couldn't wait for the breakfast hour. And when his host came in he mentioned the name on the wall. Who was this de Reszke? he asked. Did they know?

'Oh yes,' said Sergei. 'We think it was one of the old prisoners. Maybe he'd escaped, we don't know.'

Stefan's mother's teachings came back to him. 'Your great-grandfather, Stefan de Reszke ... taken to Siberia ... escaped and lived with the peasants ...'

Could it be?

He knew it was. Knew the Polish habit of tracing their names whenever they were in exile.

And what had his mother said? He taught the peasants to rebel ...

So he couldn't go back to Poland. But he could help ...

Stefan went back to Khabarovsk and sat down to write to

Tadeusz, the first of many letters, all on the same theme, freedom. *My dear Tadeusz, You are still only a boy, but old enough to understand what I am going to tell you. And I shall keep on writing to you as you get older, because you will have the chance which I do not have – to fight for freedom.*

Freedom is all. A man must be free – to think, to work, to do. And to love. If freedom is taken from you then you must fight to get it back. The time will come, so you must always be prepared.

Listen to Babcia; she will advise you well on freedom. Tell her that I know where her ancestor came, I saw his name. Tell her to teach you as she taught me, about freedom.

I shall write again, Tadeusz. And one day, God willing, we will meet. When Poland is free. Your Uncle Stefan.

In the little apartment in Gdansk, ten-year-old Tadeusz showed the letter to *Babcia*.

'Of course,' she said. 'That is what you were born for.'

'But *Babcia*. What can I do?'

'You will know when the time comes,' she said confidently.

So he wrote to Uncle Stefan, who had always been his hero. And he listened to *Babcia* as she talked of their history, of his parents.

She laughed when he and the other schoolchildren were sent to the beaches to hunt for Colorado beetles which, they were told, had been dropped by American agents, and was angry when the authorities attacked the Catholic church and arrested its priests.

'How can we be independent with the secret police at our heels?' she asked. 'Stalin stamped out all independent opinion, forced us to create a Soviet model state.' Yet Tadeusz was taught at school that Stalin was the great friend of Poland, her best ally. 'The genius of Comrade Stalin sees through all the plans of the warmongers,' the children chanted. 'Be vigilant against the aggressive plans of the imperialistic West.'

'Ha!' snorted *Babcia*, and in the summer of 1955 took him to the World Youth Festival held in Warsaw, and there he saw young people from the outside world with their music, their new clothes, and stories of life in the West. 'There,' she said. 'That is how *we* should be. That is how we will be. Stalin is dead now, Tadeusz. The nightmare is coming to an end.'

Tadeusz wished he were older. For the Poles were demanding reform, and in June there was a big demonstration in Poznan, running battles between militia and demonstrators, in which fifty-seven people were killed, Tadeusz would have liked to be there. At school he had to speak Russian, but he whispered in Polish to his friends about freedom, and when it was dark they took a pot of paint and painted great signs on walls: 'Rise up and do it again.'

He carried Uncle Stefan's letters with him everywhere. He read and re-read them all through that summer's crisis, and he rejoiced when Gomulka was restored to power in October, as Party leader.

'A peaceful revolution,' said *Babcia*. 'Achieved without any consultation with Moscow.'

'Are we going to be free now, *Babcia*?' asked Tadeusz.

Alas for their hopes. On 19 October, Krushchev arrived in Warsaw, together with leading members of the Soviet Government. Krushchev was enraged that the Polish Party had dared to change its leaders without permission, and he ordered Soviet troops to move in over the border from East Germany, from the Soviet Union, and from Czechoslovakia.

'What will happen, *Babcia*?' asked Tadeusz.

'We will fight them,' replied *Babcia* confidently. And as the Soviet Army within Poland moved towards Warsaw, the workers were called to defend their factories, while the Polish Internal Security Corps blocked the road from Poznan to Warsaw against the Soviet advance.

You must fight for freedom, wrote Uncle Stefan.

But amazingly, Gomulka faced down Krushchev in an all-night debate, and the Soviet leader flew back to Moscow. The troops returned home.

'Stalin always knew he could not impose communism on us,' said *Babcia*. '"Like putting a saddle on a cow," he said.'

'And we said like putting a yoke on a stallion,' returned Tadeusz. 'This is a great victory, *Babcia*.'

And they thought it was. Gomulka said they had finished with the system, and they believed that, at last, they were getting back to normal socialism. Collectives dissolved themselves without waiting for orders; in factories workers took control in democratic self-management. Censorship vanished; free journalism appeared, film-making, there was an inrush of Western books. The free radio was no longer jammed. Tadeusz found that religious education was returning to schools, and the Party youth organisation was abolished. Instead, Boy Scouts returned.

But it did not last. In 1957 Gomulka warned that if Poland did not remain under Communist control it would be invaded and occupied by the Soviet Union.

Tadeusz was twelve now, and a committed freedom fighter. He joined with the young radicals who still believed in a Polish revolution. He read the student magazine *Po Prostu* (Speaking Truthfully) until it was closed down. Warsaw students demonstrated, but were clubbed by the police. Repression had returned.

Uncle Stefan wrote: *Do not give up, Tadeusz. Freedom will come.*

So Tadeusz waited, and vowed to devote his life to the cause.

For the last three years Marged had received a picture card from Stefan every Christmas; and this postmark was clear – Khabarovsk. But as before, he wrote nothing but his name, and she received the cards with a mixture of joy and sadness – joy that he was well, sadness that he had obviously found a life without her. She wished he'd stop sending them, then she could forget, for she felt that after battling through stormy waters for so long, she had at last reached a measure of calm.

Martin had been tight-lipped at the defeat of their plans to buy Mordant's. He made no further trouble, but she knew he still wanted to gain control. She felt sometimes it was more than revenge. He needed to feel that he was on a level with Mordant, to erase all the snubs from his childhood – and before he was born, to his mother. 'We'll find another way,' she told him. 'Mr Walters will soon be retiring, and you can take over his job. It will be a step in the right direction.'

Martin still lived at Jack Morris's, but he spent so much time at Park Manor – when Brian was out – that Marged felt she and Martin were closer than they had been since they were children. Brian still attended many of the Board meetings, so he knew all about the workings of the factory, and doubtless passed on the information to his mother, who visited occasionally, as ever trying to belittle Marged. But Marged, at thirty-two, running the factory and supported by Martin, did not fear Adela. 'The complete businesswoman,' she would say sardonically to her reflection in the mirror, seeing only the well-groomed figure, the confidence. It was Martin who saw the lost look her eyes held sometimes.

As Mr Arnold had predicted, there had been a small slump following the rise in food prices in 1952. But Marged had carried on with the investment plan, though this meant that her own money had gone – was still going – to pay off the debts. And for a time it had been a struggle, with unemployment around.

Then things picked up. There had been a mini boom lasting until 1955. Now, two years later, hire purchase was restricted, fewer cars were bought, so again her money situation was tight.

And into this, Brian threw his bombshell.

She remembered the day, the date, 19 October 1957. She had been in her small sitting-room, which she increasingly regarded as a refuge, away from Brian's constant carping. She had made the room comfortable. The window-seat and the two armchairs she'd brought in were covered with chintz; a bookcase held paper ready for whatever she might be working on at the moment, together with a number of books she had brought in from the library and through which she was systematically working her way. Modern novels, the classics, Marged enjoyed them all. This had to be done in private, for Brian did not like her to read when he was around – understandable, she supposed – and he seldom came into the sitting-room, as he preferred the drawing-room.

She slept now in Roberta's room. At first it had been just at odd times when Brian's drinking became unbearable, for when drunk he never made any trouble downstairs, and never before Marie. He saved all his unpleasantness for her. So gradually she'd moved away, and again she refurnished Roberta's room, not so much for herself but almost as though she were trying to make up to Roberta for something.

Now it was evening, Marie was in bed, in the sitting-room a table lamp spread a glow over the darkening room. Brian entered and sat down. 'I want a divorce,' he said without preamble.

She looked up from her book, at first incredulous, then angry. Though why should she be? she wondered, even in her anger. It had been a marriage of convenience, after all.

She asked, 'But why, Brian? I mean, why now?'

He shrugged. 'Why not now?'

She put her book down and stared at him while conflicting emotions ran through her mind. Not yet forty, he was already running to fat, his face was puffy, the years of drinking had taken their toll. Brian was not a well man. She wondered if there was more she could have done for him, knowing he was a weak character, but knowing too that if she should ever praise him for something his attitude became unbearable, and he would strut and brag and put her down even more than usual. She guessed that he had deep psychological problems, too deep for her to attempt to deal with. He sat now, looking quite pleased with himself, and this annoyed her.

'What about the factory?' she asked.

'What about it?'

She thought, I should have made my share in the works legal in some way. As it is, he can just take it ... Aloud she said, trying to be reasonable, 'Well, I have been running it now for twelve years, so what do we do about it?'

Again he shrugged, picked up a book from the shelf beside him and put it down again. 'I don't care about the factory, never have. I can always sell it.'

'But you know I wanted to help buy it. I can't now. I've put all my money into the new machinery.'

'It was your idea.'

'And what about Martin? He's been working hard, too. He has some entitlement.'

'Martin. I wondered when we'd come to him. That's all you think about, isn't it? Martin. He's always here. And he's your brother. It isn't healthy, the way you two are, the way he looks at you. Oh, I've watched you.'

'You do talk rubbish, Brian. You know he isn't my brother—'

'Half-brother, then.'

'No, not even that. We're cousins.'

'Well,' sulkily. 'Whatever. I shall bring an action for divorce, citing Martin.'

'What?' Now she jumped to her feet, hardly able to believe her ears. 'You're divorcing me? Why, I've always been faithful, which is more than you can say!'

'Don't make me laugh.' He was standing now too, and

his face wore a threatening look; he must have been drinking. 'First there was Don James – oh, I heard all about it – and no doubt there were others. Colin Jackson, you've always been close to him—'

'Where on earth did you hear all this?'

But she knew, of course. Adela, who had been cultivating Mr Byers and Mr Walters ... All the time Marged had been relaxing, thinking everything was going well, they'd been plotting ...

'And Martin,' Brian was going on. 'The way you gave him his present position, the way he's always here, sometimes he's stayed the night—'

'Well, why not? We have enough rooms—'

'But you don't sleep with me now—' triumphantly. 'So you must have slept with him.'

'What a mind you've got,' she snapped. 'You know I never did. As for the reason he has his present position, you know why—'

'Do I? The silly tale you made up—'

'I did not. It's in Roberta's diary.'

'And where's Roberta's diary? It doesn't exist.'

'It's in her room—'

'There is no diary in her room.'

She stared at him now, his look of gloating triumph. What had he done? She wanted to run from the room, check ... She moved towards the door, then stopped.

'You'd really sell the factory?' she asked.

'When you leave.'

'When *I* leave?'

'This is my house.'

He was lounging now by the door. The room was almost dark, and she wanted to switch on the main light, but couldn't bear to go near him. She opened her mouth to speak, to object, then broke off. What had she expected? That he'd go, leaving her there in possession? He'd always liked Park Manor; she never had.

'I see you haven't asked about Marie,' he said.

'Well, if I have to go, Marie will come with me.'

'Oh no. I love the child, and you don't. She'll stay here.'

Now she really was dumbfounded. 'But she isn't yours ...'

'Legally she is mine,' he said.

'Legally,' she said bitterly. 'You hold all the cards, don't you, Brian? Trust a Mordant.'

'I do,' he said. 'I do.'

She couldn't bear to stay with him any longer. She went to the door, brushed past him, out, up the stairs to Roberta's room where she made straight for the bureau, opened the secret drawer.

The diary was gone.

She sat on the bed in the dark, her head in a whirl. She was to lose everything, her child, the factory she'd worked for ...

No, no, she would fight back. Try to think calmly.

She hadn't been sleeping with Martin. Brian had no proof. You had to have proof in a court of law. Just as she had no proof about Martin's real father, or for that matter, Marie's. To the law, she and Martin would be just a couple of go-getters, out to wrest the factory from an honest man ... *She brought him to their home, m'lud. She refused to sleep with her husband. They were taking over everything my client owned* ... The years of anguish in childhood meant nothing in law. Feelings, emotions didn't matter, when she stood in the Divorce Court. Only facts.

And it would be in all the papers ... How people would gloat. Especially those who'd begrudged her success – and there were many such. Byers, Walters, Adela, even some in Victoria Street who thought she'd got above herself ... Yes, it would be in the papers; everyone would be talking. Marie would suffer.

She wondered whether to tell Martin. He'd have to know, obviously, but not yet. He had such a temper. There was no point in him punching Brian on the jaw. That would only make things worse. So she went to the sitting-room in a turmoil, and wondered why she'd ever bothered. Why had she married Brian? Why hadn't she gone to live with Brenda?

She knew why. It was something deep inside her, born of her unhappy childhood, of seeing her father suffering, seeing Martin . . .

Surely Martin wouldn't lose out again?

The next day she didn't go to work. She went down to breakfast, and Marie came in. Brian was still in bed. He no longer took Marie to school, she went on the school bus. Schools had buses now; as they hadn't formerly.

'Not going to the office?' Marie asked, and Marged replied.

'No, I'm staying at home.'

'Oh.' Marged studied her daughter. Tall for her eleven years, thin in her blue uniform, dark hair, self-possessed, self-contained, she still didn't resemble Stefan – she was too dark, too thin. Adela was dark and thin, and for a wild moment Marged wondered if she could possibly have made a mistake, if Marie was Brian's after all . . . The world seemed topsy-turvy; she felt she was being spun round on a great wheel, not knowing where she would end up. Did Marie know anything about the divorce? She showed no sign.

Marie left, and Joanie cleared the table with a worried frown. Joanie guessed something was wrong, but didn't know what. Her muddled mind could not grasp reality – she was like a dog which senses trouble but cannot understand what it is about. Marged went into the sitting-room and didn't see Brian till she entered the dining-room for lunch.

And now he was startled. 'What, not at work?' he blustered.

'No. I'm not going again.'

'What?'

'Why should I? If you're selling the place, let it run down. Why should I bother? I'll tell Martin to leave. He'll find another good job soon enough. No doubt Mr Jackson and Mr James will go too. You'll have to manage with Byers and Walters.'

She ate lunch, taking pleasure in his obvious discomfiture, returning afterwards to the small sitting-room. She did ring Martin at the office, telling him she had a cold, and would be in touch, warning him not to come round to the house. Then she waited.

In the afternoon Brian came to her. He stood inside the door and she put down the book she was pretending to read. 'Look,' he said. 'I'll make a bargain with you. I don't want any unpleasantness with Marie, and a court case would only upset her, especially if you talked about me not being her father. Well, you can decide. Ask her who she wants to live with. She's eleven now, old enough to choose, I asked a lawyer.'

'Ask her to choose? But surely the Court will decide.'

'No. Not if we decide it. They could ask her.'

So he'd got it all worked out. She said: 'And you think the Court will think you're a fit person to look after a young girl, with your drinking?'

'I am never drunk in public. I never drink before Marie—' and she knew that was true. In the eyes of the Court he would be a pillar of the community, owner of a business, member of the Rotary Club, the Round Table.

She saw everything slipping away from her. She cried wildly, 'But who will look after her – and the house? Will you have a housekeeper? Another Mrs Stanway?'

'Oh no. As you told me once, those days are over. What people do now is take one of these foreign girls – au pairs, they call them.'

'And that would suit you fine, I suppose.'

Outside the wind was rising, moaning round the house. Marged stood up, went to the window, pretended to be studying the trees. Brian did not move.

He said, 'If Marie chooses me, you can have the factory.'

She swung round, wide-eyed, disbelieving. 'Have the factory?' she echoed stupidly.

'Yes. I'll just keep a few shares for income. But the factory will be yours.'

She found her hands were trembling, so she turned away again. Behind her Brian said, 'That way, it needn't be a contested case. I go to court, the case will be pushed through.'

'All decided in the backroom,' she cried bitterly.

'That's how it's done. Think about it, Marged. That way there'll be no upset for Marie, and the factory will be yours.'

He went out, and she sank into the chair again. Old enough to choose ... He'd found that out with the help of his lawyers. It hadn't occurred to her to see a lawyer. He'd known about all this, perhaps for years, then had waited till Marie was old enough ... After he'd manoeuvred Marged into the position where she had no money left to buy the factory so, if she lost, she'd forfeit all the money she'd saved and invested. No, Brian couldn't have thought all this up on his own, he wasn't clever enough. It would be Adela, having the last laugh.

For days Marged pondered wretchedly. She went back to the office, told Martin she was making a decision, but wouldn't tell him what it was about. She had to decide herself.

'There's something wrong, isn't there?' he asked. 'Why can't I come and see you? What's he been doing?'

'I'll tell you in a day or two, Martin. Honestly, you can't help me.'

Not now. No one can.

She watched Marie. Watched her talking to her 'father'. Marie had always been reserved, not an outgoing child, nor perhaps a loving child. She didn't seem to care when Renie left, Renie who'd looked after her for so many years. She didn't have many close friends, and showed little love for her mother, though she was not antagonistic. And over the years Marged had tried, had hoped that they'd get closer as Marie grew older. She had attended all the school's functions with Brian, the Open Days, the Speech Days ...

But face up to it, Marged, Marie did love Brian. And Brian loved her. She wondered drearily if Brian were doing all this for spite – yet did that matter? If it were best for Marie ...

In the end she followed the girl to bed, knocked, entered. The same room with different wallpaper, a bed in place of the cot, books, a tennis racket, dresses in the wardrobe, everything a little girl could desire.

Marie hadn't started getting undressed. She was listening to the radio that stood near the bed. She turned but did not speak.

Marged hardly knew how to begin. 'Marie—' She took a breath. 'Have you heard about – that your father and I—'

'Yes, I've heard,' said Marie flatly.

'That – that we might split up.'

'Yes. He told me.'

'What – what do you think about it?'

The child shrugged. 'If you want to go, that's it, isn't it?'

'I'm not sure I *want* to go,' Marged said, a little bitterly, reflecting that Brian had got his story in first, whatever it was, 'but if I did leave and we did split up, what would you want to do?'

She held her breath. 'I'd stay here,' Marie said. 'I like Park Manor.'

'You mean you'd rather stay with Daddy than come with me?'

'Yes.'

'But—' What to say, what to do?

Marie was talking, and it was as if she were the mother, explaining to a child. 'I could come and see you, you know. But Daddy has always been at home with me. I wouldn't want to leave him. Anyway, I look after him.'

'Do you?' Marged asked dully.

'Well, you know he can't read and all that.' How simply she talked about it, and Brian would accept it from her. 'Sometimes I try to show him, but he can't seem to grasp the words. It's as though he can't see properly.'

Marged gazed at her daughter with respect. 'You'd make a good doctor,' she said.

'Oh, I don't think I want to be a doctor, though I am interested in that sort of thing, yes.'

She wondered what Marie thought of his drinking, but hardly liked to mention it. No doubt she'd have a solution to that, too.

She went out, knowing the choice had been made for her.

She was able to tell Martin quietly, filling in the bare outline, no hysterics. She had asked him to the house, knowing it was the only place they could be alone, and they went into the sitting-room. It was a small oasis of light in the gloom of a November evening. Outside a drizzle was falling; it would soon be Christmas. Martin was clearly shocked.

'But is this what you really want?' he asked. 'To lose your child?'

'It's what she wants, Martin. Brian does love the girl, and she loves him. I don't think she loves me. To her I'm the hard career woman who didn't have time for her child. If I forced her to stay with me – that's if I could – she'd only hate me.'

'But—'

'No, Martin, I've thought it all out: Marie will stay with Brian. And he's giving Mordant's to me.'

'But, dammit, you're the one who's worked at it all these years. It's your money that bought the new machinery!'

'Leave it, Martin. It's all decided.' *Don't say any more or I might start screaming. This is the only way I can handle it.* And he understood and said no more.

★

454

Marged never remembered the next few weeks very clearly. Christmas came and went. She walked round the town like a zombie, looking at the shops. New shops now, practically all the bomb damage had been repaired. In Coventry they'd built a new shopping precinct and a modern cathedral. Not everyone liked it. *They didn't understand that we had built for our age as the old ones had done.*

People shouting and jostling, the market selling Christmas trees ... why was she walking around like this, so alone?

She went into a shop, bought a present for Marie. She must remember to give Joanie and Violet their Christmas gifts, and the cleaning woman – she could never recall her name. They'd have a party in the office as usual. They'd expect her to be there ...

Martin was a comfort. He didn't come to Park Manor now, and she couldn't visit him; they were afraid to sit in a hotel even for a few hours in case they were watched. Jack Morris had married again and now had a child, so Martin would have to look for somewhere else to live pretty soon ...

But Martin gave her his support. He was a listening ear, and when she asked: 'Where did I go wrong?' he said reassuringly, 'Nowhere, *He* was wrong.' Comforting her.

Then the memories faded and the next clear patch was when she was leaving the house. Martin was with her, helping her move, and as they stood in the small sitting-room and she turned to the door, he put a hand out and stopped her.

'You didn't have to hang on to Mordant's, you know,' he said.

'It's for the best.' She looked through the window. April the eighth. April. Blossom-time ... She'd learned a poem about that at school. 'Anyway, it's what we always said we'd do, isn't it?'

'We?'

'Yes, I suppose it's as much for you as for myself.'

He took her to the window-seat and sat her down, sat beside her. 'Do you still love Stefan?' he asked.

'Oh, I don't know. How can I when I'll never see him again?'

'Well,' now he was gazing at her intently, 'what I mean is, can you love anyone else?'

'You asked me that once before.'

'And you said you didn't trust anyone else. You can trust me, Marged. You know you can.' And as she turned towards him he said, 'It's always been us, Marged, hasn't it?'

She hesitated. Had it? Was it? Could you love two men? Of course she loved Martin, she always had. 'But I always thought of you as a brother,' she said.

But had she? Had she never really known that Martin loved her, desired her? Why wouldn't she admit it? What did she feel? Had it not been there all along, all the more exciting keeping him at a distance?

'I'm not your brother,' he said, and put his arms around her, kissing her hair, her eyes, finally her lips . . .

Outside it was spring and a bird began to sing . . .

EPILOGUE

The net curtains swayed in the breeze and Marged came back to the present day to face her grandson.

'So,' he said. 'You married Martin and lived happily ever after.' He sounded wistful.

'Brian divorced me, citing Martin. No, I didn't object. I thought it would be better for Marie that way. What did it matter? As for living happily ever after ... yes, we were happy.'

'You loved him?'

'But I always had. He'd always been part of my life.' She stopped, remembering. There hadn't been any great thrill – how could there be with someone you'd always known? It was comfortable, like an old glove ... Aloud she said, 'We just settled down together, quarrelling sometimes, as always. We lived as we'd always lived.'

'Except you didn't live as brother and sister.'

'Except we didn't live as brother and sister,' she replied equably. 'And oddly, that caused the most scandal – people thinking we *were* brother and sister.' She smiled, reminiscently.

'You were quite a girl, weren't you, Gran? Divorce, lover, scandal ...'

'The kind of girl I'd warn you against!' she said, and thought how she'd never have dared talk to *her* grandma the way young David was doing now. But things were different these days: everyone talked about sex, whereas before they just whispered.

'You came to live here?' David asked.

'No. We found a nice detached house in the posh end of the town.'

'Your dream home?'

'No. It wasn't that Martin didn't want it,' she said defensively. 'He wouldn't have cared what sort of house we had. But there was still a housing shortage in the fifties, and we had to find somewhere in a hurry.'

David looked round. 'This one, then?'

'I bought this when Martin died. No, this isn't my dream home.'

'You have the net curtains and the chintz.' David stood up, walked into the kitchen with its new shining units, then to the small-dining room at the side with its patio doors opening onto a lawn.

Marged followed him. 'A dream home has to be shared,' she said.

He strolled out onto the lawn; again she followed, and they sat on the two garden chairs. 'You say you had to find somewhere in a hurry?' he prompted.

'Yes. I had to leave Park Manor, you see.'

'Brian treated you pretty badly, Gran.' David turned his chair to face her. 'In effect he turned you out. You were supposed to be the guilty party, yet you were innocent.'

'Yes, well, that's how it was done then. And I didn't want to drag Marie through the courts, as I told you. We had to wait a year before the divorce hearing came to court.'

'And you and Martin lived together,' David said delightedly. 'I bet people did talk.'

'They certainly did.' And it had been pretty nasty, all the stares, the whispers ... Sitting through the Board meetings, seeing the knowing nods from Byers and Walters when the factory was finally turned over to her, tossing her head, pretending she didn't care ...

'Did Brian marry again?' David wanted to know.

'No. Funny, that. Adela wanted to be rid of me so that Brian could marry someone of a better class, for those born before the war still saw things in the old way. But better-class girls didn't want men like Brian now, nor a large house with no servants. Lots of the big houses were being sold off, to be turned into hotels or old people's homes. They didn't even want his money, for they could earn their own. But perhaps it was better for Marie that way.'

She paused, and David studied the flowers edging the lawn.

'We worked together at the factory, Martin and I,' Marged resumed. 'And we did well, at least in patches. There were credit restrictions in 1961, tax increases, a pay pause. But it turned out for the best for us, as Byers and Walters were due for retirement and they both decided to sell their shares to us.' She grinned, giving her face a youthful look. 'They knew they wouldn't win, so they gave up. We carried on, and our investment paid off. We were very competitive when others didn't do so well, those who hadn't invested in new machinery. It was a happy factory, you could tell from the atmosphere.'

'Nineteen sixty-one. That would be the swinging sixties I've heard about,' David mused. 'How was it really?'

'Well, Chilverton didn't exactly swing,' Marged smiled. 'But girls did wear mini-skirts and everyone sang the Beatles' songs. And yes, something had changed. The working class took over the songs and writings in a way they hadn't ever before. They called it a revolution.' She was thoughtful. 'Mind you, we did more than them in our revolution in 1945.'

They fell silent again, drinking in the peace of the garden. The sun was edging towards the west, and from the lilac tree a blackbird began to sing. 'I'll have to get something to eat,' Marged said, rising.

Back in the kitchen she busied herself with the salad, the cold chicken from the fridge, peeling potatoes.

'I never eat chips,' she said to David, when she'd put the meal on the table by the open patio doors. 'Chips were considered common when I was a child. Can't understand why people eat them now.'

They sat companionably and David asked, 'What did Brenda think about it all?'

'Oh.' Marged paused. 'As I remember she simply said we'd always been a pair.' And she'd also added that Martin always got his own way. 'But he needed me,' Marged ended. 'People didn't realise that. As for Brenda herself, Philip's business really took off in the fifties. He became well – known you must have heard of Philip Higham. There was an article about him in one of the Sunday supplements recently, saying he was one of the leading designers of the century. That's what they call them now, interior designers.'

There was a pause. David asked, 'And my mother? Marie?'

'She came to visit me occasionally.'

'So you were friendly?'

'Yes.' But she knew it was not true. Marie was never very friendly and she grew less so as the years passed. 'She was a clever girl,' she went on. 'Passed the eleven-plus which meant she could stay on at the convent, fees paid. The Welfare State benefited those with money as well as those without. She went on to university to become a chemist.' She smiled. 'I remember when she told me.'

'A chemist?' Marged had asked. 'You mean open a shop?'

'No, Mother—' in the superior tone Marie adopted when talking to her. 'In industry.' Yes, Marie had grown more superior with the years, egged on by Brian, who mocked Marged's humble beginnings. And the girl would never say much to Martin, always tried to come when she knew he was out.

Again a silence fell and the blackbird renewed his song, was answered from the woods below. Then Marged said painfully, 'It wasn't until Brian died that we quarrelled. That was in 1964, she was nineteen ...'

A terrifying time. Marged had known Brian was ill, that he hadn't listened to the doctor's warnings. Marie never told her of his condition, but she'd heard it on the grapevine – in a small town, everyone knew everyone else's business. And when he died, Marie hadn't rung her. Marged had read it in the evening paper.

She'd gone to see her, thinking the girl was upset, thinking that she could visit now surely, to help her daughter. She'd rung the bell and Joanie had answered – she'd stipulated that Joanie be kept on – and here she was, over forty now, with greying hair and stooped shoulders, looking much older. She began, 'Hallo, Mrs Mordant—' and was swept aside by Marie.

'Go away,' Marie ordered. 'I don't want you here.' And she made to shut the door.

But Marged would not be pushed away. 'I only came to see if you needed any help.'

'I don't want your help.' Marie was, unusually for her, dishevelled, her hair straggling over her face. 'I don't want you. I – I found out.'

'Found out what?' Marged asked in a whisper, though no one could hear in this secluded house, only Joanie, hovering in the background, her homely face worried, puzzled.

'That the man I've always called my father isn't my father at all.' And now the girl was sobbing, wild, uncontrollable sobs, and again Marged tried to step forward.

'Please let me in, Marie. Please!'

'No. Go away.'

'Did – did he tell you?' Had he been delirious? Could she pretend ...?

'No!' Marie almost screamed. 'No, he didn't. I found out. He had to take a blood test, and I saw the results. I

461

know my own group, so I knew he couldn't be my father. Oh,' she was crying quietly now. 'How could you? How could you do this to him?'

'He knew, Marie.'

'I don't believe you. He always said he was my father.'

'Because he loved you.'

'Oh yes, I know that. It was you who didn't love me. And now I see why. So who was my father, then? Who? Tell me, then I'll have someone else to hate besides you. Or don't you know? You're just a slut, aren't you? That's why my father divorced you. You had so many other men. He told me.'

Marged didn't speak. She would not subject her lover to a tirade of abuse; it was like speaking ill of the dead. She said: 'I'd better go. Perhaps we can talk about it some other time.'

'Oh no, we can't. Not ever. I don't want you here. I don't want you at the funeral. I never wanted you. Go away, go away . . .'

And slowly, Marged walked away.

'I never saw Marie again,' she told David. 'I wrote to her once, but she didn't reply. I read in the local paper that she'd married well and was pleased for her. She moved away, as you know, and Park Manor was sold. It is now a hotel. I never saw her – or you. As I told you, I was abroad when the accident happened. I only found out she was dead when I came back – a few days before you arrived. So—' she drew a painful breath. 'Now you can fill me in with your life.'

'Father was a lawyer,' David said. 'He was older than Mother, and when he died he left her quite well provided for. We lived in a Cotswold village.'

'Nice,' said Marged. 'Away from the harsh realities of life near the back streets. And industry.'

'Now, Gran—'

'I'm sorry,' she said penitently. 'You see, I haven't mellowed with the years. But go on, tell me about your life. About – your mother.'

'I had a very uneventful life,' David said. 'Unlike yours, Gran. My parents were happy. I never really wanted for anything, and I suppose I didn't realise how lucky I was till you told me your story.'

'Marie put a birth notice in our local paper when you were born. As you'd moved away I did wonder if she perhaps wanted me to know. Again I wrote, but there was no answer. Ah well.' She shook her head as if to shake away painful memories. 'She never had any other children?'

'Just me. I had no cousins, no one. I told her once how much I longed for brothers and sisters, and she said she wished I had them, too. So I don't think it was deliberate.'

'No. We don't seem to be a very prolific family, do we?' They sat in silence for a moment, then Marged said: 'Did she ever talk about me?'

'We-ell.' David hesitated. 'Not really. You see,' he hurried on, 'she was always very reserved, and she was perfectly happy with my father. They had a good life, so ...'

She wondered if he were covering up. Still, better say no more, let it be. 'I'm glad things went well for her,' she said. 'I really am.'

'I remember,' David was saying slowly, 'when I was about seven, it was when Martin had died and she showed me the obituary in the paper – she always had your local paper sent on—'

'Did she?' So she was still interested. Marged felt warmed.

'There was a photograph. And she said, "He may well be your grandfather." I didn't know what she meant, but later I asked her; that's when she told me she didn't know.' He paused. 'That would be in 1977.'

Marged was staring into space. 1977. Poor Martin, he'd had a heart attack. Just a year after they'd had that bad

463

quarrel. They'd been to work as usual, they came home and she'd made a cup of tea as she always did while they watched the news on television. They ate later, or went out for a meal.

It was a hot day in August; someone nearby was cutting his lawn, the smell of grass came in through the open window. The newsreader said: 'In Poland there have been student riots in Warsaw ...' and Martin turned it off.

'Leave it,' she said. 'It was interesting.'

'I don't want to hear it,' he said and angry, she flounced up to their bedroom where they had a second set, which she switched on. 'This isn't the first trouble in Poland,' the voice continued. 'There has been unrest among the workers in the Baltic port of Gdansk ...'

And Martin came in and began talking. 'Come on, we're going out—' and she was angry again and said she'd see the news if she wanted to. Of course they often rowed, they always had, but this was really bitter, and she didn't understand why. He'd said: 'For God's sake, that's all over,' and she'd answered: 'I don't think it is.' Then he'd shouted, 'You belong to me!' and she'd shouted, too: 'I belong to myself, and I shall see the news if I want to—' He could be possessive at times, Martin. She sometimes thought he'd have liked her to stay at home, but he could hardly insist on that when the factory had belonged to her in the first place, though after their marriage she'd made it a joint ownership. Anyway, it was beginning to be accepted now that women should go out to work, as it hadn't earlier. All the years that Marie had been growing up there'd been articles in the newspapers about latch-key children. She must have read them and felt neglected ...

She and Martin hadn't spoken for days after the row. That was Martin's way. He sulked, or so she told him. She read about the Polish riots in the newspapers, the way workers who played a prominent part in the strikes were sacked, including an electrician in the Lenin shipyard in

Gdansk named Lech Walesa. The Committee for the Defence of the Workers (KOR) was founded and became the best-known opposition centre in Eastern Europe ...

Yes, she'd read all that. Well, it was only natural to be interested, wasn't it? Everyone was. Except Martin.

'Gran,' David said. 'You were miles away.'

'Sorry.' She came back to the present. 'You were saying?'

'You'd miss Martin when he died.'

'Of course. We made it up later, when Poland dropped out of the news. We always did.'

Yes, she missed Martin, her companion since childhood. But she bore her loss as she had borne all her losses, straightening her shoulders, carrying on. She had, after all, been able to give Martin all he ever desired from life.

'You kept the factory?' David asked. 'Afterwards?'

'For a time. But I really hadn't the heart any longer. I remember sitting one evening, wondering what it was all about. All this talk about success, making money, hooey! What they really want is power, power over other people, power to hurt other people, power to dismiss people – that's what leads to war. I never had this desire, though I think Martin did, but I could always keep him in check. Now there was no need, so I sold up. Lucky I did, as it happened, for when the eighties came many car factories closed down, those which made machine tools, places that had been going for as long as I can remember, famous names ... So without cars there was no market for our components. We'd have been bankrupted. The people who bought Mordant's didn't keep it going for more than a year.' She was silent, watching the setting sun. Over its rim the whole sky was aflame. 'I was glad Martin was dead,' she concluded. 'He didn't see the end of the dream.'

The blackbird sang louder, a last call before the dark. David put out his hand and held hers. She turned and smiled. 'Though other dreams were just beginning. You heard about Solidarity in Poland?'

'Well, I have now. I've been reading it up. How it started in the Gdansk shipyards among the ordinary workers in 1980, how others joined with them, intellectuals et cetera. How it spread throughout, the country, with strikes and more strikes.'

'It was reported all over the world,' Marged said. 'This movement led by an ordinary electrician called Lech Walesa. In the end the government backed down and permitted the start of a free trade union – so Solidarity was born.'

She mused. 'I seem to remember Stefan saying that his mother went to Gdansk. She'd be dead now, of course.'

'Dear Gran,' David said. 'So that's why you were listening to the news about Poland when I first came.'

'It seems incredible that you arrived on the very same day as the first Polish free elections.' She looked at him. 'Well, now you've heard it all, that's the end of my story. So what are you going to do? Stay on with me?'

'Of course I am.' He pressed her hand. 'You see, Gran, it isn't the end of the story . . . is it?'

In 1989 the Iron Curtain began to crumble, and the dramas of Eastern Europe which had started in the shipyards of Gdansk nine years earlier and led to Poland's free elections, spread to Hungary, and then to East Germany.

David was living with Marged now, attending Warwick University and coming home each night in the little car she'd bought him. She liked having a boy about the house, even liked his untidiness, his clothes and records scattered around. Liked the noise, the friends who came and went, who sat and put the world to rights, who sang and danced, just as she had. It was as if she had a son of her own, the son she'd once dreamed of. With him she visited Marie's grave, and as she stood before it, said silently: 'I'm sorry, Marie.'

Together they sat before the television, when on 7 November the East German Government resigned. Permission was given for private travel, and tens of thousands poured through the Wall to West Berlin. On 10 November, they began smashing the Berlin Wall.

'Gran,' David said. 'You know I'd like to trace any relatives I might have?'

'You don't have any relatives, David.'

'Not here. But maybe in Poland—'

'I don't think so, David. Not now.'

She got up, went into the kitchen, knowing she was stalling. Not certain why.

The house was warm in winter, with central heating. Marged loved to be warm; there had been so many cold days in her youth. Women had it so much easier now, she thought as the fogs of November changed to chilly December. There was a sleety rain falling as she stood by the window and watched David drive up the hill. He burst into the house, shouting: 'Gran! Gran!'

'I'm here,' she called, walking into the dining-room.

'Gran, listen!'

'David, sit down. Tea's ready.'

'Yes, Gran.' Obediently he sat, and she smiled.

'All right, what is it now?' She loved this too, his enthusiasm, his eagerness.

'Gran,' he said. 'About my relatives—'

A little shadow moved across her face. 'Yes?'

'This morning you had a card from Stefan.'

'I have one every Christmas, I told you.' Still redirected from her old address.

'So he's still alive. And you know where he is. Khabarovsk. Could we not trace him?'

'How?'

'Have you never tried?'

'No.' She closed her mouth tightly.

'But you've never forgotten him, Gran.'

'Of course I've never forgotten, you don't forget parts of your life. But it was too long ago, David. Don't start dreaming of reviving past history, it can't be done. It's an old song that was sung. Now too much has changed, I've changed.'

'But, Gran, he is my grandfather.' And she was silenced.

Yet she hesitated. She hadn't realised what it would mean, re-opening the past, slowly and sometimes painfully. She had said it was an old song. She had clamped down on her memories again and wasn't sure that she wanted to revive them.

But David insisted. They'd drop the matter for a time, then there'd be another programme on radio or television about Gorbachev, about Poland, and it would start again.

She said, finally: 'What do you want to do?'

'I've been looking through old newspapers in the library, about Solidarity.' Triumphantly, he produced a newspaper, showing a photograph of the shipyard in Gdansk, the meeting of the workers. There was Lech Walesa, and behind him another man, tall dark-haired. 'Speeches were made also by Tadeusz Kowalski,' read the cutting.

She put the paper down. 'That's all?'

His face fell a little. 'But it's the same name, Gran. The same place, Gdansk.'

'But David, there could be hundreds of hundreds of Kowalskis in Poland!'

'We can trace this Tadeusz, don't you see? This isn't the Soviet Union. They've had more freedom since Solidarity, since the Russians left them. We could write to this man.'

She stood up and he watched her, puzzled, uncomprehending. She hardly understood herself. He said, 'You know I've been studying languages, I've done a little Russian and Polish—'

He was determined. 'All right,' she agreed. 'You try to trace them if you wish.'

She loved him. So she had to accept all of him, as perhaps she never had with Marie. Always underneath lay that resentment that the child wasn't the boy she'd longed

468

for – had Marie sensed this? So she battled with herself in the silent watches of the night, as the cold frosts of December slid towards Christmas.

David put up decorations, and Marged bought a tree. 'Now, isn't this nice?' he asked, putting his arm around her. 'Isn't this better than being on your own?'

'Go on, wheedling round me,' she said.

'Ah, but you like it, don't you? Was Stefan a wheedler?'

'N-no, not really. He was a little more reserved.'

'Like my mother.'

'Mm.' Maybe, and she hadn't realised.

It snowed in January, and every blade of grass on the lawn was separately coated with feathery frost. But March brought daffodils to Marged's garden, one of her favourite flowers; she loved the spring, symbol of hope. And as she bent over her flowerbeds David banged the car door and charged over towards her. 'Gran – I've heard from Tadeusz!'

She put down the fork, stood up slowly.

'I've had a letter. He *is* my cousin. And he knows Stefan's address!'

Now she was still.

'Come inside, let's make a cup of your tea, and I'll read it to you.' He pulled her through the door, and they sat at the table by the window while he brought the tea, and Marged opened a tin of biscuits.

'Now,' David said. 'I'll translate. First he says he is the son of Tadeusz and Nina who were both killed in Warsaw, or just afterwards, and his grandmother brought him up – *Babcia*. He says: "My Uncle Stefan is still in Siberia. After his release he stayed with his wife until she died."'

He paused. Marged drummed her fingers on the table. 'Does he say,' she asked at last, 'why Stefan stayed in Siberia? If he was released, why didn't he come home?'

'I don't know, Gran. Tadeusz doesn't say.'

Marged watched a blackbird chase a thrush away from

the bird-table. Couldn't he get out?

David said, 'Gran—' and she realised he was reading again.

'I'm sorry,' she said. 'I am interested, really.'

'It's exciting, Gran. I have a cousin! I've never had any cousins, or brothers or sisters – nothing.'

'Did you explain your relationship?'

'No. I mean, that's your private life, isn't it? I just said my grandmother used to know Stefan, so I felt we were friends. Anyway, my Polish isn't up to anything more.'

'I see. Well, go on, tell me about Tadeusz. I know you're dying to.'

And as he began to speak she could almost see the boy who grew up in the ruins of Gdansk, with *Babcia*, the boy who had always rebelled against the régime.

Uncle Stefan wrote to me and I wrote to him, and I was surprised that most of the letters seemed to get through. Because I confided all my hopes and dreams to him, and it was he who guided me all along to work for freedom. *Babcia* said that's what I had been born for, conceived in the midst of the Warsaw uprising, my mother dying . . .

Tadeusz talked of how he went to work in the shipyards when he left technical school at seventeen.

I never wanted to do anything else. I loved to see the tall ships, I used to think they sailed away to freedom . . . But I learned quite soon of the corruption of the management, knew that the economy wasn't working.

I'd always said I wouldn't marry. I wanted to devote my life to the cause, not be hampered by a wife who might hold me back. But in 1977 I met Anna. She was a teacher, had come from Warsaw, where she'd been working on a free underground newspaper called *Robotnik* (The Worker). It was an exciting time then, for we weren't allowed to possess printing equipment; it was like

Warsaw during the German Occupation. We even had a similar secret education system, and Anna worked for this. The police assaulted us, arrested some of us, but we carried on. We sat in attics and listened to Radio Free Europe and the BBC, telling us the truth. We fell in love, Anna and I, and were married.

Well, David, you ask me about my part in Solidarity. The first fateful year was 1980. Anna had the twins now, and was expecting our next child, but she still supported me in every way. There had been strikes throughout the year, but in August it was our turn. We heard that a woman, another Anna, Walentynowiec, had been sacked, 'for stealing candle stubs from a graveyard,' said my friend.

'Not for being in the Free Union, of course,' I retorted. 'We must get her reinstated, it's not fair. We must strike.'

I helped smuggle posters into the shipyard, past the security guards, demanding Anna's reinstatement and a pay rise. Then we marched through the yard, carrying makeshift banners. Oh, the sight of it! Men putting down their blow-torches and jumping down from those great ships to join us. Marching to the main gate where the Director stopped us and promised negotiations, and people wavered.

Then the sight the whole world came to know. A small man with a large moustache scrambling up behind the Director. 'Remember me?' he asked. 'I worked here for ten years. I lost my job four years ago.' Lech Walesa. He saved the strike from collapse and a strike committee was formed.

Dignity. We struck with dignity, with self-restraint. We demanded better conditions – and the right to strike. We were determined to strike for years, if necessary.

And we won. You know that, don't you, David? The government backed down and signed an agreement with the strikers granting our requests and permitting the free trade union.

Solidarity was born.

And our little Antonina was born at the same time. I thought she had been born into a free country. We talked freely, published several newspapers. I thought we were free.

Only Anna advised caution. She didn't quite believe ... She was right. Moscow began to intervene. The Polish delegation was hauled into the Kremlin before Breznev and Andropov, the KGB boss. Why was Russian no longer compulsory? they asked. How dare we guarantee private ownership? Men were arrested.

Solidarity's first National Congress was to be held in Gdansk on 5 September. I was excited, but the day before, we could see Soviet ships beginning naval manoeuvres in the gulf below. We could see them there as we listened to our speakers.

So many brilliant speakers: the last surviving general of Pilsudksi's army, who cried: 'Do not allow yourselves to be intimidated.'; the Jewish doctor, Marek Edelman, who had been a leader of the Warsaw ghetto uprising. Foreign guests, including one Len Murray from Britain.

Two months later the tanks moved in. Martial law. A military takeover. Lech Walesa was imprisoned. And so was I. Now all was chaos. Angry people protesting in the streets, squads of storm-troopers with tear gas to break the demonstrations, pummelling with truncheons, old women trapped in corners, still shaking their fists ...

But we had tasted freedom. It was coming closer. 'My prison won't hold me,' I shouted. 'I'll be back.' And I was. So was Lech Walesa.

Not immediately. The West sympathised and applied sanctions, which made things worse for us. The Pope visited. A priest was murdered by the secret police, and we were roused again.

The Party leader was General Jaruzelski, a man who'd been forcibly taken to the Soviet Union from Poland, forced to work in a labour camp as Aunt Janina and Uncle Stefan had. He was as unpopular as the rest of them, and they seemed to lose faith in themselves.

So we come to last year, 1988, and the start of the Communist retreat. There were more strikes. Lech Walesa met the Interior Minister. 'Persuade the strikers to go back to work,' said he to Lech. 'And we'll consider restoring Solidarity.' Within three days he'd halted the strikes.

Then we held our breath. There were round-table meetings in February and March this year, Lech racing round the country to suppress wildcat strikes. Yes, we held our breath ...

But everyone knows the results. Solidarity restored, free elections to be held, the Senate restored also, changes in the economy – I'm sure you know all this, David.

David paused, and Marged said, 'Yes, we know the results, but not what led up to them. I wonder how Anna managed when Tadeusz was in prison. Was *Babcia* still alive?'

'Wait a minute. Here ... *Babcia* lived along enough to see the birth of Solidarity – and of Antonina. She was well over eighty. But I think Anna would manage. She sounds the sort of person who would.'

'Mm. Is that all then, David?'

'He ends by saying: "It was a triumph, above all for Lech Walesa. In a lesser way for the lesser people, the strikers, those with the will to win. Me. Uncle Stefan. I owe Uncle Stefan a great deal, for it was he who urged me to work for reform. And now I find someone who knew him. Can we not meet and tie up the ends? With all best wishes, your friend, Tadeusz."'

David put the letter down and looked at Marged. 'We can't tie up the ends without Stefan,' he said. 'Now I have the address I shall go to Siberia, to Khabarovsk.'

Marged moved restlessly. 'I wonder why Stefan stayed there,' she said, almost to herself.

'Tadeusz didn't send a phone number, or I could try to talk to him. I shall go to see him as soon as I can. I won't have time yet. If we go to Siberia in June when my vacation begins . . .'

'Are you really going to Siberia?'

'We both are, Gran.'

'Oh no, David. Not me.'

'Please, Gran. You wouldn't let me go alone, would you? All alone in a strange country?'

'Wheedling again,' she grumbled. 'Getting your own way. Well, I'll think about it.'

He smiled, knowing he had won.

And now Marged felt she was being swept along by events outside her control, events arranged by a human whirl-wind – David.

'I've made enquiries about travel,' he told her. 'And the best thing to do is to go with a group rather than wandering around on our own. Cheaper, too. There's a trip going in June on the Trans-Siberian Railway, which will take us right to Khabarovsk. Then if we decide to stay longer we can extend our visas there – it's easier that way.'

'David,' she said. 'I'm not sure if this is a good plan. How do we know that Stefan will want to see us after all this time?'

'He sends you those cards, Gran.'

'Even so, I think you're indulging in some romantic dream. Wartime sweethearts meet after more than forty years. Forty years! It's a lifetime, David.'

'But you won't have lost anything, Gran. You can meet and come away.'

She wasn't sure. Maybe she would lose something – if only a dream. Now she had her secure memory of the past, she wasn't sure if she wanted that taken away.

David turned to survey her. 'But I'm not going for you, Gran. Stefan Kowalski is my grandfather.' And again she was silenced.

474

'I think we should write and ask first,' she pointed out. 'Before we just turn up out of the blue. It would be enough to give him a heart attack.'

'We-ell.' David considered, and she knew why he didn't want to write: Stefan might refuse to see them. 'We'll write just as we're leaving, so that he is prepared but doesn't have time to stop us.'

'You're a conniving monkey,' she said.

'I know,' he replied complacently. 'But I'm nice with it, aren't I, Gran?' He paused. 'But who will the letter be from? Do I tell him who I am?'

'Oh.' Marged paused, nonplussed. 'No,' she decided. 'We'll wait till we see him.'

'Then you must write it yourself, Gran—' And at her hesitation: 'Send a postcard, that will do.'

That almost stumped her. How did you write to a man you hadn't seen for so many years? It took several days of rewriting before she finally decided on: *Dear Stefan, We are having a holiday on the Trans-Siberian train from Moscow to Khabarovsk in June. We heard of your address from friends and would like to call on you if that is all right. Marguerite Fennel.*

That was suitably vague, she thought. The rest was in the lap of the gods. Or in David's.

'I've booked our tickets,' he told her. 'Now, on the Trans-Siberian they put you all in sleeping berths together, men and women alike. So I booked a compartment for the two of us. It costs a bit more but I thought you—'

'You thought I wouldn't want to share with strangers,' she ended.

'I didn't know what you'd get up to,' he grinned. 'I didn't want you taking off with some toyboy before we get there,' and she cuffed his ear.

She looked at the map. Khabarovsk was on the eastern seaboard, close to the Sea of Japan and to Japan itself. She gazed at the huge land mass of Siberia; Moscow to

Khabarovsk was over five thousand miles. At least it would be warm in summer – or so she hoped.

'Tell the truth, Marged,' she murmured to herself in the mirror. 'You don't want to go at all.' She looked at her reflection. She still had some colour in her hair, and her skin wasn't too bad, nor was her figure. But her face had changed. Hardened? She peered closer. This certainly wasn't the girl Stefan had known. But she missed the dignity of her bearing, the proud tilt to the head.

And, she thought, as she turned away, neither would he be the same, and that was what she feared. She'd lose the handsome lover she'd had, to gain – what?

Yet she owed it to David to go.

They set out in mid-June and flew to Moscow, thirty in the group, with a courier, Alan, who spoke Russian and seemed to know the country well. None of them was quite sure what to expect. They'd heard on the news about demonstrations, yet when they were taken to the hotel in the centre of Moscow they saw nothing.

They were forced to have a Soviet courier, too. Her name was Lena, and she was younger and less officious than Marged had anticipated. She talked openly about the reforms as she shepherded them around Red Square and, as they saw queues outside shops, admitted there was a shortage of food. As they sat in the hotel dining-room before a quite decent meal of soup, fish and a sweet (another day they were to have caviare), Marged said worriedly to David: 'I feel guilty eating well when there isn't enough food. I'm surprised the Russians don't lynch us for taking what should be theirs.' And she wondered how Stefan was faring. Did he have enough to eat?

Lena took them on the Metro, amazingly cheap, and they were struck by the beauty of the marble walls, statues and carved ceilings. But for all the *perestroika* and *glasnost*, when they went back to the hotel they noticed two men standing on one of the balconies, watching ... watching whom? And Alan told them that Russian people were not allowed in this hotel.

The next day they boarded the Trans-Siberian train.

There seemed to Marged to be a lot of pointless, pettifogging rules, such as not being allowed in the station before the train came in, not taking photographs of machinery which doubtless included trains. But when they finally went on to the platform and the great train came in, Marged watched in wonderment. This monster was to take her on a journey the like of which she'd never known before, five thousand miles across the loneliest land in the world. She shivered.

'Come on, Gran,' called David, and they settled in their compartment with its four bunks and small table, where Emma, the hefty female attendant, would bring them tea made from the boiling urn at the end of the carriage. The bed linen was clean, but the toilet was a shock. Little bigger than an ordinary British Rail one, there was no shower, and no toilet paper. They had been warned of shortages, of toilet paper, soap and bath plugs. Why bath plugs? Marged wondered.

At seven they crossed the Volga, and Marged went to the corridor to see better the wide expanse of water she'd read about so often. 'There are eight time changes between here and Khabarovsk,' called Alan. 'But the train runs on Moscow time, so we don't alter our watches. Instead the times of the meals are changed.'

The first breakfast was at 9.30, and David dressed and went into the dining car, followed by Marged. 'Did you sleep well?' he asked.

'Yes,' she replied, though actually she had not. She had been filled with apprehension. What did a man say when presented with a grandson he'd never heard about? Suppose he didn't believe it was his; suppose he just didn't want to know ...

The train roared inexorably on, keeping to its time, the

passengers having to change their times to suit, and Marged found this increasingly confusing, that the next morning, breakfast was at 7.30, though the actual time was 12.30. She soon gave up reckoning time, just went into meals when they were announced, simply noticing the days seemed surprisingly short, and it was getting dark in the afternoon.

They passed the Europe-Asia border, and Marged sat back. Green fields, wild flowers, poppies, lilies. This wasn't the Siberia she'd always visualised from pictures of Russia. She'd seen, deep snow, a white world, like something remembered from childhood, glistening magic turrets, fairy palaces, all white. But fairy tales had dragons too, and gloomy castles, dungeons ... She shivered.

They stopped at little stations where, if there was time, they disembarked and walked along the platform where bread was on sale in kiosks, and little old peasant women sat, selling home-made pies. But they had to be ready to jump back when Emma ordered. There was no guard with flag and whistle; the train just slid silently away and would not wait. People had to fit into the train and not the train to people. Marged had the strange feeling that the trains were in charge here in the wilderness; maniacal robots, taking people like Janina to places they didn't want to go, to their deaths. And Emma was its handmaiden. Was Emma afraid of the train? The driver they'd never seen. Was there a driver? There was a man who went round tapping the wheels, as in *Anna Karenina*, and even this seemed sinister ...

On and on, eating and sleeping, waking sometimes in the night to find they had pulled into another little wayside station, and they'd peer through the window to see people hurrying with their bundles and bags. Marged wondered where they were all going.

On Friday they arrived at Novosibirsk, the capital of Siberia, where, Alan told them, research was carried out at the university, where *perestroika* had been thought up in the seventies.

And when they drew up in the next station, a train passed them going in the opposite direction, and it was full of Mongolian people. Now she knew they were in an alien land, close to the Mongolian border.

On and on, past Irkutsk and the beautiful Lake Baikal, the oldest, deepest lake in the world. And then they were on the last lap to Khabarovsk.

Now they passed rivers and wide waters, plains, hills, great spaces, magnificent sunsets. Vastness unimaginable, where men were small and helpless, and could be lost for ever.

Her apprehension had grown, and with it fears of what she would find when she met Stefan. He'd been so upright, so – her mind groped for words – so honourable. He'd never really known everything about her and Martin, how they planned to take the factory, take their revenge ... He'd fallen in love with a sweet little girl and that girl no longer existed – never had.

'This is Chita,' David read from his guidebook. 'And the Onan River, on whose banks Genghis Khan was born.' Strange, alien names. Where was Stefan in all this? 'Here is the junction to Marchinsk,' David went on. 'Convict gangs were sent here before the seventeenth century ... silver and gold mines ...' and at the word convict Marged shivered. And when Alan pointed out a modern prison camp, she stared aghast.

In the morning they arrived at Khabarovsk.

They trooped out of the station, where the clock had two hour hands, one giving the train time, the other Khabarovsk time. Up to now the weather had been warm and pleasant; here in the Soviet Far East it was hot and sticky. But at the hotel Marged was given a nice airy room overlooking the River Amur - one mile wide, on the other side was Manchuria, China. Marged had travelled in Europe, but these names were strange to her; nor could she connect China and the Far East with Siberia.

And Stefan was here in Khabarovsk.

Over lunch in the hotel dining-room David asked: 'Should I ring him?'

Well, we can't just walk in,' she replied, and again apprehension rose. Supposing he didn't want to see them. That would be a laugh ... no, it wouldn't, not for David. He had set so much store on this meeting.

David went to the phone, returned. 'I spoke to him,' he said. 'He says will we come tomorrow afternoon. I think he wants to prepare. His apartment is quite near.'

'Did you tell him who you were?'

'Of course not. I just said Marguerite Fennel was here. Well,' he tried to appear nonchalant. 'They're taking us on a tour this afternoon. They seem to expect us to go.'

'Is it compulsory?' She attempted to laugh, not very successfully, and though David joined the group, she did not. Khabarovsk did not look a very exciting place; you expected to see temples and pagodas in the Far East, not utilitarian Russian buildings, shops with half-empty shelves, and goods of poor quality. And the heat was unbearable. So she settled for a walk in the hotel gardens leading down to the river. She wanted to be alone.

It was pleasant here; people walked along the embankment, and she walked too, returning to the hotel for dinner, and when a floor show was announced she went to bed early, pleading tiredness.

It was now just a matter of waiting. Having baths – there was a plug here – breakfast, David going out again to explore, she sorting out some pretty scented soap tablets to give to the waitresses, who wouldn't take tips, but would accept little gifts. She handed out the soap, feeling like Lady Bountiful, remembering that she'd known the same problem of scarcity during the war, when soap was rationed.

The war. She didn't want to be reminded of the war, the tragedies, the deaths, the suffering, it was too painful. In two days' time the group would be flying back to Moscow, a journey of eight hours, and if the meeting with Stefan did not go well then they too would fly back. And the chapter would be closed finally.

She and David lunched, and now both were quiet. And then they set out in the sticky heat. 'I found the apartment block,' David said. 'Not far away, you see.'

They reached it, stood a moment. The usual glass and concrete, and Marged wondered fleetingly why all the buildings were so functional, why they couldn't have built something beautiful, like the Moscow Metro. They went in the plain entrance, to the lift, up ...

And now David seemed to lose his nerve. He whispered, 'You go in first. I'll wait outside till you're ready for me.'

Marged knocked, and a voice called: 'Come in,' in English. She entered.

He was standing near the doorway, and the small room seemed full of light. His back was to the window and the light shone around him, keeping his face in shadow. His hair was white, his face lined and tanned from the sun. He was a little stooped.

'Marged,' he said. 'Is it really you?'

'Yes,' she whispered. 'It's me.'

'Sit down,' he said. 'I have made some English tea.' And he took her to the table by the window while he went to get the tea. And now she was able to glance around the room, plain and functional like everything here. But it overlooked the river, and it was this that sent the light into the room, the wide, wide river, with China on the other side.

He brought the tea in little cups, with milk and sugar, saying, 'I've kept these cups for a long time. I don't use them very often – we drink tea in glasses here.'

His English wasn't so good, she noted. He had to stop and search for words; his accent was stronger. As though he read her mind he said: 'You must forgive my English. I have tried to keep it up – there was a teacher at the school where I worked who taught languages, and we would speak together. But when he left—' He shrugged. 'Anyway, I didn't think I'd need it again.'

They were both ill at ease and Marged thought, This is a disaster. What can I say to him?

'Tell me about yourself,' she said.

'How much do you know?'

'Well, we heard from Poland, from Tadeusz. He said how you'd been in Siberia – in a prison. How you found Janina in the end.' She stopped.

'Yes, I found her,' he said.

'But Stefan. Why did you stay *here*? Wouldn't they let you go?'

His face was shadowed now. He said, 'She was ill – mentally ill. I sometimes think she never really recognised me. She was afraid to leave. I don't think she quite understood.' His voice trailed away, and Marged stared, horrified.

'She had been badly treated in her camp, we think raped, but she never said. She didn't seem able to communicate. But she would never allow any man to touch her.'

Marged stared, shocked, appalled. 'Oh, the poor woman. And you lived all these years with a sick wife? Here – in this place?'

'She died three months ago.'

'What a waste of a life,' Marged said. 'Of more than one life,' and for a moment she was resentful. Then resentment dissolved into pity.

There was a little silence, and she stared out over the river. She could see an embankment, neatly-laid-out gardens, people walking. 'And you?' Stefan asked. 'You married, of course. Is your husband with you?'

'No. I'm a widow. Twice. Or at least the first time I was divorced. I married Brian Mordant. He owned the factory

482

where I worked. I married him and ran the factory because I wanted to improve it.'

'I see. And then?'

'Then I married my cousin Martin – you will remember him. And we ran Mordant's together.'

'You sound as if that was most important, running the factory.'

She looked through the window at the eternal river. 'Perhaps it was.'

'Did you not have children?' he asked.

'Only one. She died. There was an accident—'

She paused. Was this the right moment to tell him? But he interrupted before she could say any more. 'I'm sorry,' he said, and the moment passed.

Again there was a pause. They were still ill at ease. Marged thought wildly, Oh, this was a mistake. I must make my excuses and go. She had entirely forgotten David. She looked round for something to say. 'Is life easier now?' she asked.

'Well, it is changing, yes. The hardliners are trying to hold things together; they jailed two Siberian journalists, and another in Sverdlovsk had three years in a labour camp for slandering the KGB. But there is a spirit of rebellion abroad.'

'And,' remembering Tadeusz's letter, 'You did your best to help it, I suppose.'

Stefan smiled. 'My apartment was bugged for some time – not now,' as she gave a hasty look round. 'And there was often the shadow following everywhere I went. But I always seemed to get Tadeusz's letters, and he mine.'

'How did you keep out of prison?' She was curious now.

'Well, the farther you are away from Moscow the better it is. You tend to be sometimes forgotten. But I have a friend in the KGB.'

'You – a friend in the KGB! *You?*'

He raised his eyebrows in a movement she remembered. 'Why so surprised?'

'Because you were so – honourable. Going back to find Janina when you could have stayed.'

Now his face was bitter. 'Honourable, me? If you knew that I'd wished I'd stayed in England even if it meant Janina dying here ... oh, I'm not so honourable.' His face twisted. 'I bribed Vladimir for information. He was in the NKVD then, in charge of the prison camp. I learned how to survive in a camp – you had to survive any way you could, or you just died and were thrown by the roadside.' He paused. 'There was no other way,' he ended, almost to himself. 'No escape, no way out ...'

Her head was whirling now. She didn't know what to think. Yet this admission somehow brought him closer; it was difficult trying to live up to a paragon. She was confused, bewildered. The sun was shining on the river, the water glittered in the heat, her palms were wet. She looked round the apartment. There was a bed in one corner, in the other a cooking ring, so he lived in one room. A chest of drawers at the far side and on that two small photographs. She could not see what they were, so she went towards them, picked them up.

The first, a young laughing girl with dark hair and an urchin face. She had given him that ...

And the other ... Mam, Dad and the family, standing in the back garden, in the days before the accident, Brenda solem, head in air, John smiling, she herself laughing because Martin was tickling her. Uncle Harry had taken this. He had a camera, a box camera, quite a luxury in those days. The old photograph brought it all back and she thought dazedly, that's me in the back streets – I never thought I'd ever be anywhere else. And certainly not in *Siberia*.

She turned, hands trembling. 'Where on earth did you get this?'

'Brenda gave it to me.'

'Oh, Stefan.' Stumbling, she went to the table, sat down,

holding the little snapshot before her like a talisman. 'All these years you kept it . . .'

'I never forgot you, Marged.'

'I know – that's why you kept on sending those cards. But why didn't you put on an address – or at least write something?'

'I don't know. I suppose because I knew I couldn't come to you. I told myself I wanted you to forget me, but underneath I suppose I didn't.'

'But you stopped me from forgetting you!'

· 'Then you hadn't forgotten me?'

'No.' It was a whisper because there was a deeper meaning in the simple words, and both knew it. He picked up her hand and kissed it, the old remembered gesture she hadn't known for more than forty years, and a surge of emotion swept over her, flushing her cheeks; the years fell away and she was a girl again.

The light streamed in from the window, the river glittered. He did not let go her hand. Then he raised it to his cheek and she felt his tears on her fingers.

She said, stroking his head, 'You were right to look after Janina, you know that, don't you? I think she would know who you were, I'm sure of it. You couldn't have left her, not here, in this foreign country.' Not in Asia, the Far East, with the river and China on the other side. This alien land.

He said, 'And you had to run the factory.'

She turned away from him then, her hand dropped to the table. She whispered, 'I've had my shadows, too,'

'Tell me about them.'

She paused, looked out of the window, the river running free. 'Stefan, the child I had . . . she was yours.'

'What?' Now he stood up, knocking the precious English cup to the floor. Behind him the river shimmered in the metallic sun. 'Mine? How could this be?'

'I knew I was pregnant when you left—'

'And you didn't tell me?'

'No. I wanted to, but you seemed determined to go back, and I didn't want to force you to stay. So I married Brian Mordant.'

'Oh, Marged ...'

'It wasn't a happy marriage.'

'And the child, did he treat her well?'

'Oddly, yes, he loved her. And she loved him. It was me she didn't love.'

'You? Why?'

She turned her face away from his searching gaze. 'She said I neglected her. Maybe I did. Maybe I put the factory first.' And now he'll hate me, he'll think I should have put the family first, she thought.

He said, surprisingly, 'And I neglected you both.'

'But you didn't know.'

'I didn't ask, did I?' He moved away from the table, and she saw that he limped a little. 'It wasn't altogether from a high-minded attempt to find Janina that I left – though that was there. It was also because I was angry at losing my country to the Soviet Union, so I hit back at you. Not so honourable, eh?' And she thought, maybe he's kept up with modern ways more than I have. No one talks about honour these days.

Now she stood up too and went to him, but did not touch him. 'Stefan,' she said softly, 'we both made mistakes. But you were honourable, even so.'

'Perhaps,' he said, and his voice was stronger now. 'Perhaps we had to carry out our life's work alone. If we hadn't, we'd have regretted it. Oh—' and his face was tormented. 'The one thing I really regretted was that I couldn't have a family. Now you tell me I had a child and she's lost to me.'

'Yes, Stefan.' She put her arm around him. 'But all is not lost.'

'What do you mean?'

'You'll see.' She went to the door. 'David,' she called. 'Come in.'

486

She stood back and watched Stefan as the boy entered, his look, first of interest, then of incredulity. He turned to her bewildered.

'Marie's child,' she said. 'My grandson. And yours.'

David took a step forward. 'All this is David's doing,' she continued. 'He would find you. He traced Tadeusz, he brought me here.'

Stefan held out his arms, and David went to him. And when Stefan stood away his back seemed straighter, his eyes were shining.

They sat and talked then, all of them round the little table overlooking the river, the changing light playing on their faces.

Marged told him the story of her childhood, the urge for revenge, all the things she could not tell him when she was young because she had been afraid of losing him. Now she *could* tell him, because the years brought tolerance and forgiveness. David talked of his life, his mother.

The hours passed. Stefan brought them soup and bread, waving aside their protests. And he told them about Siberia, trying to conceal the worst horrors of the prison camps, but ending: 'People should never be allowed to suffer in this way.'

'And are you really friends with a KGB man?' Marged wanted to know.

He smiled. 'I've never seen him since I left the camp. Though I know he is in this area, in charge of this section. Well – I did belong to a group of dissidents; we used to meet, six of us. One day we were arrested. And were released. When we asked why, we were told it was on the orders of Vladimir Primakov.'

'But why was he friendly with you?'

'Because he envied me my freedom of *thought*,' Stefan said. 'He knew my beliefs, and that I would always work for them. He envied me because that was something he dare not do.'

She was silent, thinking. 'But Stefan,' she began, 'do you think he *knew* about your letters to Tadeusz, when you urged him to rebel?'

Stefan shrugged again. 'Who knows? It's possible.'

'I heard a man talking on television, before we came,' Marged told him. He said, "The spark generated by an electrician in Poland lit a torch for democracy that spread across Europe, to Russia itself." Maybe there were other little sparks; maybe one came from Russia.'

'It's called retribution,' said David.

Now it was beginning to get dark, bringing a welcome coolness to the air. Flashes of lightning were thrown up from each side of the river, low on the horizon. Stefan asked: 'What are you going to do now?'

'We are applying to extend our visas,' David said, firmly. 'After that—'

'After that?'

'You don't want to stay here now, do you, Grandfather? After all, we don't know what will happen in the future. Come with us, meet the rest of your family.'

'Little Tadeusz,' Stefan said. 'My pen-friend.'

'Grown up now, with children of his own. You see what a large family you have. And Gran has a big house, though she is still waiting for her dream home.'

'*David!*'

Again the lightning flashed up from the horizon. 'I've never seen lightning like this before,' Marged said. 'It's like gunfire.'

'It will rain tomorrow,' Stefan told her, and she pulled a little face. 'Rain is necessary here, it cools the air. Anyway, after the rain comes the rainbow.'

Again they were silent, but now it was a contented silence, the strain had gone. On the river a boat's light gleamed. And Marged felt completed in a way she had not before, even years ago after their nights of passion. At the thought she looked at Stefan, caught his gaze, and knew he

488

was remembering, too. He put his hand out and clasped hers.

'Gran,' David asked. 'Did you ever find the rainbow you were seeking?'

She looked at him, at Stefan, as the sky grew dark and their faces were illumined by the lightning flashes.

'You brought it to me,' she said simply.